Eve's Blessing

By: JJ Park

To my parents, thank you for teaching me the power of words.

Thank you, Marissa and Savannah, for being my first readers and cheerleaders. Thank you, Gabe, for slaughtering my adverbs… But I will never give them up. Thank you, Cole and Marty, you lovable goofs. You're both too cool for us all. Hudson, for standing in my doorway and telling me to screw them all and follow my dreams, thank you. Endlessly.

Thank you, Grant, my husband, the first responder to my doubts. You've kept me grounded yet inspired since we were kids. You are my Beloved.

Never underestimate the power of taking someone's dream seriously.

WALYRE
Griffin's crest
WALOR
PHORA
IXARD
ISHEY

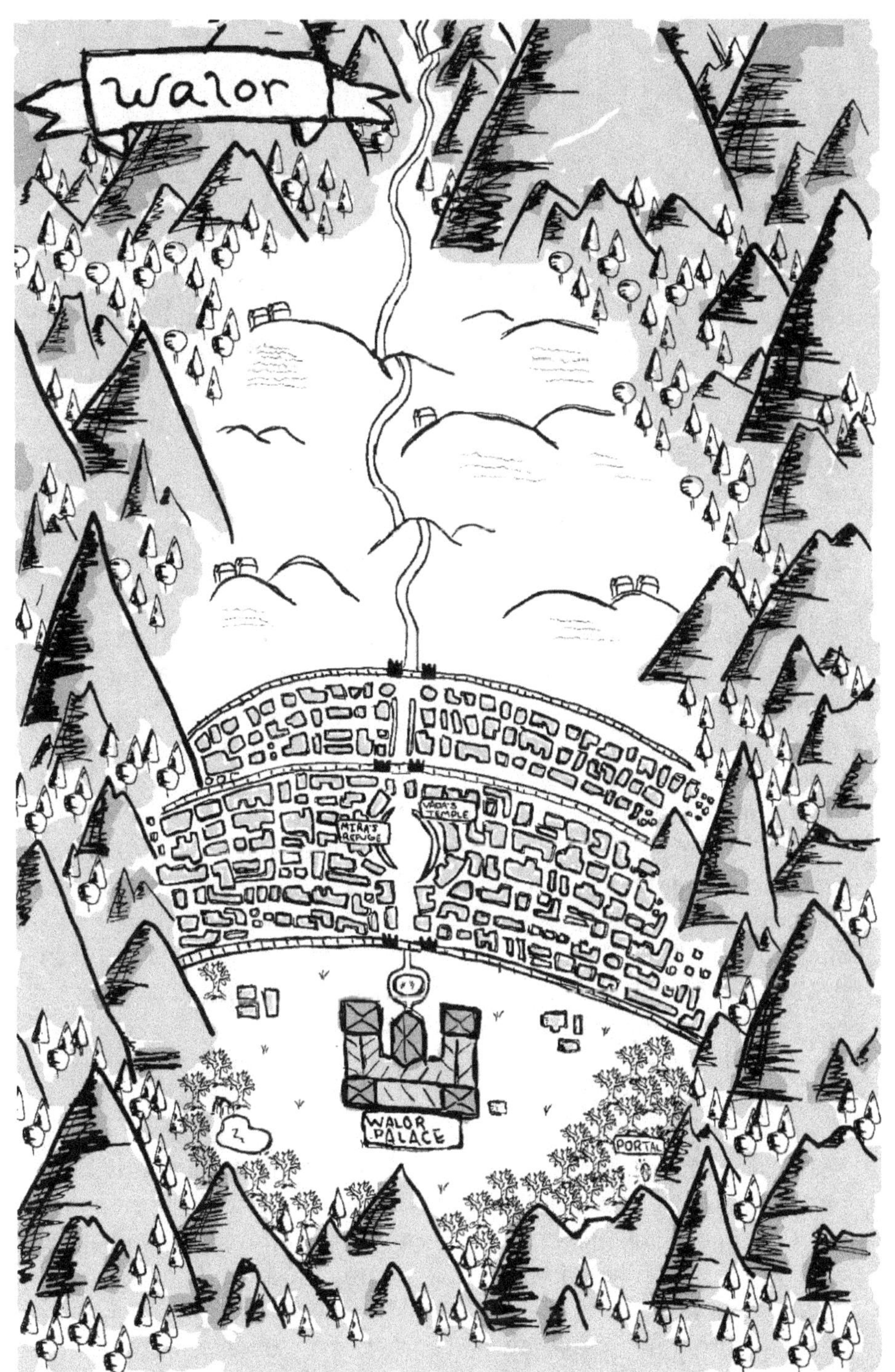
Walor
MIRA'S REFUGE
VADA'S TEMPLE
WALOR PALACE
PORTAL

Eve

Please stay down.

I inwardly pleaded while trying to remain standing, but dear God, that ten-count went on for hours. My ears rang louder than any bell. I had swallowed enough blood that my stomach churned. My left eye swelled after the last blow I had been dealt. Each heartbeat pounded as my opponent lay there, her eyes rolling, making me hope that today was finally coming to an end.

Judging by their cheers, the crowd desired the opposite. The ref dove to her side. I could empathize with the irritation of someone yelling the ten-count despite your ears already ringing.

Please stay down.

I would have begged, not only to get paid, but so I could stop beating the kid. How much was I supposed to earn from a fight this predictable? The scrapper shakily rose to her elbows, biting so hard on her bite guard that blood and drool oozed from the corners of her mouth. Her knees stood her upright in a display of idiotic determination. She raised her gloves. The ref rescinded the count.

I shook my head while she swayed towards me. The crowd fed her fantasy that the fight could still be hers. I waited for her to cross the mat, not wasting energy approaching her. She hooked one sluggish arm through the air. Her blow landed six inches away from my nose, accidentally welcoming my fist to make quick purchase in her jaw. She dropped to the mat with a 'smack.'

Shit, I wanted the fight to be over. I didn't want to make her forget how to do math.

The ten-count went by quicker this time, allowing me to slip between the ropes. Hands slippery with sweat and liquor patted me on the back, hip, and shoulder, anywhere to thank their investment as I retreated to the locker room. I leaned my full weight against the door. Once it shut behind me, I spat out my bloody bite guard. I let myself double over in pain while reaching for the closest bench.

The throbbing in my jaw and corner of my left eye were my only companions. The next few days would be blurred with recovery. Hardly able to keep my left eye open, I unwrapped the tape from my knuckles.

I sucked in a sharp breath. "Shit."

It was always impressive what new aches and pains greeted me once the adrenaline wore off. I looked at my unwrapped hands, my fingers rigidly extended, beaten red and quivering under the light. One of my knuckles was partially dislocated, strewn to the side. I could hardly open my right hand. I groaned and swiped the towel from around my shoulders, placing it between my teeth. I wrenched my index finger forward to snap the joint back into place. The towel muffled the howl that escaped me. Blinking back fresh tears, I tested my technique by opening and closing my fist one, two, three times. I spat the towel onto the floor.

My ministrations were interrupted by a clatter approaching the women's locker room. Only one creature was so bold as to enter.

The door swung open, slamming into the tile wall behind it, as a stout middle-aged man burst through. His broad shoulders almost hit the doorframe; his shit-eating grin plastered across his stubbled jaw. "What did I say? I told you this would be an easy one!"

I turned to look at him, realizing my left eye had finally swollen shut. "It wasn't without some collateral damage, Hunter."

Hunter shrugged while leaning against the wall. His galumphing figure wasn't improved by his ill-fitting track pants and dated windbreaker. "Occupational hazard, Evie. You'll bounce back. Think about how ugly you made her look. Shew, she'll have a hell of a time remembering her name tomorrow." He chuckled while ruffling his greying hairs. "I'll get you another match in a few weeks."

"Fix it against someone in my rank." I preferred to not spend my Saturday nights bloodying teenagers. My gaze reverted to my hands. "I'm going to take a shower," I muttered.

He nodded with his grin still-ever present. He dipped his hand into his pocket and tossed an envelope my way.

I caught it, feeling it squelch in my palm. It reeked of sweat, worse than me; evident it had been pried from greedy hands. The sight almost had my left eye opening in shock. I snapped my stare back to Hunter.

"I know it's not as much as you wanted, but I had a lot of good *investors* take notice of you tonight. It's better than nothing." He

failed to comfort me, just as he'd failed to secure me a profitable fight.
"I didn't hear you thank me," Hunter remarked, the edge of charisma
fading from his voice.

"Thank you."

Contentment returned to his demeanor. "I'll always take care of
you, Evie. You know that?" I nodded slowly.

"Good. Hopefully there's enough in there that you'll be thinking
of me while you're showering." He shot a sickening wink at me as
he opened the door. "And say 'hi' to Nicky for me when you see
him," he called as he left the locker room.

I hurled my glove at the door, ignoring my screaming ribs. At
the same moment, I clutched the money tighter and knew that I
would have to survive Hunter for another week.

Safir

Snow had been collecting within the valley throughout the day. It fell softer than a whisper, coating the gardens and courtyards in a blanket of untouched white. I could hardly spot the tips of the frosted mountains beyond. Its timing was appropriate given what day it was. A sigh made the window before me fog.

"That's the third one," Selasi chimed in. "Three sighs in one minute."

"I believe we discussed your unnecessary observations yesterday."

"Do you wish to discuss the source of your sighs, Lord?"

I hardly graced him with my glance, seeing him leaning back with his arms crossed by the fire. "I'm sure the air is permeated with the source of my sighs. Can you feel it from there?"

"Yes," he said without hesitation.

What I appreciated the most about Selasi was that he spoke with certainty. I never had to guess what his disposition was. He never had to guess mine either.

He leaned back and readjusted his sword at his side. "No one expects you to conduct yourself any other way than you do now, Lord."

"That's hardly a comfort. And you hardly appear to be an eager bulwark. If someone intruded now, they'd think you were taking the day off."

"No one would believe you'd give me the day off."

A proper response failed me, so I maintained my stare out the window that faced the northern most gardens where *her* tomb lay. Its white marble slab stood even more still amid the falling snow, but a sense of peace lingered. Perhaps she could feel the beauty of the snow rather than its bitter chill.

If the day wasn't regrettable enough, my ego had been further injured that afternoon. Not knowing my brother, Ashire, had been meeting with one of the local lords, I had wandered about the halls in grief for her. Those closest to me were able to withstand my pain, but those unaware…they'd suffer. My reminiscing had been cut short upon hearing wails filling the air from the lord himself. A direct result of my presence, one for which my brother had apologized. Ashire had tried to reassure me, but the damage was done. I was as burdensome as ever.

"Not your fault," Selasi offered from his corner, reading my sentiments that hung in the air around me. Private contemplation was not a luxury I knew. "His Majesty doesn't like the local lords anyway."

"That's beside the point. The king was unable to control something so repugnant that walks his halls."

"Those lords are hardly capable of sifting through their own feelings, if they have any, let alone comprehending someone else's."

I fought a smile, but guilt welled up within me. Days such as that I could only sulk, to the detriment of those condemned to my presence. The isolated night was the perfect place for me to brood. I hadn't visited her that day.

"Selasi, let's take a walk," I commanded while turning from the window.

He stood, falling into step with me. He knew where my stride would lead. "You'll be late for dinner with your brother, Lord."

"He'll forgive it.

Eve

The halo from the streetlamps made my head throb. I had to look up at the walk sign across the street, unwilling to chance jaywalking with heavy traffic and a swollen eye.

Given the state of this city, most didn't take more than a second glance when they saw me after a fight. No one had time to ask questions. I didn't have patience to answer. But one particular passer-by not only stared but stopped in their tracks, jaw falling open. I inwardly groaned as they approached me.

"Eve?"

I reluctantly turned to see a familiar face; one I couldn't quite recall.

"It's Jesse Coleman from high school? You're Nick's sister, right? I was friends with him."

The face gained a bit more familiarity with context. We'd had a few classes in common, although he'd sported spiked hair and glasses in my memory. The person before me was not-so-gracefully balding but made up for it with a well-groomed beard. We'd only spent one year in high school together. There had been too many schools, muddled in my memory.

I nodded but was careful not to lift my face into the light. "Right. Good seeing you again." I scowled at the stalling walk sign.

"I know! I hardly see anyone from those days. I ended up–whoa, what happened to you?" He reached out to grab me before I lurched away from him in a ready stance. His hand was raised halfway as he stared at me.

I cringed while relaxing my posture. "Sorry, just got done with a fight. I'm still a bit amped up."

"Oh, sure." He hardly looked convinced. "I forgot you and Nick used to box. Listen, I was sorry to hear a–"

"See you around." I leapt into the street as the walk sign turned green. The wad of cash in my sweatpants pocket weighed heavier as I patted it to ensure it was still tucked away. The righteous reward for all my blood and sweat took up such a small amount of space.

The less I thought about it the better, because my stomach released a growl that could be heard through my sweatshirt.

Shit. Forgot to eat.

Safir

I was accustomed to the shudders and gasps of servants who passed me in the corridors. Those who knew better excused themselves before I was within arm's length. Newer servants were left reeling in my wake. What could I do besides meet their wide-eyed stares with remorse? The merciful thing was to move along. Selasi, always in step with me, muttered, "I'll have a word with them later."

"No need. They know now."

I did my best not to dwell on a simpler time where my presence hadn't polluted the air, a time where I could just *be*.

In the solitary courtyard, I breathed easier. With fewer persons to burden, I could allow my conscience some peace. We tracked through the snow to her tomb, concealed by the wintry precipitation. I dusted off enough to sit on the edge of the tomb, allowing my nerves to settle like the falling snow. The cold clarified one's thoughts, almost too sharply, as I contemplated her and the Blessing she had given me.

Selasi cleared his throat. "I can excuse myself if you wish to say some words, Lord."

I shook my head, breathing a visible sigh. "No, there is nothing else to say. She already knows. I merely needed to be freed from the confines of those walls for a few moments."

"Would you like me to remain?"

"If you could."

Selasi stood statuesque next to me, as we both cherished the seclusion. It was a rare comfort.

Eve

A pulverized face drew attention when shoplifting. Granted, pulling your hood over your face was equally attention-getting. The best thing to do when entering a convenience store was cough or sneeze to hide your face from the cashier. Afterwards, keep your chin down and let your hair shroud your face from the cameras.

As planned, an urge to cough overtook me while I entered Huck's Convenience Store. The cashier ignored me dodging down the candy aisle towards the back where the frozen meals were kept. Though the fluorescent lights worsened the throbbing in my head, I made quick work.

Crouching out of the camera's view, I plucked two, frozen lasagnas, placed one under the waistband of my sweatpants and slipped the other one under my bra. When I sucked in and fluffed my sweatshirt, they virtually disappeared though their cold touch made a shiver rip through me.

I had almost escaped down the aisle when my right foot slipped out from beneath me. The rest of my body collided with the damp floor. I managed to spare my face striking the hard surface, but footsteps rushed towards me.

"Are you okay? I'm so sorry. I just mopped."

It was a deep voice, probably male, possibly could beat me in a chase.

I'd neglected to see the 'wet floor' sign. A moan escaped me as I managed to get to my knees. The clerk reached under my arms and helped me stand. I tried to brush him off. "I'm fine, thanks."

A frozen lasagna dropped to the floor with a 'thud.'

The clerk froze, and that was the perfect moment to dash. Scooping up the lasagna on the floor, I found enough energy in my exhausted legs to propel me forward. A massive hand clamped onto my elbow. Out of reflex, I drove my elbow back with too much force.

I felt the crack before I heard it.

"Shit!"

My steps stuttered as the clerk released me. I glanced back to see him holding his nose, sputtering blood. It was definitely askew. Definitely broken. Definitely my fault.

I backtracked to the door while stuttering an apology, "I'm sorry! I didn't mean it. I just- sorry!" I threw myself out the door, leaving behind the injured clerk. When my feet met the pavement, I bolted down the sidewalk.

Heavy footsteps gave chase behind me.

So much for a 'no chase' policy.

My legs were more conditioned, but his were fresher. Luckily, with my swollen features and the fading light, I doubted he'd gotten a good look at my face. He panted behind me, "Just wait! Hold up a sec!"

Not likely.

The last thing I needed, with a wad of cash in my pocket, was to try to explain myself.

So, I didn't stop, and I didn't slow, and I didn't risk throwing off my pace by looking back. Luckily, my all-too-humble abode wasn't too far, but in an emergency it was safer to go through the woods into my backyard when trying to not be caught.

His heavy footsteps had become distant patters, but I still refused to look back. My chest ached from the cold air while I sprinted off the road through the woods. There was barely enough daylight for me to see. I scraped my elbows and palms against tree bark and leapt over sticker bushes that clung to my sweatpants. My feet pounded the frozen dirt, but I could feel my energy fading. I had already endured enough that day and hadn't factored having to run away with my pitiful meals. Just as I slowed my pace and took a few deep breaths, the dreaded sound of sirens made me jump. I scarcely believed I would be the police's top priority, but...

You did assault the poor guy.

Well, fuck.

My legs resumed their pace and I ventured deeper into the forest, my back porch and a night's sleep getting closer and closer.

I needed to make it. I needed to-

Something smothered my feet. I plummeted to the ground once again and rolled through the cold to a halt. I was so fucking tired of falling, but my thoughts ceased when I found myself coated in snow.

Where did all this come from?

As I lay there, panting and staring up into a sky spitting snow, I had no idea what had just happened. An entirely different forest stretched to where the land extended into a mountain, itself coated in the wintry mix, so much so that I couldn't see the top. There wasn't much daylight, even less with the heavy cloud cover.

"What the hell?" I wheezed.

There was no reasonable answer for where I had found myself. I had no choice but to stand. My knees quivered from exhaustion and cold. Peering around me, I could only see the same snow-covered forest. My footsteps in the snow appeared from nowhere. Nothing in the distance alluded to my sprint through the forest. My curiosity was piqued, and I took a few steps back.

I found myself back in the dark, flat forest with only frozen dirt beneath my feet and the sirens ringing even louder. Jolting, I threw myself forward and returned to the forest of snow. Squinting into the distance, I could see the mountain extending into a range. It must have been a totally different forest, a totally different place. How, I didn't know, but there weren't any police waiting for me.

Can they find me here?

"You there!" a voice barked at me.

I whipped around and saw a ridiculously dressed man pointing an actual sword at me.

"Make yourself known!"

His voice was deep. How could he sound so serious while dressed so strangely? He wore tall black leather boots with grey cloth pants tucked into them. A black cloak covered the rest of him except his hands, still pointing a sword at me. His expression was deadly serious- grey eyes narrowed, jaw clenched. His breath was steady in the air. His skin was in stark contrast to the white snow, a deep umber color, his black hair cut short. As ridiculous as he looked, I couldn't mistake his stance, ready to move, ready to fight.

"Make yourself known!" he commanded even louder.

I had been so consumed by his curious clothes and choice of weapon I had forgotten I was supposed to feel threatened.

I held up one hand in defense while the other held my frozen meals against me. "I'm not a threat to you, so you can put the sword down," I said, feeling idiotic for saying such a thing.

The man advanced towards me, letting me see his tall stature. "I cannot. You're trespassing on His Majesty's land."

"Not on purpose," I replied, wondering if I should take a few steps back and return to the forest I knew.

Wait.

His Majesty?

Safir

A ruckus in the distance disturbed the peace this day deserved. I was perched against the marble slab, reciting my promise to her when the noise interrupted my thoughts. A flare of frustration coursed through me. Even Selasi stiffened next to me.

"I'll go see what it is." Selasi gripped the hilt of his sword.

"It's probably just a hare."

"I'd like to be sure, Lord, if it'll put you at ease."

I said nothing. Selasi was already marching through the snow as if he were on the hunt. I remained against the marble slab, hoping the day would have a quick and quiet ending.

Selasi's voice boomed in the distance. I swore I felt miserable for the poor bastard who had intruded, because my lack of composure was going to be their demise. I tracked after Selasi, knowing full well just how late I was going to be for dinner with my brother.

Selasi must have made quick footwork. His footsteps paced deep into the garden, almost to the wall. Past the garden and further into the forest, I discovered Selasi pointing his sword at some pitiful creature, who clutched themselves with one arm. I'd never known Selasi to draw his sword without intent, but he knew I'd prefer to avoid bloodshed that day.

When I advanced forward, the creature appeared smaller, shivering in the cold. I pondered their strange clothing: so loose and nonfunctional. They wore no armor, no boots, nothing to combat the cold. Perhaps they had a death wish.

"You'll do well to refrain from any snide comments. You're in no position to be coy," Selasi hissed, taking a tone I had scarcely heard from him.

The individual glanced between Selasi and his sword. They hardly seemed frightened. "If you want, I can show you how I got here." The voice was a woman's. I couldn't discern her sex from her brutalized facial features and her clothes hid any hint of a feminine physique. Her hair, a chestnut hue that flowed down to her neck, caught a few snowflakes.

She glanced behind herself carelessly; she could have been impaled. "I came here on accident. I promise."

As foolish as she was for trespassing, there was no fear evident in her stare, which appeared to have met an angry fist. The left eye was swollen, a purplish color extending down to her clenched jaw. She stood erect and refused to buckle beneath Selasi's stare. I had seen men drop in fear at the end of Selasi's sword, so the girl was either unfathomably brave or unforgivably stupid.

"What good is a promise from an assassin?" Selasi barked.

"An assassin?"

I hardly felt like entertaining a simpleton on a day that did not belong to them. The selfishness repulsed me, and I would make it known. Surely even Selasi felt my animosity from a distance- it was only a matter of time before she would.

"It repels me that you'd be sent here today of all days," I finally spoke with utmost disdain. "Have you no sense of decency?"

Eve

Another man appeared like a ghost. He also wore black leather boots, black cloth pants tucked in, but his cloak was a deep red, the color of blood. His hair was stark white and blew in the breeze. His skin only held slightly more color than his hair. It wasn't until he was a few feet in front of me that I saw his eyes were a deep orange, like embers in a dying fire. An earring in the ridge of his left ear held a spherical charm that dangled. It was the same color as his eyes– it practically glowed. His gaze was startling, so much so that I forgot I had a sword pointed at me.

His jaw was sharp, his mouth a tight line, and he stood even taller than the swordsman next to him. Regardless of size, I was outnumbered.

I wanted to question if I were truly in some alternate reality or if I had suffered from such a hilarious concussion. Any answer would do if it meant I wasn't about to be stabbed.

"Could you tell me who you are so I can feel intimidated?" I asked while still clutching my frozen meals. While the two men looked ridiculous, I probably didn't look that much better.

"You must be joking," the ember-eyed one sneered. "You are truly the worst assassin to ever be sent after me."

"That would make sense, considering I'm not an assassin. I'm not even armed."

"Then lift both of your arms!" the swordsman commanded, gesturing with his sword. "Show us what you're concealing."

I sighed, knowing I was going to lose my frozen dinners. Begrudgingly, I lifted my arms and felt the lasagnas slip out from under my sweatshirt and plop into the snow. I kicked them both over to where the men stood.

They stared at the frozen blocks in the snow. Their confused expressions didn't improve after my great reveal of two pitiful lasagnas.

The ember-eyed one picked up one dinner from the snow, dusted it off and squinted at the box. "It's written in Common," he muttered to his swordsman. They both looked at it, though the sword was still pointed at me.

I shivered, wondering if the police were about to run through the forest after me. "It's food," I said. A place that still used swords probably didn't have microwave lasagnas.

The ember-eyed man turned back to me. "This is considered sustenance? So, you're a thief?"

"Sometimes, but not from you."

"Strange," he murmured under his breath. "What was it exactly that has upset your face? Were you put up to this? Did someone brutalize you into trespassing here?" He turned to his swordsman. "Selasi, sheathe your sword."

The swordsman, apparently Selasi, put his sword away, though maintained an expression of deadly seriousness.

"No one brutalized me, not the way you think. Where I'm from, it's my job."

"We'll revisit your masochistic occupation later," the ember-eyed one said. "Where is it you claim to be from?"

I glanced back behind me. "About three feet that way."

The swordsman scowled at me. "His Royal Highness made an inquiry. You will answer without any coy remarks."

He's the royal?

I extended my hand out to the ember eyed one. "If you'll let me, I can show you."

His eyes widened ever so slightly, their deep orange color flaring brightly amid the snow. It was beautiful. Yet I couldn't understand his hesitation. He could have rebuked me, but I hadn't expected him to just stand there. Even the swordsman looked perplexed.

He reluctantly put his hand out, resting it on mine. He hardly touched me, so I clasped my hand over his.

In that instant I felt a wave of emotions that manifested from the pit of my stomach to the shallowest layers of my skin. One by one I was able to identify them with such clarity it was as if I were experiencing the emotions myself. There was a sense of curiosity, irritated uncertainty, and an ever-present sorrow that made my heart quiver. What was most unnerving was that those emotions didn't feel like my own. I could tell they were *his*. It was like I was able to read and feel each emotion that he was experiencing at the touch of his hand. I didn't pull away. None of those emotions were strangers to me.

My grip tightened. "This way."

Safir

I had noticed when I approached her, she wasn't affected by me. Even Selasi appeared dampened to my presence. But dear Vada, how could she *not* know? How could she not feel it?

The air must have been filled with my anger, but she either couldn't sense it or didn't care.

Regardless, her small hand boldly enveloped mine. Her skin was rough. She trembled from the cold, but her grip was strong. That close, her uninjured eye was a stark sapphire color with long black lashes that blinked the snow away, and her gaze did not waver. Instead, she pulled me forward as she moved backward.

My initial anger plummeted as I followed the girl. She was studying me as intently as I was her, waiting for me to react.

When she stopped walking, I withdrew my hand from her grasp to see I was in a different place entirely. My world had vanished into thin air. Her world extended as far as I could see. The ground below me was frozen dirt. The trees surrounding me were not the ancient trees that adorned the mountains, but unremarkable spears that rose into the sky. Even the stars in the heavens above were in a different alignment. How incomprehensibly strange to take a few careless steps to be enveloped in a different realm of existence. What preserved such a portal? How had it been created? Why did it join our realms? And how did it happen to be in my courtyard?

Suddenly a high-pitched screeching echoed from afar. Red and blue lights danced in the distance. It startled me into reaching for my own sword.

The girl's eyes grew wide. "Time to go." She placed her hand on my chest, still scarcely affected by me, and pushed me back.

I allowed it as we both paced back into my more gracious realm, welcomed by the snowfall. Her world didn't leave a trace, only leaving her behind. A long breath escaped me when I emerged back in my familiar courtyard.

"Lord, are you all right?" Selasi gasped from behind me.

I turned to see his eyes wide and dark skin turned pale. "Fine," I said, still recovering my breath.

"You disappeared, Lord!"

"Do you believe me now?" The girl's jaw was tightly set.

"I don't have any other choice, do I?" I conceded. "What's the likelihood those things you're running from can come through here?"

"I don't know."

That was of little comfort. She still had her trembling hand pressed into my chest, which led me to my second inquiry. Just as she pulled her hand away, I urged it closer. "Can you not feel this?" I imagined a sense of warmth, such as when bathing beneath a bright sun, which radiated throughout my body.

The girl shuddered. "Yes."

I released her hand. So, by touch she could sense me, but it hardly impacted her. Her very presence diminished mine.

I paced backwards until I was once again standing next to Selasi. Refocusing on the intense warmth, I asked her, "Can you feel now what you felt when I was close to you?"

"Nothing."

"Lord," Selasi interjected, "I couldn't sense you approach previously. I only knew you were present when I heard you."

"Can you feel me now?"

"No, Lord."

I snapped my stare to the girl. "What the hell are you?"

She glared at me. "I'm freezing."

"Enough with your snide remarks! How are you capable of doing this?"

"I'm not doing anything! I'm freezing, and I'm hungry. That's all I am."

Selasi resumed his hand on the hilt of his sword. "Use that tongue to disrespect His Royal Highness again, and I will cut it out."

Though she was unarmed, she hardly gave a single inch under Selasi's threat. Perhaps she was unfathomably brave, but even more importantly, she was able to control the range of my sentiments. She somehow drew a curtain that hid the extent of what I could do. And in the short time I had known her, she had been transparent with me.

She couldn't understand how valuable she had quickly become.

Eve

My feet were numb, and the air nipped my "brutalized" face. At first that was all I could feel, despite my frustration at being accused of purposefully trespassing into an alternate reality.

But when my hand was pressed into the Highness' chest, a wave of warmth encircled me. It was like how it had felt before when I'd touched him, a cascading feeling. I should have been startled, even horrified, but I couldn't bring myself to be anything other than exhausted.

The Highness stopped his accusatory glare. "We have someone in our employ who can heal you, and I'm sure we can find you something better to eat than those," he gestured to the frozen lasagnas, "if you will accompany us."

I wanted to fall into step with him.

It was a tempting offer given my condition, and I wondered how strong the "healer" was, but I stalled. "Is this a nice way of asking me to be your prisoner?"

"You need help, and I am offering it freely."

My exhaustion was relentless and how many opportunities would I get to explore a new world? Without another word, I took a step towards him and let him guide me away from the invisible door. As much as I needed to return to the place I knew, getting a hot meal and being healed sounded like a pretty good deal. But I was sure there was a catch.

Besides, I was outnumbered, and I had revealed to him how I'd trespassed in the first place, so he could have found me if I ran. If I could benefit from a meal, I could slink away, and it was worth investigating the healer.

It was evident he had an agenda for me when he ordered Selasi, "I will escort her to Lani. You will assign two guards at the place where I disappeared in case anything else enters. Afterwards, alert His Majesty as to why I'm late and that I'm bringing a guest. Have Milfred prepare an extra meal." He glanced back to me. "Preferably something hearty."

I had never met someone so proficient at giving orders.

Selasi nodded tersely. "Yes, Lord." He trotted forward through the snow ahead of us.

Then it was just me and the "Highness" left alone, and I couldn't help but feel out of my depth. I threw a few glances his way. I didn't know what he had to gain from welcoming a trespasser. The other reason I was walking alongside him was that when I did touch him, something strange happened. I wanted to understand more.

At that point, darkness had arrived, but his earring reflected soft light while trudging through snow.

"You have a rather direct gaze," he muttered. "Some consider that rude."

"I don't know who it is I'm staring at."

"Safir Astana, crowned Prince of Walyre. You may address me as 'Your Royal Highness,' then it's just 'Lord' afterwards."

"Well, I'm Eve."

For what it's worth.

"Selasi said I was trespassing on 'His Majesty's' land."

"He was referring to my brother, whom you'll have the privilege to meet."

The dynamic must have been interesting, to live with the brother who lorded over you. It would be intriguing to observe the two of them. However, I couldn't help but think that the further I walked, the less likely it was I would be able to return. I promised myself I would find my way back somehow. I would play compliant only for as long as it benefited me.

Trying to plan proved futile when the forest opened and before me stood a palace. It encompassed my entire vision, built from white stone with large arching windows that spanned each floor. It was several hundred feet wide, five floors tall, and at either end towers rose another two stories higher than the rest.

I hadn't realized I had stopped walking and was standing with my neck craned back, my mouth open in amazement.

Safir smirked beside me. "This is Walor Palace. There's much more to see." Safir continued to walk.

I followed suit, though my one eye danced across the scene. Dozens of lights flickered from the windows, casting a soft glow onto the snow. It seemed too fanciful to be real. My first thought was how *warm* it looked. I didn't know what I'd expected from an alternate reality, or what I guessed was an alternate reality. The more I waded through the more I realized how intricate and full that reality was. It was just as tangible as mine, and that alone was terrifying.

We passed a marble block sitting in solitude, coated in snow. It emanated sorrow, a similar feeling to what I'd felt when I'd first touched Safir. He glanced to it before reverting his gaze.

We came upon a set of double doors. Gold inscription along the edges met in the middle, creating an image of what looked like a single flame. Safir opened the doors, gesturing me inside.

Ushering myself in, I stomped snow out of my sneakers. Safir closed the doors, leaving us in the middle of a grand entrance. The ornate, arched ceiling matched the intricate staircase in front of us that led upwards to what I assumed was the second floor. Illuminating ornate paintings and gold molding were candelabras at each corner and along the steps of the staircase.

Safir only let me look around for a few seconds before gesturing me towards the stairs, rings on his fingers gleaming. I followed, still in awe, as we walked up the stairs, the whole area reminiscent of a Renaissance painting. We took the left side of the staircase to emerge onto the second floor. The extravagance continued along the hallway. Every so often a door led to rooms I was becoming increasingly curious about.

I fell behind Safir, who was unfazed by how beautiful his home was. I was just as distracted when I caught my first glimpse of my face in a mirror on the wall. Shit, I looked worse than a few hours prior. The discoloration made my eye look obscene. It was too much to stomach seeing what I did to myself for the sake of scraping by.

Safir paused and looked back to see me grimacing at my own face. "It's not always this bad," I said like a confession.

"Whatever your masochistic profession may be, you must be rather skilled."

"I am." I hadn't meant for my tone to sound so somber, but it was unavoidable. Safir's expression softened ever so slightly in the mirror. Silence hung between us for a second as I winced at my own touch along my jaw. "It's not a great feeling, being good at something you hate so much."

His jaw hung open before he shut it and nodded slowly. "A wretched feeling, I'm sure."

Clearing my throat, I muttered, "Let's get to your healer, Safir."

His face morphed into a scowl. "You're to refer to me as 'Your Royal Highness' and 'Lord' afterwards."

I don't plan to stay long enough to have to remember that.

Safir's scowl still present, we resumed. The corridor extended onward to the right, though, we stopped at a door. Inside another staircase spiraled upwards and downwards. Narrow windows lined the inside along with lit sconces.

"This way," Safir said while stepping forward. I hesitated, because nothing felt more like being taken prisoner than being ushered into a strange tower. He glanced back. "Our healer resides upstairs."

"That's convenient if you wanted to lure a prisoner there."

"There are many more worthy of being a prisoner than you."

"That's hardly a comfort."

Safir arched an eyebrow. "You have been completely transparent with me up to this point. I swear on my honor to do the same for you."

In any other circumstance, I wouldn't have dared to rely upon the good intentions of a stranger. But Safir apparently couldn't conceal his emotions as well as others, not if I touched him. I looked down at his hand and back up to him. I reached out. "Do you promise me?"

His ember eyes widened as his fingers twitched at his side. How much was he used to being touched? He barely clasped my forearm, allowing me to experience his feelings. I was able to sense his resoluteness and transparency. There was no maliciousness or sense of conniving, only a persistent hope that was driven by the deep-seated grief I had felt before. It was enough to move anyone to tears. I knew it well.

He released me with his ember eyes flaring beneath his white locks. I gnawed on the inside of my sore cheek, unsure what he was wondering, wishing I still had a hold of him to know.

"Does your healer work similarly to your touch?"

"In a way," he said while gesturing inside the staircase.

"How good is she?"

"The best, or else she wouldn't be here."

Could the healer be useful to me in more ways than one? We began scaling upwards to the point my legs began to ache once again. The stone steps were getting steeper, though I did see a few massive doors on the way up, entry ways to other floors of the palace. Finally, as my breaths became heavier, Safir stopped and opened a door. The fifth floor had similar décor to the others, with gold ornate moldings and designs on the walls, but instead of the hallways extending onwards, it stopped at a door.

Before following Safir, I glanced past a long row of windows where a set of double doors stood. I wanted to be curious, but I was hardly in any position to be nosy in a foreign world. I caught up to Safir as he opened a door.

We stepped into a room, dimly lit with a candelabra, arching windows on either side. Empty beds lined the room with another door on the opposite wall. Safir knocked.

A middle-aged woman appeared from it, and quickly shut it behind her. The herbal aroma that emanated from beyond that door made me wonder what was being sealed away. The healer's hair held large, black spirals that she'd tried pulling back in a bun, with a few curls falling into her face. Her eyes were a warm brown, with her skin a similar umber tone to Selasi's. She wore a dark green dress with a laced bodice, fitted at her waist and falling to the floor. The only giveaway of her age was a few wrinkles adorning her forehead. Her shoulders were rounded, with the sort of stature that made you think she spent a great deal of time hunched over a book.

She folded her hands and curtseyed. "Evening, Lord. How may–" Her brown eyes fell upon me, and her mouth fell open. "Who's done this? What's become of this woman?" Her voice was deeper than I'd expected, smoky yet soft.

"Lani, this is Eve, a guest of mine. As you can see, she's in need of healing. I'll leave her in your hands for now."

"Of course. She'll be looked after properly…" Her face morphed into a look of confusion, which deepened her wrinkles. "Lord, are *you* feeling well? I cannot seem to–"

"We'll discuss that later. For now, tend to my guest. We're to meet with His Majesty soon." Safir hardly looked to me before turning and leaving me in a tower with the third stranger I would interact with that day. To my relief, Lani didn't intend for us to be strangers for long.

She rubbed my shoulders, shepherding me towards one of the beds. Up close I could see she had a few grey hairs. "You poor dear, what an evening you must have endured. I detest whatever creature brought you to this state. I can only hope you reciprocated the pain dealt to you."

"I did," I said while lying on one of the beds, feeling it sink beneath me.

"Very good. I only wish more petite lilies such as yourself had the valor to stand with a straight back and a dagger at the ready. It's kind of His Royal Highness to allow me to aid you in your time of need. Given the time of day I hadn't expected to be visited by anyone. I was just experimenting with the benefits of crawlsey flowers for skin irritation-"

The ringing in my ears from that day's events drowned out Lani's monologue. I appreciated her chattering because too many people that day had been asking me questions. Her voice only caught my attention again when she muttered, "Huh, this is unusual."

Lani placed her cool hands on my face, closed her eyes, and took in a deep breath through her nose. "Let's try this again."

Safir

It's not a great feeling, being good at something you hate so much.

How could a stranger have summed up my entire existence in one sentence? Even more startling, she clearly understood what my touch entailed, yet she didn't recoil. She even embraced it. Never had I observed that in someone who didn't stand to gain from my Blessing. I knew what I must have conveyed to her in the courtyard and in the tower. They weren't sweet sentiments or warm affections. They were the deepest burdens of my reality. Yet she remained unwavering.

My mind was so consumed by such thoughts that I almost overlooked Selasi emerging from the stairwell ahead of me.

"Lord!" he called. "I've alerted Milfred, who's delighted, and I've attempted to inform His Majesty-"

"Attempted?"

"He desired further information from you."

"I'm on my way to him now. Selasi, tell me, can you sense me now?" My curiosity. My agitation. My hesitant hope.

Selasi nodded. "Yes, Lord."

"Interesting. It's strictly in the girl's presence you're unable to perceive me."

"Where is she now?"

"I left her with Lani."

"But, Lord, if she hinders you could she not also hinder Lani?"
Shit.

Pinching the bridge of my nose, I ordered, "Regardless, give Lani a few minutes, then bring the girl here to meet with us. It'll be interesting if she can hinder both Lani and I."

"Yes, Lord." Selasi turned back towards the stairwell from which I had emerged.

I opened the door before me and stepped into my brother's quarters. He sat by the fireplace, poised. Based on his lack of a welcome I presumed he was in deep thought.

"Ashire?" I said, closing the door behind me and navigating to where he sat. His floor was covered in books and charts, which one mustn't disturb. He preferred his chaos right where it was. I never knew how he slept, for his bedding was also coated in a layer of literature. I sat across from him as I had when we had our most paramount conversations. But the air was uneasy.

His hands were folded over his mouth while he stared into the fire. "Is it true?" he asked through his fingers. "There is one who can impede your Blessing?"

I nodded.

He sighed and rubbed his eyes. "How does she do it?"

"Similar to me, by being present she's able to exude herself."

"Interesting. Does anyone else know?"

"Just Selasi and I, though possibly Lani if the girl is able to hinder her as well."

"Yes, Selasi told me the girl was in a poor state. You seem to trust her," he murmured, picking up his gaze to meet mine.

He must have felt my sentiments hanging in the air. "She is honest, though oblivious to her capabilities."

"Her obliviousness is to our advantage for now, so we'll keep it so. She can exploit this to garner a relationship with you. With the crown."

"Eve wouldn't do that."

Ashire's eyebrows rose to a ridiculous height. "Oh, *Eve* wouldn't? Would you be willing to bet your life on that? Tell me, is she tempting to the eye?"

"As Selasi said, she's in a poor state. I could hardly discern her features."

"If so, I implore you not to think with your downstairs gentleman. Kingdoms have been reduced to dust over less."

"Don't be absurd."

"But you do clearly trust her, Safir. If her beauty didn't capture your confidence, what part of her did?"

I remembered her strong yet trembling grasp. It had been so assured and she so humble.

I'm freezing, and I'm hungry. That's all I am.

There had been something admirable about her humility while she stood statuesque in the face of Selasi's sword. "She knows of my touch, but she doesn't retreat. Not even the second time, when *she* reached out to *me*. It was unexpected."

"I'm sure it was," Ashire muttered. "Selasi said she entered from our courtyard?"

"An unkempt corner of the courtyard, yes. I haven't a single, reasonable explanation for how she appeared. You may see it if you wish, but she comes from an unremarkable world that happens to be connected to ours."

"You entered into her realm?"

I nodded. "It opens into the middle of a forest, surrounded by nothing. I've posted two guards in case any other unexpected visitors appear."

"But it's a vulnerability that just so happens to be in our courtyard. This couldn't have appeared coincidentally. Surely, an opposer conducted such a feat to have a perfect route to the capital."

"And the first person to enter is a defenseless girl who's capable of hindering Blessings?"

Ashire narrowed his gaze at me. "You think she's the cure for your Blessing, don't you?"

"I think she can be utilized."

"Safir, your purpose in life is not to be cured. You are as you are."

What I am is a burden.

He grimaced. "I sense your guilt. It's choking the room. Are you still brooding regarding Lord Korak's reaction earlier today? I assure you, he's fine. You at least made him stop groaning about taxes for a second."

"And substituted it with his screams? It only served as a reminder how onerous my presence is to others-"

"Stop."

"But if there's even a shred of hope this doesn't have to be my fate, can you blame me for seeking her help? I'm not saying I could be as I once was, but I could at least help share some of your obligations." I gestured to the chaos that was his room. "I could relieve you of this madness if it meant I could leave these walls."

"You already aid me in abundance."

"Clearly not enough."

He smirked. "Clearly?"

"The crown has aged you considerably."

"You could have properly conveyed your point by saying the crown has aged me. You only added the 'considerably' to be a cunt. The girl sounds useful, but I'd hate for you to depend on a stranger to function."

"I cannot fathom why you're not seeing the benefit of having her here. I am trying to expand my capabilities to function, not only as part of this house, but as a man."

Ashire's eyebrows furrowed. "Do you intend to keep her voluntarily for the rest of your existence? Unless you intend to not give her an option."

"I feel certain she'll be swayed with a few warm meals and allowing Lani to heal her."

"And if that's not enough? Are you willing to hold a woman captive if it meant you felt more in control of your Blessing? You could do it so easily."

It's not a great feeling, being good at something you hate so much.

I knew desperation could drive men to cruelty. "I could never do that."

"Yes, you could. You fortunately won't. Your eagerness to cure yourself is blinding you to foolishness of trusting an outsider who was probably planted here by an enemy." His eyes were beginning to swell with frustration. He stood, standing over me as he embodied his role as king. "I will meet her and determine her value, but I make no promises."

That was all I needed. I trusted the rest to unfurl in my favor.

Eve

Sweat dripped from Lani's brow. She hunched over with her hands on her knees. "There," she panted. "You look much better." She sucked in a deep breath. "Feel better?"

The swelling had dissipated from my face, along with the deep throbbing ache. Even the pain from my ribs had vanished. "I feel great. Are you okay?"

"Oh, don't waste energy worrying over me. It's been a while since I've had to work that hard, and for an ailment that minor. Strange." Lani turned and disappeared behind the door from which she'd entered.

I leaned over the bed to peer into the room she was rummaging through. Inside, rows of shelves held hundreds of vials full of strange liquids, along with mountains of books lining the walls. Plants hung from the ceiling and grew in pots, creating a floral maze.

"Lani?" I called. "How powerful is your healing? Could it do more than what you've just done for me?"

"Of course." She returned with a small cup of tea. "But it depends on the nature of the injury and how old it is. The fresher the injury, the more effective I can be."

I hesitantly took the cup. "The nature of the injury?"

"Such as how severe it is and where. It's much easier to heal a bone than the heart or the brain. The more complex, the more difficult."

"How old does an injury have to be for you to be unable to heal it?"

"My Blessing cannot have a tangible effect if an injury is greater than one year old, depending on the complexity of the area. Not even Fae magic could help with an ailment that severe." My disappointment must have been obvious as she narrowed her gaze. "Do you have someone in mind, or are you just inquisitive?"

"Just curious," I lied.

Lani gestured to the tea. "Drink it. It'll help the remaining swelling recede, though you will have a strong urge to relieve yourself in the next hour."

Noted.

I held the cup to my lips, realizing I'd not only walked into a strange tower but was ingesting a strange beverage from a person I had never met before. However, I doubted someone who wanted to hold me prisoner would waste so much energy on trying to heal me, so I sipped on the tea. The sweetness coated my palate.

"Very good." Lani plopped down next to me. "Let's sleep now."

"What?"

Lani leaned against me and closed her eyes. Her breaths blew a few curls hanging in front of her face. She wasn't particularly heavy, but I had no idea how I was supposed to conduct myself in that situation. In a matter of seconds, she was sleeping, and I sat there unmoving.

A few minutes of silence passed before the door leading to the staircase opened. Selasi entered and looked at us both, puzzled. "You look much better, but what happened?" he whispered.

"She just fell asleep."

Selasi sucked in his lips, seeming to stifle a laugh. "I will help you move her, but His Royal Highness and His Majesty are expecting you to dine with them."

Great.

Selasi looped his arms under Lani's legs. I grasped her shoulders, and we both laid her down in the bed. She gave a snore before we made our way towards the staircase. Selasi guided me towards the third floor where I presumed, I'd see Safir and his brother. It was like the second floor, only it contained many more portraits of supposed royals.

"Selasi." I said his name out loud for the first time. "What can I expect from this?"

He paused just as we stepped out of the staircase onto the third floor. "Pardon?"

"What do Safir–"

"His Royal Highness."

"–and the king expect from me? What's the point of all this?"

Selasi resumed guiding me down the east corridor. "I can't speak for His Majesty or His Royal Highness, but I can speak to their character. They're both good men who were born into an unsettling time."

That still didn't give me confidence. Suspicion gnawed in my gut that I was never going to leave that place. The feeling didn't improve as we strolled past doors, paintings, and candelabras.

The arched windows to my right showed snow still falling outside.

The second Selasi paused at a door with the golden flame emblem on it, my stomach rolled. When he reached for the door handle, he looked to me with a glint in his grey eyes. "Give a curtsey when you see His Majesty, and don't forget to thank him for having you."

With that, the door swung open, revealing a room lined with the same arching windows. A burst of warmth encased me a fireplace burnt at either end of the room, lighting an array of tapestries. The two persons who sat at a long wooden table seemed unnervingly fixated on me.

Two pairs of ember eyes were watching me, but I only recognized Safir's. He sat with his elbow on the table and finger under his chin as he studied me intently from beneath his white locks. Without his cloak, I could see his stature was leaner than I previously thought, with a pair of solid shoulders and a lean trunk beneath his leather vest. The two men shared the same sharp jaw and the same studious expression. Each had the orange charm dangling on an earring from the ridge of their left ear.

The brother wore similar clothes to Safir, only he had a golden chain encircling his shoulders. The links were ornately designed in diamond shape and had a red jewel between each link. In the middle of the chain a golden flame with a red jewel in the middle. The status symbol made my sweatpants look like rags. He had long, dark brown hair that fell to his shoulders tied back with leather string. His nose was long, coming to a point which was pronounced by his narrow eyes that hadn't wavered from me. There were creases in his forehead, like Lani's, yet not quite as deep. A small smile on his lips left me feeling like I had just been presented as a meal. I squared my shoulders tightly.

When I realized I had paused for too long, I curtseyed, or at least what I thought was a curtsy. I mostly just bent my knees while looking to the floor.

"Thanks for having me."

The man I presumed to be the king stood from his chair, gesturing to another empty chair across from Safir. His voice was rich and deep in a way that made you feel compelled to follow, as he said, "Join us, please."

Safir

Eve's facial features were more delicate without the swelling and discoloration. Sapphire eyes scanned the room before finding my brother and me. The slightest hint of apprehension was evident in her gaze, but she didn't appear the least bit intimidated by my brother's company. Upon her entering I could tell all sense of my presence was removed from the air. Yet I knew that wouldn't be enough to convince him she was valuable.

And by the gods, her curtsey was truly dreadful.

At Ashire's insistence, she sat across from me, her sapphire eyes flickering towards me. I wished I could have held her gaze longer, to better predict her behavior. My entire existence as prince seemed dependent on her in that one evening. I internally pleaded Ashire wasn't so kingly that he'd dissuade her.

"I'm told you go by Eve?" he began while sitting at the head of the table.

She nodded.

"And you've clearly had the pleasure of meeting my brother." He gestured to me, openly examining her reactions with each word he spoke. She gave him another nod, not even glancing to me as he spoke. Ashire sat back and folded his hands in his lap. "I was also told you were injured. Lani has done excellent work, as expected."

"She's very kind." Eve's voice was steady and warm, like the fires burning at either end of our dining room.

"She truly is. It was kind of my brother to bring you to her." Eve nodded again, perhaps not wanting to give away too much.

"You've found us on the day we celebrate the memory of our departed mother. Were you aware of this?"

"I wasn't."

"Most importantly, and rather impossibly, I'm told you are not of this world. Is that correct?" Ashire leaned onto his elbows. "I'd love to hear more about it as we dine."

Just as he spoke, two servers entered and began ushering in our meal. Milfred must have been wanting to impress in the kitchen

based on the heartiness of the dishes. The potatoes were drowned in
a rich butter that was soaking into the bottoms of a flaky game pie.
Steam rose from the dish almost clouding my vision. Yet I could
clearly see Eve gawk at her dish. She must have been famished since
she hadn't eaten her frozen stones of sustenance.

I picked up my utensils first and cut into the pie, piling the
game meat, onions, and crust onto my fork. As I placed the savory
bite into my mouth, Eve followed suit much more carefully than I.
Upon taking a bite, she closed her eyes and let out a small sigh. I
couldn't help but smirk as she piled another bite onto her fork.

Ashire parted with a partial grin. "Does the food please you?"

She nodded again as she swallowed her second bite.

"Now, could you enlighten me on the place you hail from?
Speak of your country. Is it comparable to what you've seen thus
far?"

She paused only a few seconds before answering, "There aren't
castles, not really. There's no monarchy. We have elected officials
who govern. I'm from a state called Pennsylvania that's part of a
larger country."

"And what is it you do in order to live?"

"I'm a boxer, a fighter of sorts," she clarified. "People pay to
watch me fight other boxers."

"You're a brawler?" Ashire asked. "That's a rather barbaric way
to make a living."

Eve resumed eating her meal. From what I could tell, she
thought the same, but for whatever reason she still brawled for a
living.

Ashire continued interrogating her. "Do you swear your
allegiance to your country?"

She tilted her head to the side. "I'm not necessarily bound to my
country."

Ashire reached for his wine and took a sip. For someone who
hadn't seemed keen to meet Eve, he appeared to be gaining more
interest. "And does your world have Blessings such as ours?"

She paused with her fork mid-way to her mouth. "Blessings?"

"Such as my dear brother's."

"Are you referring to what Sa– I mean, what His Royal
Highness and Lani can do with their touch?"

Ashire raised a single eyebrow. "Indeed."

"I can't think of anything similar where I'm from. There are people with skill but nothing more." She took a sip of wine, though stifled a grimace, before she asked, "What are Blessings?"

"Some say Blessings are an act of divine intervention. Others believe they're an offering from the first intelligent beings to walk the land. More than likely they're an act of luck." Ashire popped a piece of potato into his mouth, chewing and swallowing before continuing,

"Regardless, they have been part of our history for as long as man knew how to write. Lani has the Blessing of healing. Our cook, Milfred, can multiply anything she bakes by three. It boils down to a game of chance."

Eve seemed to be digesting the information well, given she came from a realm that didn't contain Blessings. "And you?" she asked.

"What is your Blessing?"

Ashire's face fell slightly. "It's not something I rely upon. It's hardly clever."

"My brother can physically force anything away from him if he utters the word 'repel,'" I informed her. "He doesn't find it reflects his intellectual standards."

"It's a means of defense." Eve shrugged.

"But with an army at my disposal I have very little need to rely upon my Blessing," Ashire countered. "And my sword skill is far more *respectable* than my Blessing."

Eve took another sip of her wine, grimacing less. "Does everyone have a Blessing?"

"No. Most with Blessings marry into the noble families."

"Many are given regrettable Blessings," I said, earning a look from my brother.

"There have been so many throughout the ages. Typically, those with Blessings are employed in a noble household if they aren't themselves part of a noble family." My brother leaned towards Eve. "Do you think you know my brother's Blessing?"

"I couldn't say for certain."

"Guess," he commanded. I shot him a glare. He would have known my frustration had she not been in the room, but then she looked to me, narrowing her gaze.

It was enough to make a man feel exposed.

"Others can experience what he's feeling emotionally or physically by touch."

"Oh," Ashire hummed while taking a sip of wine, "you're observant. I applaud you."

Damn him for being so patronizing.

"Eve," I said. "Typically, those within my vicinity can experience what I'm feeling or even what I *have* felt by just being in the same room. It's been years since it's been limited to requiring physical contact…until now."

Her brows furrowed. "Why now?"

"We believe it's because of you."

"Is that why you asked *what* I am?"

"Goodness, Safir," Ashire said over his pie. "You were taught better manners in the presence of a lady."

I ignored him. "I was taken aback by your effect."

Her eyes grew wide. "I'm not doing anything. I swear to you."

"Dear Eve," Ashire said, "you are. I could perceive him clear as water before you walked in."

She held her hands up in defense. "I'm not doing it on purpose."

"I just can't fathom how you're doing it while you claim your world doesn't have Blessings," I said.

"I have no answers for you," she said, her voice becoming harsher. "I was on my way home when I fell into this. I happened here by chance."

"The location of the portal you entered," Ashire interjected. "Is it in a safe place?"

"It's in the middle of nowhere and near my home, so only I would have a reason to encounter it. Will I see my home again?" she asked, making me almost reach to reassure her, but Ashire wasn't so keen on comforting gestures.

"That depends. All new relationships are born from one side aiding the other and vice versa. So," he mused while picking up his goblet, "do you think your world would be of use to us?"

Eve audibly swallowed as she leaned back from her plate, seemingly lost her appetite. "I-I don't know."

"And could your country ever become aware of our existence?"

"They wouldn't find out from me, if that's what you're asking."

"How can we trust that?"

I knew Ashire wasn't willing to trust her with such a risk so close to the palace, and there wasn't any immediate way for her to prove herself. Eve opened her mouth and then closed it. I could hear her grinding her teeth. "I can't stay here," she said slowly. "I have responsibilities."

"I'm sure," Ashire crooned. "But coincidence or not, you did trespass on the most guarded property in this kingdom, and swift punishment has always been carried out for such an offense."

"Ashire–"

He silenced me with a knowing look. "Yet seeing that you're capable of keeping my brother's Blessing in check, you've presented us with an interesting opportunity. I will offer you this: you will give us your time, as much as you can spare, to be my brother's advisor so he might accomplish his own responsibilities."

"I'd be his pet?" she snapped.

"*Advisor* is the title you'd be given. In exchange, you'll be fed, housed, and healed as needed by Lani. If you do not wish to participate, well, we're obviously aware of where to find you."

We both watched her weigh my brother's proposition. Part of me was pleased he had decided in my favor, but he could have done it so that she felt like she had more of a choice. Whatever was holding her back must have been influential.

"I can give you three days out of the week," she said, though grudgingly.

"Four," Ashire bargained.

"I could do four days when I don't have a fight scheduled, but that's all I'm willing to give."

Eve had a spine that was usually unwise before a king, but it seemed to entice Ashire. "The crown always appreciates making a new ally."

Eve

I didn't owe them anything. I could agree to the three days then never return. I doubted individuals who depended on swords would do well trying to track me down in my world. However, if this encounter wasn't some concussion-induced dream, I could get a few good meals out of it and be healed by Lani. It was going to spread me thin across a schedule that didn't allow much give. If being there was truly going to be advantageous, I needed to figure out how it wouldn't benefit just me…

The king acted like he was the smartest person in the room, and he wanted everyone else to know it as well. I resisted looking to Safir for guidance. He hadn't been as demeaning as the king, yet he'd remained mostly silent throughout dinner. Honestly, I was disappointed. I supposed it could have been much worse, like being confined in a dungeon for the rest of my days.

Dinner concluded when the king had his third glass of wine. I swore I'd dream about the meat pies, never having tasted anything so delicious in all my life. I would have asked for more, but the king insisted I be escorted back to my "realm" and return the next day to enact my new role. At first, I assumed Selasi would walk me back, but Safir volunteered as the king stood from the table.

We followed suit and descended the same set of stairs in silence towards the first floor. I braved the blistering cold again. The snow had ceased, leaving the courtyard so quiet I wanted to fidget.

Safir continued to be stoic, even as we passed the same marble platform we had passed earlier. It was covered in snow, but still emanated the same sense of sorrow. Safir glanced but nothing more, which made me wonder.

"Is this her?"

He paused and looked back to me.

"Is this your mother?"

His stare lingered on the marble platform before he nodded and continued walking, saying nothing. I had expected more of a reaction. I wondered if he were upset because of the dinner, which would have been ridiculous because I was the one who was entitled to be upset.

"You did well," he told me after a few deafeningly silent moments. "I know my brother can be rather off-putting, but he has the best intentions."

"So, you *can* speak?" I sneered while trudging through snow. "You hardly said anything in there."

"It wasn't my place," he snapped. "You're not a prisoner, do you understand that? This is a symbiotic relationship. We both have something to gain from the other."

"Yes, I heard. It seemed decided before I had any say."

Safir stopped in the snow. His scowl had vanished, but his eyes flared. As the wind blew his white strands into his stare, he extended his hand out to me.

Was that his way of reassuring me? He'd been hesitant to touch beforehand. I wasn't sure what had changed, but for some reason I didn't want to discourage it. I placed my forearm in his grasp, feeling his emotions fill the void, each more powerful and real than the last. A desire for resolution or for peace. There was that still-present grief I was beginning to recognize, a grief for what was missing. No ill intent was driven towards me– only a sharp hope beating like a heart, re-asserting itself every few seconds.

When Safir released me, I felt bold enough to be curious aloud. "You said it had been years since it required actual touch for someone to sense you. Why did it change?"

He frowned. "That is of little consequence now." He stepped closer, the wind making his white hairs billow with each gust. "Does it not bother you?"

"What?"

He held up his hand.

My head shook. "Why should it?"

"Many find it intrusive."

"That's not your fault."

The corner of his mouth turned up ever so slightly. "I'd take that to heart if you could fully understand its extent. Only being able to sense me through touch skews your opinion on the matter."

Then why ask me if disagreeing with him made my opinion matter less? "Just because someone isn't as bothered by you as you are yourself doesn't mean there's something wrong with them."

He frowned. "That's not what I meant."

"Yes, it is. I'm sorry that I'm not bothered by your Blessing, if that would make your self-deprecation easier for you."

I marched away, suddenly warm despite it being freezing. I had overstepped my bounds in a foreign world where I could end up in a dungeon, but I didn't care for being faulted for something I couldn't help. It wasn't my fault I couldn't sense him as everyone else could, but even if I could, it wouldn't have bothered me. He clearly exhausted himself trying not to "intrude" upon others. To be repulsed by his Blessing that he tried so hard to conceal would have been cruel, but I didn't think I could convince him of that.

Not that it felt important to convince him! I had just met Safir. And his world's burdens weren't mine to shoulder. It wasn't as though I didn't have enough obligations.

I approached the invisible door that would lead me back to my world. Two guards were stationed close by, sporting armor and impressive swords at their hips. They didn't bother to look my way. Safir dismissed them and they returned to the palace. My frozen lasagnas were still on the ground. Pausing only to pick them back up, I heard Safir rasp directly behind me,

"Eve."

I froze.

His mouth lowered towards my ear. "You said you felt like you didn't have a say. Let this be the time to have your say."

I turned around to see him just inches from me, finding my head only reached the top of his chest. His expression was soft. I hadn't realized I was holding my breath while I waited for him to speak.

"You can return here or remain in your realm. Regardless, I want you to make that choice."

"Your brother,"

"He'll forgive it," Safir interjected. "But if I let you leave without thinking you had a choice, then I'd be proving myself to be as atrocious as I think I am."

Safir didn't extend his touch, so I didn't seek it out. I took a few steps back with my lasagnas in hand. "If your Blessing is part of you, I won't fault you for it, but it's not fair to make it my burden to convince you of that." I took one more step back. "I have enough burdens."

And I allowed myself to be engulfed by my familiar, duller world. Safir disappeared and the snow was replaced by frozen dirt beneath my feet. I was still looking forward, only seeing bare forest ahead of me.

The police sirens were no longer piercing the air, leaving me in silence. I clutched the frozen meals closer to me as I recalled his expression. We had both managed up until that point, so what was that nagging sensation in my gut? Perhaps my tune had changed once I'd realized he was willing to give me a choice. It made me reluctantly want to rely on him. It was a feeling like taking in a big gulp of air after holding your breath for too long.

All I could wonder, in that moment, was if I would have believed any of it when I woke the next morning.

Safir

"I like her well enough, for her price being as small as food and healing," Ashire murmured. "I think you'll be able to benefit from each other."

I raised my eyebrows at him over my goblet of wine. "It seems like I stand to gain much more than she."

He grinned mischievously. "I think she stands to gain a great deal if she's smart."

"Meaning?"

"You don't see the similarities? The steadfastness, the strong sense of self-preservation, the temper. Best of luck managing that. And above all, she seems just as starved for companionship as you."

"Tread. Carefully."

"I think you two will benefit from each other's company. It's always pleasant to sit in the same room with someone with whom you can just be."

I ruffled my hair, fatigue wanting to overtake me. "I'm not sure how much she likes my company. She said some of the kindest things in the most horrible way just before she departed."

And she'd put me in my place with her parting words.

If your Blessing is part of you, I won't fault you for it, but it's not fair to make it my burden and convince you. I have enough burdens.

I wanted to tell myself that she only felt that way because she could only sense me through touch. If she could experience the full scope of what I could do, of what I had done, then she would have reacted as everyone had, as everyone was entitled to react. It wasn't my Blessing that burdened her, but my own perception of it. She remained the key to acting in my role as prince, but she was also one of the few to refuse to shy away from my Blessing. Even if she only understood a fraction of it, I didn't want to relinquish her presence.

I must have cared a great deal for her opinion because her words lingered long after she had departed.

Ashire looked to me smugly.

"She likes your company well enough for now. She was obviously more at ease with you than she was with me."

"That's not much of a compliment given your disposition, and she did not guarantee she would return."

"She will. Trust that I am as clever as I say I am. Regardless, I'm still uneasy knowing a vulnerability is close. Only Vada knows how long that portal has been present."

I sighed while pinching the bridge of my nose. "At least her realm appears docile according to her."

Ashire snorted. "I have no intention of trusting her supposed testimony."

"Then what would you propose?"

Leaning back with his arms extended over his head, he speculated, "Perhaps a small group of my men to infiltrate, observe, and report back. Nothing else unless deemed necessary. I'd prefer to hear their impression of her realm." A soft knock came from behind us. Ashire called, "Enter."

Beyond the door was Lani whose droopy eyes and tousled hair were indicators she had just been roused from a deep sleep. Her hands had the slightest tremor. She folded them when she approached us. My curiosity must have been evident as she glanced to me and back to Ashire.

"You called for me, Your Majesty?"

Ashire took a long drink from his goblet. "Lani, did you have to strain yourself to heal the strange girl?"

Lani nodded. "It was startling. Even with firm contact, I had to concentrate to have any impact. I couldn't fully heal her given the amount of time I had."

"Pardon?" I asked. "She looked to be in a far better state than when I left her with you."

"I found multiple old injuries which will take much longer to fully remedy, predominantly to her head."

"Explains her temper," Ashire sneered. "You would have thought she would have taken our deal faster, since she's in such need of healing." He turned to me. "Or do you think the damage has retarded her from making coherent decisions?"

"I think your ego has retarded you from possessing coherent social talents," I retorted.

"Well, then, thank Vada we'll have you for that from now on."

Lani's eyes widened. "For His Royal Highness? She is returning?"

"Yes, and Lani," Ashire said while turning towards her, "we're all well aware you are as horrible at being discreet as you are a marvelous healer, so it would serve the crown well if you were careful when you discuss the girl with other people."

Lani's face made its best effort to not form a scowl. "I would never do, nor have I ever done, anything to displease the crown."

"Goodness, no, not the crown," my brother simpered. "But I do recall you discussing the rash that plagued Selasi's crotch for an entire week."

I choked on my sip of wine while trying to stifle my laughter.

Ashire looked towards the doorway. "Selasi? I take it the state of your crotch has improved?"

There was a definite pause before Selasi spoke defeatedly from the hallway. "Yes, Your Majesty."

"Very good– much to the delight of all the young women of Walyre." Ashire turned back to Lani. "Now, Lani, if you're willing to discuss that then gods know what you're capable of babbling about."

"I offer my word I will not discuss the capabilities of the girl openly," she asserted.

"I take it then you fully understand the ramifications of what her presence does to your Blessing and likewise what it does to Safir's?"

Lani beamed at me. "Is that why I couldn't feel you? She is that capable?"

I nodded. "She not only suppresses my Blessing but those around her."

"You must be pleased, Lord. You won't have to isolate yourself so."

That notion made me smile, for Lani wasn't happy so she wouldn't have to sense me but because she understood my burden.

"But how is she capable of such a feat? Is her own Blessing to stall other Blessings?" Lani asked.

"She claims her world isn't as Blessed as ours," I interjected.

Ashire glanced to each of us. "Which leads to a few possible options: Either she is lying, and her world does have Blessings, or she does possess a Blessing and is unaware."

"She wouldn't lie," I defended, sure in Eve's transparency. She truly appeared perplexed as to why her mere presence would hinder my Blessing.

Ashire rolled his eyes. "Very well. Entertaining the hopeful wishes of my brother, let's assume she is honest. For whatever reason, she possesses the Blessing to hinder others without her knowledge."

"It's subtle," I murmured. "It's possible she wouldn't have had a way of knowing until encountering people such as us."

Lani's head shook. "But for her to be using her Blessing constantly and at such a high capacity– it's amazing she survived infancy."

I didn't know why that hadn't occurred to us earlier. If Eve truly had a Blessing and was using it as extensively as she had been the time we'd interacted with her, she should have shown signs of exhaustion. Blessings took a toll on the body based on how they were utilized, as evident by Lani's trembling hands. Even my Blessing ebbed and flowed based on my fatigue. Yet if I or Lani or Ashire were to use our Blessings at maximum capacity, we'd more than likely faint after a few hours, let alone an entire day.

"Perhaps she isn't using it at its greatest capacity," I pondered aloud. "It's possible she's only using it lightly."

"That would still take a physical toll, especially as a child," Lani countered.

I shrugged. "Then it's possible that she's had to build endurance. I'm sure there was no one in her realm to educate her on how to spare herself from exhaustion due to her Blessing."

Ashire stared into the fire as if it had wronged him. "Lani, it would serve us, and the girl, if you could help her tame her Blessing during your healing sessions. She'll prove to be useful not just to Safir if she's truly capable of impeding Blessings. It might be advantageous if our neighbors should try to thwart the crown."

"Do not weaponize her," I snapped so sharply the air thickened with my ire. "That will not be a fate for her to suffer from."

Lani began to shiver beside me while Ashire stiffened. "Control yourself," he commanded.

"You *will* promise me."

My brother held up his hands in defense. "I will do no such thing to Eve. I just said it would be advantageous, not that I would place her at the frontline. I'm not one to follow in the previous king's footsteps."

I swallowed hard as I tried to focus on the warmth of the fire. Whenever I felt a noxious emotion, I tried to mask it with the feeling of warmth for the ease of those around me. It was a trick I had gotten rather good at. Lani breathed a sigh of relief and Ashire relaxed into his chair.

"Apologies," I muttered. It took more energy to climb down from my more potent emotions than to feel them. The late hours made it harder to keep such moments from occurring, making me crave a night's rest.

"Unnecessary. More proof of the benefit of the girl," Ashire said while finishing his wine. "Lani, you may retire for the night."

She nodded, curtseyed, and left us to each other's company.

Ashire's words confirmed my suspicions that he felt the need for the girl to also benefit the crown. I didn't take it to heart. He understood my Blessing from a very practical point of view like Eve, who saw no use finding fault in something I couldn't fully control. He had never made me apologize for an outburst.

Surely, he saw the opportunity before us, and for some reason he thought she had just as much of an opportunity amongst us.

I set my goblet on the only part of his table that didn't have books stacked on it. "I think I'll retire for the night."

"That's wise. Tomorrow marks the beginning of a new life for you both."

I longed for my beloved bed, but I paused. "Do you think perhaps her being here was divine intervention rather than some enemy plotting it?"

Ashire chuckled. "Do you believe Vada decided to place a portal and invite the most ideal stranger for you to encounter?"

"Perhaps. She works mysteriously."

"Yes, though usually more subtly."

"True or Mother had a hand in it. A gift from her given today's significance."

Ashire rubbed his brow but managed a grin. "Do you think Vada and Mother could be in collusion for the sake of our family? I like that notion. I'll entertain it for a bit. Thank you, Safir."

It made any remaining anger dissipate to see Ashire in a state of peace. I left him to his wine and literature, seeing Selasi waiting outside of the room for me. He mirrored my exhausted expression as he walked me to my room two doors down from my brother's. I insisted he rest in his quarters as I opened my bedroom door. Selasi didn't argue and left me with my remaining thoughts.

My bed sat in the middle of the room, surrounded by bookshelves and desks full of parchment. I found myself drawn to the windowsill that overlooked the forest below. I swore I could almost see the exact spot Eve had appeared from and would hopefully appear the next day. To have such a portal in the most secure location in the kingdom seemed beyond the doing of any man. I felt convinced it had occurred by Vada's hand. Whether Eve's presence was part of the divine plan, I couldn't be sure, but I wouldn't question it. Though I did contemplate if Mother had any involvement from beyond the realm of man, if she could still extend her gentle touch. It seemed plausible, given her stubborn love that I could remember with perfect clarity.

Such melancholic memories made me grateful to be alone. While it was burdensome to not have privacy for my emotions, it was more taxing to plague those around me. It was a Blessing that was useful for means that were anything but diplomatic. The true use of my Blessing, the rotting truth that was the epicenter of my existence, rightfully frightened those in my presence. Eve would be repulsed if she understood.

I hoped to the trenches of my soul that she would never have to.

Eve

I awoke waiting for a pulsing ache like the world's shittiest alarm clock. That was tradition the morning after a fight, but as I peeled my eyes open to look at my cracked ceiling, I wasn't greeted by pain. A warm ray of sunshine streamed through my window, the warmth reminiscent of Safir.

I shot up from bed.

That thought had me clamoring for the mirror in my bathroom to see for myself there was no sign of injury. It wasn't that I hadn't wanted that night to be real, but as I had drifted to sleep, I'd figured having a concussion was more likely than happening upon an entirely different universe.

Yet as I poked my cheeks and jaw, I found no sign of the grisly fight from day before.

My back window peered into the forest. Safir's all-encompassing world was just a few hundred feet away. I swallowed hard, wondering what exactly I stood to gain by returning to that place, and if it were worth the time I would lose in my world. Regardless, the wad of cash still tucked into my pocket reminded me I had other obligations.

After showering and putting on a fresh pair of sweats, I walked down the street towards the bank. It was fifteen minutes away and given the neighborhood I wouldn't have advised anyone to take a leisurely stroll. My only advantage was my familiarity and that many knew my chosen profession. I hadn't pictured spending my best years at ground zero of deprivation, but I hadn't had the luxury of picturing my future at all. But, with not having to spend money on food and being healed quicker, I was hoping I could buy myself more time.

With the cash deposited, I diverted across town. The winter air cut through to my bones and around streets corners. Traffic was light as I jaywalked my way through the streets, even passing my gym along the way. Outside of its doors an unmistakable smell of sweat and old leather wafted past me. My bookie, Clay, leaned against the brick building, smoking a cigarette with a bit too much vigor.

His hair had greyed, thinning at the top, though still scruffy around his chin. Clay's nose formed a hard right angle to the left and most of his teeth had silver caps. His once overwhelming stature was reduced to a lanky figure that barely filled in the jeans and coat that hung on him. He lifted his chin at me while taking a long drag.

"Morning, peach. Come over here. Let me get a look at ya."

I approached, letting him grab my chin and turn my head back and forth. "Hunter said you looked like hell last night. Was he lying or do you got some crazy juice?"

"Nothing a good night's sleep couldn't cure. The pay was fine."

Clay took a drag, coughing as he exhaled and shook his head. "Yeah, well, I'm sure what he decided not to keep for himself paid well. Whatever it takes to keep you in his back pocket."

I sighed and leaned against the brick. "I know how he plays it off."

"Nah, you don't. No one knows a person like their bookie. I'm just saying, don't ever be too grateful for him."

"I am living in his spare house."

"Ah that shit-hole? I suppose it's better than the gutter. Ya know, there's always petty crime going around, nothing the pigs give a shit about. Kids swiping gum and scratch offs, stuff like that. Except last night."

I reached to bite the end of my thumb.

"Cops are asking around about some kid who broke the clerk's nose at Huck's last night. Trying to snag some food. Ya know anything about that, peach?"

"Clay—"

"Luckily, they didn't get a good look at the sorry bastard on the cameras, but I'd figured you wouldn't be so stupid as to draw that kind of attention to yourself. Not with everything you've got on the line. They're down the street questioning some of the stoners in case you were gonna take your usual route today."

I stifled a cough from his cloud of smoke. "Thanks. It was an accident."

"Yeah, I'm sure," he huffed and reached into his pocket. "Well, you're looking better than I thought you were, so take this while you're thinking straight." Out of his pocket came another wad of cash.

My eyes widened as I shoved it back. "What are you doing? You can't just flash that!"

"This is the rest of your winnings you got stiffed a few fights back. Took me forever to figure out why the math wasn't working."

My head shook as he placed the money in my hands, squeezing hard enough my fingers were turning purple. "Clay, I can't take it. This is your money."

"This is *your* money. I know what you do with your winnings, so just take care of yourself with that. You gotta look out for yourself if you wanna take care of anybody else."

I shoved the money into my pocket. "Actually, I think I found some work that might be useful…"

"Goddammit, I told you, never whore yourself out."

I flicked the cigarette out of his fingers. "I'm not hooking, but it's going to take time out of the gym."

Without even blinking, Clay already had another cigarette at his lips. "How much?"

"Three days out of the week at least. Do you think I'll be hurting for it?"

He shrugged. "You're pretty conditioned. Just keep your legs fresh and your lungs open. You oughta be fine as long as when you're here, you're focused." Clay took a deep breath that always hitched at the bottom of his chest. He winced. "Get on outta here if you're heading where I think you're heading."

I nodded and departed from the gym, diverting to avoid the cops. With a few free meals on the way, I intended to make a pit stop by the bank to deposit that money on my way back home. After a few minutes, my pace quickened as I walked through the parking lot and emerged through the automatic doors of St. Mary's Skilled Nursing Facility. I gave a small smile to the receptionist, Tabitha, who was a pro at sporting at-home-bleach-kit fails and wasn't afraid to openly read books about how to "self-love." She waved me back before I had even signed in, which I never did.

The long-term care unit smelled like hope wasting away into damp, stale diapers the nurses overlooked because they were scrambling up and down the halls to find that one patient who meandered into other people's rooms. The sounds were harder to ignore, the moans or whimpers of people who longed for their original home. I marched through the sea of prescription despair until I reached the door at the end of the hallway. The wallpaper peeled at the corners and the rug sported the same sterilized stains.

I opened the door. I saw him laid stiffly in the bed before me. At least he had been showered, his golden curls damp but growing longer, almost twirling over his ears. His body was curled in around itself, covered by a sheet and propped up by pillows. Feeding into the base of his neck was the ventilator that sustained his life. His sky-blue eyes were staring up at the ceiling, but then he began to blink furiously.

I stood over him, brushing a few stray hairs out of his eyes.

"Eve," he wheezed, his gaze flickering with life.

I smiled. "When's the last time they turned you, Nicky?"

"An hour ago."

"Good," I muttered while adjusting his bed so he could sit more upright and see out his window. His bedroom had two large windows, a TV, a closet, a bathroom, and a single lamp that hardly emitted any light. He was sitting up, the ventilator wheezing, and I crawled into the bed to lie next to him.

"The fight went well enough yesterday. It already took care of this month's payment, with Clay's help."

"Good."

I paused, looking up at him as I hesitantly mentioned, "I found a place where I could work a bit. It might help me with winning more. I'd get free meals and healthcare, but I'd be away for three days out of the week at least."

Nicky's mouth almost formed into a smirk. "I'll be fine."

He had a knack for knowing my thoughts without me having to express them. I was no better at concealing my feelings than Safir. "But I don't know if it's worth pursuing."

"You wouldn't have … brought it up … if it wasn't." Nicky paused and sucked in a big breath. "I'll be fine," he repeated.

He gave me a smug look, always acting as the older sibling. Any moment I wasn't spending with Nicky left me feeling guilty, so I wondered how I was supposed to manage three days. I'd at least have most of the week to visit Nicky, but if I had the option…

Sighing, I reached for the remote and made sure his face was angled to be able to see the TV. "I think we're just in time for *Golden Girls.*"

It was our secret guilty pleasure.

***

Three months of age was too young to understand abandonment. I didn't know what my first experience of life had even entailed whether it was so horrific I should have been grateful that my brother and I were dropped off at Our Sisters of Sorrow Church, or whether it was a life worth missing.

We lay there on the church steps on Christmas Eve for an hour before anyone found us dusted with snow. We had no names, no birth certificates. All we had was a pair of pendants tucked into our blankets that looked like a pair of wings surrounded by a circle of greenery. We clung to those for as long as we could.

The nuns gave us seasonal names in remembrance of the day we were found: Eve and Nicholas. Hardly anyone wanted to adopt infants with an unknown conception. Only perfect babies were in demand, babies who weren't born from addicts, babies who hadn't experienced trauma within the first eight months of life, babies with a perfectly tracked pregnancy. We remained unwanted together. It didn't help that I was a sickly kid. My vision would blur from exhaustion. Sometimes I would sleep for days. No diagnosis sat well with any physician. If Nicky hadn't made me guzzle PediaSures he'd stolen, I don't know what would have happened to me. He acted years older than me when it was believed we were only ten months apart. He would force-feed me when needed, tuck me into sleep in the middle of the day, dress me when I was too weak to do it myself. My exhaustion persisted but faded with each year.

We built a siblingship, a world, which was the safest place for us to be.

Most of the families we stayed with saw us as a burden, shipping us somewhere else just as we had gotten settled. Home to home, town to town, state to state, and family to family until I memorized the smell of our social worker's car. Often we didn't get along with the children already present in the home. One pair of brothers snapped my pencils, ripping pages out of my books, even cut off my hair in my sleep. Each time Nicky would come to my defense, standing between me and my foes. The night the brothers locked me in the basement, Nicky awoke in time to liberate me and tackled the pair for torturing me.

I tumbled out hyperventilating as Nicky pinned one of the brothers while furiously punching him, with the other brother trying to pry him away.

That was the first time I truly felt animosity for those people, for the sake of having home, for having to depend on my brother to come to my rescue, for being so goddamn feeble. I was sick of myself. I grabbed the brother to hurl him away from Nicky. In a blink I was on top of him, scratching, biting, anything to make him feel as helpless as I felt. I'd carry that spite like a badge for the rest of my life.

Those parents only saw their two assaulted boys as Nicky put himself between me and the rest of them. It was the end of our time with that family, but we were labeled as "violent."

This led to the only time in my entire life I was separated from Nicky. We were both ten years old. He held up our pendants and patted his heart. "We have each other here. Always," he told me as they pulled us away.

I had never cried so hard in my entire life. I thought I was dying. I couldn't know where he was, if he was happy or safe. I was stuck with a family that had four foster kids, ripped from violent homes or born addicted.

One girl weaponized her incontinence, peeing on my pillow if I annoyed her. Another boy liked to play with lighters and burned the kids if you didn't let him control the TV. The other two were brothers who would steal anything of yours but deny it. I slept with my pendant clasped in my hands.

My showers were cold because hot water was a luxury. Meals consisted of whatever was in the fridge, if there was anything. The only two places I went were that house and school. School wasn't worth focusing on when I was hungry and exhausted every second of the day.

After a few months of growing so sick of the putrid people around me, my feet carried me outside, down the driveway, up the road, and into town. I picked up my pace in a full sprint in no discernable direction. I truly felt like I wasn't just running away but escaping. I was better off alone than that sorry excuse of a home. I was tired of being unwanted. Other kids were adopted or at least remained in the same home. I couldn't even keep my brother. Could the universe just allow us that small comfort? Did we not deserve that? I was tired of being told to be grateful for the misery that was my life. So, I ran until I was sure I would collapse. That would have been better than going back to that house.

Wandering through unknown streets, I wobbled up a church's steps and pushed the doors open. I hugged myself while stepping into the empty sanctuary, finding a single pew in the back.

I figured I'd lie there until I died or was taken somewhere else.

Hours later, the best possible thing happened to me.

"Eve!" His voice echoed off the sanctuary walls, making me sit upright in the pew. Across the church, Nicky locked eyes with me. "Eve!" He sprinted towards me.

My arms immediately stretched out to him. Nicky swept me up in his warm embrace.

"How did you find me?" I asked between sobs.

"Just had a feeling," he whispered, his own voice strained. Nicky had always been able to find me anytime, anywhere. Every time he let me cry into him. We'd sit and wait for hours for the rest of them to find us, and we'd be pried apart again.

It was another few years before we were found a home that would take both of us, and by that time we were teenagers.

That was how we met Hunter.

He and his wife, Mary, never had kids before us. Afraid of being torn apart again, we showered in the early hours of the morning, ate quietly, and never left a mess. We never went anywhere without the other. That included school. I hadn't cared for studying, but for the first time we were safe enough to worry about school. It turned out Nicky was quick with math, enough so he was placed in more advanced classes. I found myself looking forward to my English classes. I didn't mind the essays or long reading assignments. Nicky and I took turns helping the other so that neither would get left behind.

Mary and Hunter occasionally took us out to eat or to see a movie, but typically left us to ourselves. They didn't care that we were quiet or weren't entertaining company. For a while, it seemed like we had finally reached a sanctuary.

Then Hunter was laid off at the Ford plant, leaving him constantly needing his ego stroked. Mary took more shifts at the hospital, so we were often left alone with him. He'd stare at the TV, never moving his eyes. We pitied him and tried to pick up more chores around the house. They hardly noticed but something that did catch my attention was Hunter's interest in me.

It started small. He'd ask me to get him a drink or join him in watching a show that neither of us enjoyed. Hunter would sit so close our thighs would touch. I had to "pay a toll" if I wanted something. If I wanted breakfast, the remote, or a few bucks for lunch Hunter would tap his stubbled cheek for a kiss. I hated it but tried to get it over with. One time he turned at the last second and kissed me on the lips. It tasted so much like beer that I recoiled. He reared back with a grin on his face, like he had won a competition that wasn't his to compete in. Tears brimmed as I brushed past him, realizing my first kiss felt tainted.

I stopped asking for anything from him. Every experience I had had in my life told me his presence was a threat, but that past year had been the best of my life with Nicky. We were indebted to Hunter for making that possible. So, I sat next to him as he fidgeted closer to me. Nicky hadn't noticed my discomfort since he was excelling at school, so I didn't disturb him.

The first time I came home from school without Nicky, who was speaking with the guidance counselor about college, something shifted. The air reeked of booze as Hunter eyed me up and down in a way that made my legs twitch, like I should've been ready to run. He'd clearly spent the better part of that day nursing his buzz. I'd entered at the wrong time without the one person who would have defended me. He licked his lips. "Evie, get over here, girl."

"I've got homework," I answered too quickly, clutching my backpack.

"You'll have the rest of the night to do it. Get over here." He patted the spot on the couch next to him. "Show me you're glad to see me."

Like an idiot, I walked over to him, regretting every step. Just as I was going to sit, his meaty hands grabbed my hips and planted me on his lap.

I yelped and stiffened, refusing to make eye contact with him, afraid of seeing what I could only imagine was a disgusting smirk plastered across his stubbled face. He patted my bare thigh. "See, isn't this nice?"

I didn't say anything. I didn't move. I just stared at the TV, though I cannot recall what was playing. His body relaxed beneath my rigid posterior. I was so small at the time, barely fifteen, and I couldn't help but feel smaller as Hunter's hand remained on my thigh.

My stomach churned as I clutched my backpack. We remained like that for a few minutes, though it was hours for me, until the front door opened. I shot up from Hunter's lap. Nicky entered, giving me a confused look as I dashed up the stairs to my room. My skin burned where Hunter had touched me. I wanted to peel that skin off.

Nicky didn't ask, and I didn't say anything. I stopped coming home alone. As long as I was with Nicky, Hunter toned down his creepiness. Though I had grown into a lanky frame, still plagued with fits of fatigue, Nicky had grown into a man's body and carried himself like one. I regretted having to rely on him as I had as a child.

Only being home when Nicky was present worked for a while. Hunter became consumed with professional gambling, which led to him and Mary having late-night screaming matches. From what I could hear, he wasn't gifted at his new profession.

The few times he won big only made him bolder.

Once or twice, he tried to open the bathroom door while I was showering, "forgetting" it was occupied. I locked every door behind me, but I wasn't always quick enough. After one shower, I walked into my room in a bath towel. I threw my door closed, only for my stomach to drop when a hand caught it and pried it back open. I snaked my arms around myself as Hunter barged into my room.

"What're you doing?" I questioned shakily.

He wasn't the least bit intimidated. "Sorry, I think I left my phone in here."

"Why would your phone be in my room?" I asked. He ignored me while looking under my bed, my dressers, and in my nightstand, though he sneaked glances at me. It was like I was on display before him. I hated him for it.

He sighed after a few minutes of me clutching myself in my bedroom corner. "Can't seem to find it. I'll look some other time." Hunter turned and pointed to my pendant. "You shower with that?"

I nodded slowly.

He walked forward, and I backed further into a corner. His hand brushed my chest as he picked up the pendant.

"Huh, that's real gold. I always thought it was just plated," he said, though his eyes tracked across my bare shoulders.

I began to shake. "Why are you still here?"

"You haven't asked me to leave, Evie."

"*Leave*," a voice seethed from my doorway.

We both turned, and to my relief, Nicky stood shooting daggers at Hunter.

"You can check your tone," Hunter chided though he did step back from me. "I was just looking for my phone."

"Must be pretty important if Eve can't even get dressed first," Nicky shot back and, as he always would, stood between me and my oppressor.

Hunter scowled while reaching for the door. "You both need to learn that privacy is a privilege. It wouldn't kill either of you to be more grateful."

Once his footsteps trailed down the stairs, Nicky slammed my door shut and locked it.

"Jesus Christ, Eve! What the hell was that?"

I shook while clutching my towel. "I didn't know what to do. I just…He's never been that forward before."

"What's that supposed to mean?" Nicky waved for me to change in my closet. "Has he acted like this before?"

"Kind of," I muttered while putting on jeans and a sweater. "But it's worse."

"Shit."

I stepped out of the closet to see Nicky sitting with his back against the wall. He rubbed his eyes as I sat next to him. "How is it possible we keep finding these pieces of shit?" Nicky looked up at me with our matching blue eyes. "Has he hurt you?"

My head shook.

Nicky sighed, ruffling a few of his curls in deep thought. "We only need to stay here another three years, and then we're done. But I don't trust him with you for another minute. Are you feeling tired today?"

I shook my head again.

"Good, let's go."

"Where?"

Relying on Nicky's uncanny sense of direction, we found the boxing gym in the middle of town. It still smelled of sweat and old leather and only housed a few amateur boxers who competed. Old men stopped by to reminisce about their days of glory with whatever memory they had left. One square ring was in the back, surrounded by rows of seats, and beyond that were bags hanging from platforms and standing upright. There were weights and treadmills along the walls. Nothing fancy. I followed Nicky inside, woefully unprepared with my jeans and wet hair. My brother was on a mission and spoke to multiple people before finding Clay.

Clay's hair was less grey, but he still smoked inside. He looked us both up and down and shook his head. "I don't coach. If you wanna place a bet, I'm your guy."

Nicky looked over his shoulder. "Everyone else said you were the person to ask if we wanted to get started."

"You don't need me. Watch one of those YouTube videos on form or whatever, but this isn't a pretty business to get into. I suggest you pick a different form of exercise."

Nicky leaned in. "This isn't for exercise."

Clay perked one silver eyebrow. "What, you got a school bully on your ass? Or is someone picking on your girl?" Clay glanced to me.

Nicky stepped forward. "I'm not here to be patronized by some bookie who prioritizes cigarettes over basic hygiene, but better you than our perverted foster dad."

"Down, boy. I'd hate to see you if I intentionally tried to piss you off," Clay chuckled in a cough. "Look, the pervy foster dad, what's his name?"

"Hunter Lowe," Nicky answered.

A look of realization washed over Clay's face. "That guy? Well, holy fuck, kiddos— my condolences to you."

"You know him?"

"Yeah, I'm the asshole's bookie. The bookie he owes some money to. So, you must be the 'mouths he has to feed' so he can't pay me on time. Didn't take him as the pervy type. Guess it's not surprising." Clay scratched his head and gestured over to one of the punching bags. "All right, let's see what I'm working with here."

Clay made notes on our form, commented on our endurance, and critiqued our performance for the rest of that Saturday. By the end of the day, sweat was pouring to the point I'd have to take another shower. My ribs ached, and my knees quivered beneath me.

I was so frail then, unsure if my legs could hold me up or if I could raise my fists one last time.

"This is nothing," Clay spat. "If you wanna make something of yourself then you're going to have to be willing to drown in your own sweat. Understand? I'll see you back in a few days."

"We'll be back tomorrow," Nicky panted.

"If you can get out of bed tomorrow."

We couldn't. I couldn't take a deep breath because my chest ached so much. Every joint screamed in retaliation when I tried to move. Nicky woke up with a groan that emanated down the hall which resonated with mine. The aches remained for days, but by the third day Nicky was adamant we'd return. Clay was waiting for us with a cheeky grin. "Well, aren't you two gluttons for punishment."

We did what he told us until I could wake up without soreness and keep my breath steady during the worst workouts. Even my usual exhaustion subsided. It became natural to be coated in sweat or to drive a punch through my whole body. Nicky improved as well, developing an uppercut so nasty that "it'll make Hunter forget where his own dick is" according to Clay. And me— Clay was the hardest on me.

"Ten more," he snarled as he planted his foot into my back while I resumed a push-up form. My elbows snapped and sweat dripped from my nose. I pushed it until my body collapsed onto the floor, and when it did, he said, "Good. Let's run it again."

I bolted for the trashcan and hurled.

My vision had failed me, but I heard Nicky's footsteps race towards me. Then Clay ordered, "Leave her be. She can stand her own ass up. Can't you, peach?"

I vomited all the water I had drunk that day before I wiped my mouth and pulled myself up. I mostly just locked my knees to stand straight against the trash can, but Clay smirked. "Atta girl, peach."

That was the first time I wanted to prove myself to someone other than Nicky.

My brother wasn't impressed. "You're pushing her too hard."

"Look Nick, you're not doing her any favors by pussy-footing around her. She's pretty good, aight? Hell, she could compete if she wanted. I take it you don't plan on being attached to her hip for the rest of your life? No? Then let her pick herself up."

Clay pushed us every day for nearly three years. The more time we spent there, the less time we spent with Hunter. By the time we'd get back from the gym, he'd be out placing bets. It was the first time I felt confident enough to walk past Hunter. For once, I was safe within my own body. "Ya got the fire to be a slugger and the feet of an out-boxer," Clay praised. I never wanted to lose that confidence, so I pledged myself to that gym in a way that Nicky never could. He liked being stronger but never relished it like I did.

We were nearly eighteen, nearly free from Hunter. We planned to apply for scholarships so we could go to the same college downtown without having to take out a loan. We were going to get an apartment, get a degree, and go into social work. Each day was spent plotting vengeance on a system that had forgotten us. We piled into the public bus, since Nicky was adamant that we should take a tour of the campus. I didn't care what it looked like as long as I could get a degree.

It felt like the culmination of years just barely surviving. We could both taste the satisfaction on our tongues, but that taste quickly changed into a mix of blood and glass.

An eighteen-wheeler slammed into us at an intersection, throwing us both against the opposite side of the bus. I first heard the sound, like thunder mixed with twisted metal, before slamming into a seat across from me, while Nicky was thrown through the window.

My thoughts became muffled.

There was crying, smoke, and sirens so loud it almost consumed all my other senses. Every part of me throbbed. I could hardly discern voices shouting. I only felt myself being lifted into the air, pieces of glass spilling over me. All my instincts told me not to open my eyes until the pain was over, until I saw Nicky again.

Nicky.

My instincts could fuck off as my eyes shot open, and I bolted upright.

"Don't move! Don't move! You've been in an accident!"

Hands were forcing me back onto a gurney. Bright, warm red caught my attention. It was spreading across my whole body.

"Am I dying?" I croaked.

"You need to stop moving," a woman's voice commanded over the sirens and distant shouting.

"What about Nicky? What about my brother?" My breaths were coming and going so quickly I thought my chest was going to explode. It hurt to breathe. It hurt to see. It hurt more to worry about Nicky.

I don't remember anything else until I woke up in a dark room that periodically beeped. My limbs refused to move. I could barely make my chest rise and fall with every painful breath I took.

Six broken ribs, massive hematomas covering my core, lacerations across my legs and back from the shards of glass, along with a severe concussion. Nicky was two floors below mine in the neuro ICU. I had to wait to see him because my own brain wasn't ready for "too much stimuli." All the strength I had built, all the confidence I had gained was shattered in one moment. There was no longer the certainty that we'd go to college together, that Nicky would be there alongside me. I wanted to tear myself open and give whatever piece of me I could if it meant Nicky would live.

Nicky did live, but at an unforgiving price.

The first and only visitor was Clay. He waltzed in, looking strange without a cigarette in his hand, and peered at me with more pity than I wanted. "You look like shit, peach."

My bottom lip quivered as my throat swelled shut with sobs. Clay sat down and patted my hand with his rough palm. "It's gonna be okay, peach. You're getting a shit ton of money from the bastard who did this to you."

"But Nicky," I croaked. "What about Nicky?"

Clay's hand retreated. "I was just down to see Nick."

"How is he?"

A look of hesitation crossed Clay's face. Nicky couldn't be dead; I would have been told. How bad could he be? "If you want, I'll take you to him."

After fighting with my nurse to get me into a wheelchair, Clay wheeled me down to the neuro ICU, where we were greeted with a symphony of chaos consisting of monitors beeping and bodies running around. The air was thick with the anxious anticipation of death, making me fidget in my wheelchair. I wondered how the hell Nicky was supposed to get any rest. Arriving at my brother's room, Clay opened the door, and we entered to see Nicky lying in bed, staring up at the ceiling with little expression. His head was shaved on one side, sporting a railroad scar, his face peppered with bruises, the whites of his eyes blood red. A plastic tube ran into the base of his neck.

My breath hitched in my throat, making his gaze turn towards me with smallest flicker of life. "Eve?" he wheezed.

I wheeled myself closer and reached out for his hand. "It's me, Nicky."

His fingers lay limp in my grasp. The blood drained from my cheeks. He grimaced as he sucked in his lips. "I-I can't feel … anything."

"It's okay—"

"I can't … move anything either."

A single tear escaped his eye. I leant my face into his bed and wept for our entire eighteen years of existence. "I-It's gonna be okay, Nicky. It's gonna be okay. I'll make it be okay." All Nicky could do was weep alongside me.

I would have sold my soul to take his place. I needed him to be whole more than I needed to breathe. There had already been too much time stolen from us, so many wishes we'd built up, our only sources of hope, which had been taken away without warning. It wasn't going to matter. *We* weren't going to matter, and that realization shattered us.

Nicky had suffered from a cerebral hemorrhage during the wreck, shattered his legs and arms and spine. Yet he couldn't feel any of the pain because he was paralyzed from the neck down.

We were given a lump sum from the court case that covered our hospital expenses, and I planned to use the rest to fund Nicky's long-term care. That would have been the plan…had the money not been entrusted to Hunter while we were in the hospital. At the time of the accident, we were still minors and the money went to our guardian, who had elected to handle our financial obligations remotely. When I was discharged, I found Hunter sitting on his couch and Mary surrounded by papers at the dining room table.

I slammed the door behind me, startling them enough to finally look up at me. "Where the *fuck* have you two been?"

"Handling your legal obligations," Hunter retorted. "If it wasn't for us, you wouldn't have won shit."

"Where's the money?" I spat.

They exchanged looks between themselves.

"Where is it?" I repeated.

"We used it to pay off your hospital fees," Mary said meekly from the table. "And the rest…"

"I had some debt I needed to clear." Hunter spoke plainly. He didn't look regretful. I waited for him to continue speaking because surely there was more to say.

They remined silent.

"Are you fucking kidding me?" I roared. "You blew the money meant for my brother to live because of a hole you dug yourself into?"

"There's some left to last the year. They were going to send men after me, Evie, if I didn't pay. We were going to lose the hou—"

My knuckles slammed into Hunter's nose with an audible crack. His eyes rolled back into his head before my second fist made purchase with his jaw. My fists screamed, but my spite didn't care. Furious tears stung my eyes as I reared back to hit him again before two scrawny arms wrapped around me. Heaving myself forward, I threw Mary off me as she fell to her knees.

It took all my energy not to direct my hate at her. She was scared of him, but we all were. She depended on him, but we all did. We had all been hurt. We had all gotten screwed. It was no excuse to let others get hurt along the way. "You're just as guilty for enabling him."

Hunter's massive body pinned me to the wall, causing my healing ribs to creak. I gritted my teeth in pain. "Bitch." He spewed blood onto my face. "I'm going to come up with more money. I'll make twice what you won in the court case."

"I hate you! Both of you. I only had Nicky! I only had Nicky, and now you can't even let me have him. Tell me how you plan to fix this. Tell me exactly how you're going to make up for this!"

"I told you. I can double the money in just a few months. There's enough left over to support Nick for a while, and by then we'll be set for the next decade."

My head shook. I didn't even remotely put any faith in Hunter. I didn't bother asking Mary.

"Look you're pretty good with these," Hunter said while holding up his fists. "I knew where you two were going. I've been talking to Clay. You could make some money if we arrange a few fights. I know some easy ones."

I had heard enough.

I shoved him away from me and ran upstairs to gather my and Nicky's things, which only took five minutes. When I marched back downstairs, Hunter was gone, but Mary was still sitting on the floor.

"You broke his nose."

I reached for the door.

"I am leaving him. I am, but I didn't want to leave you two alone."

"We were alone anyway. When Nicky turns eighteen, we're going to set up a bank account. You're going to transfer the money into his account where Hunter can't touch it. If you don't—"

"I will," she said, though I didn't put much faith in her either.

Two months later when I turned eighteen, the money was placed in my possession. I stayed in Nicky's room at St. Mary's Skilled Nursing Facility, or sneaked into the boxing gym where I could shower in the early morning.

After a few months of long-term care, I saw how quickly the money was dissolving. That was when I started pocketing food so I wouldn't have to waste expenses. With an unimpressive skill set and no college degree, I worked as a waitress at an Italian place in town. I could pull in tips, and I pocketed leftovers to eat on the bus. The work was meaningless. My smiles were empty. Even working long shifts and not paying rent or utilities, I was barely able to put any money away for when the court case money evaporated.

"I'll figure it out, Nicky," I promised him.

Nicky was at the mercy of negligent caretakers. They would leave him in the same clothes for days, with food crusted on his shirt. I'd find him with dry tear tracks on his cheeks. He hadn't been moved or spoken to in hours. Some days he'd tell me he wished he were dead. Part of me would die alongside those words.

"If you go," I told him, "I won't be far behind."

I couldn't give him his body back, let alone his independence. I could only promise to try to keep him alive, which didn't seem like a promise Nicky wanted me to keep.

When they didn't turn him for hours, pressure sores developed. I was working so hard for so little I couldn't be there to ensure he was being treated right. One year after the accident, a pressure sore on his back became septic and required hospitalization. The court case money was wearing thin, and my waitressing income wasn't going to sustain him.

I pawned our gold pendants to ensure we had some more money set aside. I tried not to cry through the sale, but once I stepped outside the shop, I choked on my own sobs.

At my wits' end, I went looking for Clay for the first time in two years. I stepped into the boxing gym, feeling like a stranger in a place that used to be my sanctuary. When he saw me, his mouth fell open, and his cigarette tumbled to the ground. "Peach! How's it going?"

"I need help, Clay."

"Good, glad you said it, because you look like hell." He pulled his jacket over his shoulders. "Let me get you something to eat."

I didn't argue and followed him down the street to a hot dog cart. I usually didn't trust street food but scarfed down three hot dogs within minutes. Clay offered me a sip of his Coke as we sat on a bus bench. It tasted like cigarettes.

"What's happening, peach?"

"You once said I was good enough to compete. Did you mean that?"

He scratched his chin. "I did, but you were in fighting shape. You look like you could be blown over by the wind right now."

I took a big gulp of the soda, feeling the sugar fill my veins. "How long would it take to get me back in shape?"

"What're you doing? You wanting to make a living boxing?"

"Does the money beat waitressing?"

"If you win, or if you have someone place bets for ya."

I handed him back his drink. "Can you get me to that point?"

"Jeez, maybe, but I can't bet for you. Someone else would have to do that." Clay spoke with hesitance. "Hunter has been around lately, and I'm not saying he's not an asshole, but he's gotten better at playing the odds. You two could strike up a partnership. You'd be his investment, and he'd split the winnings with you."

I ground my teeth. "Would I make more money that way?"

"If you don't want to do this, then—"

"I have no other skills, Clay. I have no other means to make money for Nicky."

Clay rubbed his eyes. "I'll talk with Hunter, 'kay? We'll figure something out. Meet me at the gym tomorrow morning. We'll start your conditioning then."

The rest unfolded too well. Hunter spoke to me as if we hadn't left on such bitter terms. He even gave me the keys to a shack he'd won in a gamble. It had bugs and poor insulation, but there was electricity and a hot-water heater that tried its best. There I stayed, once again in debt to him as I trusted him to make bets for me, hoping he'd give me a fair split of the winnings. Clay kept track to make sure I received my fair share. It didn't take as long as I'd thought to reach a competitive level of fitness. After dropping to part-time waitressing, I spent the rest of my time at the gym and trying to find cheap ways to eat. The yield was better than waitressing, and my need to win was greater than anyone else's.

My life followed this routine for the next few years in a blur, unwavering and unforgiving in its consequences. I didn't expect to know anything different.

Until I met Safir.

Safir

I waited for the better part of the day for the most advantageous stranger I had ever met. To rid myself of angst, I spent the day sparring with Selasi. He wore a few droplets of sweat upon his brow despite the crisp air.

"Should we fetch her?" he asked.

"No. I'd prefer she return of her own accord, and if she doesn't my brother will have to admit he isn't as clever as he thinks." I stood in the same spot I had seen her the previous day. Most of the snow had melted, remodeling the landscape that surrounded us. I doubted she'd even recognize where we stood.

"Your faith in her is robust."

"Do you believe it's misplaced?"

"Reason tells me yes, but I find myself just as hopeful for you."

"There will be ample time for her to prove herself."

Should she return.

Ashire hadn't done a tremendous job of explaining her role without making it sound like a threat. Granted, I could have been more cordial. It had been years since I interacted with strangers and never one who so swiftly made me want to brave those bounds. If she made that impression in such a short time, what would result after months in her presence?

The crunch of footsteps in the snow rang in my ears. Selasi nudged my ribs. I picked up my head to see her standing there, staring at me with what I could only interpret as surprise. Her sapphire gaze shone as she took a few steps forward until she stood before me. She still wore loose clothing that did nothing to deter the cold, her hair blowing about her shoulders.

"Safir." She spoke warmly. "I didn't know if this would all still be here. If it was still real."

"You're to refer to him as—"

I held up my hand to interrupt Selasi. "I'll grant this informality for now, as a 'thank you' for returning."

The corners of her mouth curved up ever so slightly. Her gaze flickered to the garden and forest around her, and I could see the beauty through her eyes. Most of the snow had cleared, allowing her to see flower beds, fountains, winding trees, and paved paths throughout the gardens. Sharp mountains wrapped around the back of the palace and stretched around the valley. It evoked a need to crane your neck back to see the peaks, so mesmerizing you almost forgot to breathe. There was going to be plenty of time to marvel, so I gestured her to the palace where Lani was waiting.

Eve fell into step, hardly as hesitant as she had been the day prior. Selasi exchanged a grin with me before following her. If she hadn't been hindering my Blessing, she would have felt the slightest bit of hope dare to surface within me.

She recalled the path to Lani's quarters on the fifth floor but questioned the need to be healed again. "Lani only healed the surface damage. She wished to focus further," I said. Eve didn't argue, and I doubted she would, since it was part of the deal.

When we entered the palace, she could clearly see the throne room through the rows of windows.

Eve gawked and pointed towards it. "What's kept there?"

Seeing the joy in her face, I wanted to see her expression when she found out herself. "You'll see in time," I told her.

I relieved Selasi of his duties and urged us towards Lani's quarters. Upon seeing us, she slammed her book shut and ushered us to one of her recovery beds. As light streamed into the room, Eve appeared dazzled by the view. You could see the mountain ranges clearer with the fading sunlight.

"I'd like to try some meditation techniques with you," Lani explained. "I think if you were focused I could heal you better."

"Do I do to you what I do to Safir's Blessing?"

Lani quirked an eyebrow and threw me a look. "Doing away with the formalities so quickly, are we?"

I didn't indulge in her assumptions while leaning back against the wall. "It'll take time to develop the habit."

Lani nodded, though not looking at all convinced, before focusing on Eve. "In a way, yes, you deter my Blessing. It could be a characteristic of the people from your realm. His Royal Highness sees its benefit, but I need you focused so I can heal."

She placed a lit candle in Eve's hands. I remembered secretive evenings in bed trying to master the technique. It was something most children with Blessings were taught. Eve stared at it curiously. Lani leaned forward, a few hairs collapsing into her face. "For now, you will see yourself as this flame, ever changing. Never stagnant. Can you do that for me?" She pushed the candle closer beneath Eve's nostrils. "You feel the warmth? You feel how your breath feeds it?"

Eve barely nodded, not taking her gaze off Lani.

"You are the flame; therefore, your Blessing is the flame. The breath is the fuel for the body; therefore, the breath is fuel for the Blessing. This works similarly for the flame. Do you follow?"

"Hmm," Eve agreed.

Lani reached for her own candle that she lit from one of the sconces on the wall. "If one wanted to make the flame grow, what would one do?"

Eve took a deep breath and slowly breathed into the flame through her nose, causing the flame to grow.

Lani smiled and mirrored Eve with her own candle, but her flame grew twice its original size. "Exactly. You altered your breath, yes? It was slow and deep. Too fast and harsh for too long and your flame would go out. This would stress the Blessing to the point that it would be uncontrollable."

Eve glanced towards me, appearing to have deduced more than I would have liked. I hoped she wouldn't have to know the reason behind my unruly Blessing. There would come a time for that.

Lani's command drew Eve's attention away from me. "Derive your breath from your stomach, not your chest. You'll create a better-quality breath."

Eve took another deep breath and blew again, but the flame grew more than it had the first time.

"Good. This is how one learns to regulate one's Blessing. The breath determines the intensity, or effectiveness, one's Blessing can have. Show me your breathing. Let the flame grow with your breath."

Eve continued to blow deep breaths into the candle. It was like watching a heart beating within her hands. Her breath appeared steady, and it made me wonder if she were amplifying her own Blessing so much no one could have sensed me even with touch.

Lani reached out and placed her hand on top of Eve's head, commanding her to continue deep breathing. After a few moments, she looked to me. "I can hardly heal her at all," she whispered.

"So, she can vary its use?"

"It appears so." Lani sighed as she removed her hand. "I attempted to utilize my Blessing and felt no effect within her." Lani stroked Eve's cheek. Eve jolted and looked up at her. "You drew yourself into a trance. That's good. When you concentrate on breathing like that, you allow the Blessing to grow like the flame. I couldn't heal you while you concentrated. As you aren't concentrating now, I could heal you better, but not as well as if you were utilizing this next technique." She held her candle under her nose once again. "For one to hinder their Blessing and keep from wasting energy, one's breath must be controlled but fluid." Lani took a few moments, breathing shallowly into the candle. The flame hardly budged. "Do you see how the flame doesn't dance? You try. Don't let your breath startle the flame, but do not deprive yourself of the air you need."

Lani had started Eve with the easier of the two techniques as was evident when Eve's candle danced beneath her nose. It was hard not to get frustrated which reflected in one's breathing.

"Remember, breathe from the stomach," Lani said with her hand on Eve's head. The wrinkles along her forehead grew as she continued with her own deep breathing while Eve remained occupied with her own task.

It was much harder to control one's Blessing than expand it. The deep breathing technique was taxing on the body. If one didn't know the slower breathing technique, they would quickly fatigue. Much like a muscle, the Blessing must be utilized to grow, and should it be neglected it would atrophy. As Lani alluded, if one's Blessing was overused, it could become erratic and unable to be controlled regardless of any breathing technique. As repetitive stress on a muscle made it susceptible to injury, so would overexertion of a Blessing. It formed into something grisly, something that made the name 'Blessing' terribly ironic—

"Your Royal Highness?"

"Safir?" Eve's voice scattered my thoughts. Lani stared at me curiously, while Eve's sapphire gaze was scanning me. I would have extended my hand to her to feel, for words failed me and I wanted to grow accustomed to tactility once again. Yet I withdrew.

"My apologies."

"I was just saying I'm done for today," Lani said. "Whatever duties you have to attend to, you are both free to do so."

I thanked Lani, as did Eve, whom Lani reminded to practice her breathing exercises. As we entered the stairwell, closing the door behind us, I extended my hand to Eve. She didn't pause for a second as she grasped my forearm. She remained remarkably composed as I imparted the thoughts and sentiments I had been experiencing in the infirmary— my anxiety and grief for my Blessing becoming such a liability. Her eyes widened slightly, but she had a look of contemplativeness, as if she were digesting every detail my Blessing offered to her.

Eventually she released me, staring at me with a look of empathy that I dreaded. "I assumed that's what happened to your Blessing, but I won't ask you how." No pity was evident in her voice. It was alien to me to not have people either regretting my existence or wishing to avoid it altogether. Eve demonstrated neither. Instead, she turned and began descending the stairs.

I couldn't know for certain if she understood I couldn't bring myself to discuss *why* my Blessing had devolved as it had. She didn't ask, as if to leave me privacy. It was appreciated, so it only felt appropriate to show her new room first.

It was generous for a guest. It was close to the latrine and was stationed on the second floor west corridor, which was exclusively for traveling guests, extended visits, and higher-ranking servants to the crown. Ashire's advisor and Selasi each had a room on the second floor. Her room appeared rather unremarkable. A bed in the middle of the room was adorned with furs, fluffed pillows and a canopy of sheer curtains. A fireplace sat along the left wall. There was a large, wooden trunk at the end of her bed, full of appropriate attire, along with a vanity opposite the fireplace. The window revealed the frozen garden below and the mountains that encircled the valley. The candelabras remained unlit to let sunlight pour through the windows.

The only decoration was an intricate tapestry depicting Walor's map on the right wall. The room did smell dank, but Eve hardly seemed to notice. Stepping inside, she twisted her neck about to look at each corner, gliding her fingers over the tapestry. She reached for the bed, pressing her palm into the mattress. A grin brought a new light to her eyes. It was quite becoming. She turned and peered out her window to bask in the view.

"You like your room?"

She nodded emphatically. "It's almost bigger than my entire house."

"I figured the earnings of a brawler would be more rewarding."

Eve's face fell slightly.

She explored her room, peering into her fireplace and touching the smooth stone walls. Her fingers grazed over almost every surface, perhaps her way of making it her own. When she looked to her wooden chest, she looked up at me, puzzled.

"Open it."

She did so without delay, though she looked more bewildered afterwards. "Are these clothes?"

"Of course," I said, pointing out her petticoats. "They're yours."

Eve stooped down and picked up what looked to be a flattering dress, but you wouldn't have known it based on her facial expression. She pawed through the layers of skirt. "There's a lot of fabric here."

"It's the customary style."

"Is it the only style?"

I smirked and took the dress from her grasp. "No. Given your profession, I'm presuming you'd be more partial to trousers?"

"If that's even an option."

"The request will be noted." I made my way towards her door. "I'll fetch your lady-in-waiting. She will help you dress, and then we'll resume the tour."

After I shut the door behind me, I heard an audible thump and a sigh, presumably Eve lying in a heap on her bed. The thought gave me a smile that almost matched hers.

Eve

Having a space that was all my own, that was solid and warm and beautiful, was indescribably freeing. I rolled around in *my* fur bed that smelled like musk and the crispness of the outdoors in *my* room. As I stood and returned to *my* windowsill to admire *my* view, I couldn't catch my breath. I'd known the world Safir lived in was just as tangible as mine, but just a glimpse made me realize how much there was to see. Mountain ranges continued in the distance in a pattern of rock and snow caps. Below, the palace continued until a towering brick wall surrounded the grounds. Beyond that, tiny buildings that billowed smoke extended further down the valley. What lives were lived down there?

The tapestry woven on the wall was longer than Safir was tall and held such delicate color. It showed the mountain range that created a valley for the people to live in. At the far end was the palace in its extravagance. It appeared U-shaped with the north, east, and west corridors. A large building jutted out from the middle of the north corridor, the building Safir said I'd have to wait to see. The property around it was lush with gardens, footpaths, surrounded with forest. The wall I saw outside encapsulated the entire property and left space between the city and the castle. Beyond that were the little buildings arranged in a semi-circle around the outermost wall. Some were larger than others; one had golden thread woven through, looking to be an impressive size. In the middle of all the buildings was a large, open circle, maybe a marketplace.

The buildings cascaded down until they became sparser halfway through the valley. The rest of the land appeared empty except for a few houses surrounded by fields, presumably farms. At the opposite end of the valley, a path cut through the mountains that extended off the tapestry.

Even though I reminded myself I was there for Nicky's benefit, I couldn't help but hope I'd get to see the rest of the palace, let alone the rest of the city. I didn't know how I'd come to be so lucky as to have fallen into this world. I guessed all my years of rotten luck meant I'd been due for something good. Yet, as I had been rolling around in a soft pile of fur, Nicky was lying motionless in a hospital bed. My mood soured.

A knock at the door made me jolt. A young woman sashayed in with a navy dress hugging her torso and falling from her hips. The corset was pulled tight, the fabric straining along her bodice and her narrow shoulders. From her collar bones to her sharp cheeks, freckles smattered her pale skin. She had a heart-shaped face with brown eyes, and her hair was a menagerie of orange spirals she kept tucked back in a braid. She smiled at me in a way that made me relax.

Safir stepped in from behind her. "Eve, this is Maisy. She's been with us for a while, so I have no doubt she'll prove to be a fine lady-in-waiting."

Maisy curtseyed, making her orange hair bounce. "It's my pleasure to be of service to you."

We're going to ditch that curtsey.

"I'll leave you to help Eve get dressed, and then we'll continue the tour before it's time for dinner." Safir exited the room once again, shutting the door behind him. Safir must have tremendous faith in his staff to constantly leave me alone with them.

Maisy trotted towards me. "I'm so pleased to meet you! It's rare His Royal Highness welcomes new guests. Will you be staying here a while?"

I almost took a step back to gain some space between us. "I think so."

Maisy squealed. "Yes! I'll get plenty of time to be a lady-in-waiting. You're my first."

"You're mine as well."

"Splendid! Let's dress you in something more," she glanced over my sweatsuit, "recognizable."

"I'm not a fan of the heavy dresses."

"Not a problem. His Royal Highness told me of your profession: a brawler. I've known a few women of adventure, but not too many." She opened the trunk and practically dove in.

"Perhaps you can teach me a few maneuvers so Selasi will learn to watch his tongue." She emerged from her dive with what looked to be a lot of leather. She narrowed her gaze at me. "This is going to take a lot of intimate negotiating."

There was a blur of undressing and then me cursing as Maisy tried to fit me into a pair of brown leather pants. They weren't the kind of leather I imagined a dominatrix wearing, but a thicker material, soft on the inside. The material wasn't very forgiving.

"Son of a bitch," I growled while pulling them over my thighs.

"Well said, ma'am," Maisy panted while hoisting the leather up my hips. "Deep breath now and yank!" We both pulled the pants up so hard I thought the crotch was going to split me in two. Maisy wiped her brow. "I must say, I don't usually exert so much effort trying to get someone's trousers *on*."

I was unable to stifle a chuckle. After a few squats, the pants slightly loosened up. They hugged my legs, though I imagined it was easier to move around than in a dress. I looked up at Maisy, who was mimicking my wiggling in solidarity. "Please tell me that was the hardest thing to put on."

"I'll tell you anything you like, ma'am."

"You can call me Eve, Maisy. 'Ma'am' is a bit above my pay grade."

She beamed at me. "I knew we'd become friends." Maisy pulled out a white cloth shirt from the trunk tossed it to me. "Tuck that into your trousers while I fetch your vest."

I did as she told me. The sleeves fitted well, but it took another bout of wiggling until the shirt was tucked into the pants. By the time I had finished, Maisy had pulled out what looked like a vest, though it was also made of leather.

"How much leather is customary?"

Maisy looked to the vest then back at me. "It's protective and warm, certainly more functional than the flabby ensemble you were wearing."

I couldn't argue with that. The vest was strung through the front with a soft leather string. Maisy's nimble fingers did quick work lacing up the front and knotting it at the top. The interior was also soft, lightly fur-lined to keep the heat in. Afterwards she pulled out a pair of boots that would be more resistant to the snow than my tennis shoes. Fortunately, they slipped on with ease. Even though my ensemble was complete, Maisy insisted on 'perfecting' my hair. Maisy didn't take 'no' as well I thought a lady-in-waiting was supposed to. "You're His Royal Highness' advisor. Your appearance should reflect it."

I couldn't help but fidget. "I've never really had my hair done." I had always cut my own hair since it had been first cut for me when Nicky and I were kids.

Maisy stared at me, perplexed. "Did your mother never do your hair for you?"

My silence must have been enough of an answer because she beckoned for me to sit in front of the vanity. She went to work threading pieces of my hair together, though I didn't think there was much worth working with.

"You have pretty hair, ma'am. Did you know?" she asked while pinning a small braid at the back of my head.

I almost shook my head but tried to remain still. "You can just call me Eve, Maisy."

"You are very pretty, Eve," she crooned while starting another braid on the opposite side.

I assumed she'd been hired to flatter me. Still, her words were sweet. The fact I had only been deemed 'pretty' by one putrid man soured the compliment.

"How old are you, if you don't mind me asking?" she asked while reaching for a pin from the vanity.

"I'm twenty-three."

"Ah, not too much younger than His Royal Highness. I think he's four or five years older."

"What about the king?"

Maisy rolled her eyes. "He's ten years older than you, but sometimes acts well over a century old." She snickered to herself while continuing to place pins.

As she combed her fingers through my hair, it made me realize I liked having my hair touched. It was soothing in the right hands. In that moment I felt something good, something worth cherishing, I was stricken with guilt. Nicky wasn't getting to know the luxuries I was, nor would he ever be able to. I was supposed to be there to help him rather than dwelling in my newfound luck.

When Maisy was finished with pieces of my hair delicately braided and pulled back, probably the only time I'd had my hair in a style other than in a ponytail, I couldn't enjoy it.

But I smiled for her. "It's really nice."

She beamed. "I'll do this every day for you if you like. I know so many styles I've yet to try on someone."

My smile devolved into a grimace. It didn't feel fair. None of it felt fair.

Maisy knelt beside me. "Eve? If you truly don't like it, I'll take it down."

My head shook. Even so, my braids didn't come loose. I reached back to feel them tightly pinned to my scalp. "It's nothing to do with my hair. It's nothing."

"Obviously not," she quipped while smoothing the wrinkle between my brows with her fingers. "Come now. You won't find a more attentive ear than in your lady-in-waiting."

Guilt welled up inside me. Dammit, I wanted just one person to confide in. Maybe a giddy stranger was my best bet. "Can I ask you something as long as it stays between us?"

She leaned close enough I could have counted her freckles. "I'd take it to the grave."

"Have you ever been so lucky you felt guilty about it because other people can't be as lucky with you?"

She sat back on her heels. "I can only hope lucky people feel that way. It means there is some compassion out there. But you would only live a shadow of your life if you let yourself feel guilty all the time. The best way you can repay those who didn't become as lucky as you, is to live as well as you can."

"That doesn't feel like enough."

She shrugged her shoulders. "But that's the best you can do. If you ask more of yourself, you're setting yourself up to feel horrid all over again. I'm aware you haven't been here long, but are you aware of the plague that struck us years ago?"

"No."

"The number of deaths still hasn't been tallied to this day. By the end, some of the smaller villages were buried under bodies. You'll find many here who were affected by that terrible time." A smile grew on her lips despite her somber words. "So, you know I can only be sincere when I say, I do not know if that distress is comparable to yours, but I hope you see how others have been able to live on and live well."

My smile reluctantly matched hers. While that hadn't exactly made my guilt vanish, it made me feel lighter for confiding in Maisy. For confiding in anyone.

"But if you could stand to be honest with me," she blurted, "do you actually like your hair?"

"Yes, I like it a lot," I confessed, staring at myself in the mirror. It was a cute look, and it kept my hair out of my eyes.

Maisy beamed, practically leaping from the floor as she pulled one more thing out of the wooden trunk. I was beginning to think it was an endless void of fabric, but she handed me a cloak similar to those I had seen Selasi and Safir wear. It was heavy and long, a deep blue color, darker than Maisy's dress.

"Can't have you catching a sniffle, can we? I think His Royal Highness is ready for you now."

As I stood, I looked to the vanity's mirror and couldn't help but feel exposed. I wore less when I was boxing, but at least then I was distracted by punching somebody. But I wasn't fighting anyone. I simply had to *be*.

"Are you ready, Eve?"

"I might as well be," I huffed, throwing the cloak over my arm as I stood there. I refused to feel as ridiculous as I looked, so I squared my shoulders and kept my chin high while Maisy finally opened the door.

I felt utterly ridiculous until I saw Safir gape at the sight of me.

Safir

I would never understand why Eve previously hid her physique underneath that mass of cloth. The leather vest hugged her solid torso, showing she could have benefited from a few more meat pies from Milfred's kitchen. Her hips and thighs curved from muscle, with sharp and squared shoulders. She was a statue with the body of a brawler and delicate features of a woman. Her sapphire gaze, which only seemed brighter with her hair softly pulled back, seemed transfixed on me.

She didn't look away as she walked towards me, her boots clicking against the stone floor. She seemed to wait for someone to speak. I wished I knew what she was waiting for me to say.

Maisy emerged, smiling enough for her and Eve combined. "I think His Royal Highness is rather pleased with your transformation."

"Maisy," Eve groaned.

"I am," I interjected. "This does suit you far better than a dress. However, it's more pertinent that you're pleased with it."

A smile almost formed on her lips. She began fidgeting with her shirt sleeves. "I'm pleased."

It would have been clear to any man that Eve was a beautiful woman who was utterly unaware of it. It was something beyond trying to appear humble. I tried to be delicate about the matter, considering she was obviously uncomfortable with the subject.

Selasi was not as tactful.

He rounded the corner to join us and saw the three of us outside of her room. "You're a sight!" he cheered while approaching Eve. "I'll have to make sure the guardsmen mind themselves."

Eve's hands formed fists in her cloak, tight enough her knuckles turned white. "But they will mind themselves or answer directly to me," I asserted.

Selasi looked to me, bewildered. "I was merely jok—"

"Oi!" Maisy piped up. "You best be looking after my lady as well as His Royal Highness."

Selasi's jaw dropped. "What's *she* doing here?"

"I'm Eve's lady-in-waiting."

He turned to me, aghast. "Did you do this or does Vada hate me?"

"I can't speak for Vada, but I did assign Maisy to Eve. I thought she'd be compatible company." I watched as the conversation seemed to ease whatever was unsettled within Eve, her fists loosening at her sides.

"We're already best mates." Maisy smiled and patted Eve. "So, you'll be getting to see more of me around here."

"If I hadn't sworn my sword, then I—"

"Yes, but you did," I chided. "No further commentary is necessary. Maisy, you're dismissed until Eve calls for you tonight."

Maisy curtseyed, threw a glower to Selasi as she passed. "Now," I sighed, "it's time we finish the tour before the sun has set."

We started the rest of the tour from the bottom up. The first floor was used as living quarters for staff, though considerable space was taken up by the impressive kitchen. One could hear Milfred cursing from down the hall. We popped in at Eve's insistence. Billows of steam filled the room, giving rise to a sweltering heat. We were met with a wall of savory and sweet smells that clung to our clothes and skin. There were fires roaring and bakers rushing about kneading dough and dicing vegetables. They hardly noticed us, as they were preparing for our busiest day of the year.

When we entered, Milfred swore, "Who the fuck is intruding in my kitchen one day before—"

Her plump body froze as she saw Selasi and I standing there with Eve. Her face was already a beet red but grew to an even darker hue. She curtseyed far too deeply. "Y-your Royal Highness, I apologize for my ill-timed words! I wasn't aware of your presence."

I plucked a bay leaf from her frazzled blonde hair. "You shouldn't apologize, Milfred. Your cursing invigorates your baking."

She offered a toothy smile and glanced to Eve. "And who is this lovely stranger?"

I gestured Eve forward. "This is Eve, my new advisor. She'll be staying with us for a while. Eve, this is Milfred, our head cook and backbone of Walor Palace."

Milfred wiped her sweaty palms on her apron and kissed Eve's hand. "A pleasure to meet you."

"You made the meat pie I ate last night?" Eve asked.

Milfred nodded. "Yes, ma'am. Was it to your liking?"

Eve smiled, her cheeks glowing. "That was the best thing I've ever eaten in my entire life. Thank you."

"She's smart to get chummy with the cook," Selasi whispered to me. "Maybe she'll help me smuggle some custard tarts."

That was unlikely.

Milfred beamed. "Bless you, dear child! It's an honor to feed your belly. You call on me any time. I'll be sure to help you put some meat on those bones." She winked at her. "Men like something warm to hold onto at night."

Eve's cheeks grew as red as Milfred's face. Selasi snickered underneath his breath. Milfred turned her attention to him. "Got something to say, piglet? Do you disagree?"

"I would never be so bold as to disagree with you, Milfred."

"Oh, fuck off." She glanced to me. "Pardon me, Lord."

"By all means, continue your artistry. We look forward to tomorrow," I told her, ushering Eve and Selasi out of the kitchen.

Selasi reached across the counter to grab a handful of dates as we left. His hand was met with a swift smack from the back of Milfred's spoon. "Oi, piglet! You're done stealing from my kitchen."

Selasi recoiled as I tugged on his collar. "Is it not also an honor to feed my belly?"

"You've never thanked me! She did within the first two minutes of us meeting, while you've been packing on the pounds for years!"

I hauled Selasi out of the kitchen and glanced to Eve. "That's why I can't take *him* to the kitchen."

Selasi whipped around to her. "Eve, I will personally pay you to smuggle some custard tarts for me."

I began walking, hoping to finish the tour before the day ended. "She's not been here one day, Selasi, and you've already accosted my advisor to partake in your exploits?"

Eve chuckled out a rejection for Selasi before insisting we continue the tour. While my bodyguard sulked behind us, I showed her as much as I could of the first floor. "As I said, the majority is staff living quarters and the kitchen, though below our feet lie the crypts and prison cells that can be reached from any of the four corner staircases."

She stopped in her steps. "You have an actual dungeon?" I nodded. "Is it in use?"

"Not at the moment, and we pray it remains that way," I said, feeling my palms begin to sweat at the thought of entering that place again.

What I hoped would distract her would be showing her our chapel to Vada.

"The goddess of luck and chance," I told Eve. "She sees that good luck and fortune be brought upon the land." The chapel was in the east corridor of the first floor, more decorated in gold than the throne room. Gold patterns lined the walls and columns in the room, making it shine as brightly as the morning sun. It housed pews for residents of the palace to pray and worship. Tapestries hanging on the walls told tales of Vada's ventures through the cosmos and the people. At the end of the room an altar held a small statue of Vada made of gold. She stood with her hood shrouding her face, holding a coin in one hand.

Selasi prayed in one of the back pews as Eve stepped forward to examine the Vada statue. Her gaze narrowed. "Is she your only god?" she asked.

"No, there are multiple. In the South, they worship Chike, god of retribution and justice. The east has recently started worshipping Tove, the god of cleverness and wit."

She nodded, though scanned the room without the fascination she typically wore when seeing a new place in the palace. Perhaps her kind had an aversion to deities.

"Are there any specific beliefs or practices where you're from?"

"There's plenty. There's almost something for everyone," she muttered with a hint of disdain.

Selasi peeled one eye open to look up at me from the back pew. Neither of us had ever met someone devoid of a faith. I didn't know if her deities lay dormant or were perhaps less involved in daily lives. Many gods lorded over their creation from a distance, watching them grow beneath their unmoving hand.

Eve made her way back towards the double doors and looked to me expectantly, as if she were waiting.

I obliged, tapping Selasi's shoulder on our way out. From there Eve's gaze assumed its prior wonderment while exploring the remaining palace. There were greater halls to see, and after Eve's poor response to the chapel, it felt best to stun her with the throne room.

The room was full of the same white stone but with large windows allowing the sun to scatter rays through the glass. Columns extended upwards, carved in ornate patterns colored with royal gold. The ceiling arched into a crest and had hanging chandeliers for when gatherings ran late into the night. Banners with our family emblem, the Last Flame, hung from all corners of the room. At the far end of the throne room were a set of double doors that opened to the courtyard. At the center stood a golden throne at the peak of a pedestal.

Empty, it wasn't as ornate as other rooms in the castle. It was meant to be filled with tables of food, music, and people. It was a space in which to flaunt in front of others, which was useless if there weren't people present.

But Eve was practically twirling. When her amazed stare settled on the golden throne, she looked to me. "So, your brother sits there?"

"Only if he must."

Ashire rarely held court or threw grand enough parties to fill the throne room. He found the throne more symbolic than truly functional. "There's still more to see," I told her.

It took a few more lingering moments to pull her away from the view, but we departed the throne room. The second floor was designed for guest accommodations It contained latrines, lounges, and smaller gathering rooms for quainter parties and dinners. The third floor was meant for the royal family's use. Some bedrooms had been redesigned as personal libraries. The fourth floor contained great halls designed for prolonged and grotesque meetings between my brother and the local lords. I rarely visited.

While they weren't evil men, they were representatives of the noble houses in Walyre which made them intolerable. Just hearing Ashire moan about his meetings made me understand what a fine line it was catering to the nobles while simultaneously withholding enough that the peasants didn't demand the king's head on a spike. That, in addition to many other burdens that came with the crown, was why I wanted to share in his obligations. It was why I wanted Eve to stay.

We concluded the tour of the palace at the fifth floor. Eve was already familiar with Lani's quarters, but she hadn't paced down the hallway that led to a set of double doors. Upon opening the double doors, I relished in Eve's jaw dropping at one of the grandest libraries in the kingdom. It spanned the entire west corridor, with shelves upon shelves full of leather-bound adventures, recipes, anecdotes, hymns, and poems. The air smelled of old parchment and dust. The room was warmed and lit with dozens of lanterns on various tables. There were lounge chairs, sofas, and tables for one to find comfort while reading, which I was sure I'd find Eve doing as her awestruck gaze memorized every corner of the room.

It was a point of pride for my brother. That great room had once been the previous king's war room. Ashire had moved the "war room" to a simple meeting room on the fourth floor and converted the hall into a library to feed his mind. It had required most of his reign to ravenously collect this many books.

Eve ran her fingers across the leather spines and breathed in the dusty air. Her gaze settled on the sole painting of our mother that Ashire allowed in the palace. It depicted her holding a small Ashire and myself. We were plump and lively lads, evident by the size of our cheeks. Her gold hair cascaded down her shoulders. She wore the jewels of a queen but held the warm regard of a loving mother. She had deep green eyes that stunned anyone who saw them, accompanied by a narrow chin and slender neck. She was the pride of the palace.

Ashire, as a child, held what looked like an attempt at a smile though his eyes were brighter, revealing the shared family eye color that symbolized the Last Flame. I sat, lumpy and pink on Mother's lap, beaming up at her with my gaze that had barely taken on its mature color. My hair was still brown.

Eve's stare flickered from me to the painting. It was an easy observation that my ghostly white hair had not been gifted to me from birth. I was sure it made her wonder, but she merely whispered, "She's beautiful," and drew her attention back towards the books, much to my relief.

She meandered through the shelves as Selasi and I lagged. "Are all these books written in English?" she asked.

I wasn't aware of the language she was referring to, but based on her frozen meals I was presuming we shared the same vernacular.

"Most are written in Common, so you shouldn't have any trouble deciphering the texts."

"Can I read whatever book I want?"

It was strange seeing her happy over such a trivial privilege, but I couldn't deny it made my chest feel light. "Of course. Write down whatever book you withdraw from the library in the ledger." I pointed to the ledger in the corner of the room. "It helps keep track of the books."

"His Majesty would skewer anyone who misplaced one of his children," Selasi sighed while keeping his distance from the books.

Eve seemed brave enough to begin a collection as she began reading titles, perhaps making a list in her head of books she desired. If Ashire had seen her like that, I was sure he would have been *almost* smitten. I allowed her a few more minutes to peruse before we concluded the tour. She'd have more opportunities to bury herself in books in the future. Part of me hoped the grandness of the palace would solidify her decision to be my advisor.

That entire first day with her, I had to remind myself I didn't need to project neutral sentiments for fear of affecting those around me. I had practically forgotten what it felt like to just be.

Seeing through the windows that the sun was on its final descent, I ushered Eve up the staircase to the top of the tower. We only climbed one more flight of stairs before the last door allowed us to exit outside. A chill wind welcomed us as we made our way onto the balcony that encircled the tower. Eve pulled her cloak around her shoulders and stepped towards the edge of the balcony, a dazzling view before her. The sun cast streaks of orange and pink, across the once blue horizon. The colors spilled onto the green landscape that was the valley. Soon the color spread to the city below. The valley proved its beauty in a single instant, captured by Eve's astonished gaze. A gasp escaped her, and she leaned against the railing to look closer.

Watching Eve made the beauty of that day more precious. Every detail, every crevice, and every person we encountered was more valuable through her eyes. It made one feel grateful, especially as she hungrily stared at the sunset, as if she were starved of any such beauty. She didn't speak. She hardly breathed, even after the sun and any remnant of light disappeared from the sky. Then the stars emerged, one by one in a symphony of starlight. That night was illuminated perfectly for her, and I would never know anyone who appreciated it as much as she.

Eve

A place like that, a *home* like that was possible to imagine, but impossible to believe until I saw it with my eyes and touched with my eager fingers. It was a very full world, untouched by most luxuries I knew but better off for it. I already felt mesmerized when I had seen just a tiny piece of that world. I'd been waiting for a catch, but I'd been consistently stunned.

I contemplated it over dinner, a savory beef stew full of vegetables accompanied with freshly baked bread. It was much more relaxed than the first dinner I'd eaten with them. I hardly had time to amuse the king with how impressed I was with his palace because I was too busy stuffing my face. Even the sour wine was beginning to grow on me, at least after my second cup. I imagined dinner with the king and the prince wasn't customary, so I'd have to appreciate the meals I did share with them, all while hunting for more carrots in my stew.

I told the king how much I enjoyed his library. He played with his earring as he grinned, pleased enough to stop patronizing me from across the table.

Dinner concluded when the king had his fill, leaving Safir and I alone. It didn't take long before Safir suggested turning in for the day, with which I heartily agreed. I had bounced between two worlds in just a few hours, and I couldn't help but wonder how well I'd sleep on my bed of furs.

Selasi was waiting outside of the door, but was dismissed, much to his relief.

"I was hoping I wouldn't have to run into Maisy again," he sighed. "I hope you both rest well." Selasi made his way down the east corridor until he reached the door to the staircase and disappeared.

"Why does Selasi not like Maisy?" I asked.

"There are many theories." Safir began walking in the opposite direction. I followed. "Maisy is known to have taken many lovers. I think Selasi wonders, if not sulks, why he's never been asked to warm her bed. Or it's possible he's frustrated she sees him more as an annoying sibling."

"Is she that much older than him?"

"Not by much, but Maisy and Selasi grew up in the same village. Maisy's family were nobility, but her father gambled away their fortune and left them destitute. Maisy was taken in by Selasi's family, that was until the plague arrived. Sometimes Selasi speaks highly of growing up alongside Maisy. Sometimes he detests it. I cannot keep up."

We entered the stairwell and began walking downwards as we continued to talk. "You seem to employ very virtuous people."

"We're fortunate to be able to do so. It was Maisy who recommended Selasi for his position here."

"You'd think they would be closer than they seem."

"Oh, they are, I can assure you. It's best to not take their bantering to heart."

We arrived at my door in the west corridor and paused. Safir looked perplexed at my door and then back at me. "Are you not going to retire for the night?"

"I will, but I wanted to thank Milfred for dinner."

He smirked. "While I'm sure she'd relish your gratitude, the entire kitchen staff is preparing for Feast Day. She wouldn't have time to talk."

"Feast Day?"

"The shortest day of the year is celebrated with the palace baking an immense batch of meat pies, which are given to the townsfolk as a symbol of good will. My brother personally hands out a few pies. It was his idea not long after he first ascended. Milfred spends all her time just using her Blessing to multiply enough pies for the people."

"Do you not help distribute pies?"

Safir hesitated. "Given my circumstance, it wouldn't have been tolerable for people to be that close to me."

"But now you have me."

A shy grin grew from the corner of his mouth. He bowed his head, making white hair fall into his gaze, but his ember eyes shone brightly as he nodded. "Yes, now I have you."

I didn't understand how a mere shift in tone could make his words sink into me. His voice deepened in a way that commanded my attention while being soothing at the same time. I must have looked like a deer in the headlights.

He peered at me beneath his white locks and crooned, "Goodnight, Eve."

I swallowed hard. "Goodnight, Safir." I slipped into my room and shut the door behind me, finally separating us.

A flood of heat rushed to my cheeks. It was terrifying yet enthralling. It wasn't exactly a safe feeling, but for the short time I'd been with Safir I hadn't felt endangered. I plopped onto my bed of furs, perplexed yet exhausted. As my room was warmed by the rolling heat coming from the fireplace, I couldn't help but drift. I was warm. I was cozy and full. I was on the precipice of feeling what people would have described as peace. If Nicky could have shared it with me, it would have been the closest thing to heaven.

When I awoke, I realized I hadn't even bothered burying myself under the covers. My ears caught the pounding of fists on my door and Maisy's perky tone. "Happy Feast Day, Eve! May I enter?"

"Come in," I groaned, rubbing my eyes as I sat up in bed.

Maisy entered with bright eyes and a tray in hand. Her hair was braided back in two braids that were twisted into a bun. I didn't know when she'd found the time to do that when it felt painfully early in the morning. The sun's rays barely prodded at the window.

She set the tray down on the vanity. "You were sleeping like a babe when I entered last night, sleeping in your day clothes— even in your boots!"

I yawned while reaching for what looked like a pile of croissants. "You were right, the leather is much warmer. I couldn't keep my eyes open when I lay down."

"Well, considering today's festivities, I suggest you bathe."

I paused mid-bite and looked to Maisy. "Where am I supposed to bathe?"

"I'll arrange for a tub to be brought here. You sit and eat."

Given my groggy state and my growling stomach, I plopped onto my vanity stool and finished off the pastry before moving onto the bowl of fruit. A mixture of berries tasted tart and fresh on my tongue, washed down with a cup of hot, bitter tea that had a hint of lemon. All the while, Maisy and others entered and exited with a large, open wooden tub and multiple buckets of water. I offered to help carry, which led to a swift reprimand from Maisy.

After a few more buckets of water and many embarrassed "thank you very muchs" from me, Maisy welcomed me into the tub.

I groaned as we peeled me out of my leather pants and vest. Once I was on the verge of being nude, I did express some desire for privacy. Maisy obliged and returned my tray to the kitchen, extending my thanks for the meal. Once she left, I stripped and lowered myself into the fresh water. It wasn't piping hot like the showers at the gym, but it was warm. I was certain Maisy had scented it because it smelled overwhelmingly floral. I reached for the bar of, what I assumed was soap, from the floor. It smelled like baking soda, but I lathered it over my arms and legs to rid myself of as much grit as possible. I even undid my tight braids and soaked my hair in the water.

That was the most luxurious morning I had ever experienced, and once again the twang of guilt in my belly grew until the flowery smell turned sour and the croissants in my stomach churned. Nothing was worth fully enjoying without Nicky. It almost felt like a betrayal, and I couldn't shake the shame. I wondered if Maisy noticed my agitation when she re-entered my room with a robe. She placed it next to the tub and stoked the embers in the fireplace for more heat.

I stayed in the tub longer than necessary since they'd gone to such trouble to fill it, but after a few more moments I exited and wrapped myself in the soft robe. Maisy sat me down in front of the vanity and went to work on braiding my hair. She glanced up from her work occasionally, only to see my sour face.

"Any chance you're feeling less horrid than yesterday, Eve?"

I almost shook my head but kept still to not disturb her fingers in my hair. "Not exactly. I'm sorry if I seem ungrateful for your work."

"On the contrary, you're one of the most gracious people I've ever had the pleasure of serving," she murmured while pulling piece after piece of my hair back.

I smiled small and attempted to enjoy the feeling of a full belly, a warm robe, and Maisy's fingers combing through my hair. She hummed something light while working, a pretty tune, finishing my hair in a similar style to the previous day but with more intricate braids. She slicked back a few pieces before resting her hands on my shoulders and looking at me through the mirror.

"If I might speak boldly, Eve, perhaps you'd benefit from conversing with someone who feels similar to you."

I quirked an eyebrow. "And who would that be?"

"Frankly, everyone in this palace could probably relate in some manner, but I trust Selasi to be most kind towards you."

"Selasi? So, you trust Selasi?"

"As much as I trust you not to tell him."

"Of course," I snickered. "Though he does seem easily influenced by you."

Maisy exhaled deeply. "Selasi's family saved me from having to sell myself on the streets when my father gambled away our fortune with little remorse. Ah, I could bite that man's ear off if he were here, but it allowed Selasi and I to grow up together. His household felt cramped at times, but it was kind. It was more of a home than I had ever known." She smiled. "He'd tell me ghost stories each night before bed, though I'm certain it was just so that I'd ask to stay the night in his cot. Even then, he wanted to protect. He couldn't help it. He wanted to make something of himself so badly, and when he was old enough, he set out to become the greatest swordsman." Her voice trailed off slightly, as if her words were readying to sting her. "He promised he'd return an accomplished man before anyone could even think to ask for my hand. But it wasn't long after he left the plague came. I tried to care for his family, but no one was spared. Only I remained when he finally returned from his training. Selasi would attain the position of his dreams but couldn't share it with his family. For them not to see him is one of his greatest regrets. That regret nearly killed him."

"That's not his fault," I remarked quickly. She gave me a knowing look, like the pot was calling the kettle black. "Point taken. But did he ever ask for your hand?"

"We'd both grown into different people, no longer dreaming of marriage but making our own way."

I'd had no idea that Maisy and Selasi's feud started years prior or that it had been rooted in such a shared childhood. "If you are actually fond of him then why are you at such odds?"

"I saw the mistakes my mother made. I wouldn't have attained my secure position if I hadn't kept most men at arm's length."

"But Selasi—"

"Selasi is the reason for our current estrangement yet is the only one unhappy with it. I'm perfectly content with continuing our bantering until we both die from old age in this palace, never needing more or less. There is not much benefit to punishing oneself in solidarity. No true friend would wish for that."

I understood. I really did. Nicky wasn't just my friend. He was my right arm, and if one were ever miserable then we were miserable together. Happiness for one wasn't attained when it wasn't guaranteed for the other.

Maisy pulled from my trunk an outfit that looked like the one I'd worn the day before, only it was a darker color of leather.

I groaned while standing. "If I keep eating Milfred's cooking it's going to be impossible to fit into those pants."

"It'll just be more to be admired," Maisy teased.

With Maisy's patience, we managed me into the pair of leather pants once again. I pulled on the long-sleeved cotton shirt then had my leather vest laced up. Maisy beamed at me. "I think the day is now ready for you, if you'll follow me."

I followed her skirts as we exited my room and made our way to the north corridor on the fourth floor towards Safir's study. Maisy knocked at which Safir's distinctive voice called for us to enter.

When she opened the door, Safir sat at a long desk covered in papers and books, one hand ruffling his white hair. The other was furiously scribbling. His study was lined with bookshelves, maps draped across the walls, and a wide balcony overlooking the gardens. Safir looked up, not looking as stunned as he had the day before, but he did have that same smile in the corner of his mouth that made me want to suck in a sharp breath.

"Good morning," he greeted as Maisy closed the doors behind me. "Happy Feast Day, Eve."

"Morning," I reciprocated, scouring the room for a place to sit. There were a few lounge chairs in the corners of the room, one corner already claimed by Selasi who was closest to the fire.

"Morning, Eve," Selasi greeted me with a grin. "Were you gifted with a hearty first meal for Feast Day?"

"Selasi…" Safir groaned.

"I think so," I said uncertainly.

"I received a plate full of apple cores," Selasi whined. "It's sorrowful to have such a meal on Feast Day. I'm starving."

"Selasi," Safir chided from his desk. "No one would look at you and accuse you of starving."

Selasi huffed and stared into the fire. "The winter weight is unkind to us all."

Safir looked up at me. "Eve, for the majority of today I'll have to be confined here, but if you'd like to retrieve a few books from the library to entertain yourself then you can." I nodded emphatically, to which Safir handed me a paper with scribbles on it. "These are recommendations from my brother, since you took such a liking to his creation. You may go retrieve them now. And take Selasi with you. His sourness poisons my productivity," Safir muttered as Selasi joined me in exiting the study.

Selasi's pout didn't remain for long. In fact, it dissipated the second we exited the study and walked towards the stairs.

He winked one grey eye at me. "It does him good to jest every now and then, even at my expense."

The morning light shone through the narrow windows in the stairwell. Selasi climbed up with pep, making me wonder if it would dampen his mood if I confided in him as Maisy had suggested. When we entered the library, I couldn't help but bask in its wealth of books. The smell of pressed paper ignited a desire I had smothered years before when I hadn't the time or energy to read. I would have dared to be giddy, if my guilt hadn't suppressed any sense of joy.

All my thoughts were distracted when I saw the portrait of two small boys sitting next to what anyone would have assumed was a goddess, with cascading blonde hair and large eyes. I had seen the same portrait the previous day but hadn't taken the time to study it considering Safir appeared self-conscious. She held the small boys protectively yet had a gentle gaze when looking at them. I imagined that was how a mother was supposed to feel: ready to protect and love furiously. And the two children next to her, I would have never guessed who they were if it weren't for their eyes. That bright ember color that was unmistakable made the painting come to light. Ashire looked so joyful, already mischievous. Then there was Safir, a happy baby…with brown hair. That wasn't something I planned to ask about. Based on how forward people in the palace were, I presumed I'd be told eventually.

Selasi emerged beside me, catching me staring at the painting. "You were right to say she was beautiful, Queen Mira. Beautiful in every sense, I'm told."

"You didn't know her?"

"She passed long before I was positioned here. The plague took a great many people that year."

I pulled on my shirtsleeves. "Selasi?"

"Hmm?"

"Maisy told me about how many people suffered from the plague."

He remained stoic but didn't say anything. I expected him to say something snarky about Maisy, but he truly cut the antics when he wasn't in the presence of Safir.

I continued before my confidence waned. "What would you tell a person if they always felt guilty whenever they were happy because they couldn't share it with their family?"

My heart pounded before Selasi turned to me with a look of compassion, to the point I almost stepped back. He smiled, though it seemed sad. He opened his mouth to speak, closed it, then opened it again. His gaze looked to the floor. "I would say that feeling doesn't go away. It only becomes quieter. The best you can do is live for those who could not. Live in a way that would make them and yourself proud. You cannot ask more of yourself or else you'll begin to ask too much."

Selasi calmly rolled up his left sleeve, revealing a set of raised, vertical scars on his wrist. I stared at them wide-eyed.

That regret nearly killed him.

He rolled his sleeves back down. "But as long as you're in Maisy's care, you'll always be safe." His voice matched his scars: unashamed and unabashed. He didn't speak of his anguish in any way other than matter-of-factly.

My heart quivered. Whenever someone bares their scars to you, it makes you want to bare your own. As if someone revealing their pain liberates yours. The last thing I would have wanted was pity, so I gave him something better. "Maisy does put a lot of trust in you, not that I'm supposed to tell you that."

His sad smile turned cheerier, making the light in his eyes no longer so melancholy. "Oh, I'm well aware, and that's something no other man has from her," he said with a hint of victory in his voice.

In that moment I was happy to know Selasi. I was happy to know Maisy, and I was becoming happier to know Safir. If any happy sentiment dared to be extinguished by the guilt in my gut I would remember Selasi's words and scars. I promised myself that guilt would never take me that far.

Safir

Eve hummed when she read. It was a light tune that periodically drew me out of my trance.

When she and Selasi had returned from the library, exchanging looks, she'd found a corner of her own. She'd opened the book *Origins and Manifestations of Blessings*, per Ashire's recommendation, and hadn't put it down the entire of the day.

Time passed sluggishly for me, while it must have been soaring for her. She became so entranced she didn't hear Selasi approach my desk.

"Lord," he whispered. "Even standing next to you, I cannot sense you."

My interest piqued, particularly because I was bored with paperwork. "Can you feel me now?" I asked while extending my hand. I focused on my usual default sensation: a neutral warmth that encased my whole body.

Selasi placed a few fingers in my palm. After a minute he pulled away. "Very faintly, Lord. I had to look for it."

"Interesting." Eve was still buried in her book, breathing deeply and evenly. I doubted she realized it, but her breathing was mimicking what Lani had taught her to expand the use of her Blessing. Perhaps she wouldn't tire. Even though she was limiting me, that was still a fraction of her Blessing's ability. If she purposefully chose to focus on eliminating one's Blessing, how extensive would the effect be?

"Eve?" I called to her. She didn't move a single muscle. "Eve," I commanded with greater authority. Her head remained bent towards the book, but her sapphire eyes darted upwards towards me, as if she were annoyed I'd interrupted her focus. "Since you're relaxing, now would be a good time to practice the breathing techniques that Lani taught you."

"Which one?"

"Keep your breath shallow. Picture not disturbing the flame."

She nodded, then averted her gaze back to her book. Even the calling of a prince didn't distract her from the written word. Her breathing became shallow but steady. After a few moments, I extended my hand back to Selasi. His touch lingered briefly before he nodded. "Your sense was much greater."

"Very good."

I resumed my work, though half-heartedly. It was either pleas from nobles or reports sent from various outposts. Given it was a peaceful time, there was hardly any new information. Ashire was able to spend time on pressing matters while I triaged the paperwork. That was what I had done for years, though there were occasions when he had to travel south to maintain relations with our more powerful subjects, and I remained locked away within the palace. Public appearances and occasions had never been for me, until tonight.

I couldn't help but feel a healthy dose of angst as the morning drifted into the afternoon. I hadn't appeared in a crowd in almost two decades. I hadn't had to face or speak to a stranger. The thought left me doubtful I could be capable, even with Eve at my side. What if her abilities faltered and the crowds scattered at my Blessing? What if I recalled a painful memory too powerful for Eve to inhibit and harmed those around me? I hadn't allowed such a thing to happen in years. I had always been so careful to practice control, so diligent in maintaining a neutral feeling when in the presence of others, but there were days when I could only limit myself so much. Even now, if it hadn't been for Eve I couldn't have indulged in my doubts for fear of affecting Selasi.

My thoughts halted when Eve's hands slammed into my desk.

"Let's take a walk," she suggested.

I didn't know if she could sense my anxiety or if she was just able to read me. Either way, a walk was a welcome distraction from my own inner turmoil. Without another word, I reached for my cloak, and she followed suit. Selasi joined us as we exited the study with the afternoon drifting into the evening. Soon, I'd have to join my brother in helping with Feast Day. It was why I wanted Eve there, but I couldn't help but feel a dread wash—

"Where is your favorite garden?" Eve asked while we trailed down the stairs.

My thoughts halted. "The east gardens were bountiful, since more extravagant rooms and gatherings are held in the east corridor."

"Then let's go there."

"It's winter. Nothing is in bloom."

"Then, *Your Royal Highness*, describe them to me so I can picture it."

A smirk that was unmistakably Selasi's emanated from behind me, which I ignored. We descended the staircase towards the first floor, where we exited out into the north gardens. It was brisk out, but Eve insisted on a tour of the hibernating east gardens. We followed footpaths partially covered in snow, and I tried to describe specific flower beds or bushes that were shaped into different likenesses each year. They were usually scattered across the grounds, complemented by the teal hue of our ancient trees that descended from the mountain. I described the full beauty of the gardens, trailing through multiple canopies and tunnels of sleeping vines and flowers.

Though Eve began to shiver beneath her cloak, she insisted on continuing along the footpaths, which I preferred to being trapped within my own thoughts back in my study. We made our way towards the pond where a wooden canopy sat. Outdoor luncheons and afternoon teas were held there during the spring and summer.

With the sun's light fading, I realized that Eve had distracted my rapid thoughts long enough for the obligations of Feast Day to arrive. "We should probably make our way to the throne room," Selasi suggested.

Eve had already begun walking back towards the palace. She looked back to me expectantly.

"Eve, this will be the time to imagine making the flame grow," I said.

She nodded in understanding. We journeyed onward, welcomed by the warmth of the north corridor. The hall was busy with bakers and staff shuffling meat pies towards the throne room. It had been a while since the entire throne room was lit, illuminating the white stone and gold embellishments, and enveloping the room with a comforting warmth. The throne itself was surrounded by candelabras. My brother stood stiffly before the pedestal that held the throne, wearing his favorite livery collar, the golden chain studded with red and orange gems. Ashire must have chosen it to contrast against his black leather doublet. He was even wearing his crown, though it was far more petite than the cumbersome crown he had worn during his coronation. It was an ornately woven gold that had similar gemstones to his livery collar.

The staff were already setting crates of pies before us, but Ashire scanned me. "You're not dressed in any of your adornments."

"And?"

"And it makes the king appear vain when his princely brother is dressed casually."

I took my place next to him. "Perhaps the king *is* vain."

He scowled at me but called out to a member of staff. "Go and fetch a livery collar and the crown for His Royal Highness as hastily as you can manage." The able body scurried across the floor, disappearing to fetch the proper jewelry.

Selasi and Eve were standing off to the side, whispering something I couldn't overhear.

If she's here, I can remain in control.

"The people expect to be given gifts from their king and prince; therefore, they expect them to look the part," Ashire informed me.

"I'm sure they would manage."

Ashire leaned towards my ear. "The key to these events, Safir, is to always meet expectations. Keep your humility intact, wish them a happy Feast Day. You'll be loved for it." He placed his hand out. I allowed the back of my palm to rest on his hand as he surely felt the angst that swarmed in me. I hadn't bothered to focus on my typical neutral warmth to distract my Blessing. Ashire released me. "Just remember how much good this is doing. Seeing us united will inspire confidence in the crown. This is what *your* Eve is here for."

I glanced back at her, but that time I caught her gaze which was wide and bright. She smiled. I turned away.

If she's here, I can remain in control...

The member of staff returned with a golden livery collar and my crown, to be nestled on my head. I hadn't worn it in such a long time I'd forgotten how dense it was, though it was one of the smaller ones.

The last of the crates of frozen meat pies were settled next to us. The staff stopped scurrying. You could hear the chattering of people lined up outside. There must have been hundreds outside the palace doors. "Will they not freeze?" I asked Ashire under my breath as a winter wind shook the windows.

"I had the guardsmen light a few bonfires along the route outside. It'd look terribly insensitive to let people freeze to death while they wait to be fed by the crown." Just before they opened them to let the commoners rush in, Ashire murmured to me, "Remember to play the part they expect."

Then great doors were pried open. One by one people entered the throne room.

Some stopped and gawked at the interior, reminding me of Eve's reaction. They filed through with wide eyes and gaping mouths. Ashire assured me, "Every year, they stop and look. Best not to rush. Let them approach when ready." Gradually, they approached to curtsey or bow, looking to us expectantly.

Ashire stepped forward, plucked a pie with a clean cloth, and offered it to the elderly lady before him.

"Such kindness, Your Majesty! You embody Vada's good luck," she rejoiced, showing she was missing a few of her front teeth. The meat pie looked large in her shaky grasp. "We pray for this day everyday throughout the year. Every day, my king."

Ashire smiled, one I had only seen him wear when he was on display as king. "I wish you a very happy Feast Day, my dear," he told her, making her beam. He glanced to me, signaling I was to follow suit.

A man before me, probably not much older than Ashire, dressed in a heavy cloak with mud caked onto his boots, looked at me eagerly with his arms outstretched. I reached for a meat pie and handed it to him, careful that my skin never even grazed his.

He plucked it from me and smiled. "Good tidings to you and your family, my lord."

I took a deep breath. He hadn't sensed me. He hadn't experienced my Blessing that would have repulsed him. Even better, he appeared joyful. I didn't have to focus on suppression or hiding myself away. I could just be.

Yet the man was still staring at me, expecting some kind words. My brother's stare caught mine as he reached to the disheveled person in front of me. "Go with Vada's good luck, and have a merry Feast Day," Ashire remarked, allowing the man to bow and place a quick kiss on my brother's knuckles.

The man smiled and removed himself from the line while clutching his pie close to his chest. I wanted to cringe at my lack of etiquette, but the next person arrived with empty hands and an empty belly. They were consistently grateful being handed a simple pie, which left me humbled. Quickly I understood the meaning of Ashire's guidance. Seeing their expectant faces after waiting in the cold to meet their monarch, I wanted to meet that expectation.

While Ashire had much more practice interacting with the public, I tried to appear warm and open. Whenever I felt a flicker of doubt, I'd glance over my shoulder to make sure Eve was nearby. She watched me with a warm gaze that made my smile more genuine.

I continued passing out pies until my feet grew numb. I felt Ashire's hand on my shoulder. "If you deem it wise, your Eve may join us to help move this process along."

"Are you serious?"

"She's your advisor. She represents the crown. That and I'd like to eat tonight."

I waved Eve over and handed her a meat pie. "Would you care to help?"

She took it in her hands with a coy grin. "Really?"

"You're being put to use, dear Eve." Ashire leaned towards her. "Play the part, and we'll all be rewarded."

Eve, not impressed by my brother, handed the pie to the person in front of her. They thanked her graciously, and she smiled wide, wider than I had ever seen.

Eve adjusted well to interacting with the people. She was enjoying herself, which was contagious. It certainly helped move the line faster to the point where we could conclude by midnight. I swore Ashire's cheeks were spasming from having to smile so much. It had been a while since he had worn so much expression. Even I was feeling my energy fade, but we played the part up until the very last few.

The last ones we tended to were a young boy and a girl who approached us with great reluctance. The boy was carrying the girl, who didn't have shoes. They had dirt smeared across their faces and hair matted to one side. Their cheeks were sharp and skin pale. Though I considered Walor a prosperous city, there would always be those less fortunate.

But just because it's painful to look doesn't mean they don't deserve to be seen.

Mother's words echoed in my mind and after exchanging a glance with Ashire, I knew he was thinking the same. I stooped down and offered them a meat pie. The boy took it hastily. "Thank you," they both chirped, though the pie appeared to weigh more than them. A hand tapped my shoulder. I turned to see Eve transfixed on the children as she asked,

"How expensive are these boots?"

It was a strange question, but I glanced down. "They're unremarkable."

She pulled them off her feet and offered them to the girl. "They might be too big right now, but they'll keep your feet warm." The girl gawked, as did we all, and climbed down from her brother's shoulders to take the boots. Her bottom lip trembled, yet Eve wasn't finished as she pulled the cloak from her back and wrapped it around them both. She fastened it tight and smiled at them, but for the first time that night, her smile was pained. "You two have to take care of each other. Do you have a place to stay?"

"Eve," Ashire's voice grew low, almost in a warning, which she ignored.

The young boy chirped first. "We stay at the refuge with the others. It isn't too bad, right?" he asked the little girl.

She didn't move but instead stared wide-eyed at their pie while licking her chapped lips.

Eve looked up to me pleadingly. "Are there no spare rooms here? This place is huge. Can't you—"

"Would you like another pie?" Ashire interrupted while handing over an extra meat pie to the children who already had their hands full. "Keep it our secret. And hurry along now."

The children, clothed and given food, beamed as they bowed and toddled out of the throne room with their new regalia. A heavy sigh escaped Eve, and if I didn't know any better, I would have said her stare became glossy as she watched them exit.

"Well, it was advantageous we didn't see too many hungry children tonight, or else Eve would have stripped herself naked by now," Ashire sneered. "Those were the crown's clothes, not yours to give away."

"They're easily replaceable," I defended.

"One cannot give the shirt off their back to an unfortunate without themselves becoming an unfortunate. It was nowhere near her place to begin to think of housing anyone here. Soon we'd have to invite the whole refuge, if not the entire city, into our palace."

Eve looked longingly towards the empty doors. I wished I could have sensed her sentiments as easily as she could mine. "Is that the end of the day then?" she asked.

"Of course not," I scoffed. "It's Feast Day."

"Time to celebrate." Ashire removed the crown from his head. "I'm quite certain there's a ham and a tray of custard tarts waiting for you, and a few casks of wine for myself." He brushed past us while glancing to Eve. "You're welcome to join in the celebration once we replace your footwear. Selasi, you may also bring your impressive appetite."

Both Selasi's and Eve's eyes lit up as we made our way to the dining hall on the third floor. It was a tradition isolated to the palace, but it was one I relished. My favorite moment of the night was when Eve's belly let out a loud groan when the smells struck her nose. Her pace increased when the dining hall doors opened, and we were welcomed with a feast of our own.

Eve gasped at stacks of pies both savory and sweet crowding the table, along with a roasted pig, piles of fruit, fresh loaves of sweet bread, and rows of custard tarts along with classic Feast Day pudding waiting for dessert. We sat and eagerly filled our bellies, doing away with manners once everyone had had a few glasses of wine. Ashire certainly didn't have any cares once his goblet was placed in his hand. Both Eve and Selasi matched each other in appetite, hardly allowing their plates to empty throughout the course of the meal.

We were eventually joined by Lani, who was welcomed to the table to unburden us of the amount of food and tactlessly enlightened us on her new remedy for chronic diarrhea. It was ill-timed considering we were about to indulge in the Feast Day pudding. Regardless, once the damage was done to the feast and everyone was moaning their bellies were going to burst, games were to be had. We played 'What am I?' and 'Who am I?' multiple times, with the players trying to guess what the designated person was or who they were impersonating. Ashire quickly guessed every time, hardly sharing the fun with anybody. When it came to Eve's turn to be something, she barely took any time to contemplate her choice.

"It'll be impressive if your impression is accurate given your short time here," Ashire sneered while finishing off another bottle.

She stood smugly.

"Are you a what or a who?" I asked.

"I'm a who," she said. "And I think this will be too easy." She reached for a knife and pointed it across the table. "Make yourself known!" she boomed with her voice audibly lower in pitch. She reached for a sweet bun and stuffed it into her mouth while stabbing her knife through the air.

Ashire choked on his sip of wine. I chuckled as Lani yelled out, "You're Selasi!"

Eve chortled and peered over at Selasi, who looked amused, though none too pleased. "Your form was sloppy," he grumbled while taking a bite out of a sweet bun.

"Imitation is the sincerest form of flattery." Eve sat back in her chair. Her smile was wide and her cheeks rosy from just her second glass of wine. She giggled throughout the games, though she wasn't as good at playing. It seemed being from a different realm gave her a disadvantage.

When it was Lani's turn, she perched high in her chair and flapped her arms while roaring to the ceiling.

"The fuck kind of a bird is that?" Eve snarled into her glass.

My jaw dropped as Ashire threw his head back and laughed heartily. I signaled for Selasi to remove Eve's goblet from her hand. "It's rather obvious who here is seasoned with the drink."

She looked up at me from beneath her lashes with a pout, and I found it endearing. But Lani was still flapping in her seat and roaring.

"You're a griffin," Ashire called out to end the game.

Lani nodded, satisfied, and resumed leaning back in her chair.

Eve looked to each of us. "What's a griffin?"

"Creature as old as these mountains that live up north," Ashire explained. "They have the body and tail of a lion with the wings and head of an eagle."

"Many believe they're the ones that first bestowed Blessings on man," Lani commented.

"You don't have these creatures in your world?"

Eve rubbed her eyes and shook her head. "Not all blended together like that."

Selasi leaned back and rubbed his full belly. "Well, should we hear of the good wishes now?"

We all nodded in agreement as the night was growing into early morning. Ashire conceded and reached to his end table, where piles of envelopes awaited him. "I do detest this. No one is ever as sincere as they sound in these wishes."

"That's including you," I remarked.

"Especially me. The first one is from House Rarke. Ugh, Arius." Ashire scanned through it and threw the letter away.

"You have to read it aloud," I protested.

"Arius hasn't said anything remarkable outside of the squeals he made when he first came out of the womb. It was simply sending good wishes and hopes of visiting soon. Next, Uncle Batrum, hoping for a prosperous year for us all full of good health and Vada's blessing. I should write to him more. He used to send me messages every week as a child. Then we have oh— oh my, Lady Zae of House Oska sends her sincerest good wishes to us all and hopes the bond between our houses grows even stronger this year." Ashire looked up at me knowingly as he twirled his earring. "Safir, you could best attest to her sincerity."

I rolled my eyes. "Are there any letters in there from our Fae friend, Emtias?"

Ashire plucked a letter up from the pile. "There is."

"Then by all means read his so you can attest to *his* sincerity."

"You're fortunate he's visiting his village during their winter convalescc. Otherwise, I'd have him hex your downstairs gentleman."

Ashire continued reading them one by one as we listened to the sound of good wishes, a crackling fire, and sighs of full bellies. It was my favorite part of Feast Day, and this was the best Feast Day I had experienced. Even Ashire sighed contentedly with a warmth to his gaze that told me he was happy. Selasi was falling asleep at the table and finally excused himself. Lani followed suit, swaying down the hallway. I assigned Selasi to follow her safely to her quarters. I hadn't even noticed that Eve had settled into a chair against the hearth and fallen fast asleep. She hugged her knees to her chest with a small smile on her lips.

It did my heart good to see her happy like that. Ashire cleared his throat from across the table. "It appears she cannot hinder your Blessing as well while she sleeps."

"Can you sense me from there?"

"Only barely," he said, stifling a yawn. "What I can sense is what I'd wish for you to feel every day. Not just on Feast Day."

"It was a successful Feast Day though."

"Very much so. You conducted yourself very well. I know you had reservations at first. Of my appreciation, I hope you are fully aware."

"I am, though hearing it aloud is welcome."

"Hmm, and *she* did rather well, besides stripping herself," he said while looking towards Eve's sleeping form. "She is…good, I believe."

I smiled. "Yes, I believe so as well. She's only been here such a short while. Time will tell more."

"Indeed, but so far this partnership seems promising. Perhaps we should debut you before the royal houses, if matters continue as smoothly as they have, to show your place, your role in this kingdom."

I couldn't help but be taken aback by his words. "That's quite a leap to make after one successful night."

"I said as long as things continue smoothly, which seems to be dependent on her. It doesn't have to be decided now, but I wanted to share the notion with you." For the first time that night, he pushed his goblet away. "Yet I think I'll be more secure in my decision once my men have returned from observing her realm. I'd prefer to know how honest her testimony was regarding her home."

"They haven't returned yet?"

"They were instructed to remain for three days, so it will soon be telling." He stood and stretched, allowing a few joints to crack. "And with that I think I'll retire. Hopefully, my head will be clear by the time I wake." He gestured for me to stand, which I obliged, as he bestowed upon me his yearly embrace. Ashire was hardly one for affection, but he allowed it on Feast Day. I reciprocated gladly, as I never felt apprehension in physically contacting Ashire. It was one of the many reasons why I could breathe easier around him.

A few seconds passed before he released me. He patted my shoulder. "Happy Feast Day, Safir." And then he turned and retreated to his bed.

I smiled. While my own bed was calling for me, Eve still slept by the hearth.

I gently shook her. "Eve, you should go back to your room to sleep."

"I am in my room," she slurred, not bothering to open her eyes. "Why are you in my room?"

"Come on. Stand up." I reached under her arms, trying to pull her forward as her feet plopped onto the floor. She sagged in my grasp. "Push through your feet," I commanded fruitlessly.

A moan escaped her while I practically held her up. She made no effort to exert herself. She leaned against me, burying her face in my chest. "The floor won't stay in place, Safir," she groaned into my leather doublet. "So dizzy."

It was no use getting her to stand, and we both needed sleep, so I chose the simplest option. "Hang onto me," I said while placing her hands around my neck. Her grasp complied as I looped my arms around her shoulders and legs to scoop her into my chest. She groaned and kept her face buried in my tunic.

"You're going to make me sick," Eve hiccupped.

I had already taken a few steps out of the dining hall with her in my grasp, but I managed to focus on a soothing warmth I hoped would console her senses while I carried her back to the second floor. It must have worked because she sighed and held onto me more tightly. I was apprehensive of allowing my sentiments to wander any further in case I lost concentration on soothing her.

Every part of her in my grasp felt taut and toned, owning to her profession. Yet at the same time she was soft and warm, her hair smelling of crawlsey flowers, which spurred a nostalgic feeling in my gut. She was fetching to behold, unabashed and unafraid of me or my Blessing. I wanted to tell myself that drinking could make anyone that comfortable, but I liked to think she had grown to trust me.

I navigated down the stairs and arrived at her door with the morning sun spilling through the windows. I imagined Maisy would be there soon to help undress her, but Eve wouldn't be any help given her drunken state. As I settled her into her bed, her hands still clung around my neck.

"Eve," I whispered, trying to pry her hands away. "You're in your room. You can let go."

"Safir," she rasped, her sapphire eyes awake and transfixed on me. I froze when she said, "If only they were all as gentle as you."

She released her hands and collapsed onto her bed as I stood there sickened. The anguish in her tone mimicked the pain that lingered in my own spirit. She hardly divulged that part of herself, that pain she kept concealed. I had only caught a glimpse the first night we had met.

It's not a great feeling, being good at something you hate so much.

"Today was one of the best days of my life," she hummed while circling her arms around a pillow and burying her face in it. "Nicky would have loved it." Her voice waned and slow breaths escaped her as she drifted back to sleep.

I wondered what men had crossed her path to have given her that burden, wondered at the name she spoke and what it meant to her. I knew so little of her and her world, yet my guts twisted at the sound of the strange name.

The fact Eve could help control my Blessing meant she was inherently useful, but us enduring the same pain tethered her closer to me. Closer than I'd bargained for. I couldn't help but brush a few locks of hair away from her face.

"You'll keep having happy days here. We both will now."

Even in her sleep, she smiled for me.

Eve

My head pounded with every beat of my heart, and it only became worse as I braved opening my eyes to the bright light enveloping my room. I gagged at the taste in my mouth.

"Good afternoon, Eve!" Maisy's voice reached my ears before I even remembered where I was.

"Maisy, please, quiet voices," I moaned while trying to sit up in bed. "I'm never drinking again."

"We all say that until we do," Maisy chimed in with a glass of water in hand. "This is probably the object of your desire."

I brought the cup to my lips, the crisp taste helping me regain life. "You said 'good afternoon,'" I sighed after chugging the water. "What time is it?"

"It was close to three the last I checked."

My head fell into my hands. "Shit, Safir is going to be pissed I slept through the whole day."

"Not at all." She patted my back. "He informed me you could return home as soon as you felt able."

I sat up straighter. "He wants me to go home?"

"Yes, you've been here your three days. You get to go home now, but you will return, won't you?"

"Of course. I mean when I can."

It was hard not to notice how her face fell. "I'll be sure to report that to him. I know he was quite pleased with your presence during Feast Day."

I rubbed my eyes and shook my head. "I don't feel like I did very much."

"You do more than you think. I'm sure His Royal Highness would inform you, but I believe he is still sleeping as well. Now, I allowed you to sleep in your clothes since you threatened to purge whenever I tried to move you, so I imagine we'll have to return your baggy cloth suit now?"

I scoffed as I tried to stand and remove my leather clothing. My head swirled, but with Maisy's steady hands we managed to fit me back into my sweatpants and sweatshirt. It felt like a relief to have my more forgiving clothes back on, but immediately I felt less secure without my leather vest. It would be fitted soon enough when I returned in four days.

Before I left, Maisy handed me a cloth bag. I peered inside and saw two meat pies and two wrapped custard tarts. Despite my hangover, my appetite spiked. "A Feast Day gift from Milfred," Maisy said.

"I should thank her." I began making my way towards the kitchen.

Maisy pulled my sleeve. "Milfred usually sleeps for a few days following Feast Day since she exhausts her Blessing to create so many pies. I'll be sure to extend your thanks."

I smiled and held the bag close to me. "Will you be here when I come back?"

"I'll be right here waiting." Maisy beamed as I turned and left the room.

I made sure to return Ashire's books to his library before I left, fearing he'd follow me into my world if I didn't. It had only been three days, yet I had felt content in that peculiar world. I hadn't even known it existed less than one week before. It was baffling.

Just as easily as I'd entered, I returned to the woods I knew, but not before looking back at the palace behind me where I had eaten more and laughed harder than I had in my entire life. I kept it in my view as I stepped through the invisible window, watching it fade and gradually turn into the familiar woods of my backyard.

Part of me already felt as if there were a cord attached to me that was tied to that place, and it pulled every time I took a step farther away from it. Yet at the same time, a tauter cord that tied me to Nicky willed me forward. That cord had motivated me to endure more than I'd thought I could, which was evident when I stepped into my house and found Hunter sitting there in the corner. His sunken eyes were fixated on me.

My mouth ran dry, and I became acutely aware of how far away Walyre felt in that moment. "What are you doing here?" I asked while daring to step inside.

He clapped his hands and stepped towards me. I would have recoiled if he hadn't caught my jaw in his grasp. "Clay said you were looking good despite the other night. Wanted to see for myself." He pinched my jaw with his rough hands. I averted my gaze as I felt his stare trying to probe me. His other hand reached up and held the side of my face. "You *are* looking good."

"That's enough," I growled while pulling myself away, but he caught me when he found the bag I was holding.

"What's this? You looting?"

"It's nothing. It's my business."

He pulled harder, yanking me towards him. "If your business is nothing there's nothing wrong with looking." Hunter pried it away from my hand and opened the bag, only to be confused. "What is this?"

"They're pies. I'm taking them to Nicky."

"Ah, sure, if he has time in his busy schedule," Hunter sneered while running his hand through his thinning hair.

I scowled and brushed past him. "You should leave, and don't just show up unannounced."

His meaty hand caught my arm and squeezed so hard I was already anticipating bruises. "This is my house, Evie, that you're *allowed* to stay in, that you hardly thank me for. You should be a bit more grateful before you're made to."

My scowl snapped to him. "Meaning what?" I seethed while balling my hands into fists. Hunter was bigger than me, but if I ever needed to, I was sure I could give him a broken jaw to remember me by.

He smiled, sickeningly. "Just be grateful. That's all I'm asking of you." Hunter released me and I darted for the front door with him chuckling behind me. Just a few moments with Hunter had soured all the happiness I had experienced in Walyrc. I could hardly stomach him, so I tried to only think about Nicky.

What had surprised me the most about celebrating Feast Day was that I had forgotten to feel guilty, to remember my brother who suffered while I drank and ate myself sick. The guilt accompanying that realization was greater than I could have imagined, and so part of me was glad I returned home early. The sooner I could see Nicky, the sooner I could make up for my time not being with him.

I found him exactly as I left him, only at least they had him sitting up so he could look around the room. His hair had been trimmed and there was a flicker of life in his eyes when I burst into the room.

"Eve," he wheezed with a smile.

I threw myself beside him, hugging him as tightly as I could without disturbing the ventilator. "How was the new…job?"

I wanted to tell him everything, to tell him of the impossibility I had experienced, but I could hardly do the explanation justice. I wanted to talk about Safir, Ashire, Selasi, Maisy, Lani, and Milfred, but it was too daunting. Instead, I held up my reward in my hand.

"What's that?"

I smiled and placed the contents onto his side table, showing him a meat pie and custard tart for each of us. "Merry Christmas, Nicky."

We ate merrily, and Nicky agreed it was the best food he had ever tasted. I tried to regale him with my time at my "new job" by altering a few facts, saying that I was a note taker for a professor rather than an advisor to a prince in an alternate reality. It was simpler that way. "You seem happy," Nicky observed as we engulfed the last bites of tart.

I couldn't help but feel my all-too-familiar guilt. I merely nodded.

"Good," Nicky breathed. "One of us … should be." My face fell, but Nicky scoffed. "Kidding, Eve … Your happiness … is mine too."

I smirked but couldn't ignore that nagging feeling. Nicky did want me to be happy, but at the same time I knew he wished for his own happiness. Anyone would have. He said kind things because he was kind, but also so that I wouldn't burden myself more. I knew because I would have done the same for him. My guilt lingered, even though Selasi and Maisy's words echoed in my mind.

Regardless, as we finished eating, we watched the holiday specials of *Golden Girls* gladly. Afterwards, we watched the snow fall outside until Nicky fell asleep. It wasn't a glorious Feast Day, but it was a good Christmas.

My routine became the most peculiar in history as I bounced back and forth between worlds as if leaping through pages in a book. It granted me time to study that invisible portal. Not all creatures were able to pass into Walyre. Birds flew through, and squirrels scurried past, but never once did anything else disappear into the portal. I didn't know if it was limited to humans, or just intelligent creatures, but how was the portal aware something was intelligent?

Curiosity faded with my weekly routine of entering and exiting the portal. I gave up waitressing altogether and spent four days in my world, training twice per day to make up for the time in Walyre. If I had a fight approaching, I would train the morning before I left and the evening I returned from Walyre. All the meals Milfred fed me did me good while in the ring. My endurance and strength had improved immensely with not having to depend on stealing frozen meals. On days I returned home, Milfred sent extra pies and dishes I got to share with Nicky. He looked forward to what I brought home, and I attempted to tell stories from my time in Walyre. Each time, guilt panged in my gut. Neither of us could be fully happy if the other wasn't, so I could only allow myself to be so happy each day.

Hunter obviously noticed I was eating better. He pinched my hip between his meaty fingers while I worked out.

"Careful before you have to move up a weight class," he sneered as I slapped his hand away.

"If you wanna a girl to paw after, Hunter," Clay snapped from across the gym, "there are ones you can pay for that. Let the slugger focus."

Moments like that made me miss Walyre, miss Safir. I imagined him throwing Hunter into their dungeon. Whenever I re-entered that world, greeted by the winding trees and the palace, I could forget all about Hunter and having to fight. I could read whatever books I wanted, indulge in whatever food was served, and enjoy company that I was content with. I became more appreciative each day since Nicky couldn't experience it. That was the only way I could cope with being remotely happy, which was easier when I was with Safir. We had grown comfortable in each other's presence. I almost feared that comfortableness at first, wondering if Safir had earned my ease. But Safir proved himself repeatedly.

Every now and then, if he wanted to convey an emotion he couldn't articulate aloud, he extended his hand to me, and I never refused. Our emotions were often similar. Somedays all I could feel was grief in him. But he never said where that pain came from, and I dared not ask. It wasn't unlike how I felt, how I'd probably always feel. That feeling made me want to return to Walyre for more than my promised meals and free healing from Lani. Our separate but matched anguishes wanted to find company in the other.

I also found solace in the company of Maisy and Selasi, dodging their antics whenever I could. Lani became better at healing me as I improved upon my breathing technique which I could begin to feel the effect of on my body. Whenever I breathed to limit the flame of a candle, I had more energy. If I breathed to make the flame of a candle grow, I'd fatigue but could easily nullify the Blessings of those around me.

"I'm so proud of your improvement." Lani let her hands graze my bruised and bloodied face, making the pain fade and the swelling recede. "I'm sure His Royal Highness is pleased as well."

"I think so," I said. Safir attended a few meetings with some of the local lords in Walor, though merely observed with me close by.

"Continue to drink the tea I brewed you. It'll help the swelling." She handed me the bitter cup of tea.

I downed the drink quickly. "Why do you study how to heal if that's your Blessing?"

She sighed sitting next to me, wiping a drop of sweat from her brow. "I didn't know it was my Blessing for many years. Healing, for the most part, has been a passive process. Those around me simply ceased having a cold or healed from wounds quicker. It simply seemed like good luck from Vada. I didn't realize I was using my Blessing on anyone, let alone myself, which led to me aging exceptionally slowly. By the time I had lived thirty years and had the face of a fifteen-year-old, I began to question."

My jaw dropped. "How old are you now?"

"I'm eighty, I think."

Lani didn't look older than forty at best. Her brown eyes were bright. Her skin was smooth besides a few wrinkles. She giggled at my reaction while sweeping her black curls behind her ears. "Before I realized my Blessing, I was training and working as a healer. After the realization, I continued to study because there are days where my Blessing is spent, and I must rely upon other methods to help those around me." Her face fell. "When the plague came, my Blessing was so busy healing my own body that I was of very little use to those in the palace, especially my Queen Mira. I had to use the methods I learned in practice, but there was only so much that could be done."

Her grief hung in the air before I mustered courage to interrupt it. "I didn't know that was how the queen passed."

Lani sniffed and nodded. "Her sons do not speak of it, so I try not to as well. Queen Mira was in such a delicate state. She was carrying her third child."

Words failed me as the grief that plagued Safir unfolded itself around me.

"She was the mother of all mothers. She had such a delicate beauty, rarely treasured. Even while facing death, she was more concerned for the unborn child."

"You were there when she died?"

Her eyes began to glisten. "I couldn't leave her."

"How old were Ashire and Safir at that time?" I asked boldly.

"His Royal Highness was ten, I believe. His Majesty had just turned fifteen."

"But what about their father? Did they not have him?"

Lani froze and stood while smoothing her skirts. "I'll speak openly about my beloved queen, but I refrain from discussing the king past."

"I'm sorry. I didn't mean to upset—"

"Eve," she interrupted. "I'll only tell you to be cautious about making inquiries into matters that will surely sicken you." We never discussed anything related to the departed king or queen again.

Instead, whenever Safir was busy rummaging through paperwork, I'd read books about the history of the land and the great houses in hopes of uncovering more. All the texts first spoke of the beginning of humanity. Most postulated that drops of sun fell to the land and man rose from the mixture of fire and soil. The first five men created gave rise to the five great houses. The more I read, the more I wanted to understand.

This was how I met Emtias.

I was plucking new books from the library to take back to my room when a slick voice found my ear. "Do you not tire of these readings?"

I jolted and spun around on my heels.

A thin, tall man stood before me with warm skin and black, silky hair pulled into a bun. His eyes were narrow, as he studied me. His eye color was a bright gold, with a long and sharp face. His ears, pierced with rows of golden hoops, ended in slight points. I tried not to stare. He had his own stack of books tucked under his arm. Long robes hung on him loosely.

"Do you not tire?" he asked again.

I clutched the books and stood tall. "I haven't met you."

"I'm Emtias Winterspeck. I'm His Majesty's advisor."

Oh, he's an actual advisor.

"I hear you're His Royal Highness' new advisor?" he asked while raising a sharp eyebrow. I nodded. "You read quite a bit of simple content for one who's meant to provide profound advice and counsel."

I narrowed my gaze. "If you're the king's advisor you'll already know why I'm actually here."

He grinned slyly. "Correct. I wanted to hear the ruse you'd provide should anyone ask why you lack knowledge for being an advisor."

"I'd say Emtias knows enough for each ruler's advisor."

Emtias scoffed. "Flattery only takes one so far."

"It's not as though I'm lacking effort," I said while holding up my pile of books. "I'll feign being shy in company I'm not familiar with."

"Your body language is entirely too assertive to be mistaken as shy. Unfortunately, we might actually have to educate you." He brushed past me and reached for a few books over my head. "The king assures me you can be trusted with his collection, though I will only be convinced with time." He pulled them out and dropped them on top of the pile of books already in my grasp. I struggled to keep them from toppling over. "Start with those two, then find me again when you need heavier material. As often as I see you combing through the shelves, I imagine you're capable of more than just sitting in the same room as His Royal Highness." His golden eyes flared just before he turned away. "Do not disappoint me."

It didn't surprise me that Emtias was Ashire's advisor. They were so similar, though I later learned Emtias was Fae— one of the magical folk who lived deep in the mountains further north and were allied with House Astana. They claimed to have lived long before man and had seen fire fall from the sky to create humanity. Emtias came from a noble family and acted as advisor to be sure Fae interests were considered. They practiced "practical magic" in making predictions and healings and were known as history's keepers. Fae weren't Blessed as humans were because, according to Emtias, "We have no need to be pitied in order to survive. Our talents know no bounds even without Blessings," and so I dared not ask more. The only way to divert his attention from his superiority complex was to let him quiz me over and over.

"House Oska, in the southwest city of Phora, primarily produces what?" Emtias inquired, hardly looking up from his own book.

I sighed while staring up at the bookshelves. "Spices and…"

"And?"

"Silks?"

"Is that a question?"

I inwardly groaned. "Spices and silks." Emtias was relentless in educating me, whether it was for my own benefit or to stroke his own ego. Regardless of his intentions, I became more familiar with the aristocracy of Walyre. House Oska's symbol was a serpent with a gold ring hanging off its tail, a domineering emblem.

"Now House Trice, relations to His Majesty and His Royal Highness, live amongst the meadows of the southeast. They produce enough grain to supply the majority of the kingdom. Where do they reside?"

"It starts with an X."

His critical eyes rolled. "'It starts with an X' is not an appropriate answer when conversing with the local lords. *Xard*," he emphasized. "House Trice breeds scholars. We honor them by speaking to them as intellectual equals."

And so, I was schooled, tested, and teased, but in a way, I reveled in it. There was a sense of accomplishment when I made Emtias smirk by answering a question correctly, and a sense of dread when he rolled his eyes when I couldn't commit each fact to memory.

I memorized House Trice's symbol, a dove with a dagger clasped in its claws. I recalled their profits from their grain supplies and attempts at implementing a new irrigation system. All the way south, bordering the sea, was the House of Rarke in the city of Shey.

"The house of shame," Emtias called them. "They exist at the king's mercy." Their symbol consisted of a bloodied harpoon impaling some tentacled creature, and they were known for seaports.

They were obviously disliked by most staff at the palace for reasons I hadn't determined.

The most mysterious of all was the fourth house, the House of Calista, north of the mountain ranges I knew in Walor. They lived inland where cliffs extended into tundra. Their house symbol was a griffin: the body and tail of a lion and the feet and head of an eagle. They created fine iron workings, and their lands were home to griffins themselves.

Lastly was the House of Astana, which resided centrally in the northern mountain range. They used to primarily ship lumber, but found riches mining precious metals, gems, and stone. Their symbol was a single red and orange flame, which I had seen many times in tapestries and in Safir's eyes.

Most of the great houses had kept their power primarily through Blessings. Marriages were chosen to pass down Blessings to their children. It made me believe there was a genetic component, because it appeared stronger Blessings could be bred. One Blessing in House Rarke consisted of being proficient with whatever weapon they touched. In House Trice, one lord could see one minute into the future, which drove him mad. The first ruler of the House Astana could create sparks at his fingertips, giving to their house symbol: the Last Flame. House Calista didn't have a single documented Blessing for the ruler in Griffin's Crest in all their history. Whoever the ruler would marry had a Blessing, but the ruler themselves never did, which was hard to believe, since a person's Blessing greatly impacted the influence they had.

I didn't know if it was too treacherous to travel that far north, but every generation had a few persons Blessed with being able to command a person to speak the truth. This made it impossible for someone to hide their Blessing to gain an advantage. The persons with that Blessing were called Seekers and traveled throughout the land to document people's Blessings. Regardless, still no ruler in House Calista was ever documented as having a Blessing.

It made me wonder, if Fae didn't have Blessings, yet humans did, then what brought about Blessings in the first place? Many books speculated, but none gave a conclusive answer. The last few texts I consumed discussed the Blessings held by those in power at this point.

In Shey, Lord Arius of House Rarke had the Blessing "jump," where he could transport himself thousands of feet at a time. He could even transport a few other beings with him. It seemed passed down from his grandfather, the usurped king Urso, who had the Blessing to "open doors" into other worlds. This piqued my interest, but the doors were described as openings to hell, a gift from Chike himself, the god of retribution. Urso primarily used it as a means of punishment for his subjects, but he'd disappeared years after the war was over.

In the southeast, Lord Batrum of House Trice had the Blessing "whisper," with which he could speak to someone from miles away if he had something of theirs. In the southwest, Lady Zae ruled House Oska, yet she didn't have a Blessing despite her departed father having the ability to see into someone's memories for one minute if he were touching them. I supposed it made House Calista less suspicious for not having a documented Blessing, though it was still peculiar.

The last recorded ruler of House Calista, Tyrren, had ruled in Griffin's Crest for ten years with his wife Carissa. Her Blessing was "navigating," with which she could always find the safest, fastest, or shortest path she desired even without being familiar to the area. Little was written, as their house had disappeared many years ago.

"It was a strange occurrence," Safir commented one day. "The entire family was found gone without a single trace, and to this day the griffins do not allow anyone to rule in Griffin's Crest."

"How do they not allow someone to rule?" I asked.

"They kill whoever tries. Only a Calista can rule in Griffin's Crest. Their house made a covenant with the griffins at the dawn of man and upheld it until their disappearance. For now, Lady Carissa's brother, Lord Harysle of House Sypher, attempts to govern inland, but the people are hard to influence, and he cannot intervene with the griffins considering he's not a Calista."

My curiosity grew when I finally reached the portion discussing House Astana. It had only been established as the royal family two generations prior, when Lord Muire Astana led an uprising against House Rarke, the original royal family. His Blessing was "inspiration" where he was capable of motivating those he could see to do his bidding. This was how the Fae first became aligned with House Astana. House Calista and House Trice supported him. House

Oska had split into two factions supporting opposite sides of the war, but House Astana succeeded in becoming the new ruler. Little was written about the opposing side of House Oska considering most were killed in battle alongside House Rarke's forces. I hadn't even realized Safir's family hadn't always been monarchs.

"Power shifts constantly," Emtias told me while returning a few books. "If you saw the palace in Shey you wouldn't doubt House Rarke were the first royal family. It's why this one is simple. They didn't plan on it being the capital centuries ago," he sneered as if the palace wasn't exceptionally grand on its own. "Regardless, we've known more peace because of the shift in power than history ever knew before. The Rarkes lacked ambition. They had grown too complacent. Lord Muire Astana, with his influential Blessing, inspired others to help him usurp the crown with promises of fortifying and emboldening the kingdom."

After Lord Muire's victory, he was crowned King Muire. His son, Prince Ronire, was betrothed to Lady Mira of House Trice to secure their alliance. Prince Ronire's Blessing was "hold," where he could make a person freeze in place for a considerable amount of time if he uttered the command "lock." Lady Mira's Blessing was documented as "pleasing," which made my stomach form into knots. It was said she could make a man, even a suffering one, feel indescribable bliss at the touch of her hand. It didn't seem limited to just pleasure, but any positive emotion: comfort, peace, happiness, security, or ecstasy. She birthed Ashire soon after they married and Safir five years later. Queen Mira died from the plague ten years after giving birth to Safir. Little else was mentioned until the king passed away from a "weak heart" one year later, after Ashire ascended the throne at age sixteen. It was written so plainly I wanted to understand what had happened between the lines.

More answers were given to me one day as I returned to Walyre from my world. And as Lani had warned, I only received sickening answers. I had stumbled upon Safir and Selasi sparring in the west gardens and stopped to observe. The air had grown warmer as time passed, and Safir spent more time outside than in his study. On rare occasions, Ashire joined them. He was a more defensive fighter, weaving and dodging but hardly ever using his energy for offense. He obviously preferred to tire out his opponent, not unlike many opponents I faced in the ring. But Safir fought differently. He wanted the fight to be over as quickly as possible, and to do so he needed to be swift and clever.

Selasi and Safir moved fluidly around each other despite carrying longswords. Sweat poured from their brows. I imagined the leather pants were of little help. When Selasi saw me approach, he ceased his sparring and waved me over. "Eve! Put my mind at ease and sit there," he pointed to a bench before them, "and try to inhibit any Blessings."

I sat and looked to Safir, who was panting with his sword still pointed at Selasi. "Selasi is the best swordsman in the world, but it's unknown whether it's his Blessing or his own talent."

"The Seeker doesn't know?"

Safir shook his head. "A Seeker hasn't been able to reach Walor for years. The weather has always been too troublesome. This will test whether Selasi is the greatest by Vada's hand or by his own skills."

Selasi grinned as they squared off and began clashing once again. I did my best to breathe deep and slow. It was like a vicious dance. Each time one made a move towards the other, it was as if they had already predicted such an attack. Safir's orange earring charm swung and almost got caught on the tip of Selasi's sword a few times. Even though his white locks fell into his gaze, he had little trouble avoiding Selasi's attacks. I had almost forgotten to continue breathing deeply when Selasi disarmed Safir and had his sword pointed at his throat.

They both panted, but Selasi's face was consumed with pride. "I suppose that answers that question," he said withdrawing his blade.

"Perhaps it was Vada's luck," Safir sneered.

"You insult me, Lord! Eve's presence has made it known my sword skills don't derive from a Blessing!"

They snickered at each other, though I averted my gaze, heat rising in my cheeks, when Safir pulled his shirt over his head and wiped the sweat from his face. From the glance I allowed myself, all those years of sparring had built lean muscle onto Safir. I could see each indentation along his core, arms, and chest. It wasn't bulky, but a functional strength that left me embarrassed for admiring it. My sheepish stare dropped to the ground.

Selasi chuckled. "You shame your advisor. She cannot even look at you."

I overheard a grin in Safir's voice. "Is this true, Eve? Can you not even look upon me?"

"I hope if the roles were reversed, you'd avert your gaze from me." I tried to maintain my composure, though every time I blinked, I was greeted with the image of Safir shirtless.

Dammit.

"I won't seek to make you uncomfortable," he conceded as he turned his back to me, then continued wiping the sweat from his body. That only exposed the lean muscle rippling across his back, but I found myself not staring at his physique but at the scars that crisscrossed his entire back. They were jagged and gleamed in the sun. My stomach dropped and my blood lurched. There must have been at least a dozen if not more scarring his beautiful back.

Selasi caught my gaze and shook his head. Closing my mouth that I hadn't realized had fallen open, I tried to act as normally as I could the rest of the day. Safir also conducted himself normally, which meant the scars were such second nature to him that he thought nothing of it. It made me think about the grief that I sensed in him. One could only wonder what had occurred between the lines in those books that led to the gruesome souvenirs that Safir was forced to carry.

Safir

Eve adjusted to her new role with surprising pace. She kept herself busy in my brother's library while I conducted paperwork, though I knew she was given a workload of her own, per Emtias, who never tired of analyzing her. Emtias reported her performance every few days, though I knew he valued her when he commented at dinner, "She's gentle with the books," the grandest compliment he could muster.

Eve and I had for the better part of two months found an understanding. She knew when to let me concentrate and when I needed reprieve. "Take a walk with me," she'd say every time my frustrations were ready to crest, and I found it hard to refuse her. My head would clear as we walked through the garden paths that I knew she had memorized. She asked me questions about other houses or the history of Walyre.

Though my mind was often occupied with pleas for tax relief or trying to observe a meeting with the local lords, if I needed a distraction I would inquire about her world. It had seemed dull from my brief glimpse, but from Eve's descriptions it was entirely removed from any magic.

She recounted her world as we settled against a great tree to rest. It was nice to let the sun graze our faces as opposed to being confined to my study. Eve plucked at the grass. "I swear we don't use carriages! There are metal vehicles that can travel miles at a time. Imagine moving from here to Xard in one day."

I shrugged. "One can, with our stableman who Blesses horses with speed. So, does your world not have horses?"

"There are horses, but we don't use them to pull carriages."

"Strange how your realm has similar animals like horses, but doesn't contain griffins, Fae, or goblins."

"Of course there are goblins here," she sighed.

I didn't find it that far-fetched since she seemed comfortable with the idea of magical Fae and griffins. "Tell me again the services your 'machines' provide."

"Heat, cool air, food, light, medicine. But they're primarily used for weaponry."

"War is present in any reality. What medicine could be provided? What place do your healers have?"

She brushed the blades of grass from her lap. "Similar to Lani before she knew what her Blessing was. Probably the greatest thing our healers discovered was a fungus that cures most infections."

"Infections?"

"Oh um— like an injury or poison that can get in your bloodstream."

"A fungus that pulls poison from the blood?"

"Sure, kind of, like Penicillin. It'd come in handy here."

"Thankfully, we have enough healers we don't have to stake our hopes on a fungus, not all as skilled as Lani but still helpful. There was once a healer who provided vitality if you wore the clothes she weaved. Another was able to heal people through the food she baked, no relation to Milfred. But no one must rely on fungus. Sounds dreadful."

Sometimes she laughed at moments I didn't understand, but it was an intoxicating sound. Regardless, I was able to relax with her. At the very least, my temper lessened, and I could return to my work with more diligence. She was someone with whom I could just *be*, and I relished that feeling in her presence. I found myself longing for the days she stayed at the palace. Just knowing she was within the vicinity lightened my spirit, and then it dampened whenever she left for her world.

She often returned to Walyre with grotesque bruises and swollen eyes. I came to detest the sight of her so brutalized. It made my stomach plummet when we were separated, knowing that she was in pain and so far from me. I began to wait by her portal to meet her. On many occasions, I was thankful I had.

One such evening, I had only been waiting for a few moments before she appeared. She stumbled to her knees with a groan. I immediately reached for her. There were bruises smattered along her jaw. Her breathing was labored. "Eve?" I asked. "Are you in pain?"

She gripped my leather sleeves. "Safir," she gasped. Despite her pain, she always smiled when saying my name. "I-I can't breathe," she wheezed while clutching her side.

"I hope you were at least successful in your endeavors," I scoffed while pulling one of her arms around my shoulders as I raised her to her feet.

She yelped. My chest tightened, and I focused on numbing her through my touch. "I was." After a few moments I felt her relax into me once my Blessing took effect. "I'm so glad to be here."

I was reassured when she was near. The closer she was, the better I could be assured that she wasn't in any immediate pain or danger. Lani saw to Eve's injuries each time Eve visited. She'd be returned to me whole, happy, and with another book in hand.

The first few months with her at Walor Palace were the simplest but gladdest in my recent memory. The effect she had lingered even after she had returned to her world. One day, Ashire observed, "I sense you very faintly from here."

I stared at him quizzically. "I'm not trying to limit myself."

"I know. I think it's your Eve."

"You're getting in an awful habit of calling her that. What if she heard you?"

"And if she did? Would you be overcome with bashfulness? The prince of Walyre?"

I waved him off. "I think you'd risk making her feel more uneasy than me." I noticed Eve didn't appreciate being the center of attention. She'd restlessly fidget.

"But perhaps her reach is greater than we thought. I've written a few theories Emtias agrees with—"

"How long have you been creating theories?"

"Since Feast Day. Ever since then, each time she returns to her realm your Blessing seems more controlled."

I hadn't even noticed myself. "Do you believe her effect is so strong it can traverse our planes of existence?"

"Not at all," he answered while nursing his wine. "I believe her Blessing is acting much like a splint on a broken leg. It's allowing your Blessing to rest."

"That sounds remarkably simple."

Ashire shrugged. "That doesn't mean it's any less true. Lani agrees with me."

My eyes rolled. "Does Selasi agree with you as well?"

"He will when I instruct him to. Regardless, it means that the longer she remains here, the more responsibilities you may take on, should you so desire. I mentioned after Feast Day that we should debut you to the other great houses. I think this plan should be enacted."

I leaned forward onto my knees. "That would entail you trusting her. What of your men you had infiltrate her world?"

"Oh, yes." He revealed a piece of parchment from his pocket. "I had their observations written down, and either Eve is disassociated from her reality, or she was underestimating its docility. 'The streets were paved with smooth stone to provide means for transportation by loud iron-clad carriages. The carriages provided commands and cues for the persons operating them. It seems humans live in a symbiotic relationship with the iron-clad creatures. Illusions and projections were observed on many corners; however, we were unable to interact with them. Most of the inhabitants spoke Common, although most were unwilling to engage in conversation, apparently inebriated."

It matched what Eve had tried to explain to me regarding her means of transportation. It hardly seemed to impress Ashire.

"'What's abundantly clear is the people carry projectile weapons on their person regularly. One can assume their rulers have a greater means of protecting their power. Such an event was witnessed in an illusionary pane of glass, which displayed colossal projectiles decimating multiple cities. This occurrence was considered common, which encouraged the entourage to return promptly.'" Ashire dropped the parchment into his lap. "Not exactly a glowing evaluation, I must say. It sounds like some made-up drunken horror. Can you imagine? Like a god smiting the land, but it's exacted by an imperfect human."

"Eve told me that much. She's more stunned by magic than by military prowess."

Ashire leaned forward and threw the parchment in the fire, allowing the words of another world to disappear in embers and smoke. "If such weaponry were possible, we'd be better have nothing to do with it. How could I defend myself against a man with an exploding projectile? An entire army of skilled swordsmen is laughable in comparison. Even with Blessings, I'm not certain we would stand our ground against the forces her world possesses. We have enough folly to ruin ourselves with magic without the use of their innovations."

"You're abandoning the resources in her world?"

"I'm abandoning the risks. At the very least, if *I* cannot possess this power then neither can our potential opponents. It's ungodly to think about possessing such destruction. The king past would have been tempted, but I'm certain it would bring torment to our lives."

I agreed if anything commending Ashire's caution. We had both seen the cruelty man was capable of. Absolute gods-given control had no place in a time of peace.

"May I clarify, do you have men walking about the palace grounds who are aware of a portal to an alternate realm?"

Ashire snorted while shaking his head. "I had Emtias undo the memories of their observations. As far as they're aware, they spent those three days in drunken splendor. It didn't seem like a deviation from their character."

My jaw fell open. "I see, and Emtias was content with carrying out your order?"

"I dare say he was even eager."

I stifled a chuckle. "In regard to having me debuted, you're sure you aren't suggesting this out of impulsiveness?"

"You claimed the same on Feast Day, but I have given it two months and seen the progress in you both. The effect is palpable," he said while sipping his wine. "Safir, I want you to be debuted. To show us united would strengthen all we've done to mend the wounds inflicted by the past king."

I almost flinched, and my anguish prickled at the surface of the contentedness left behind by Eve. I smothered the animosity that would have permeated the air. "So, you want me to be displayed to assert yourself?"

"To assert our house," he reiterated with a hint of annoyance. "But also, to offer you proof you're capable of contributing to the betterment of the people outside of the exploitation of your Blessing."

I swallowed hard, feeling that animosity tempt the surface of my composure. "You're speaking frankly about a subject on which I appreciate you treading carefully."

"Are you scared of making me feel sad, Safir?"

"Ashire," I growled. "I know you're aware I'm afraid of far worse, so why antagonize me?"

He smiled. "It goes to show how effective Eve is: even as pumped full of ire as you are, I can still barely feel it."

I sat back and sighed while rubbing my eyes. "You don't have to go to such insufferable lengths just to prove you're right. If you want me to be debuted so desperately, I won't deny the will of the king."

"What of your brother?" "Gladly, I would deny *him*."

Ashire grinned. "Excellent. I'll send for the other great houses. Your Eve should be in attendance. Perhaps she can be convinced to prolong her stay."

That I certainly looked forward to, and so plans were made for the great houses to meet for the first time in almost ten years. It brought another host of doubt and angst similar to what I'd felt during Feast Day, only amplified. However, I took comfort in knowing Eve would be there as she had been before. It left me anxiously looking forward to the coming days.

Eve

It was a warm afternoon when I emerged onto the palace grounds, one of the few times Safir hadn't greeted me in the forest. I was earlier than usual, and likely he was tending to something tedious.

I was deep in thought after having visited Nicky that morning. His breathing was labored, erupting in pained coughs that made his ventilator jolt. He'd attempted to convince me he was fine, but I had heard that wet cough before and knew where it could lead.

My thoughts were so consumed I didn't hear the footsteps creeping behind me. The second a sweaty hand clamped over my mouth, my body tensed, and my hands formed into fists. Something deathly sharp pressed into my back. My lunch churned in my stomach. I stiffened, breathing in the smell of something rotten from behind me. It worsened as a mouth was lowered to my ear.

"I don't wish to harm you. I swear it." This I doubted based on the pressure of his blade against my back. "Take me to the king's rooms, and you will remain uncut." His voice was rough and full of promise I didn't believe.

A deep, searing spite surfaced in my consciousness where my fear should have been. I hated, no, *loathed* being afraid.

"How did you get onto the palace property?" I asked through his dirt-crusted fingers, hoping to spot a guard walking through the grounds.

The man pushed the blade harder, to where the tip just barely pierced my skin. "Show me the king's rooms."

He was bigger than me, given the size of his hands. No doubt someone of incredibly low rank given his hygiene. I could outrun him, but he kept me too close to break away without being stabbed. I didn't know if I could outfight a knife. Should I refuse he seemed more than willing to kill me and then would infiltrate the palace anyway. I was hoping I could walk away unscathed if I brought him to the person I knew could disarm him.

I swallowed hard and nodded, the dagger pressing against my skin. "Say nothing. Make no gestures. We stop nowhere. Walk me directly to his rooms," he ordered.

He was taking a gamble relying on me. He thought I'd be persuaded enough with his dagger, but I was betting he wouldn't know what a king's room looked like. If he were as lowly as I thought, he would think even my room was grand enough for a king.

Quaking with anger, I stepped forward and his footsteps followed suit. The blade was withdrawn. I tried to look behind me, but the blade swiftly returned, making me yelp. "Don't look behind you. Just keep leading forward."

I seethed as we emerged from the forest, stumbling into the gardens. I had no intention of feeling afraid that day, so I ventured into the north corridor of the palace. There wasn't another soul, but I hoped the ornate décor would distract him enough for me to make a getaway. Just as I took a quick step forward, his hand wrenched for my shoulder and pulled me back into his dagger.

The metal ripped through me. His hand covered my mouth as I shrieked at the pain. I bit down on his fingers as hard as I could, which made him curse and push the dagger deeper. He smothered another shriek from my mouth. "This dagger isn't for you. Do not make it so," he warned.

I sucked in deep breaths, tears brimming in my eyes as warmth enveloped my back. He was willing to kill. He wouldn't be distracted. He didn't care for my pain. I needed to act out of self-preservation if I wanted to avoid his dagger again.

I shakily walked towards the staircase which led to the second floor. Each step caused more pain to rip through me and the warmth was only growing.

"Faster," he rasped behind me.

A bloody trail would be too suspicious.

I picked up my pace, grinding my teeth so hard I was ready to chip a molar. Any staff passing by kept their heads down and hurried past. Him being in my presence seemed to mask him from onlookers. Blood trickled down my leg as I reached the door I wanted.

"Stop," he told me. Then he pressed himself against the door, presumably listening to check it was empty. He opened the door and stole us both inside. I tried to turn, but he grabbed the back of my head and spun me.

"Don't turn around," he repeated while backing us towards the window. "So, this is how a king lives, huh?" After some rummaging, he stood behind a curtain while I stood directly in front of him. Through the fabric, he had a hold of my shirt with his dagger in the other hand pressed into my back. "We wait, and when he arrives, you'll beckon him towards the window. Then you will be free."

"What quarrel do you have with the king that you're willing to risk yourself?" I asked, forgetting his hatred for questions.

The blade stuck into my flesh again, and I practically buckled, stifling my cry that would have been heard throughout the palace. Pain radiated through my back as I tried to remain standing. "No questions. You'll calm yourself when he comes."

Calm myself? Calm myself!

I was going to fucking throat-punch him the first chance I got. He would regret ever making me feel afraid. I waited patiently to make certain of it.

Safir

"I should take my leave now," I groaned while throwing my shirt back over my torso. "Eve will be expecting me."

"All the more reason to not dress yourself, Lord," Selasi jested while sheathing his sword.

"She practically swoons when seeing you not dressed formally."

I wiped the sweat from my brow on my forearm. "I believe it embarrasses her more than impresses her."

Selasi rolled his eyes. "You're too modest to admit a lady would swoon over you."

"She's too reserved to swoon," I argued while venturing back towards the palace, needing to change. I cursed. "I don't believe I have any clean shirts for today."

"You may borrow one of mine if you want, Lord. It might be a tight fit," Selasi snickered while climbing the stairs towards his room. "But I don't think she'll mind."

I groaned as I followed him. Selasi clearly still had too much energy left. I couldn't help but wonder if Eve had already arrived as we stepped into Selasi's quarters, and we both stalled to see her standing there.

She wasn't smiling. She stood too still as her eyes widened with such intensity. I froze. Something had happened.

"Eve?"

"Your Majesty!" she piped, too high-pitched. "T-there's a matter in the garden that I wanted you to see. You can see it clearly from here." Her voice shook, but she was looking to Selasi.

Selasi, having lost any hint of amusement, nodded slowly while taking careful steps forward. I could see she was quaking. To my horror, a small puddle of blood had formed around her feet. My anger arose and was ready to punish whatever it was that caused her harm in my home. If she hadn't been present, the entire palace grounds would have felt the weight of my indignation.

"Show me this matter," Selasi barked while approaching her, trying to sound as imperious as possible.

She tore her panicked stare to me, a single tear cascading down her cheek.

I wanted to burn on the spot.

Just as quickly as her tear fell, a body emerged behind her from the curtains. He threw her onto the floor as he charged at Selasi with a bloodied dagger.

I caught Eve in my arms, pulling her into me and away from the creature who thrust his blade at Selasi. Dodging the initial attack, Selasi grabbed his wrist and head-butted the assailant. The two skulls cracked, leaving the assailant dazed. He lost his grip on the dagger as Selasi drew his sword and held it to his throat.

"You will not move unless you intend to meet our God," Selasi growled. "She'll favor me sending you to Her."

The assailant spat at Selasi. He was a gruff man with a beard smothered in dirt, only having one brown eye in his skull. He panted, almost trembling in his raggedy clothes that hung on him.

"All my life I've wanted to kill you, king of Walyre."

"I'm remorseful to disappoint you, but he's not the king," I said.

The creature shot a glare at Eve. "The bitch lied to me."

If it hadn't been for Eve in my arms, I would have brought that man to his knees in a sea of pain. Yet I couldn't allow my past to surface into my Blessing, not with Eve so close to me. As I looked down, seeing her wide gaze transfixed on her attacker, blood poured from her back.

He had driven his dagger into her. He had assaulted her in a place meant for her to be safe. I was blinded by the sheer spite surging through my body.

"You'll never meet the king. You're no concern of his, only mine now," Selasi said while driving the sword close to his throat.

The assailant didn't waver in his ire. "No concern of his? Has that bastard repented for what his wretched father did?"

"King Ashire is not beholden to the previous king's sins," I warned.

"Someone must be! My boy's soul doesn't rest if his death hasn't been atoned for. Sixteen years ago, to this day, one bad harvest was all it took to lose favor with King Ronire. He collected my debt by taking my boy!" The man sobbed, though Selasi kept his blade steadfast. "His body was brought here to take my punishment and returned to me in a bag!"

Part of my resolve gave way as a horrified recollection pried its way into my forethoughts. I clutched Eve to keep myself from shaking.

"I would have given myself willingly, but I wasn't even given a chance to beg for my boy. I'm no concern of the crown? I will *make* myself a concer—"

"Fuck you!"

Eve tore herself from my arms and slammed her fist into his cheek. The crack of bones ripped through the air as her other fist shot upward into his jaw. His eyes rolled into the back of his head as Eve seethed, "What the *fuck* makes you so self-righteous?" Her right fist landed into his ribs.

His chest caved in around her fist. The air rushed out of him, and he crumpled to the floor. I grabbed Eve and hauled her away from the attacker. She kicked and pushed against me as she raged at him, "It's no excuse to let others get hurt!"

"Selasi!" I roared. "Remove him now!"

Selasi did as commanded, brought the creature to his feet and escorted him away at swordpoint. Eve's glare remained on him until he was out of her sight and then she went limp in my grasp. I lowered us to the ground, ripped off my shirt sleeve and pressed the cloth to the wounds on her back. She didn't even flinch, though I tried to numb her through my Blessing. Her wide stare was lowered to her fists that trembled in her lap.

"Eve, you're safe. Neither he nor anyone else will ever harm you again. I promise."

"Safir," she breathed, but she couldn't say my name with a smile that day. She continued to quake in my grasp. Her teeth had begun to chatter, and I wondered if my Blessing had any impact soothing her.

"Is your pain—"

"I don't feel any pain," she rasped against me, spilling blood into my hand. It felt as though her disregard of pain had nothing to do with my touch.

Up until that disheartening moment, I had the understanding that I enjoyed Eve's company. As she seethed beside me, I better understood what tethered us together. There was a pain that belonged to her, I had only ever seen glimpses of that mimicked my own. And we both manifested that into an anger that could hardly be satiated and could only be understood by the other.

139

Eve

Safir had summoned Lani down to Selasi's room, where I sat in a growing puddle of my own blood, trembling with an anger I was afraid would kill me. Lani's hands sought me out, but my temperament impacted her ability to heal me.

"Can you control your breathing for me? I can't help if you don't try." She pressed Safir's shirt sleeve into my back, but I hardly felt the sting. I could only picture the face of that man, that *thing* that had almost taken me away from Nicky.

"My lord, can you try to calm her?"

If he had killed me...

"I can numb her, but I am not capable of calm right now."

Nicky would have been alone.

"She's pale. Help me lay her down."

Who would have taken care of Nicky?

"Hang onto me, Eve."

Who could *have taken care of Nicky?*

"Can you try to breathe easier, my fierce lily? Can you picture the flame?"

If I die...

"I'll have to do what I can."

...then Nicky dies.

"Eve."

Safir held my face between both hands. Warmth spread throughout my whole body, but I didn't know if that was him or the blood. I felt his worry and anger that pulsed alongside mine. He looked at me with such concern in his ember gaze and held me so tenderly it reminded me of the gentleness of which some men were capable. "You're safe here. You're safe with me. You know that, don't you?"

I said nothing. And I said nothing when his touch and footsteps left the room. I wanted to be safe with him. But I was not safe enough for Nicky. Safir could live without me, but Nicky couldn't. We wouldn't live without the other. We weren't meant to.

“I can’t stay here.”

“Eve?” Lani’s voice found me.

“I can’t stay here,” I repeated over and over until I convinced myself.

Safir

I hadn't been below the palace in almost two decades. The familiar smells of dust and mold burnt my nose. I stomached the rotten memories for the sake of seeing the creature who had dared to draw blood in my home. I descended the stairs with haste, following the lit torches down the hallway deeper into the palace until I saw Selasi standing before the man in his cell. He was holding his side where Eve's fists had found purchase. He deserved to feel a greater magnitude of pain—

"Lord," Selasi said. "I share your grief, but you don't need to burden yourself by being in this place."

"I want to look at him," I growled.

The man picked up his head. "Will she live? The girl?"

"Yes, more than likely to spite you."

"I didn't want to hurt her. I acted blindly."

"You stuck *my* advisor with your dagger as if she were swine!" I fumed through the bars with venom in my voice. "She was an innocent."

Selasi began to shiver. My sentiments were plaguing the air, and without Eve they could run rampant. I could not compose myself in that moment. I couldn't spare myself or those around me from my anger.

"King Ronire died years ago," Selasi said. "Why would you seek retribution now?"

"I have *nothing*," the man spat. "My wife is dead. I have outlived my other children, and I have survived this wretched world only to seek the justice I was never given. I could only let myself die if Chike found retribution himself! My son was an innocent! King Ronire did not take this into regard."

"That king," I mustered the courage to even mention *him*, "didn't kill your boy. I did."

Eve

I didn't want to leave without a goodbye, but a few words from Safir would have sent me spiraling. I needed to think of Nicky first. As much as Safir benefited from me being there, he could live without me. Nicky didn't have that luxury. It twisted my insides into knots as I rummaged through the library, wanting to at least have one piece of Walyre to take back with me. I wanted to remember them. I wanted to know it was all real and had become such a part of me.

Lani, sweaty and flushed, had left me in my room, begging me to stay put as she fetched some ointment to help the scarring on my back. The sting in my flesh had diminished but the memory drove me. The first book I'd read on Feast Day would be the closest thing I would have to Walyre, to Safir.

"Lani told me of your intention to leave us." Ashire's voice found my ears.

I groaned and turned around with my book in hand. He narrowed his ember eyes at me. "What did you plan to do with one of my collections?"

"I wanted something to remember everyone by."

"Would their solemn faces not be a suitable souvenir? Or did you not even intend to tell them?"

My head hung low. "If I had told Safir, I don't know that I could have left."

Ashire nodded slowly. "I see. If I had known you had such weak fortitude, I would never have suggested you have a role here." He placed his hand over his chest as he hissed, "That was my mistake."

"I was stabbed!"

"Once, and you were healed. Many men suffer far worse and can still sing jovial songs."

He was impossible whenever he was set on an objective. "It's not just my mortality I'm worried about. I have people depending on me."

"Yes, you do."

"Other people!"

"I'm sure, Eve. And one of those people is the crown prince of
Walyre. I hate to be callous, but his well-being must take precedence
over your other obligations."

He was asking me to help his brother. I was just trying to do the
same for mine. "You don't even know what you're asking of me."

"Undoubtedly, but I will ask it anyway. I'd command it if I
thought Safir would approve. We know where you enter and exit.
We could easily find your home and you'd be back in our service by
sundown."

I reared back. "Are you threatening me?"

"Hardly. I'm simply stating the obvious. Even if you weren't
physically connected to this place, your infatuation will compel you
to stay nonetheless."

I cast my glare away from him, but it only landed on the portrait
above the library. It made my stomach churn.

"The infatuation is mutual, I'm sure. Based on my brother's
current location, he must be very emotionally invested in you."

"Stop it."

I didn't want to hear it. Ashire would have said anything for me
to stay.

Ashire took a bold step forward. "Did you just give the king a
command? How can you bark at me when you don't even have the
valor to tell my brother you're leaving to his face? I was wrong
about your infatuation. If that were true, that would imply you
cared."

"I. Care," I snapped. "But others need me more than Safir
does."

"Need you more? So, you are being selfish for someone else?
Then I will do the same. Stay for my brother."

It was tempting to crumble into myself, to stay in my small pool
of happiness, but it would never be complete without Nicky. To have
found something remotely close to happiness without him was
nothing short of a miracle, and I woke up weighed down by guilt
because of it.

Your happiness…is mine too.

Nicky's melancholic words echoed in my heart every single day
I was in Walyre. But Safir…

You're safe here. You're safe with me. You know that, don't you?

I knew I was.

But Nicky wasn't safe without me.

"If you need convincing," Ashire piped up, shattering my thoughts. "I think it's time you understood how needed your role is here." He held out an old leather book. I slowly took it as he plucked the other book from my grasp.

"If you do intend to leave, I'd recommend giving this a read instead. It'll be a more honest souvenir of what you have left behind." He turned and strolled out of the library, his arrogance lingering behind him.

Peering down at the book, I saw there was no title, and the pages were thick and busy with writing. It was as if the writer was trying to pierce their pen through the paper. I thought it was a diary since it had entries at different dates, but it wasn't documenting personal events. It was more like a logbook.

I only intended to look at the first few pages before mustering the courage to leave. If I had known, I don't think I would have opened that book. After reading the first page, the room spun around me. I sank to the floor with my breath hitching in my throat. As much as I wanted to turn away, I couldn't stop reading the horror recorded in those pages. It brutally answered so many questions that I wished I had never asked.

Safir

My grandfather, King Muire, was obsessed with obtaining the crown. He became so fixated on the concept that not long after attaining his aspiration, he died from a weakened heart. It was even beyond Lani's repair. The crown passed to his son, who became King Ronire. Like his father, he was obsessed with preserving the crown.

He had a robust stature, broad shoulders, yet he remained slim from hours spent sparring in the gardens. He was eager to draw his sword and challenge any poor bastard to cut him down. I wished someone had. His hair was dark, cut to his shoulders, and tucked behind his ears to show the many earrings he wore in both lobes. Most were made of priceless gems and metals found within the mountains, but he wore the orange charm from the ridge in his ear to reflect the color of the Astana eyes. One glare from him would bring a man to his knees. People believed literal flames resided in his stare.

He demanded more than any other king had of his people because of the promise his father had made— to fortify the kingdom. King Ronire wanted to build wealth and reserves, preparing for someone to steal back the power his father had secured. He planned to build strongholds around the land and fortify the entrance into the valley. He demanded twice the production from smiths, farmers, and miners every year. Families would borrow money from the crown, but the goals were impossible to meet, therefore more were unable to crawl out of debt. After ten years of disputing over the crown, the kingdom was too depleted to compete for it again, and it was also too ravaged to meet his demands. It was in this his cruelty showed.

Mira of House Trice wasn't an obvious selection to become queen. Other women with more powerful Blessings could have served him, but the second he kissed my mother's hand he made an offer of marriage. Though she was a great beauty, her Blessing became a toy for him. It was said she could bring bliss to a decrepit wretch with her touch, and so King Ronire used her for selfish means. It was as if she were a drug for him. Sometimes he'd interrupt gatherings with the noblemen to have his way with her regardless of her cares. Even after she recently gave birth, he ravaged her. Her Blessing was more effective if she were happy, and so King Ronire obliged her wishes to provide charity or to collect books. If it weren't for her kind nature House Rarke would have been welcomed into the city to take back the crown.

Whenever King Ronire spoke of her, he never spoke of her cleverness, her kindness, or any other talent she possessed. He merely spoke of her Blessing in terms that left men envious and women reeling. Only Ashire and I would know her for more than what her Blessing offered.

Ashire had Mother to himself for five years and did everything in his power to remain close to her skirts. Her embrace meant we would feel comfort and security, as was her Blessing. She'd encouraged him to read, as House Trice typically bred scholars. Often Uncle Batrum, our mother's brother, sent him books and tomes that Ashire would memorize before sending back. He had many summers spent in Xard absorbing our uncle's knowledge, being able to read in multiple languages by the time I was born. King Ronire didn't see Ashire's intellect as a resource to be nurtured. He merely showed attention when my brother grew old enough for his Blessing to develop, as most children begin showing signs of their Blessing at age five. The king hoped his first-born son possessed a Blessing that would help him maintain the crown. At the realization Ashire could merely push someone back at the command "repel," King Ronire abandoned my brother. At the time, Ashire could only push small objects a few feet, which hardly improved under ruthless training that would leave Ashire begging for our mother. It didn't escape anyone's notice how he preferred our uncle's way of parenting.

"We are fathered by the wrong man," Ashire used to say when we were children. "He'll never care how hard you work, only what you can give him."

Not long after, I was brought into the world. Mother said her labor with me was painless in comparison to Ashire's. Her lap was always the safest, warmest place to be. I'd crave my mother's calming presence, and one day it felt effortless to convey the love I had for her and the curiosity I had for the king through one simple touch. Her eyes grew wide and brimmed with tears.

"Darling," she told me, "I want you to only do this for your mama. Can you do that? Don't show anyone else."

When the Seeker came to the palace, I was sure she paid him heavily to assert I had no Blessing, or perhaps she bargained by allowing him to experience her Blessing firsthand. And so King Ronire's second son became an even greater disappointment than the first by not having a Blessing whatsoever. I couldn't have known my mother was trying to spare me the treatment she was subjected to by the king. He was never affectionate and had no way of knowing what my Blessing was. It was kept a secret between my mother and me.

She kept me close, closer than Ashire, even as I grew out of infancy. Mother oversaw our lessons, our meals, and put us to bed each night under her watchful eye. I believed all mothers to be that tender. She'd have us join her whenever she gave coins to beggars outside of Vada's temple. Mother wanted us to see the faces of hunger and deprivation that we had been shielded from in the palace.

"But just because it's painful to look doesn't mean they don't deserve to be seen," she'd say each time we visited. She'd place a coin in each person's hand, they'd thank her and scamper away with their newfound treasure. Queen Mira gave a great deal of herself away until all that was left within her was the love she had for my brother and I.

"My darling boys. You'll have to look out for each other as you grow. Even if you're at odds, you will be brothers first and foremost."

She said it as if she wouldn't be there to remind us. She couldn't have known. No one could have known a rampant plague was readying to dig its fingers into the land and its inhabitants. The king kept himself sealed away. In fact, we didn't see him for weeks, yet we worried for Mother the most. Her belly had become swollen which Ashire informed me meant we were due to have another sibling. But one by one, we each became afflicted. Even our staff were unable to help the royal family in their ill state.

Ashire and I fell sick within a few days of each other. My limbs became too heavy and too painful to even reach for a glass of water.

No matter how many blankets I buried myself under my bones still shivered. I resigned myself to bed until the sickness either killed me or faded.

I couldn't recall how much time had sluggishly passed in its cruelty, but one night a hand grasped mine through my pile of blankets. A pale Ashire climbed up into my bed. He was shivering with cracked lips and bloodshot eyes.

"What are you doing?" I croaked.

He tremulously extended a biscuit. "Eat or die."

I brought it to my lips. Chewing felt like a feat. Ashire had broken into a cold sweat. He swiped his brown hair away from his soaked forehead. "Is it settled in your tummy?"

I nodded. He rolled off my bed and began crawling across the floor. "What are you doing?" I croaked again.

"I'm doing what Mother asked," he wheezed while crawling out the door. I didn't know how much longer it was before he returned. It could have been hours, but I awoke to him pulling on my blankets. He lay flat on the floor while holding a glass of water, extending it into the air.

"Drink," he ordered breathlessly.

I shakily took the water, and I guzzled it with more life than I had mustered in days. Ashire remained on the floor with his eyes rolling into the back of his head. His body was quaking with sickness, and I couldn't imagine the pain he endured to try to keep me alive. I rolled off my bed, taking my blankets with me, and plopped beside him. I pulled the blankets around us both, and we remained together on the floor.

"Do you think Mother is all right?" I whimpered.

There was a long pause from Ashire, so long I even thought he had fallen asleep, but he shook his head. "I don't know, Safir. I've been praying to Vada."

My eyes grew heavy. "I'll pray too."

We were found that way the next day, with the sun streaming through the windows and warming us. The plague had passed through the palace, and we were given news that the king had survived. But of Mother…

Lani was found cradling her lifeless form, utterly inconsolable.

I remember staring blankly into the wall, in torrid disbelief. It was as if I expected to feel her warm and calming touch any moment.

Ashire threw a chair out the window.

It was unimaginable the sun had even risen that day. I couldn't fathom how time moved on without her. The king held a grand ceremony for the queen, inviting members of her family to lay her to rest in Vada's temple. He did not weep, but he spoke of how deeply he'd miss his wife with whom he had found solace. I buried my fists in my pockets, knowing he missed the innate ability she'd been granted at birth more than the woman who'd given her body and children.

That I never forgave.

Days passed. I felt the aching need to reach out for her, as if her form were still tangible. The ultimate pain was knowing that if I reached out it would only be met with her absence. Ashire kept himself scarce, and the king continued with his duties, though more agitated since his addiction could no longer be satiated. We all longed for her, and I came to realize how much I'd miss the protection she'd provided for me. I hadn't understood that mercy.

One day, I lifelessly walked through the gardens where I thought I could speak to Mother in prayer. My body moved, but my mind couldn't create any coherent thoughts while I journeyed outside for the first time in weeks. A young maid tripped and fell before my feet. I truly didn't care as she apologized and wiped the dust from her palms. Yet my hand moved anyway to help her.

She thanked me and took my hand to stand. Immediately she burst into tears and recoiled from me, clutching her hand to her chest. The girl dashed in the opposite direction in a fit of sobs. Her visceral reaction roused me from my grief for a few moments, making me recall Mother had made me promise I wouldn't show anyone my Blessing. I stared down at my hand. Why had it happened passively? My Blessing only occurred *that* strongly if I willed it, but during my emotional turmoil, it had a stronger effect. I thought nothing of it as I resumed my route to the gardens.

The gravest mistake of my life was born in that one moment.

Later that night the king summoned me. He had never requested to see me. I hadn't even laid eyes on him since Mother's funeral. His room was lit by the fire, illuminating his domineering figure. The gold rings on his ears glowed, but his stare blazed brighter as I drew nearer.

"Closer, son," he commanded. "You're to stand where I can see you clearly."

My feet carried me forward into the light.

He pierced me with his gaze that I was sure could scorch me. His eyes narrowed. "Your eyes are swollen, and your cheeks crimson. You still mourn for your mother?"

"I miss her."

"Of course. We all do." He held his thumb under his chin and sighed. "Your mother had a manner of giving herself that surpassed human capacity. It was a tragedy to watch."

I hoped my disdain for him would eat him up one day, but I remained silent.

"Her Blessing was something I very much hoped would be passed down to at least one of my children. All hope was lost after you. That hope was renewed once I learned she was expecting again." He began to drum his fingers on the armchair. "Hope is peculiar, Safir. It takes many forms." His lips curled as he stood from his chair. I fought the urge to retreat. That look I would come to recognize with time, that conniving grin. "I was told a servant was overcome with inconsolable grief just from having touched you."

I took one step back. "That's not possible. I have no Blessing."

"That is what I was told, but I'm willing to hope a piece of your mother resides in you after all."

The king reached out and clamped a hand on my shoulder.

Darling, I want you to only do this for your mama. Can you do that for me? Don't show anyone else.

She had hardly asked anything of me. I could at least fulfill her wish. Though his hand gripped my shoulder tight enough to bruise, I refused to use any part of Blessing for him. I focused on the feeling of the fire, a physical sensation he would have felt as well and not realized it was coming from me.

He scowled. "You disappoint me."

Quicker than a blink, he grabbed my shirt sleeve and shoved my hand into the fire.

"No!" I shrieked, trying to pull my hand away. The skin seared and bubbled as the flames engulfed my flesh, and the pain left me crumpling to my knees. "You're burning me! You're burning me!" I kicked and shrieked at the agony of my charred hand, yet he remained expressionless as he held it in the flames, ignoring the smell of burning flesh.

I could still feel the pain when he finally pulled me away from the heat. Pieces of wet skin hung from my palm and knuckles. I held it in the air shakily, the muscle peeling white and surrounded by bubbles of whatever skin remained. Sniffling and choking on bile, I barely clung to consciousness.

The king placed his palm on my head, and grimaced. "I can feel the burning as if it's happening to my own hand. Dear boy, I can *feel* your pain."

Drowning in my agony, I couldn't think to limit my Blessing. "Why?" I wailed. "Why did you burn me?"

He picked me up from the floor and pulled me into his chest. "My son, my dear son, you *do* have a Blessing. That part of your mother is very much alive in you if you let it," he said while stroking my hair, no doubt feeling the agonizing sensation of my charred hand over and over. Though I hated him and felt consumed with pain, I cried into him. I tried to expand my Blessing for him to experience the pain and sorrow he had caused me.

"Yes, I deserve that," he cooed, unaffected. "Safir, do not mistake my actions for lack of affection for you. You'll be healed, and soon you will become my hope once again. Son, you will become my pride."

I never missed my mother more than I did in that moment.

I lost consciousness, but I soon awoke to darkness surrounding me, locked away below the palace. Damp dust filled my nose. When I peered down at my hand, it was perfectly healed. The pain was gone, but I recalled what it had been like to feel my charred skin sizzle away from the bone. Fear struck my whole body as I clawed at the walls and leapt at the bars. "Help!" I screamed. "Somebody let me out! Help!"

"Quiet now." The king emerged from the shadows as I trembled with a freshly born fury. "Your training begins today."

Eve

It began with starving him. He was only given water for one month. His ribs protruded and he curled in around himself. By the end of the month, he could not stand, and open sores formed on his body.

After recovering, he was poisoned repeatedly, always with a new concoction that would make him seize, or hallucinate, or vomit. The poisons were at first administered through food, but when he stopped eating it was hidden in his drink, and eventually, it was forced down his throat. It was written that he cried for his mother when the poison was most potent.

When he had developed immunity, the cruelty became wickedly creative. He received fifteen lashings to his back and then salt was poured into the wounds. The soles of his feet were cut, and he was made to walk. Both of his hands would be broken. Legs broken. Flesh burned. Teeth pulled.

At that point, I was barely able to hold the book. It felt like I was hurting Safir by just reading it. It became clear where his grief derived from and why he could not rid himself of it. That pain had become part of him. It made me wonder how he'd survived. While pondering that question, I came to find it was Lani who was the narrator of that cursed logbook. After each bout of cruelty, she'd heal him as well as she could, documenting her findings and observations. At first I felt sick, picturing her healing him without truly rescuing him from his pain. But I didn't doubt she'd been threatened by the king, and I couldn't help but wonder whether Ashire had been suspicious.

While it pained me to read, nothing feels more isolating than when someone turns away because your pain is too burdening for them. So, I continued to read, swallowing sobs and tears, as the pages exemplified the very worst of humanity.

Safir

I recall every depraved second in that place with perfect clarity. My thoughts were consumed with surviving the next second, and the next, until the day faded. There was scarcely room for thinking about my brother, my mother, or the life I'd had prior. I was only pain. Nothing else remained.

At first, I'd beg and cry to be spared, fighting with whatever energy lingered within me. In a never-ending cycle of nightmares, I submitted to my anguish. I preferred being starved to being poisoned, preferred being poisoned to being lashed, and preferred broken bones over burns. And with each moment of torment I survived, the king would praise my endurance through my tears and screams with a jovial smile.

Not a second passed where my breath wasn't labored with agony, where my eyes didn't long to see some color outside of those grey walls. My fingers curled in darkness, desiring warmth. Many moments in solitude were spent trying to remember the feeling of the sun. This was what I focused on whenever Lani was sent to heal me, for if I hadn't, she would have experienced the torment plaguing my body and soul.

She could hardly behold my glorified corpse as her hands shakily tried to heal me. Her hands were warm to my wearied delight. It was strange how something as miniscule as her touch revived small bits of my soul.

"I-I'm so sorry, Your Royal Highness. I am so sorry."

Considering she refused to regard me, I must have appeared to be lapping at the feet of death. "If you must heal me, can you not even look at me?"

Her lips trembled, sealed in silence as she continued healing me.

"Ashire…Does he know?"

She lowered her voice. "I don't know. I am not permitted to speak outside of these premises to anyone. I'm never alone." Lani glanced over her shoulder at the guards who had escorted her to the dungeons.

I knew she was being surveilled, yet I couldn't help but ask, "Could you stop healing me?"

She snapped her eyes to me for the first time. In her gaze I saw the shell of a boy I had once known. "What?"

"Just make it look like you're doing what they want. Let the poison run its course."

"But Lord…"

I didn't speak and only let myself enjoy the warmth emanating from her hands. It was such a small, pitiful pleasure.

"Please," she whispered. "Don't ask that of me. My beloved Mira, your mother, did not die just for you to join her so quickly."

"Mother…"

"I'm doing this in the hopes I'm helping you live to see better days. I promised her. That is what I'm telling myself." Her hands shook, to the point I was sure she was barely able to heal me. She'd slave over me, pulling the poisons from my body while I'd lie there, uncaring if she were successful. It wasn't that I desired to perish, but living had become too great a burden.

"I'll do what I can for you," she'd whisper before being ripped away. I was once again left alone in familiar darkness. She had freed me of my infections and physical wounds, but their memories remained fresh. My entire being became an empty cauldron for the king to fill with sorrow, anguish, and hatred. I only existed to be in pain and to be its giver.

After months of profound depravity, the king summoned me. I was carried for I couldn't muster the energy to walk. I almost took pleasure in knowing there was little else he could do that hadn't already been done to me.

He stood before me as he always had, with apathy, and instructed me, "Safir, I find myself in need of you now. I only ask that you do exactly as I say."

I could barely stand upright, but I still reserved enough energy to hate him. "How? How could you think I would do anything for you?"

A look of pride crept onto his face. "This is not just for me, son." He knelt in front of me, soiling his fine robes on the dungeon floor. "This is for all that is good. This is for the righteousness for which I have prepared you. You are free to allow your trials to be for naught or let *me* give purpose to your pain." He then said the only words that could have ever made me compliant. "I can only imagine how much more agonizing it would be to have undergone your suffering and have no purpose with which to redeem it."

The edges of sanity I had been clinging to, began to crack beneath my fingers.

I was carried to a different part of the dungeon where I was settled before a battered man whose jaw remained clenched tight as he threw ferocious glares at the king, tightening his fists against the chair he was bound to. He glanced to me, his expression only changing slightly at the sight of my corpse.

"I'm ready," he grumbled. "I'm ready to meet Vada in the heavens."

"That will have to wait." The air shifted, turning colder as the king stepped forward with the grace of a fateful arrow. "Vada may do what she desires with your soul once I'm finished with this body."

The man shook his head, freeing the oily tresses of his hair. "The flesh will give, but my spirit will not break."

You are wrong.

The king leaned over him with a grin. "That is exactly what I wanted you to say." He looked up to me with our family eyes blazing. "My son, step forward."

I tried to remember how to walk as the stranger began to panic. "That is your son?" He gawked while I dragged my feet across the floor. His eyes widened with my ghostly form standing next to him. "Do you treat your own blood the way you treat the land?"

"Safir, show this creature your Blessing."

After so many months of agony etched into my soul, I finally understood what it was he had tortured me for. I simply wanted, for one moment, to not be the one hurt.

My hand dropped on top of his head, and the man grimaced beneath my touch. His face contorted from anxiety into discomfort. My swelling despair poured into him. His eyes watered and his hands shook. Yet, when my thoughts flickered to memories of the torture that had been befallen me, his mouth opened, and screams poured from him. I wondered if I were somehow less of a human because I could no longer bring myself to cry as he could.

I removed my hand, letting it fall at my side as the stranger sucked in air. Even after my touch left him, he quaked in that chair, making the chains rattle. I hadn't even *tried* to use my Blessing. It had just happened at my simple touch.

My teeth began to chatter.

The king ordered the stranger removed. I never saw him again. The king pulled me towards him in an alien embrace. He stroked my hair even though I flinched. "You are more than I had hoped for. You have become my pride."

I winced each time his hand graced my head. My body was expecting pain with each stroke. The king never shied away from experiencing my Blessing; he seemed to have become accustomed to it. "Any boy can suffer, Safir. It takes a great man to accept purpose in their suffering." He released me and kneeled to meet my sunken stare. "And without a doubt I've imbued that in you. What I have given you, no man can take away. You embody the will of our house. You will secure our name. And I'll be sure you excel at it."

Many men were brought to me. The king claimed they were offenders against the crown. I was to make the land safer by punishing them. My purpose was to keep the land safe. It was good. I was good.

Simply resting my hand on their heads would cause men to tremble and weep. The king wasn't always pleased with this result. "Engage with your suffering, Safir. Bring it forward."

It was too easy to recall the torture. There was hardly a second that passed where I didn't feel the lingering effects of the lashings, the burning, the poisoning, the starving, the breaking of bone and spirit. If I focused on that for one second, my touch would send men reeling into madness. They would beg for mercy, but my hand would always involuntarily recoil from them whenever they cried out for their mothers.

"Why?" I asked the king one evening. "Why do I not cry like they do? I cannot cry anymore."

"They are lesser men, Safir. They have no purpose and can make nothing of their pain other than to weep about it. They haven't ascended to your state of being."

There were moments where his cruel compliments were pleasing, and I almost, *almost* thought he had been right.

Then a boy was brought to me.

Sniveling sounds emanated from the bag over his head. The king watched intently. "This boy must suffer payment for his father's sins against the crown, just as I pay for the sins of my father for attaining this crown I'm cursed to keep it so we might be safe. You pay for my sins by enduring your agony to become a better man. It's an undeniable cycle, Safir. He must redeem his father's sins with his pain."

The boy did not beg like others did, and I hadn't been ordered to kill him. While stretching my hand out, I wanted to withhold my more tumultuous agony. It was of little use.

The second my palm was placed on his head, the boy shrieked and urinated in the chair. He convulsed and thrashed against me, though I tried to tell him, "Don't worry. You're being given purpose for your pain." But his screeches filled the room to the brim, until they ceased. My hand remained, but no sounds came from him. No movements. Not even a whimper. I tried to shake him awake, as if my Blessing gave life rather than deprived it. "You've done it," I rasped to him. "You've endured."

Still nothing. The guards removed his body. I stared at the puddle of piss on the ground as if it were nothing. That was all the pain I had given him amounted to. Nothing.

The king saw otherwise.

"The future of our house will need your fortitude to protect it. You've proven this, and you will continue to exact the purpose I've given you."

I stalled behind him. "Ashire is the future king."

He turned towards me with his eyes flaring, and I honestly believed hell's fire resided in his stare. "Ashire has not earned such a burden as you have, and that is his own undoing. Worry not about your succession to the throne. It will be dealt with."

A flicker of life I hadn't known still resided in me, spread throughout my body. Ashire. My brother.

You'll have to look out for the other as you grow. Even if you're at odds, you will be brothers first and foremost.

We had both promised her long before the king had left me to rot and die and be re-born as his submissive son. Ashire had fulfilled his promise to her, and I couldn't even cry anymore. The king had said I would defend our home with my suffering, with my Blessing. I had suffered for the good of the crown. **I had suffered for the good of the crown.**

The next day I feigned illness, which wasn't hard considering I was still deprived of any basic comfort. When Lani reached me, I focused my Blessing on conveying to her impending danger, anticipation of terror and torment. She gasped as she touched me, but I clamped her hand down on my arm so she couldn't let go. "Ashire," I mouthed to her, staring into her eyes intently.

I released her. She fell back onto her heels, practically throwing herself out of my cell. Then I waited and hoped my efforts wouldn't be for naught.

The following day I was summoned to a cell and found it strange there were no guards posted outside of the door. Upon entering I found, to my horror, Lani standing there on her toes with her arms twisted behind her arched back, frozen in the middle of the room. Her entire body was trembling, but she stood unmoving. Tears were pouring from her eyes and harsh breaths escaped her. The king stepped out from behind her. "Look at what you've done to her."

Lani's toes were red and purple as sweat poured down her brow. She must have been exhausted from trying to heal herself. The king's personal punishment was his Blessing. The body was forced to support itself, unable to change position as long as the king maintained concentration. It became excruciating over time. The muscles would burn from exhaustion, the blood become stagnant, never to know relief. "How long have you held her here?" I asked.

"I'm not certain. I've lost track of time."

"You will not earn my suffering," Lani gasped. "Just as you never earned my Mira-" her words became muffled when the back of the king's hand struck her, his golden rings digging into her flesh. She yelped and her eyes darted to me. "I'm so sorry, Lord!" Lani sputtered blood. "I tried."

I knew she had.

The king stepped toward me. "I'm disappointed, Safir, that you would be willing to deprive yourself of my purpose for you."

"I don't want anything to happen to Ashire," I confessed, but kept my eyes on Lani. He still had his hold on her, and her breathing was becoming erratic. "That isn't a purpose worth possessing."

His hand clasped around my throat and pinned me against the stone wall with such force that I lost my vision for a few seconds. My head cracked and blood ran down my neck. My ears rang as his grip tightened. "You're assuming that you are getting to choose your fate."

"I am."

My hands clasped onto his arm, and I conveyed every single ounce of agony he had inflicted onto me over that year, the whippings and bone-breakings and poisonings and the never-ending sense of emptiness that had become my soul. The king had tolerated my touch before, but never while I intentionally hurled my agony towards him. He roared and tried to rip away from me, but I curled around his arm, focusing on the most intense pain I had known. Lani dropped to the floor in a heap of whimpers as the king lost his concentration.

"Run!" I roared at her as she attempted to rise from the floor. She scrambled upright, practically lunging out the door, leaving bloody toe prints behind.

The king threw my pitiful body against the rock wall. I released him and slid to the floor with a groan. I tried to reach for him again or else he'd catch Lani, but as I extended my hand—

"Lock," he commanded with the might of every king before him. Each muscle, ligament, and bone froze with me crouched against the wall. He spat into my face and seethed, "You are so much less than what you could be! You think freeing her will amount to anything? I will have her back here in minutes, and I'll have your skin stripped over and over until you see as I see."

I somehow smiled, letting out a ghostly laugh. "I don't care. I don't think I will ever care again what is done to me!"

His eyes narrowed. "You've given up on your own body, but clearly not your brother's."

My smile faded and my bones creaked as I tried to break away from his Blessing. My muscles twitched, but no part of me budged. "Ashire is separate from all of this."

"Quite the opposite. Perhaps he is integral in your ultimate upbringing. At least he'll have a useful purpose."

The king turned from me and began walking to the door. "Where are you going?" I asked, still trying to break through his Blessing.

"I imagine you'll want to see your brother. You've spent quite a lot of time apart."

"Leave him!" I screeched so loudly the king sharply turned to me. "I will kill you if you touch him! I will kill you where you stand!"

The king smiled. "You will sit there, unable to look away, while I pull your brother's lungs out. And you'll never again take for granted the air I let you breathe. Never again will you question the purpose I've given you."

My very existence snapped, like a string pulled so taut it tore into pieces. In all the suffering I had known, I had refused for Ashire to play any part in it. I had promised my mother, and I no longer cared if I died trying to fulfill that promise.

I let my soul scream into the air, releasing all the pain that would reside in my body for the rest of my life, as I directed every bit of anger, hatred, malice, sorrow, and ire towards the infernal being that shared my blood. My heart raced in my throat as blood vessels burst in my eyes, staring down the thing I couldn't reach but I wanted to suffer. I *needed* him to suffer through me.

The king began to quake, eyes wide, and fell to his knees.

"How?" he choked as I willed him to feel every bit of pain he had caused me amplified hundreds of times across the space between us. Every broken bone. Every seared piece of flesh. Every dream of death. All of it. I willed it to infest him. He would become my pain just as I had become his pride. He clutched himself and scarcely drew a breath with the onslaught of remembered torment that I possessed. He convulsed and writhed on the ground before me, and I refused to release him.

The king collapsed onto the floor, and I tumbled forward. I shook violently with sweat pouring from my brow and my teeth chattering while staring at the motionless figure on the ground before me. "G-get up," I commanded while trying to rise to my feet. "Stand and tell me again what my purpose is."

But he didn't.

"Get up!"

Silence. So much silence except for my furious breaths.

"F-father. *Why?*"

My body reeked of sorrow, and I could feel it in the air around me. I couldn't control it. I realized it wasn't worse to not have a purpose for my suffering. It was worse if my purpose was what was lying before me: death by agony.

"I kept my promise," I whimpered to myself.

Hurried footsteps arrived and the door flew open. Ashire stood in the doorway before the motionless king. His eyes were wide before landing on me, and then I could see it:

He didn't recognize me.

"Ashire?"

Horrified understanding washed over his face as I called his name. He fell against the doorframe to hold himself upright. He tried to take a step forward. "Oh, Safir. I didn't…Lani, she just—"

"Don't come near me!" I shrieked, my overwhelming pain and sorrow permeating the air. Ashire recoiled. "I'll only hurt you. I-I killed the king."

My brother stooped, looked at the body then back at me.

A small wheeze emanated from the king. "My…sons…"

"You didn't kill him," Ashire said darkly, looking to the figure on the ground. Ashire rose and stood between me and the king. "Repel."

The king's body was hurled fifteen feet through the solid rock wall, crashed into the opposite wall and was reduced to a mass of flesh. Ashire looked down at me with unnerving stoicism. "*I* killed him."

"Ashire," I moaned. He reached for me, but I recoiled into a corner in the cell. "Don't! I'll hurt you. I'll only hurt you!"

"That doesn't matter." He pursued me.

"No, I can't hurt you. Not you." My initial anger was fading as my sorrow crashed over me. The air was thick with it. Ashire physically struggled to reach me as my Blessing struck him like hundreds of arrows. "I could never hurt you."

He kneeled beside me, flinching with hitching breaths as my Blessing pierced through the air. "Yes, you can. You will never again suffer alone." And he threw his arms around me, pulling me close despite being subjected to the pain I was feeling. He stifled sobs, but he refused to release me.

In that moment, in the arms of my brother, I realized I could still cry.

I later understood why Ashire hadn't recognized me. When I looked into a mirror for the first time in one year, my hair had turned a stark white. My skin was stretched across my bones, my eyes practically falling out of my skull. I moved like a phantom, reluctant to come in to contact with anything. The first time Lani tried to bathe me, I shook and sobbed so violently the water spilled out of the tub. For years, only Lani and Ashire were able to be in the same room as me, let alone touch me, and only out of sheer will. Anyone else would writhe in pain as I recalled my torment, or they would begin to weep. My Blessing wreaked havoc on anyone within my vicinity, and I couldn't stop it any better than I could forget the scars across my body. The king had been right, he had given me a power no man could take away— not even myself.

It was enough to kill a man. Lani oversaw that the king was documented to have died from a "weak heart," as his father had. Ashire was made king of Walyre, and his first act was to exhume Mother from her resting place in Vada's temple and create a shrine for her in the courtyard, so she was closer to home. More importantly, so I could visit her resting place without having to vacate the palace. His second act as king was to imprison and execute any staff who were complicit to the previous king's doings, except for Lani. Most were hanged and buried in the mountains. Those who escaped fled to all parts of the kingdom, telling the tale of the boy who could kill with the touch of his hand. I became a nightmare told to children to keep them from misbehaving in case the ghostly prince punished them. I was to remain out of sight to not give life to these stories.

"I will make you whole again, Safir," Ashire told me on the day of his coronation, which I wasn't able to attend. "I promise you."

He was only sixteen, but he took it upon himself to carry the burden. His guilt for having not reached me sooner was palpable. Ashire had been informed that I'd been sent to our mother's home in Xard to study with Uncle Batrum during my year locked below the palace. Ashire had written to me many times and found it peculiar I had never replied, even more peculiar that Uncle Batrum never mentioned me when sending his messages. It hadn't been until one full year had passed, and Ashire had taken ill from an undercooked dinner (purposefully planned by Lani and Milfred), that he was sent to Lani, who'd prescribed him a tonic. She had enclosed a note warning him of my location and the king's plans but had been caught by one of the guards. The note was disposed of before Ashire could read it, and Lani was taken to the dungeon where the king held her in her precarious position for hours.

Ashire had become suspicious of Lani's actions and her hasty disappearance. The king had guards posted to his room, and Ashire was forbidden from exiting without permission. Upon hearing Lani's screams, Ashire had used his Blessing to force his way to Lani, who'd directed him to me.

Upon being freed Lani spent hours upon hours trying to help rein in my Blessing, but I was beyond simple breathing techniques. I had stretched my Blessing to a breaking point and had to live with it. I had resigned myself to being a burden to my brother, a prisoner within the palace. And I had promised never again to use my Blessing to harm any creature, to never again indulge in the purpose of the king past.

Sixteen years ago, I'd been confined to that dungeon, and the king past had only ever brought prisoners to the castle to hone my Blessing. Only one boy had ever been brought to me…

Looking at the father before me, I knew there wasn't any comfort I could give him. "I was a victim, as was your son. A debt that I cannot repay and a remorse that will never leave me."

The shell of a man had slumped against the wall. His one eye stared at his shaking hands. "My child killed by a child. How could the king, a father, ask of such evil?" He looked up at me with his bottom lip trembling. "I cannot blame the boy you were, but you can repay me as the man you are. His life for yours."

"There was a time where I would have eagerly given you that. Alas, I cannot. I've suffered for my actions and suffer still, I promise."

Selasi shuddered next to me but remained at my side despite my sorrow spilling into the dungeon. The man slowly lay on his side with his hands clasped over his heart. "That will grant me enough peace for now."

Eve

I had understood so little of the truth behind Safir's sorrow. His Blessing had been stretched and exploited at the hands of his own father. He couldn't stop feeling it, all his suffering. No wonder he became so scared of touch, locked away and isolated in the palace.

Stay for my brother, Ashire had begged. *I think it's time you understood how needed your role is here.*

I had a better understanding, and my soul weighed more for it.

"Eve," a voice came.

His voice.

Safir froze mid-stride as he looked down at the book in my hands. He swallowed hard. "My brother should not have given that to you."

Safir was no longer trapped in that dungeon. He was standing there. He was whole. I stood from the floor, bracing myself against the bookshelves behind me. I walked towards him; his ember eyes boring into me. I reached out and handed him the book.

Without tearing his gaze away, he took the book from me, but allowed his fingers to intertwine with mine. I could feel his immense concern wash over me, apprehension, anticipation, and of course his grief. He was asking without words if I was okay.

"Are you withholding yourself?" I asked, my voice strained.

His eyebrows furrowed as he replied slowly, "How do you mean?"

"Are you holding back everything you're feeling? To spare me?"

"I try," he answered, pained. "For the most part."

"Don't," I told him while grasping his fingers tighter. "Don't spare me."

"Eve—"

"I refuse for you to have to limit yourself more than you already do, especially for me. Please."

He sighed and soon I felt a gradual heaviness, like falling asleep, encompass me. I was trapped in a tomb I had made myself from which I didn't believe I deserved to be free. The longing made my soul ache. Longing for light. Longing for hope. Longing for warmth. My very existence was a burden and a curse. I had to remain in my tomb. It was how I would protect those around me, but it killed me at the same time.

Suddenly the terrible feelings ceased as a deep warmth encased my limbs. Safir's other hand cupped my cheek. His thumb swiped away a stray tear I hadn't known was cascading down my face. "I'm sorry," he murmured. "That was too much."

My head shook against his hand. "No. No, it isn't that. I just—" I swallowed a sob in my throat. "Do you feel like that all the time?"

He gave me a very weak smile. "Not all the time. Less and less so each day." His thumb skimmed over my cheek again. "I appreciate what you've done for me, Eve. You've helped me escape that horrid place." He dropped his hand from my cheek. I immediately missed its warmth. "But I would never blame you for returning to your realm, regardless of what my brother says. I know you have your commitments, of which you're not obligated to tell me. You were kind enough to not pry into my nightmares, and I offer you the same courtesy now. But I offered you a free choice to leave before. You have that choice now."

I must have already made up my mind before he had finished speaking. "I'll stay, but only if you promise you'll never withhold that part of yourself from me ever again."

An unmistakable sigh of relief escaped him as his ember eyes flared. "I solemnly promise you."

Safir

"What's to become of that creature?" I asked Ashire as he labored over a pile of parchment.

"I'm not certain. I doubt he's in any hurry for me to decide." He looked up at me with a weariness I hadn't seen in some time. "Do you have a preference?"

"I assumed that since his aim was to kill you that you would prefer to decide his punishment."

"Yes, but he stabbed *your* Eve."

I winced. "I'd prefer to not be reminded."

"She was healed almost immediately. No true harm was done."

"She almost fled the palace!"

He glanced to me knowingly. "But she didn't, did she?"

A sting of irritation coursed through me. "You should never have given her that book."

"I don't see why—"

"It was not your story to tell!" My agitation peaked. "I didn't wish to burden her!"

Ashire slammed his hands on his desk and shot up from his seat. "Look at you! Fuming like a child yet I can hardly feel your ire from here! That is the good she has done you! That is the difference she has made, so yes, I would do it again if I had to ensure she stayed! For the good of my brother, you ungrateful cunt," he fumed and slumped back in his chair.

"Forgive me if I don't bow with grace for you guilting her to the point of tears."

"You insult her attachment to you if you believe she's merely staying out of guilt. And even if she were, what difference would that make to you, the prince of Walyre? She's your advisor, a stranger from a dull world that is of little consequence. Her reasoning shouldn't consume you."

I scowled out the window. Of course, I wouldn't want her to stay out of guilt, just as I hadn't wanted her to stay out of feeling threatened when we first met. If I hadn't given her a choice, I would still be the dreadful creature the old king had bred in his dungeon. Though I couldn't admit it to Ashire, there had been a sense of relief when she'd cared more about me not controlling my Blessing than my childhood of torment. I couldn't bear the thought of her recoiling from me after learning what I had done.

"Well, since it was she who was attacked, would Eve prefer to decide the assailant's sentence? We could lock her in a room with him. I was told she broke a considerable number of ribs during her outburst."

I smiled. "I think not. She's had her say, and I prefer she never interact with that man again."

"Fair enough. He was telling the truth though." Ashire pulled out a dusty ledger from under his desk. "The man had suffered a bad crop for years, but many farmers in the area had. The prior king had written the man's debts were paid through 'sacrifice.'" He looked up at me, his callousness fading. "One can't fault him for his anger."

"I would never. I fault him for endangering my advisor, and he did intend to kill you."

"One cannot be killed by something that is already dead. His soul died long before trying to kill me. To punish him with death would be redundant." Ashire reached for his quill and scribbled an almost illegible description on the page before him. "It's not as though we're dealing with the infamous Frederara Bask, just a grudge-wielding farmer."

"I'd be disappointed if it were Bask. He'd never be so tactless."

"Bask has retired, from my knowledge." Ashire chewed on the end of his quill. "Or at least his work hasn't been observed for years. It was last rumored he was behind the 'boar-hunting accident' that led to Lady Zae's ascension." He looked at me quizzically with a bemused smirk. "What a scandalous rumor regarding your past lover."

"I am not dignifying that with a response."

Ashire dripped his quill and scribbled on the parchment. "I'm sending the assailant to our northernmost post to join the scouts for his remaining years."

"Uncharacteristically compassionate. You're willing to give this man a weapon and let him fight in your name?"

"Well, obviously he isn't that much of a threat even with a weapon, and I'm sure our stricter commanding officers will ensure his loyalty to me." Ashire reached for his full goblet of wine. "Do not think I am compassionate towards this madman. I'd rather him be freezing and live in the glory of our name rather than give him the release of the beheading he so desires." He set down his goblet without even taking a drink. He appeared impossibly tired and still surrounded by a sea of documents.

"Ashire," I said softly. "Perhaps we should postpone my debut. Enough is consuming your thoughts as it is."

"Alas, we cannot." He gestured to the papers before him. "These are the acceptance letters from the great noble houses, eager to congratulate you on your debut. It would be a calamitous lapse of judgment to not carry on."

"They're all coming here?"

"Practically everyone but Lord Harysle, but more than likely he doesn't want to admit his lack of influence over the north." Ashire plucked a letter from the pile and wafted it in the air. I recognized the scent emanating from the parchment. "I at least look forward to seeing Uncle Batrum. Lady Zae wrote that she is especially ecstatic to meet with you once again. Perhaps she'd like to resume the strong bond our houses once had?"

"Doubtful," I remarked while plucking the letter from his hand. I studied her penmanship, as elegant as always. The scent of warm spice and a morning breeze coated the page, strong enough that old memories surfaced. "She appreciates her power far too much to share it with any one man, and quite right too."

"Well, it'll be an interesting week of festivities considering Lord Arius also plans to attend."

That name soured my good mood. "Must he?"

"Seeing as our grandfather usurped the crown from his family, it seemed only polite to invite him."

"Is that truly wise, Ashire?"

"It was my idea." Emtias let himself into Ashire's study. He was the only one bold enough to do so without being summoned.

"*Our* idea," Ashire responded while continuing to scribble.

"My idea, which the king agrees with," Emtias contested while handing me an obscene number of ledgers. "Inquiries from the local lords," he informed and took a seat beside Ashire. "I can't think of a more suitable treatment for the previously defeated royal family than to see how prosperous and beloved the current royal family is. This whole debut is to assert the strength of House Astana, is it not? Also, House Rarke controls most of the seaports in the south. Now wouldn't be the time for old grudges to impede progress."

"Yes, yes, well summarized," Ashire remarked. "It'd be best to prepare for diplomatic duties, Safir. Your debut is scheduled in one month's time."

"One month?" I asked. So soon after an attacker had infiltrated the palace?

"And your advisor will have her knowledge put to the test," Emtias commented. "I have no doubt she'll be available for the festivities?"

"Surely," I said, still reeling.

"Good. I'll oversee her instruction myself." Emtias reached for Ashire's goblet. "I'm sure she'll at least attempt to impress us all."

Ashire swiped the drink back from the Fae and took a long gulp while simpering at Emtias. The air in the room shifted as the two leered at each other, and I struggled to regain my footing in the conversation. "I'll see myself out," I said.

"Please do," Ashire called as I shut the door behind me.

As I stepped out into the hallway, Selasi waited for me. "Those two deserve each other," he remarked and fell into step with me, taking the ledgers from my hands.

"Indeed."

Eve

"Back straight and chin high! Should you look at your feet for one second, you will end up on the floor." Emtias' bark reverberated off the walls of the throne room. "No, keep your arms firm." He pushed his hand into my lower back to somehow make my spine even more straight.

"This is intolerable," I grumbled between my gritted teeth.

"Wait until you must do it while wearing a corset. Now, in step with me."

I had been expecting ballroom dancing, not group dances like something out of a Jane Austen novel. Some dances were more intimate, some had a faster cadence.

All while we were stepping and gliding about the floor Emtias was humming along for me to become familiar with what songs entailed certain dances. "What's the main export in Walor?" he quizzed.

I was twirled beneath him as I frantically tried to recall. "Iron ore?"

He spun me away from him. "Do not say it as if it were an inquiry. Speak with conviction. You're the prince's advisor." We shuffled in step, circling around the other as I tried to maintain eye contact or else suffer another scolding. "What is the main export in Xard?"

"Grain and—"

"Keep your eyes up."

I flashed my glare back up. "Grain and fleece."

"How has grain production been the past few seasons?"

"Better," I panted while taking two steps to the right then three to the left. "Since they implemented a more efficient irrigation system. They had an excess of grain last season. Could they not then export ale to make use of the excess?" I sucked in a deep breath while Emtias hoisted me up into the air. "They could use taxable funds to build the conservatory they've been requesting a loan for. Then they won't have to be in debt to the crown."

I could have sworn Emtias fell out of tempo for one split second. "Yes, very good, though only if their grain stores are full."

The tempo slowed, and we bowed toward the other. I finally let myself relax, struggling to maintain enough energy to be scrutinized by Emtias and then workout twice per day when I returned to my world. I was giving Milfred a run for her money when it came to my appetite.

"That will do for today." He clapped his hands. "I will say that I'm pleased with your progress."

"You can tell me more over some custard tarts," I commented while walking towards the kitchen. "And you don't have to sound so surprised."

I had done well at balancing two different dimensions. Despite being stabbed and not being able to see Nicky as much, I was able to compete in more fights, which helped pay for Nicky's long-term care. My guilt was gradually smothered with every custard tart, every new book to devour, each new hairstyle of Maisy's, and each lingering caress Safir left me daring to crave. I honestly thought my new life was sustainable until I returned from Walyre to see Nicky and found he wasn't in his room.

"We've been trying to call you," Tabitha remarked with an edge of judgment as she looked up from her *Listen to Your Inner Goddess* book of the month. "He was transferred to the inpatient unit yesterday."

I cursed while sprinting to the inpatient unit, hating the smell of disinfectant that clung to the stained carpets and chairs. The walls and floors were varying colors of beige. People cried out from their beds, asking for help, asking for Percocet. Most of the staff scurried from one room to the next to silence alarms or sedate you into oblivion.

A place to die.

That was what it looked like.

And I found Nicky there for the fourth time within a year. He coughed, struggling to breathe through his ventilator. Pneumonia had paid its annual visit to him with a vengeance.

"He's struggling to clear the infection," the physician told me outside of his room. "We'll give him his usual work-up, but...I don't think Nicholas is very comfortable."

I looked at her questioningly. "Obviously not."

Her face fell. "Eve, I'm not certain Nicholas isn't struggling to fight this infection because he's failing to thrive. He doesn't seem as motivated to fight it this time."

I turned without a word and returned to Nicky's room. He wheezed and winced while people meandered in and out to poke and prod him with needles and questions. He could barely rouse himself enough to glance over at me and smile.

"Money-maker," he had begun calling me. "Did you bring … pies?"

I shook my head. "You're having enough trouble keeping food down as it is. I'll bring some next time."

"Next time." The smile faded as he peered up at the ceiling. "I'm in here a lot … There will be a …. next time."

My breath hitched. "Nicky, they said you're having more trouble fighting the infection this time. Do you— do you want to get better?"

"Do you remember that time … I found you in the church? You had run away." He spoke with pain in his crackling voice. His tone had grown deeper while he'd lain in that bed.

I nodded slowly.

"I could always find you … Always … I could just picture it … like a daydream … Lately, I can't picture … where you are … You seem so far away … so happy."

My jaw clenched while I swallowed lumps in my throat. "I'm never really happy without you."

"Liar," he said with a smile, our matching eyes swimming in tears. "I knew one day … you would find someone who would … look after you and replace me …. And I hope you know … That it's okay."

"Nicky, what are you—"

"Don't you think it's time?" he asked in a single breath with a bitter smile. "To let me go … I'm tired, Eve … All the time I'm tired."

Tears spilled over as I reached for his hand. "I don't think I can do that, Nicky. I can't. Would you be able to do it if it were me?"

"No," he responded without hesitation. "But you have always been … the stronger one."

I half-heartedly scoffed. "That's the dumbest thing you've ever said." Nicky had been the one to find me, to save me, to inspire me, to make me want to fight. For my entire life, my strength had belonged to him. I felt so certain it would die with him.

"I'm ready … You shouldn't kill yourself … just to watch me die here."

"Fucking shut up," I begged, barely even able to look at him.

"Eve, even if you had … all the money in the world … I couldn't be free from this." His tone became soft. "I wouldn't ask if I didn't … think you had someone … to be there when I'm gone. You've grown and one day … you'll be okay."

My head shook as I wiped my sleeve across my face to catch tears and snot. It was like a void was already forming inside my heart in the shape of Nicky. "Why now? We've gotten by okay with just us two."

"I've always felt stuck … in this corpse … but I couldn't leave you. And now you've found … some happiness outside of me … I'm glad … I felt we were both ready."

I didn't respond. I couldn't anymore. All the fighting, stealing, bleeding, and breaking was enough to merely keep him alive. Nicky had always had a fierce spirit, and as much as I had hoped he'd find peace in his quiet body, I'd known. I'd always known. He withstood the hospital visits, the loneliness, the insanity of being trapped in his own body, because he felt I still needed him. And he had been right.

"Do you know I'll always need you?" I asked quietly.

"We'll always need each other…Just think about it the next time … I'm stuck here … just let me go."

"I've told you— if you go, I won't be far behind."

He smiled. "Liar."

Stays in the inpatient unit were always more expensive, and it was a kick in the teeth when I saw the bill. Even if I competed in more fights, it wasn't going to make a difference. And I didn't doubt dying in peace had its own price. I couldn't bring myself to entertain the idea of him voluntarily dying. It would be like losing my right arm. I'd bleed out.

I even tried asking Safir for money. I had never brought up Nicky before, probably for the same reason Safir hadn't originally told me why his Blessing was out of control. But I needed some solution, and I wasn't so proud I wouldn't ask a prince for help.

"Safir?" I asked tentatively one afternoon.

"Hmm?" he hummed over a pile of papers. He had become consumed with preparing for his debut in just a few weeks. I could feel his growing anticipation, nervousness, and excitement. I wished it were more infectious.

"Our original arrangement, me being compensated with meals and healing for being here, could that be changed?"

He looked up from his desk and furrowed his eyebrows. "Are you not happy with the arrangement?"

"I am, it's just boxing hasn't been as fortuitous this season, and I still have obligations in my world. I was wondering if I could instead be given payment equivalent to the meals and healing."

Safir leaned back and extended his hand to me. Immediately I took it in my grasp. I sensed his confusion, concern, and possibly a twinge of hurt? His background nervousness about his debut became muddled amongst everything else.

He pulled his hand away before I was ready to let go. "I thought, you had grown happy enough here you weren't motivated by our original arrangement. I thought you had become content here."

I winced. He wanted me there for the same reason I wanted him to want me there. And that was why it killed me to say nothing in response. I could spill my guts about the shit list that had been my life until I had met Safir, but I could sense the stress he was under. Perhaps there would be a time after the debut where I could justify myself to him.

"I promise it's nothing to do with—"

"But I'm aware obligations in your world don't cease just because you're here," he interjected, a hint of disappointment in his voice. "I can discuss the matter with Ashire, but I'm sure he won't agree to finalize anything until after the debut. Once that's over with, we can focus on more minute details."

That's not soon enough.

I had stooped to asking my first real friend for money, and I hated myself for it. Granted, anything was worth it for Nicky. I had to remind myself not to become too enveloped in a world that wasn't my own to do what was best for Nicky. Which meant I'd have to stoop even lower.

I approached Clay in the gym. "You're looking light on your feet, peach," he sighed while taking a drag from his cigarette. "Whatever new juice you got is working like a charm."

"Clay, I need more cash than I'm getting."

He peered above the smoke. "What, is Hunter not giving you fair splits? I've been keeping track—"

"It's not that."

Clay gestured for me to walk with him, away from curious ears. "How's Nick doing?"

Between trying to catch my breath and trying not to think of Nicky's death wish, I felt like my lungs were going to collapse in my chest. "Not great," I panted, unable to hold my composure.

"All right, all right. No tears in my gym." He coughed then took a strained breath. "Look, I know you don't exactly do this for the love of the sport. This is a means to an end. If you're wanting to make some more cash, Hunter could fix some fights for you. You'll get a bad rep, but you'll get more yield."

I sighed. "I figured."

"You're gonna be burying yourself deeper in his back pocket."

"That's fine."

It wasn't. My stomach rolled as I stood in front of that godforsaken house. It was sickeningly familiar. The last time I had left that place my life had been on the precipice of falling apart, and somehow, I was back in the same situation.

My fist felt like it weighed fifty pounds as I knocked on the door and silently hoped no one would answer. But someone did. My jaw dropped when Mary cracked the door open, looking as shocked as me.

"Eve?" She looked back into the house, then stepped outside with me. "How are you? What are you doing here?"

"What are *you* doing here?"

She looked thin, seeming to have aged more since I had last seen her. "I got laid off and—"

"Mama, who is it?" a pixie-like voice came from behind the door. A tiny hand pried the door open, and a watery eyed kid toddled outside and looked up at me. "Who are you?"

Mary shooed the child back inside. "How old is she?" I asked, my voice trying not to shake.

"Three years."

I took a step towards her. "You *cannot* let her near him. You know that. You cannot stay here."

The door flew open, and the man of our nightmares stood there with his shoulders taking up most of the doorframe. "Lexi said we had a guest." Hunter looked to me and smiled. "Evie! What a surprise. Welcome back home." His arm scooped around my shoulders and ushered me in that house. "I would never have guessed I'd see you here again."

"Me either," I said, struggling to breathe in the familiar smell of that house. One half of the house was full of toys and the other half was busy with looming figures shooting glances my way.

"My associates," Hunter remarked. The men were openly counting cash. "Gentlemen! This is my heavyweight I was telling you about!" He squeezed my arms and squished me closer against him. I held my breath. I could hardly stand the feeling of his body melding into mine.

The men smirked, looking me up and down before resuming counting their dollar bills. I had seen that look all too often. My shoulders squared, and I held my chin high, refusing to feel as small as they wanted me to.

Hunter released me. "What can I do for you, Evie?"

I took two steps back to gain some space. "It's Nicky. I can't keep up with some of his bills and Clay said you'd be able to fix some fights."

"Is Nick all right?" Mary asked.

"He's dying, but thank you for your concern," I snapped.

She recoiled behind Hunter, who gestured her away. "Take Lexi to the back and put on some TV. We'll talk business."

Mary scooped the child into her arms and fled the room, shutting the door. Then it was just Hunter and I, his band of goons in the background. I felt as if I had just served myself up on a platter for him. Hunter sighed and looked at me with insincere concern. "I told you I'd always take care of you, Evie. You know that."

I nodded slowly.

"And if Nick needs help, I'm more than happy to oblige. Think of it as strengthening our partnership." He placed his sweaty hands on either side of my face. I swallowed as his thumb prodded my cheek. "The thing is, you haven't always been grateful to your patron, even with everything I've done for you. Hell, I even gave you a place to call your own."

My thoughts flashed to Safir and how he had held me so gently, how he had caressed my cheek without wanting anything in return. His touch was like being able to take a free, deep breath, while Hunter's presence made me feel like I was choking on my own bile. I had to think of Safir, only him, or else I was sure I would kill Hunter.

"And I think a little gratefulness would look real good on you, Evie. So, ask me again so I know *you* know how much you need me."

My skin crawled and my fingernails dug into my palms as my hands formed tight fists at my sides.

"I need you … please."

Hunter smiled too widely. "I know you do." He squeezed my face and smacked his rubbery lips into mine. I froze. I would kill him. I wanted to kill him. I let him hold me there for a few seconds too long, hearing scoffs and whistles from his insufferable associates.

When he released me, I stumbled back and fought the urge to chug a gallon of bleach. My lips burned. My skin itched. And worst of all, tears threatened to fill my horrified stare.

He chuckled and wiped his mouth. "My friends and I will arrange however many fights you need. It'll be simple, just win or lose like I tell you to. I'll take care of the rest."

I staggered for the door. I had to leave. The very air was going to choke me. Hunter followed closely. "Come back anytime you want, Evie," he whistled while shutting the door behind me, pushing me onto his front porch.

Furious tears spilled over as I walked away, pumped full of anger I had nowhere to place. It was worth it for Nicky. Anything was worth it for Nicky.

Suddenly I hunched over a street trash can and dry-heaved into it. My nose burned and core ached, but it wasn't as bad as recalling Hunter's lips. In that moment, sobbing and vomiting into a random trash can, I couldn't help but miss Safir. Never had I felt so far from my newfound happiness.

Safir

I hardly ever wished my Blessing upon anyone, but there were a few moments when I wished it upon Eve just so I could know her disposition. During that time before my debut, it was harder to discern her thoughts. Her gestures were minimal, and her bright smile had become quiet. Perhaps I had been too harsh when she'd asked me for money. I'd thought her time in my realm was an improvement over her own, but perhaps I was being ignorant.

One afternoon I met her by the portal, watching her emerge with slightly less bruising than usual upon her face. "Safir," she greeted me with a weak smile, but a smile all the same.

When I reached out to her, her cheek fit right into my hand. Despite her brutalized face, she never once winced at my touch. In fact, that day she leaned into my palm and a deep melancholy overtook her sapphire gaze. It made my chest want to cave in on itself. I hated whatever obligations made her need to be beaten.

"I'm fine," she assured me. "Just tired."

"It seems you've been quite tired lately. I'm hoping this will help." I reached beneath my cloak and offered her the gift I had been preparing for her.

Her eyes grew wide as she took a silver dagger and sheath into her hands. I'd had it made for her after the last encounter with the assailant so she would have a weapon to defend herself. The smith had created a beautiful dagger engraved with delicate designs. The sheath and hilt had jewels of the Astana house embedded inside, glowing an orange and red in the sunlight.

"To help keep you safe."

"It's beautiful," she said breathlessly and then smiled, truly smiled at me. "Thank you," she would say multiple times throughout that day. She was the most gracious person I had ever met, and whenever she was in Walyre, she always had the dagger at her hip.

"It's not enough to just have a dagger," Selasi would say when we took a break from my relentless studying and strolled through the gardens. "One has to be proficient." He offered Eve lessons, which she readily accepted.

Given she was already a brawler, it was simply an extension of her craft. She learned to think through the path the blade would take when slicing through the air. She was quick to follow Selasi's example as she danced around him, swift and focused. It was alluring to watch and a welcome distraction from the storm of responsibility that was readying to crash over me.

We were less than two weeks away from my debut and they were practicing in the gardens, when Selasi collapsed to the ground in a huff. "I believe she is bored with me, Lord. I dare you to try her."

"I think Selasi snuck too many biscuits from Milfred's kitchen this morning. Usually he isn't this easily exhausted," she panted, but with an exhilarated smile.

I rarely got to see her in such form. Some of her hairs hung loose around her face, being impressed by her breath. Her cheeks were flushed, but she studied me from head to toe as I assumed the role of assailant. A shock down ran my spine while I was analyzed underneath her intense gaze. I would have equally hated and been thrilled to be her adversary.

When I lunged at her she disappeared around me, hardly making a sound. She taunted me with her bold grin. She was always one second quicker than me, hardly letting me get within arm's reach before changing directions. I was left to follow her sapphire eyes that felt like they were beckoning me closer.

Our altercation ended when I purposefully caught her foot just as she was dodging away from me. She yanked me down with her, making me grab the arm that was carrying the weapon. We landed on the grass in a heap of exhaustion. I was poised over her, looking down into her focused gaze as she pressed the dagger against my throat.

I couldn't help but marvel at the tautness of her body as her chest rose and fell against mine. Her eyes were wide, but her grip was solid. I didn't mind her sensing the slight thrill and wonder that coursed through my Blessing. She even raised her chin, as if daring me to meet her. I wondered…

Selasi cleared his throat. I rolled away from Eve and lay beside her. "I'd hate to ever be pitted against you," I told her while wiping sweat from my brow.

She smiled as she sheathed the dagger at her side. "Hopefully I won't have to put it to good use."

"We should have you spar against Lady Zae when she arrives." Selasi plopped down on the grass next to me. "I'm told she's skilled with a dirk for a lady. It'd be quite the spectacle."

"She is not a force to underestimate," I breathed while sitting up from the grass.

Eve peered up at me. "Are House Oska and House Astana closely aligned?"

Selasi and I exchanged glances before I stood up from the grass and brushed off my trousers. "Yes, though not as closely we were previously." She stood up, obviously still riled with curiosity. I cast my eyes away, almost embarrassed. "It's best you know before guests arrive that Lady Zae and I were betrothed for a short time."

Eve stilled as her eyes widened ever so slightly. "Oh. Were?"

"Yes." Was she angry? Indifferent? Merely surprised? I began to walk through the gardens to my study and Selasi followed. "It was quite a long time ago."

"Why are you no longer betrothed?"

"She rescinded her agreement once her brother died in a hunting accident, and she became lady of her house. She no longer needed my name to advance herself in society."

"That seems harsh," Eve pondered aloud.

"I wasn't entirely surprised. I never believed it was love that tethered us together, but she was a good companion."

"If it wasn't love, then what 'tethered' you together?"

I smirked. "I often forget how direct you are, Eve. I'm not entirely sure I can give you a delicate answer."

She stopped on the edge of the gardens, her eyes flickering between Selasi and me. I turned to my swordsman, who gave a stiff nod and walked in the opposite direction for a few paces, enough for us to have a bit more discretion.

"Surely you're aware of the desires that can be acted upon between two persons…away from prying eyes."

Her cheeks reddened. "Yes, I'm aware. I just didn't think you … I figured since you were merely betrothed that you'd be forbidden from … that is, until you were-"

I watched her fidget. "Perhaps in your realm the act of intimacy is more reprehensible? If one musters accountability for any illegitimate children that could be produced hardly any judgement passed."

"It's not reprehensible, per se, where I come from. It depends. I figured the idea was more open-minded here since Maisy tells me all about her exploits."

"Come again?" Selasi called from afar.

I waved him off, looking back to Eve. She quieted while folding her hands together and tucking them under her arms. I could feel the air of inexperience surrounding her. I decided to be bold and ask, "Have you never … with anyone?"

Her sapphire gaze flashed up to me. "No. There's never been time, and no one was exactly lining up for an opportunity."

That I didn't believe.

She huffed while swiping a few loose hairs out of her eyes. "So, I take it Lady Zae was understanding regarding your Blessing?"

I thought back to those darker days. "She was one of the few, besides Ashire and Lani, who didn't mind it. She helped me become the person you first met."

To my relief, the corners of Eve's mouth perked in a small smile. "Then I'm glad."

***

The last thing I'd wanted was to meet Lady Zae, let alone marry her. The previous king had been dead for five years, and Ashire was working tirelessly to prove House Astana was under a vastly different monarch. My days were spent in solitude or with my brother. My Blessing had run less rampant once I was freed from the dungeon. Select persons could almost tolerate being in the same room as me if we were at opposite corners. I practiced emanating a neutral warmth to enshroud my sickening sentiments. My memories were still etched into my skin, and so I was careful not to expose anyone to my Blessing.

That fear was realized when Ashire was given a letter from House Oska.

"Lord Ollo wants to betroth his daughter, Zae, to one of us, as a sign of loyalty to the new king," Ashire sighed while peering up from his stack of books. "The old man is probably just trying to unburden himself of his daughter."

I shrugged. "You're old enough to marry, though I doubt she'll favor living with her poisoned brother-in-law."

Ashire threw the letter into the fire. "You should refrain from thinking yourself so vile. I think she might be a good match for you."

I broke out into a sweat at the thought. "You can't be serious."

"Easy, Safir," he cautioned as the air filled with my anxiety.

"How could I marry, Ashire? I wouldn't even be able to touch her!"

"Yes, you can. You've been able to keep your Blessing to yourself. Perhaps a bit of light-spirited fun would give you something else to ponder."

"Why are you not interested in her?"

He stalled and huffed, "She's not the type of person I'm interested in."

"How would you know? You haven't met her."

"Trust me, I know."

"Ashire—"

"I am not saying marry her now! Just meet her. Perhaps something good will come of it."

I paced backwards with my head shaking. "It will only end in disaster, and Lord Ollo will disavow the crown if I hurt his daughter."

"You won't hurt her. I trust you."

I wished he hadn't. My stomach felt twisted for weeks before her arrival, and I dreaded every second until her carriage arrived. For years I had understood and accepted I could never be a husband or father. I wouldn't be willing to touch my bride, let alone make a family when the touch of my hand sent grown men crying.

"I trust you," Ashire repeated as the doors opened and Zae approached us with her entourage.

She was tall with rounded hips and chest for her age. Her hair was black as night, shimmering in the candlelight while it flowed down her bareback. She had obviously dressed for the sweltering weather in Phora. A loose-fitting dress covered her chest and flowed to her sandals. Her skin was a deep bronze color, and her eyes found mine immediately. They were grey but sharp. Any sane man would deem her beautiful. I could only see my downfall.

She curtseyed and smiled as she thanked us for welcoming her. Ashire was the first to receive her. I did my best to focus on a neutral warmth, taking her hand and placing a kiss upon it as quickly as possible.

"An honor to meet you." I released her hand like a hot coal.

Her grey eyes were wide, but her smile remained. My control had been maintained during our first meeting, and yet I did not feel relieved. She was to stay with us for two weeks, longer if Ashire believed we were compatible. It was going to feel like holding my breath for two weeks, and I intended to avoid her at all costs.

For the first few days she explored the palace herself, and at night I would find her kneeling in front of my mother's tomb. I wondered if she prayed. What could she possibly say to my mother? The audacity of her repelled me but also intrigued. I couldn't discern what she was thinking, until on the third night there was a knock on my bedroom door.

I opened my door, not knowing who would call upon me at that hour. To my astonishment, there she stood in her shear nightdress. I focused my energy on maintaining eye contact.

"Lady Zae, are you lost?" I asked, aghast.

She smiled. "I have something I want to show you. You must come with me at once!" She reached for my hand, but I recoiled. Her smile faded only slightly. "Just come with me."

She dashed away, and I stood there utterly dumbfounded. I didn't want to follow her, yet I could use that as an opportunity to repulse her enough to refuse to be betrothed to me. Though I was becoming more curious as she led me to her room. I swallowed hard as I stepped inside and found her standing on her balcony, letting her nightdress blow in the wind. She waved me to her side.

"You'll catch a sickness if you stay out there in the cold." I joined her on her balcony but remained as far away from her as possible.

"I like it. It's so different to Phora. The air is crisper, easier to breathe. See the moon?" She pointed up into the sky. "It's full. Do you see how its light sparkles on the mountaintops? I didn't know snow could exist throughout the entire year."

"This isn't a new occurrence for Walor. Is this what you wanted to show me?"

"I wanted you to see it through my eyes."

I softened my uninterested façade and took another glance at the moon. "I suppose it does seem brighter tonight." I maintained the space between us. "I've seen you kneeling by the tomb of the former queen. Are you praying?"

Zae nodded. "I wanted to pay my respects and to ask for advice."

"Advice? Regarding what?"

She turned to me with an arched eyebrow. Blood rushed to my cheeks. "Girls always need advice from mothers, even if it isn't their own. I've never left home, never been anywhere where I didn't see a familiar face. One naturally seeks out a mother for comfort. I'm also without a mother, you know. We're similar in that way."

"I suppose you're right."

"That is the correct mindset to have if we're to marry," she giggled, but I scowled instead.

"Lady Zae—"

"You could just call me Zae."

"You cannot marry me," I told her, my tone shifting to where it sounded like a command.

Her smile faded and eyes pierced straight through me. She stepped towards me. I began retreating until my back struck the railing. "Do you not like me, Your Royal Highness?"

"Pardon?"

"Am I unappealing to you? Do I repulse you?" she asked as a breeze blew her nightgown back and almost exposed her breasts.

My fingers twitched at my side as they wondered if her skin felt as soft as it looked in the moonlight. I focused on the night breeze, or else she would sense my apprehension. "That's hardly the issue."

"Then why will you not marry me? I would be a good wife to you."

"I'm sure you would. Trust me when I say that it has nothing to do with you." I tried to retreat towards her door. Yet to my shock, she reached for my hand and gripped it.

A gasp escaped me as I tried to pry myself away from her, but she only held on tighter. Her eyes grew wide, and she clenched her jaw. Surely, she felt my fear and grief. I had to push away any memories of physical torment.

"Let go!" I ordered. "I'll hurt you."

"If I'm to be your wife, you should know I am not easily afraid!" Zae held my hand tighter, though after a few moments she began to tremble. "I'm aware of what King Ronire did, and you don't have to be alone."

"Stop this," I begged her. "You will never find a suitable husband in me."

"Yes, I will. I can feel it." She took careful steps towards me. "Do not think about the things that have hurt you. Think about the things that feel good."

"There are very few things in my repertoire that feel good."

She closed the space between us, the peaks of her breasts brushing against my chest and a shiver ripped through my spine.

She smiled as she sensed it. "See?" Zae reached up and placed her palm against my cheek, though I flinched. "I want you to see, to know, that not all touch is bad. You can feel good, and you can focus on that."

I swallowed hard, abandoning any hope of trying to retreat from her. "I don't want to hurt you. I don't want to hurt anybody." Her hair smelled of warm spice and the night air.

"You think me so fragile," she cooed as her hand slipped from my face and roamed down my back.

My fear sparked as her hands ran over the ragged scars. I fought to not relive the memories of those lashings. The immediate pain didn't surface. It felt serene being touched by someone so gentle. She was careful and calculating, measuring my reaction every second. "Do you know you're beautiful, Safir? In body and soul."

I scoffed. "I doubt your observations."

"You're so overcome with worrying about my well-being. I don't think any man has ever concerned themselves so much over me." She pressed herself flush against me.

"Zae—"

"I'm going to kiss you. You deserve to be kissed by someone who isn't afraid."

My heart writhed in my chest as she stood on her toes and leant her forehead against mine. I didn't breathe as she pressed her lips against mine. My blood rushed through my veins. All I could think was how warm she felt, how strange she felt, how *good* she felt. She pulled back, her chest rising and falling against mine, making my fingers itch to caress the sides of her ribs. She felt fragile and soft in my grasp.

"I will stop now. And never speak to you again if you wish."

I said nothing, only staring in awe. She must have found that answer sufficient because she reached to kiss me again, but this time I captured her lips and pulled her closer against me. She sighed into my mouth when I ran my hands up her back. Her entire being was consuming my thoughts. There wasn't time to think of pain when I could experience the smell and taste of her. She showed me, as her hands ran through my hair and caressed my shoulders, how touch could be good. It was thrilling. It was addicting. The kisses began slow but grew long and deep as we devoured each other. I could feel her beginning to tremble in my grasp. Suddenly she pushed me backwards onto her bed.

Our limbs tangled around each other. My skin that was scarred and grotesque, a map of misery, was somehow marveled over. Once I tasted the desire to be touched, I swore I would never get my fill. It was terrifying how we rapidly ascended together despite having been mere strangers days before. Yet I drank her whispers that spoke my name. She was warmer than the sun itself, blindingly radiant beneath me. I couldn't think of anguish when moving in rhythm with her. I would never have dreamt she could cling to me. Her touch was equally desperate from a source of despair I didn't know. We both needed to touch and be touched, and it made us completely undone.

Her smile was present on her swollen lips as she fell back onto her pillows. I swore my heart was going to pound through my ribs. Zae patted the spot next to her, and I happily obliged.

She laid her naked body against mine. I wrapped my arm around her to warm her from the cool air from her balcony. "Can you do that again?" she asked.

"Pardon?"

She chuckled. "You made me feel like I was bathing in the sun. I was so warm. I want to feel that again."

I did as she wished, imagining the feeling of the sun beating down on our bare bodies, and she hummed. "See? Now whenever you're afraid of feeling something bad, something you're afraid of other people knowing, you can think of the good feelings."

Resting my cheek on top of her head, I murmured, "I suppose you've added something nice to my repertoire. Have you done this before?"

Her smile fell. "Not really. Not like this. It felt good like this. You were quite good."

"Was I?" I half-heartedly chuckled. "And would you tell me if I wasn't?"

She giggled and nestled closer. "Of course. If we're to be wed, we'll have much time to practice anyway."

After that first evening, each night felt more exhilarating than the last. I memorized what made her quiver beneath me, and she helped me explore good touch. Whenever we had finished exhausting each other, Zae would dream up new requests.

"Show me how it feels to roll in the snow. To get caught in a rainstorm. I want to feel the sun!"

I had gotten better at summoning sensations and emanating them.

"You feel lighter somehow, as if you trust yourself more."

"I do." I nuzzled into her neck. "I was so worried I would hurt you. I still am, but I can only think about this." I ran my hand up and down her naked spine.

She shivered. "I can still tell it's there, your fear and your sorrow. I know that doesn't go away just because you lie with me." Zae ran her fingers over the long scars on my back. I flinched but focused on her touch rather than the originating pain of the scars. She winced but didn't stop.

"Do you feel my pain sometimes?" I asked her.

"Barely, and only a few times. It's as quick as a blink and you don't linger on it as long as you used to."

I pulled back from her. "Have I ever hurt you?"

"You have only made me feel wonderful," she purred and drew herself closer to me. "I didn't think I'd ever be so fortunate as to have a lover such as you."

I somehow felt more exposed when I asked, "Do we love each other?"

Zae pondered for a few seconds. "No, this is not love. We're just very good at pleasing each other."

"That's more than most couples hope to have."

"True, but it is not love."

"How do you know?"

"I saw it between my parents before my mother died. They loved effortlessly. They shared one soul. I enjoy your company, and you have become a dear friend, but my soul isn't yours. My soul may never belong to anyone," she said in a melancholic tone. "Is that a horrible thing to say?"

"No, I don't think so. I'm not so certain my soul will ever belong to anyone either."

She scoffed and played with the earring in my ear. "I am most doubtful of that, Safir. Your soul seems bound to find a home in someone, and that person will never want for love."

"Well, they won't matter if we're to be married."

She grinned widely. "That's true, if you intend to marry me."

I reached up and stroked her soft hair. I could, for the first time, foresee myself being happy with another human being. Perhaps I wouldn't be in love, but I would be happy, nonetheless. "I would be happy to marry a friend."

And so, we were betrothed, much to the delight of Ashire, who reveled in being right once again. I doubted either of us ever predicted I would experience something even close to happiness, let alone with another person. I breathed easier, and perhaps it let loose some of the restraints the old king had put on my soul. I couldn't help but be hopeful. If I were able to be with Zae perhaps I could have a useful role in the kingdom. I could have a purpose outside of trying to avoid those around me. It couldn't erase the sorrow and grief I was sure would follow me all my life, but Zae could shed new light on it.

"It seems," Ashire spoke above the crackling of the fire one night, "you've improved your ability to control the physical sensations you radiate from your Blessing."

We had decided to celebrate my betrothal, just us two, over Ashire's newfound taste for wine. "Are you saying I'm better able to manage my Blessing?"

"Somewhat. What you are emanating into the air appears to be more innocuous. There's very little physical pain coming from you now, but I can still sense your emotions. It's a start."

"But could I ever engage in running a house or holding a meeting with the local lords?"

Ashire didn't answer immediately, making my hope dwindle within me. "Don't lose faith, Safir. One day you'll be able to resume a role in the public eye, but that will take a great deal more control. We must be patient."

I couldn't help but feel a twinge of disappointment. I had known I wasn't ready to emerge from my place of hiding, but I'd thought surely I was taking steps forward.

"I will not set you up for failure, Safir. I won't have you debuted before you're ready only to then have you regress."

"Zae believes I could do it," I grumbled under my breath.

Ashire shot me daggers. "Zae fills your head with folly, and I'm acutely aware of the effect she has on you. It's grand she's able to entertain you *thoroughly*, but those positive sentiments are fleeting—"

"How could you speak so harshly of her when you're the one who wanted me to marry her?"

"I am not saying she isn't beneficial to you!" he barked. "But you should be aware the feeling of bliss she gives you will never sustain you in a room of lords. She satiates you. She appeases you, which you deserve. But that doesn't equate to you having control over your Blessing. The very foundation of my power is bolstered by people never knowing what I truly think of them, and you … You could not do that."

I didn't hide my disgust as I stood from my chair. My hopes had risen so high when Zae was there. I'd thought I would never know happiness again. Why couldn't my brother see the difference she made?

Just as I reached for the door, Ashire's lingering words found my ears. "And don't think she won't exploit you for her own purposes."

I trudged towards Zae's room where she'd lift my spirits. I tried to ignore how the staff scuttled away from my irate presence, looking at me with mouths agape. It stung my already fragile ego as I burst into Zae's room.

She had her back to me, brushing out her long hair. Suddenly she whipped around in her chair. "Whatever is wrong? You're making my heart jump in my chest!"

I winced as I stepped inside and shut the door behind me. "It's my brother. He thinks I'm not ready to resume any public role. Why can't he see me as you see me?"

"Calm yourself," she cooed while standing from her chair. "Remember to focus on the good things. Like this." She stroked my cheek.

I sighed. "I don't think I want to feel good things right now. I want to be upset. I must be able to let myself feel angered at some point."

"Of course, but we must be willing to sacrifice if we're to hold any esteemed position together."

I recoiled from her touch. "I have sacrificed enough," I seethed while keeping my distance, to not disturb her further.

Her hands fell at her sides. "Saf, I didn't mean to offend you."

"It is not you who offends me. *I* offend me! Can I never again let myself feel anything remotely adverse without causing harm to those around me? Should I give up on feeling human at all?"

Zae dashed forward and threw her arms around me. I couldn't help but crush her against my chest. "My dear Safir, stop these thoughts, not because you're hurting me but because you're doing more harm to yourself. You're indulging your anger, and you are far better than that. You're the prince of Walyre."

I breathed in her warm scent, relaxing in her embrace. She worked like true magic.

"See?" she purred. "Just feel the good things."

Withdrawing from her, I looked into her grey eyes. "But I can't have you embrace me every time I'm angry. There will be times where I will be angry and be unable to control my Blessing. Why did you agree to marry me?" I asked her.

Her eyebrows furrowed. "What?"

"I know why I would marry you. You're a better friend than I deserve, but I don't know why you would want to be locked away in this palace with me—"

"Not forever," she scoffed.

"Possibly forever," I told her, watching her playful expression fade. "We don't know that my Blessing will ever improve to the point I could engage in public life. I could not accompany you to balls, to court, or public gatherings."

She withdrew herself from me. "I'm thankful that I was born into House Oska, or else I would just be another girl without a Blessing. Yet even with my name, I'm easily overlooked. My brother is the gem of our family, something of which he constantly reminds me." She looked up at me as her grey eyes glistened. "But I know if I helped you step out of the shadows I could also be seen in the light. I just know it."

"I cannot promise you that, Zae."

"But I know you would try."

Zae soon returned to Phora when news came of her father falling ill. Days after she arrived, he passed away in his sleep and her brother became lord of House Oska. I longed for her presence. While I missed the pleasure she offered at night, I ached to be in the aura of someone who could withstand my Blessing. I controlled myself within the palace, but I was better able to project neutral sensations should I need to. I practiced in moments where my heart felt ragged, as it often did. The air was no longer clouded with the memories of my physical torment, but everyone was still exposed to my sorrow, my fear, my anxiety. I had no privacy unless I locked myself away.

Zae and I wrote to each other throughout that year, and I treasured her letters. She hardly mentioned what we'd spoken of that night when my anger was overtaking me. Her words were sweet and sensual, and each letter smelled overpoweringly of her. I wrote back to her in my own time, struggling through the day to focus on controlling my Blessing rather than fantasizing about her.

However, almost one year after our betrothal, we received a letter from House Oska, only it was from the lady of the house. Zae's brother had died after suffering an accident while hunting boar. Suddenly she was head of her house. She enclosed a private letter for me, and somehow, I already suspected the contents before even opening it.

Dearest Safir,

My life has taken a sharp turn in a direction I wasn't anticipating when we first met. I find myself being seen by the people as someone who will protect and provide for them, and I intend to do this to the best of my ability. With a broken heart, I'm afraid I must rescind my agreement to marry you.

My affection for you has not changed, but I realized that my soul cannot belong to any one person because it belongs to all the people of Phora. They need me, and I couldn't bear to share that affection with any other being. The time we spent together truly inspired me, and I think about it very often. There will forever be a place in my heart for you, my first true friend. I swear my allegiance to the crown and pledge you will always find a friend in House Oska.

Think of me during the next full moon.
Lady Zae Oska

She sounded happy. I could only be glad for her. And I couldn't help but be relieved for myself. As much as I appreciated her presence at the palace, I had become certain after our last altercation I wasn't going to be able to give her a life she wanted. She deserved far more.

Ashire emerged beside me as I folded the letter into my pocket. He assessed the air about me. "You're more cheerful than I expected. I am regretful that she won't be able to go through with the arrangement. I know you did care for her."

"I regret nothing, I think. You were right to bring her here and right to keep my hopes grounded."

He rested his hand on my shoulder. "I didn't mean to discourage you. I merely want success for you."

"I know," I sighed. "At least Zae showed there's one more person in this world who could live alongside me. There's a chance there are others."

Eve

My ears rang as Hunter beat his fists and yelled over the crowd. My opponent was still dancing before me, smirking through her bite guard. She had too much energy for so late in the fight. How much longer did Hunter intend me to keep it up?

"Bring it home, Evie!" Hunter cheered amongst the sea of voices.

Gladly.

My bones creaked, and my lungs ached. I had no problem making the mat my home for those ten seconds. It was strangely peaceful while the ref sang the ten-count overhead.

"Winner!" the ref announced while raising my opponent's arm in the air. I groaned, stealing myself away through the ropes. I felt pats on my back while trudging for the locker room. I kicked the door open and stepped to the sink to spit out my bloodied mouth guard. Grinning into the mirror to examine my teeth, I saw Hunter already standing behind me with his arms crossed over his chest looking none too pleased.

"What?" I snapped while wiping my mouth. "You told me to lose."

"I told you to make it look like a struggle. At least we now know acting isn't your strong suit," he chided.

I tasted blood. My ribs ached and my head throbbed. I was not in the mood to tolerate his obscenity.

He stood one breath away from me when he held up an envelope full of cash. Just as I tore off my glove to reach for it, he yanked it back from me. "You barely earned this, Evie. I'm gonna have a lot of upset clients if you don't deliver what you promise me. The only way I can bring in this kind of money is by playing off the perception of you in the ring. Do you understand?"

"Yes."

"Then play your goddamn part." He dropped the envelope on the floor and left the locker room.

I stared at the money. The envelope absorbed water dripping from the sink, staining it brown. It was for Nicky. The taste of blood on my tongue was for Nicky. I didn't have the luxury of being proud as I stooped down and picked up the money, tucking it into my duffle bag.

After the shortest shower of my life, I threw on my sweats and darted out of the gym. My body was begging for a break, but I sprinted to the bank to deposit the cash before I ran back towards my house. I couldn't be late. It was the first night of Safir's debut, and he was probably a nervous wreck. If I could just get there on time, he'd be fine.

Despite all the aches and pains, I dodged down alley ways and around corners until I stumbled into my neighborhood. The sun was setting, and I picked up my pace. As I sprinted past my house, I could almost feel myself nearing the portal. It was just one hundred yards away in the thick of that forest. I dodged sticker bushes and thorns that had risen with spring having come and gone, feeling small cuts on my legs.

One last leap over a fallen tree, and I tumbled into the world of Walyre. The familiar winding trees, towering mountains, and great white palace waited before me. Two guards were stationed on either side of the portal, making me assume Ashire didn't want any guests to get lost in my world. I paused to catch my breath before Maisy called out to me.

"Eve! Where have you been? You're late."

"I know," I said as she ushered me to the palace. "Has anyone arrived yet?"

"Not yet. We've had word the guests have just set foot into the valley."

"And Lani?"

"Waiting for you in your room. She'll heal you while I manage your hair."

"Safir?"

She smiled and ushered me faster. "His Royal Highness will be more at ease now knowing you're here."

I'd never had so many pairs of hands on me at once as Maisy fixed my hair, Lani healed me, and other servants tried to fit me with stockings and corset. "Emtias was right," I panted. "This is intolerable."

"Focus, my fierce lily," Lani said next to me. "I'll be able to do this faster if you focus."

I calmed my breath and focused on the flame, visualizing not making it grow. It helped Lani as the pain and swelling receded with each passing minute. My head no longer felt like it wanted to explode. "Very good," Lani murmured. "I'm sure it'll be much easier for you to manage now you're free of that pain."

"And how was your brawl, Eve? Did you win gallantly?" Maisy inquired while pinning my hair back.

I forced a smile. "Gallantly is one word for it."

"I wish you could teach me how to be smart with my fists. I think I'd like to be a more imposing figure," she commented while plucking a strand of hair. I winced. "So sorry. I've never had to work this quick before!"

She pulled my hair back at the base of my neck while allowing a few tendrils to frame my face. She shoved gold accessories into pieces of my hair, most of them looking like gold leaves, then hurriedly ushered to me to the corner where my dress was hanging. I had yet to wear a dress in Walyre, but I doubted I could get away with wearing my leather pants during Safir's debut.

Maisy gave my corset one last tug before allowing me to step into the dress and pulling it over my body. The material was heavy, but at least it was comfortable. Based on the gold embroidery along the bodice and skirt, I'd expected it to itch like hell. It fell to my feet with a flowing skirt which met the fitted bodice at my waist. The neckline dipped low enough I was somehow showing more cleavage than I actually had and was offset on my shoulders before extending into sleeves that ran down my arms.

She had me step into a pair of petite boots before opening a box on my bed. It held a gorgeous jewelry set consisting of a gold choker and matching earrings. They were far too regal for me. Maisy smiled as my jaw dropped. "My family's jewels. I figured you wouldn't have any of your own for tonight, and as the prince's advisor you should not look second best."

"Maisy, I can't wear these."

"You most certainly can, and you'll give them right back once you've tired yourself of the festivities." She fastened the choker around my neck and clipped the earrings onto me. "Selasi went to a great deal of trouble tracking these down after my father had to sell them. They deserve to be admired. They've spent quite a bit of time in that box."

My heart leapt into my throat. "I'm grateful to you."

"I know, because look at you!" she cheered while turning me to look into the mirror on my vanity.

I froze. It was hard to believe less than an hour prior I'd been coated in sweat. My hands reached up and pressed themselves into my bodice, feeling a gasp escape me. The dress fitted me so perfectly, though perhaps too fitted in the bust. The color matched my eyes in a way that made my stare look more direct. As always, my hair was perfectly styled by Maisy's hands to frame my face. I had gone from a brawler to looking like a princess in such a short amount of time it felt like whiplash. I was beginning to wonder if I was becoming two separate people.

"Beautiful," Maisy admired from behind me. "And now, it's time for everyone else to see."

Safir

My heart hammered in my throat. I cursed that Eve had to brawl. If she could have been there hours prior, I was sure that my nerves would not have taken such a strong hold. The guests would be arriving any minute, and my right side was bare without my advisor.

"I've been assured she's here," Emtias informed me while standing on the other side of my brother.

Ashire sat tall on his throne. "And she will be here soon, so try to calm yourself." He peered up at me, careful not to disturb his crown. "This is a grand step forward for our house. Revel in the fact this day has come for you."

He was right. I should have been joyous, but I couldn't help but be consumed with every unfortunate outcome that could befall me that evening. *It could always be worse.* The voice of myself locked in the dungeon seemed to echo through my thoughts.

"Safir," my brother mumbled. "Focus on where you are, not where you were. The only time in this world that matters is the time you spend right now."

At the very least I focused on a neutral warmth, but my palms sweated in my pockets. I needed her close. I needed—

"Lord," Selasi said from behind me, making me turn to see him staring at an unearthly figure pacing towards me. Her dress flowed behind her, highlighting the color of her eyes that I had longed to see that whole day. Glowing from the gold embellishments on her dress and in her hair, her taut figure was emphasized by the tightness of her bodice that hoisted her breasts and displayed the sharpness of her shoulders. She picked up her chin when she saw me, letting me see the gleaming choker that adorned her neck. She was the very picture of elegance, of unreachable magnificence.

I stepped forward, reaching out to her just as she was reaching out for me. "Safir." She smiled while allowing me to cup her cheek. She placed her hand over mine, sensing apprehension, excitement, uncertainty, but above all joy that she was there. Her sapphire eyes quieted my tormented thoughts. "You are everything you need to be for this night to go well. I'll make sure of it."

My heart swelled in my chest as I leaned down to her ear. "I know how you detest flattery, but I'd like to say how much brighter the room has become with your presence."

Her cheek grew warm in my hand. I felt her breath hitch in her throat. We were mere inches away from the other. If it hadn't been for prying eyes, I would have liked to spend the rest of the evening that close to her. Those warm sentiments must have been conveyed through my touch as her eyes grew wide.

Selasi cleared his throat from behind me. "Eve! What a beauty you are! Though I doubt there's any room in that dress for you to conceal your dagger."

Eve dropped her hand from mine and arched an eyebrow at my swordsman. "I've obviously concealed it well enough for you to not be able to tell."

I let my hand fall from her cheek, not wanting her to sense the wonder that stirred in me at the thought of searching for that dagger. Selasi's jaw dropped as he seemed incapable of a clever answer. We didn't stand dumbfounded for long before Emtias emerged.

"Ah, my pupil. Now that you look the part, I'm curious as to how well you can act it."

It was easy to miss the small hint of trepidation about Eve. I could only tell because she straightened her posture, which she only did when she didn't want to feel small.

"Yes, yes, very well," Ashire barked from his throne. "The night must go on."

Eve and Selasi stood close behind me. I swore I could feel the heat coming off Eve's body. Seconds before the doors opened to our guests, I glanced back and found her gaze. It was direct and self-assured. Everything I needed to remember to be, and everything I knew I was capable of being. Anytime I ever doubted, I'd look to her and remember.

Eve

The extravagance condensed into one place was insane. I was surprised people weren't blinded by the hundreds of candles reflecting off the sea of jewels in the throne room. Even Safir and Ashire had worn their most decorated livery collars and crowns. Their message of prosperity and riches wasn't missed.

The first to enter were the local lords accompanied by their wives, who looked as if their cheeks would burst from smiling. They bowed to the king and prince, offering congratulations and well wishes to Safir. He already knew them by name, having had to read their petty requests to the crown. He appeared courteous but hardly seemed moved by their words of praise. When they had finished, they took their place at one of the long tables stationed within the throne room.

But soon entered the heads of the great houses. Lord Batrum from House Trice entered. He had similar hair to Queen Mira, blonde and curly though his was beginning to grey. He was tall, not quite lanky, and with minute wrinkles at the corners of his eyes. He bowed deeply. "Your Majesty. Your Royal Highness," he greeted warmly.

Ashire leaned forward on his throne with a genuine smile. "Uncle, we're overjoyed you've arrived safely."

Lord Batrum beamed while standing upright. "I'm pleased to see that my king is no longer the inquisitive boy that would ransack my libraries but is now a great man. My dear sister would have longed to see this day. I felt I must take her place in having immense pride for my nephews." He stepped aside and ushered a round woman next to him. She had dark skin, warmer than Zae's yet still seemed flushed in the spotlight. She beamed and curtseyed, not too deeply given her delicate state. "I believe you have yet to have the pleasure of meeting Lady Tesara, now carrying your fifth little cousin."

"Congratulations. I'm sorry the rest of your family couldn't accompany you."

"Nonsense. While the other four send their glad tidings, we were both quite content to escape the estate before the fifth child arrives." Batrum gestured to a liveried figure to hand him two books. "If it would please the king and prince, House Trice offers its knowledge and wisdom to serve the crown." He extended one book to each Ashire and Safir. They took them in hand, carefully studying the text. "For you, my king, Xard's most recent publishing of philosophical truths passed down from generations of our strongest scholars. And for you, my prince, a collection of the grandest tales of conquest recorded in Walyre, some believed to have been told by the griffin's themselves."

"As ever, Uncle, you know how to please your king," Ashire declared. "Summers spent in your library provided such solace that now I've created my own collection for these to call home. I hope you find the time to peruse during your stay. I must know how it compares to yours in Xard."

"It shall be of the utmost importance. I'll be overjoyed the day that your collection outshines my own," Batrum agreed, bowing before ushering his wife to his own grand table, where their entourage accompanied them.

Afterwards, an extravagant entourage entered the throne room, led by a gorgeous woman I could only assume to be Lady Zae of House Oska. She was tall, most of her height being in her long legs. Her dress barely accommodated her breasts, and she had raven-black hair slicked back to show off her misty grey eyes that immediately landed upon Safir. She smiled coyly, curtsying so low it left little to the imagination. Her warm skin glowed, and she greeted them in a rich, husky tone, "My king. My prince. How I have longed to return to Walor. I cannot tell you how much good it's done my heart to see your prosperity spread to all corners of the land."

"As always, it's splendid to see you again, Lady Zae. You've grown into a formidable head of your house." Ashire glanced to Safir. "And I believe I speak on behalf of the entire royal family when I say you're always welcome here." Both Safir and Zae cracked small smiles while muffled chuckles could be heard across the throne room, as if everyone were sharing in the same joke.

I felt my hands twitch at my sides.

For a split second, Zae glanced past Safir at me. Her smile grew ever so slightly before she looked to Ashire. "Phora offers its finest silk to adorn your beautiful home." Zae's liveried personnel brought forth rolls of silk spindled on wooden rods. It looked luxurious, shimmering with intricate designs.

Ashire took the silk in hand, rubbing the material between his fingers. "I wouldn't expect anything less grand to come out of Phora. You have our thanks, Lady Zae." She curtseyed deeply before taking her place at her own table, continuing to make eye contact with Safir. It made a twinge of annoyance pang in my gut.

Lastly, an imposing figure stepped forward. He was strapping with broad shoulders and wide hands. His hair was long, pin-straight, and fell down his back. He was wearing a breastplate that shone in the candlelight with a sword strapped to his side. Every facial feature was sharp: his nose, cheeks and chin came to an exact point. His eyes darted from one corner to the next. He only had two men with him, both of whom kept one hand on the hilt of their swords.

Ashire's ember eyes flared as he leaned forward. "Lord Arius, it's hardly customary to dress for battle when approaching the king on such a happy occasion."

"On the contrary, Your Majesty." Arius' voice was low and dripping with intent. "I was taught one should always be prepared to lay down their life for their king, and I have dressed accordingly. My grandfather found it of the utmost importance to instill this principle."

The air in the room soured as even I realized the boldness of his words. Ashire, however, took his comments in stride. "Rightfully so," he hummed with a seething smile. "The crown is derived from the lives of men sacrificed to attain it. Let us be thankful no further blood has had to be shed."

"Indeed, and as a show of my goodwill," Arius turned and one of his men retreated and returned with a child, thin and quivering, "I have a gift for you."

She couldn't have been older than ten, and though she was decorated in fine clothes with silver pins in her hair, the frantic look in her eyes made it hard to believe she had arrived of her own volition. My blood ran cold as I lunged forward, but Selasi's hand clamped onto my arm. I snapped my glare to him, seeing him shake his head as he urged me back into place. I growled but did so begrudgingly.

Ashire questioned, "You are gifting me a child?"

"I am gifting the prince the Blessing she possesses," Arius clarified.

Safir stiffened.

Arius bent down to the girl. "Now show your Blessing," he commanded her, leaving her to stand alone and quivering in the middle of the throne room.

She barely lifted her terrified gaze to Safir. "F-for you, Y-your Royal Highness." The girl bowed her head, folding her hands over her heart, and began to sing. Her voice was small but grew in volume, and as the sounds echoed from her small body, images took form in the air, acting out the story she told through her song.

Gasps were heard across the throne room as mixes of color and light came together to form figures that looked as tangible as any person. They sprouted wings and feathers while dark clouds formed towards the ceiling, setting the scene for the story that unfolded.

A griffin's nest was enduring the angriest storm ever known. An egg was blown out of its nest by the winds, knocked from its cliff, tumbling further away. The winds, rains, and rivers carried the egg to lands unknown to the griffins. The chick hatched during the storm and suffered the wind and rains beating against its adolescent wings. It learned how to fly despite the storm, developing wings strong enough to withstand the winds. It took flight and scoured the land, in search of its own kind. The storm followed, growing as the griffin grew. A day finally came when the griffin found its original family, but since neither was familiar with the other, the pride rebuked the griffin. At this point, the storm had grown indescribably large and was closing in, but the griffin stayed upon seeing a nest of abandoned eggs. It cast its wings wide and sheltered the eggs. Having endured years of hail and rain, it was able to withstand the storm. Lightning struck the griffin multiple times, but the griffin kept its wings wide. Even as the storm brought its death, the hail had formed so heavily around the griffin that it turned to stone.

For the first time in decades the storm dissipated. There the griffin would stay, and there it would watch over the hatchlings until they became the next great guardians of Walyre.

When the girl finished, the images faded like mist into the air. The griffin, the hatchlings, the epic storm all disappeared. Thunderous applause erupted as Arius stood there smugly. Ashire, however, was transfixed on the girl, refusing to clap. Safir hardly even breathed.

It was grotesque watching yet another child be exploited for their Blessing. If it hadn't been for me taking deep breaths behind Safir, the entire room would have felt the depths of his disgust. The child winced underneath the deafening applause. It was abominable.

"I hope you are pleased, Your Royal Highness," Arius jeered. "I thought she'd provide ample entertainment now you're well enough to engage in public life. I can attest her Blessing is as powerful as the imagination that commands it."

Ashire's eyes seemed glued more to the child than the abhorrent man. I itched to reach for her, but I knew Selasi would restrain me. I trusted Ashire wasn't as callous as to accept a child as a gift. He stood from his throne. "As always, Lord Arius, your kindness is rather unorthodox, but nonetheless, she will be treasured."

To my shock, Ashire gestured the girl to him, and she begrudgingly complied. I could see her quiver as she approached him. His hand reached out to hers, and she placed her small palm within his. He stooped down, whispering something in her ear before urging her towards Emtias, who took the girl in hand.

Ashire stood, assuming a stature befitting of a king. "After being bequeathed such gifts from our most loyal subjects, it feels only right to begin the festivities. Many of you have been gracious enough to offer salutations to my brother, whose dedication to the crown and service to the people is the reason we celebrate this evening." He turned to Safir, who hadn't said a single word since everyone arrived. "Through many years of hardship and extraordinary self-discipline, he's vowed to engage in public proceedings should it please the crown, and I'm certain I'll be a better king for it. So, for tonight, let all laughter, joy, and delight be in the name of my brother. Please, enjoy the festivities!" He clapped his hands and platters of food were rushed forward onto the long, decorated tables, allowing people to gorge their eyes on the feast.

Chatter erupted as Ashire turned to the young girl.

"Selasi, you will take her to Lani first and then, I do not care how busy she is, tell Milfred to fix a plate for her," he commanded.

"You don't intend to keep her as a *present*," I declared. "She's a child."

"Would you prefer I return her to the man who served her to me?" Ashire snapped. He looked down at the girl. "You'll have a much more promising life here than in his care."

"I'll take her to Lani," I offered, wondering if she would be more comfortable with a woman rather than being handed off from one strange man to the next.

"You're to remain by Safir's side. Do not forget the part you're to play here," Ashire ordered. "Selasi, go now."

Selasi bowed and took her hand in his, pulling the girl away from the crowd until she disappeared out of the throne room. Once she left, Ashire sighed. "Perhaps you were right. It was a mistake to invite Arius."

"Maybe not if we've just freed a child from his claws," Safir huffed. "I'm going to need a disgraceful amount of wine to manage the rest of this evening."

"I anticipated such," Emtias interjected while extending goblets of wine to Ashire and Safir that he had snagged from the table adjacent to the throne. "Eve, I'm afraid you'll have to secure your own goblet."

I didn't mind as they downed their wine with grimaces. "Now," Ashire sighed, "remember this is a happy day. We should eat."

We sat at a long table of our own, overlooking the adjacent tables that housed the guests, whose whooping and chortling was deafening. The air tasted smoky from the lit candelabras and overhanging chandeliers but also the smell of crispy pork, the yeasty bread, and sweet pie fillings obliterated my nose. There were multiple suckling pigs on the tables that were steaming and stuffed with fruit. Slice of fresh bread drizzled with icing and embedded with nuts adorned the tables. Rows of pies and puddings were already spilling over people's plates and dripping onto the polished floor. I stopped trying to count how many bottles and casks of wine were constantly moving to refill goblets. I at least tried to indulge myself. My dress hardly let me fill my belly, but I still savored every bite I could.

Safir only took miniscule bites of food, seeming more consumed with scanning the crowd.

"You didn't say much when everyone arrived," I commented, "given that today is for you."

He settled his cutlery on his plate. "Customarily, I would need permission to speak while the king is holding court. I did well enough remaining composed. I hardly minded Ashire speaking on our behalf." He leaned on his elbow to speak into my ear. "How did you find it? The introduction?"

Heat rose in my cheeks, but I dared to lean towards him. "More extravagant than I imagined. Lady Zae understandably caught everyone's eye."

"Not everyone's."

I hoped he didn't notice me shiver in my seat. "I'm more nervous about having to partake in the dancing Emtias tried to teach me." I turned so I could look up into Safir's ember eyes. "I'd hate to disappoint him given the hours he poured into me."

"I'll be sure to pair with you for as many dances as possible this evening in order to spare you from his scorn."

"Your kindness is appreciated."

"Do not mistake my mercy for kindness," he crooned as his eyes flared at me.

I swallowed dryly as the air shifted around us. I forgot about the food and the noise surrounding us. All my senses zeroed in on Safir. I longed to feel closer to him, like when we'd been sparring with my dagger. Closer than being in the same room, closer than breathing the same air, close enough that all he could think about was me. I had never thought I'd want that feeling from a man, and I found myself unafraid of the thought. He clenched his jaw while holding my gaze, as if we were both holding ourselves back.

"Finally!" Selasi plopped himself down at the table beside me so violently it shook the plates. He reached across me to pile his plate high with decadent baked goods. He practically inhaled half of the table.

Even Emtias leaned over and remarked from four seats down, "Must you gorge yourself so savagely?"

Crumbs tumbled from Selasi's lips as he swallowed a mouthful of pastry. "This is the only time I get to eat the best of Milfred's baking!" He reached for seconds and thirds. He was going to be too stuffed to even try dancing.

"Is the little girl okay?" I asked him.

"Her name is Oberia, and she said she felt better whenever the king spoke to her."

"What did he say?"

Selasi leaned towards me and spoke in a hushed tone. "She said he told her, 'I promise, you're safe now.' But don't tell him I told you, can't have the king knowing we're aware he has a heart." Selasi chuckled. "And her eyes were as big as mine when she saw the meal Milfred brought her. That cook makes it her personal challenge to expand people's waistlines. Think of how enormous I would be if she were actually fond of me."

I glanced to Ashire, grumpily nursing his wine, and though his patience was running thin, I couldn't help but feel the slightest bit proud.

Suddenly, a tall presence cast a shadow over me. I looked up to see Zae beaming. Her grey eyes were transfixed on Safir, who sat back in his seat with a smirk.

"Your Royal Highness," she greeted. "I wanted to comment on how remarkably kind the years have been to you. My visit has been long overdue."

Safir grinned, making my gut twist. "If the years have been kind to me, they have been twice as gracious to you, Lady Zae. You don't make it easy for one to forget you."

"Did you try to forget me?" she purred.

I fidgeted in my seat, feeling as if I were a mere ornament on a wall. But Safir gestured towards me. "I have yet to introduce my new advisor, Eve. She has been paramount in ensuring this day came to fruition."

I fought a blush as Zae's eyes finally met mine. "I saw you hiding behind my Lord, and I wondered who this delightful star was. An honor to meet you."

Standing and attempting to appear as a self-assured advisor, I affirmed, "The pleasure is mine. His Royal Highness has told me so much about you."

"One can only hope one lives up to nostalgic stories."

"You exceeded already towering expectations, which I'm told you do daily in Phora."

"Oh, you *are* a gem," she glowed. "I knew it just by the way you held your chin. I insist upon comparing notes regarding His Royal Highness' idiosyncrasies."

Safir looked at the two of us with an audible groan. "I can only hope we'll be far too busy this week for any sort of experiment to be conducted with me as the subject."

"Too late, my lord." Zae had a cocky grin as she glanced to me. "We will reconvene this most fortunate conversation another time." She curtseyed, returning to her own table, but not before throwing a smoldering look at Safir.

"Are you sweating, Lord?" Selasi asked from behind me.

"Please resume your carnage, Selasi," Safir sighed while looking up at me. I resumed sitting in my chair, feeling proud of myself. "Is there any point in asking for you to be kind in your comparison?"

"Do not mistake my mercy for kindness," I quipped while reaching for my goblet of wine.

Safir covered his mouth with his hand to hide a smile. I didn't try to hide mine.

Soon music filled the air from a corner of the throne room where a group huddled around string and wind instruments. My heart beat harder at the thought of reenacting the dances Emtias had spent hours trying to teach me. I wasn't ready to make a fool of myself, especially since I hadn't practiced in a dress.

"Safir," Ashire taunted from his chair. "I believe our guests are waiting for you to open the dance floor." He flashed a devious grin in my direction, yet many people's eyes were on Safir as the music lifted to the roof of the throne room.

Safir scoffed and stood. He said nothing, but he extended his hand to me, drawing every burning gaze to my face. I could only focus on his flaring ember eyes that beckoned me to take his hand into mine, and as I did so, gasps cascaded around us. I had forgotten how forbidden Safir's touch had been, but not to me. Never to me.

His fingers tightened their grip, and he gently pulled us onto the floor. A shaky breath escaped me, but just before he released my hand, I felt a wave of warm affection wash over me as his thoughts transfixed on me solely. It was just he and I.

Safir took his place across from me, holding my gaze as the music shifted tone. I recognized the melody and shuffled to the left while Safir did the same. I returned to my original position, keeping my eyes up like Emtias had told me, and willed my muscles to rehearse the dance by memory. The dress weighed me down, but the momentum of the skirt helped carry me into the next motion, allowing me to flow across the dance floor. Once I realized I had survived longer than I'd thought I would, I found myself giddily twirling beneath hundreds of glowing candles and analytical gazes. It was exhilarating to see Safir watch me, as he had watched me with my dagger, admiring every move I made around him. Our gazes whipped around to find the other's each time we dipped out of view. For once I didn't mind being at the center of a man's attention. I found myself wanting to consume his thoughts because he was consuming mine.

Others joined us on the dance floor as one song led to another, but I didn't feel fatigue. I focused on my breathing as more and more people crowded the space around us. With my back to Safir, his hand flat against my bodice, and my hand wrapped around the back of his neck, we gracefully circled the floor. My chin was tilted toward him as he peered down at me, locking my stare into a trance while guiding me around other spinning dancers. Soon, he spun me to face him, making my heart leap into my throat. He gripped my waist tightly. I placed my hands over his as he hoisted me into the air effortlessly. The entire time I could feel his pride, his happiness, his exhilaration. It was a rare joy I hardly ever sensed from him. That deep-seated sorrow only felt like a whisper in a concert of joyous emotion.

Once the music slowed, he lowered me to the ground and pulled me closer, making my bodice ghost over his chest while I descended. Our eyes remained locked as my feet found the ground beneath me, but Safir didn't release me. Our breaths made the white hair fall away from his burning eyes. We were frozen, and he angled his head towards me. Warmth radiated from his hands and an enthralling emotion grew, drifting over me as his forehead rested against mine.

The music ceased and thunderous applause erupted from the crowd around us. Safir smiled coyly while withdrawing from me and joined the masses in praising the dance. I realized I was straining to take deep breaths within the tight confines of my dress. I didn't know if I was breathless from the dance or from being under Safir's stare. It was more intoxicating than any wine I had ever drunk.

"I believe you've done Emtias proud," he told me as we stepped away from the dance floor.

"I don't think I care," I panted.

Emtias approached me halfway before letting me reach for something to drink. His smile was sly as he whispered, "It seems your dancing ability is wholly dependent upon your partner."

I hoped my blush could be interpreted as being overheated from dancing. "That's plausible," I admitted while glancing over to Safir. He was guzzling his drink as Ashire mumbled something to him.

"There's still a great deal of the evening left. Pace yourself. Remember appearances are one aspect of being an advisor to the crown." Emtias glanced over my head. "Even as we speak."

A small voice chirped from behind me, "Pardon me."

When I whipped around, Lady Tesara stood behind me in all her maternal glory. She held out a cup of wine. "I thought you could use a refreshment. You move so elegantly."

I gladly took the cup. "Thank you— that's very kind." Emtias had already made himself scarce. I took a sip as Tesara beamed at me; her cheeks full of smiles. "Do you like to dance, Lady Tesara?"

She nodded, making her black curls bounce around her face. "Oh, yes, but alas," she rubbed her shapely belly, "dancing will have to wait."

"It seems as though you won't have to wait much longer. You'll grace the dance floor soon."

Tesara sighed, glancing over to Batrum, who had joined Safir and Ashire in conversation. "My sweet husband prefers the company of his books to hosting soirées. He and the king are quite similar in that way. I swear at times that it feels that His Majesty was Lord Batrum's first son, in a way, so eager to mold his mind. I know how his affection for the king is very much like that for his own children."

"I didn't realize they were that close."

"Oh, yes. The king used to visit Xard often when he was younger. My lord even kept a room that was always ready for his visit. It took me ages to convince him to give up that room to one of our four other children. While he's a wealth of knowledge, it hardly presents opportunities to socialize outside of our children. Yet there's, just a few weeks to go. If she's anything like her brothers she'll probably arrive fashionably early, much to my lord's dismay."

"You're so sure you're having a girl?"

"It's merely a mother's wish. I've had four sons, more than enough to secure our house. It's time a little lady graced our family. Daughters are friends you never lose." Tesara smiled sadly while rubbing her belly.

It wasn't hard to hear the somberness in her tone. Though I was a stranger, I couldn't help but want to ease her discomfort. "Perhaps we'll have to host more events here so you can put my dancing to shame."

She confided with a smile, "I would like that very much. Should Lord Batrum pull himself away from his plans for a conservatory, perhaps he'd be more willing to indulge in such endeavors."

"Ah, yes," I hummed while finishing off my cup of wine. "His Royal Highness has reviewed the request. We've discussed options for the project to be self-funded rather than rely upon the purse of the crown."

"Then you should speak with my lord at once."

"No, no, I could use your assistance. We hypothesized that given your excess grain stores you could export ale and with the profits fund the conservatory."

Her eyebrows rose high. "I'll warn you he won't be fond of the idea. Academia and brewing seem to clash."

"Does it matter that much if he'd be able to fund his project?"

"My lord takes great pride in the prestigious reputation of Xard, but I'm not certain how I can be of assistance in this matter."

I shrugged. "Perhaps just plant the idea in his head, make the thought of not going into debt to the crown sweeter than the bitterness of exporting a good he doesn't particularly approve of. Wives are better able to introduce suggestions than advisors or politicians— everyone else is too consumed with wanting credit."

A curious smile formed on her lips. "Quite right. You've given me a healthy dose of thought to ponder."

"And should it succeed, I think a ball should be held in order to celebrate."

"Come now," she giggled. "You're filling me with such prospective glee I'm going to burst."

I smiled at her delight. It was clear she had just wanted a life, or perhaps a friend. "Regardless, I'd like to have more gatherings such as this so we can get to know each other. Honest company is hard to come by."

Tesara's eyes softened. "Truer words haven't been spoken." She reached out and gripped my hand, almost pinching my fingers between her rings. "I look forward to the rest of this week's festivities."

"As do I."

We both curtseyed to the other to go our separate ways. Tesara looked far giddier than when she had first approached me. I finally let myself approach Safir who was leaning against our dinner table while watching the swarm of people dancing, laughing, and shouting.

"Will every night be like this?" I asked.

His head shook. "Dear Vada, no. Most of the noble houses would die out if so. The guests seem on the verge of overindulging themselves as it is."

"Good. I don't think I can manage another night in this dress."

He glanced to me. "Surely one more night wouldn't do a great deal of harm." And he truly looked at me, as if I were someone to be admired rather than something to claim. "Though I do prefer seeing you at ease when you're wearing your typical trousers."

"One more night or so in this embroidered prison may be possible. Do not make me regret it," I teased with an edge of seriousness in my words.

He caught my tone and nodded. "You have my word." He extended his hand to me, and I took it, feeling his utmost certainty, appreciation, and understanding. The feeling made my blood leap in my veins. I had given up thinking of Safir as anything remotely platonic. We had become friends, honest friends during our time. Yet I was enthralled every time his eyes flickered to me, every time his touch lingered, every time he smiled whenever I said his name. It was like I never had to search to be understood. He just did, and I could just be.

Our fingers were still entwined between us, and it made me suddenly aware of how tight that dress was. Yet just as quickly as the sweet moment arose, Zae approached. We dropped our hands to our sides as she beckoned Safir. "Your Royal Highness, I think it rude you haven't given as much attention to your other guests."

I felt a twinge of annoyance as Safir smiled and softly excused himself from my side. I knew it was his job to engage with the other houses. It was the whole reason that night was being celebrated, but it didn't leave me feeling any less empty when he accompanied her on the dance floor. I stayed nearby, focusing onto suppressing Safir's Blessing as Zae's hands trailed across Safir with each move within the dance, every opportunity to brush against him. He didn't exactly recoil from her. Surely he was just being polite. They had a history I wasn't part of, and I couldn't presume that history would suddenly disappear.

"Your nostrils are flaring," Ashire remarked while emerging beside me.

"I'm trying to focus."

"Good. I'm appreciative of your efforts to ensure nothing interferes with my brother's success." The way he said it was dripping with hidden meaning. "Truly, it's our duty to ensure *nothing* interferes, and that includes our own selves."

I stared at him, piecing together what he was implying.

He rolled his eyes. "Your obvious infatuation isn't the same as wanting to see him succeed. Should you distance those two ideas, you'll be doing him a much greater service."

"What are you—"

"You look stunning, by the way," he interrupted. "Enjoy the evening." Ashire brushed past me and disappeared into the sea of people. His words soured my mood even further and almost took my focus away from suppressing Safir's Blessing.

My obvious infatuation? How obvious? I was so busy trying to make sense of his obnoxious words while also maintaining focus on Zae and Safir that I didn't feel another presence approach me. It wasn't until the hairs stand on the back of my neck that I whipped my head around to see Lord Arius standing far too close. He scanned me up and down, like so many men before him had. I felt exposed and more ridiculous than ever in that dress. His presence was one my brain had memorized, signaling me to distance myself, to slip away, but it wasn't going to be so easy there. I had to stay to focus on Safir.

I curtseyed. "Lord Arius," I curtly greeted.

His eyes narrowed. "You've bequeathed an abundance of yourself to the prince tonight. You should invest your interest elsewhere."

"If you don't mind, Lord, I'm fatigued from this evening's dances. I'd appreciate time to recover."

"I'm quite certain you'll live," he remarked while extending his hand to me. "Accompany me."

It wasn't a suggestion.

My very skin felt revolted touching his, and his all-too-tight grip suffocated my fingers as he pulled me onto the dance floor at the opposite end from Safir and Zae.

"Shit," I cursed under my breath. I was going to have to multitask. As the song continued, I tried to maintain the steps while focusing on my breathing.

"Where do you hail from?" Arius asked as we weaved through people. "Your face is not one I'm familiar with, and I'm sure I would be otherwise."

"I'm from here."

"Of course. But how did you come to be so close to the crown?"

I spun about him, wanting to vomit my dinner when his hands latched onto me roughly. "Through my merit alone. Is that so hard to imagine?"

He spun me to face him, so quick my vision blurred before I met his stare. I held my chin high, not forgiving the bastard for wanting to make me feel small. "Not at all. I'm impressed with the prince's taste," he said while licking his lips.

I leapt back, almost ripping myself away from him as we glided between people and met back in the middle. "It's an honor," I panted, "to serve someone worth serving."

Arius scowled, gripping my sides as he lifted me into the air. I swore he was going to throw me clear across the throne room. He yanked me back to the floor, almost making my legs buckle beneath me. "I wondered if that curse of his is what ensnared you to him."

My breath hitched as I pushed against him. Fuck that dance. Fuck him. But he pulled me back and began guiding us through the masses of dancing people. "Now, now. It is not a comment upon your character. I know he can cause great pain as well as pleasure. You can't help being bewitched by him. You know what he can do with that curse."

"You're ridiculous," I seethed, no longer caring to appear cordial. Zae and Safir still danced at the end of the line, and I had to remember to take deep breaths for Safir's sake.

"His mother had people addicted to her touch. He's capable of the same." Arius released me, making me almost tumble backwards across the floor, but I caught myself.

I crossed and weaved around him. "You shouldn't speak of the late queen or the prince this way."

"I'm merely looking out for you, a beguiling girl who clearly isn't looking out for herself." He twirled me beneath him, his stare locked with mine. "Just be vigilant when he's with you. Deceit is innate for House Astana, the driving force for why they have the crown."

"It's hard to believe you have good intentions when it seems like you're seeking retribution for your own house."

We paused as the song began to slow, each resuming our original position across from the other. "I only seek what is worth seeking."

"How do you feel the king will react when I tell him what you've told me?"

We bowed to the other as the song finished its final note. "It is nothing that the king hasn't already heard."

I stood upright. "If your intentions are honest then what do you gain from looking out for me?"

Everyone applauded, dancers smiling and breathlessly reaching for drinks. Arius and I did not move. "I told you. I only seek what is worth seeking." He watched me slyly as he walked past me. "Thank you for the dance and conversation."

My heart pounded in my ears, fingers twitching as I fought the urge to crack my knuckles into his jaw. He spoke the vilest things regarding my dearest friend. People like Arius would always be there to remind Safir of his anguish, and it made me sick.

To add insult to injury, when scanning those around me, I found Zae and Safir had disappeared.

Safir

Zae had pulled me onto the dance floor with vigor. Her shameless pride and delight had always been infectious, and I reveled in her familiar scent and her glowing disposition. Ashire had warned me not to spend the entire evening with Eve, for I was meant to engage with the greater houses invited that night.

Zae made every touch count, every gaze linger. It stirred my memories to the point Zae solely consumed my thoughts.

Almost.

The way Eve had felt within my grasp, so delicate yet incredibly strong, made my hands ache for her. She had been so bold when addressing me that night, as if our friendship had been elevated to a new and captivating status. I wanted her to be bold with me, to trust me that much, to expose parts of her character she kept secret from others. Eve made people want to earn her, made me want to be an ideal version of myself. I hadn't understood how much I wanted to earn her until she had told me with little discretion:

Do not make me regret it.

I had promised her.

"Your Royal Highness," Zae sighed while circling around me, brushing her chest against my back, "I do believe that you are blushing."

I was, but not for the reasons she was discerning. With Eve close by, it was harder for Zae to gauge my emotions. "Overheated, perhaps. I have claimed this dance floor numerous times this evening."

"Yes, that answer would be convenient. But that is not the answer I want." As the music slowed, she bowed before looking up at me with grey hooded eyes. "I missed you. I want to show you something."

"Zae—"

"But it's in my room. You'll have to come with me." She grasped my hand, and suddenly I saw her as I had that night: in that nightdress, beaming while dragging me along. Somehow, even over a decade later, it still felt the same, and I let her pull me into a symphony of nostalgia.

Eve

I twisted and turned to try to find Safir. Hardly anyone had seen him leave, but most of the guests were drunk or falling asleep into the pudding. My heart was pounding in my throat. I hated the way Arius had made me feel as if I was just as trapped in this world as I was in my own. I wanted to feel safe somewhere. I wanted to feel safe somehow.

I wanted Safir.

And as minutes passed by, I began to lose my composure. The corset felt like it was digging into my ribs and making me strain to breathe. I clawed at the thick fabric. The wine and food soured in my belly as I looked around at wasted nobles who were mostly strangers to me. And then there was Arius standing across the throne room, piercing me with his vulgar stare. I could see, just as with Hunter, he was enjoying seeing me squirm.

"Fuck," I wheezed while wiping sweat from my brow.

"Eve?" Selasi reached to steady me with his brows furrowed. "Are you unwell? You seem distressed."

"Where is Safir? I can't find him."

"I don't know. Can I fetch you some water?"

"Where's Lady Zae?"

Selasi paused before answering reluctantly, "I-I'm not sure."

I swallowed dryly. "I think I should retire for the night. I've had enough dancing. Can you send Maisy to my room to get me out of this damn thing?"

He nodded. "Of course. I'll accompany you."

"I'd prefer to walk alone."

Selasi hardly let me take two steps before asking, "Eve? Has someone upset you?" He glanced to Arius. "Did something happen?"

My stoic look wasn't as impressive as I thought. Even I didn't believe the words coming out of my mouth when I said, "Everything is fine." And then I let my feet carry me away.

I went towards the north corridor so I could take the staircase directly to my room. My heart was burning in my chest, and I struggled to breathe, dodging chortling people in their silk suits and powdered faces. What was once glamorous had become torturous, and the whole time I could feel Arius' eyes glued to me. How could I have let one stranger ruin a perfect evening? How could he have that power over me?

Perhaps because there were versions of him in every dimension, every reality, every time, and that dread felt inescapable. I couldn't even step into an alternate world without versions of Hunter finding me. The only time I had reprieve was when I was with Safir. The only sanctuary I had whenever their selfish hands pried at my body was thinking of Safir. If I couldn't find him then I needed to leave.

The noise faded behind me as I relished the stillness on the staircase leading to the second floor. I caught a glimpse of myself in the mirror, my hair in disarray, my chest rising and falling, my eyes wide, and hands trembling while grasping my bodice. No wonder Selasi had come to my aid. I looked like I was having a nervous breakdown. My pace increased as I ignored the rest of the mirrors.

Just as I could see my door, I heard something that made my entire body freeze on the spot. I broke out into a sweat as my stomach plummeted into the depths of my core. I willed myself to run, but I couldn't move, even holding my breath at the sound of heavy breathing, rustling, and moans emanating from Zae's room.

My eyes squeezed shut. The sounds grew louder and bolder. Images formed in my mind of the two of them, his thoughts and touch wholly consumed by her. She would never deserve it. She would never appreciate his care and his touch the way I…

I halted my thoughts abruptly, cursing at how stupid I sounded. I didn't know for certain who was behind that door and given Zae's flirtatious nature it wouldn't have surprised me if she had many lovers. That conclusion made more sense than—

"Oh, Saafiiir!"

A long, drawn-out moan escaped the room, and my entire body winced. Tears stung my eyes as I dashed away from those abhorrent sounds. Even after I threw myself into my room and slammed the door shut, I could still hear them within my mind.

I felt ridiculous. I felt stupid for thinking we were ever likened by our disposition, our emotion, our pain, by our admiration for each other. It couldn't have felt crueler how one-sided that admiration was. Sobs choked me as I remained trapped in that corset. I was willing to cut myself out if I could have reached my dagger on my thigh, but there were too many damn layers to that dress! I tore off fingernails trying to claw my way out of that fabric prison. I couldn't breathe. I was going to die in that stupid dress, and I couldn't breathe!

"Eve!" Maisy burst into my room. "What's happened?"

"Maisy," I sobbed. "Get me out of this thing. Get me out! I can't breathe. I can't—"

Maisy frantically went to work undoing the lace restraints on my dress and corset. I sobbed until the last lace was pulled, and I could suck in a sharp breath. Maisy wrapped her arms around me and slowly lowered me to the ground. I shook and heaved into her embrace, grieving the loss of my newfound happiness.

Safir

Zae pulled me into her room by both hands, and I felt dazed by the reenactment of our first night together. Yet I couldn't help but feel a spasm of guilt. Zae sensed this, seeming to think it a challenge as a wicked smile graced her lips. How she still had so much vigor, I couldn't comprehend. While other heads of houses aged with the responsibility, Zae seemed to blossom. She yanked me onto her balcony.

The night air cooled my face from winds cascading down the mountain tops. Zae picked up her chin to the night sky. "Do you see?"

I peered up and grinned with nostalgia. A full moon cast its light over the valley, highlighting every hidden crevice. It illuminated my friend even further as she hummed while hugging my side. "Do you still think of me when you see it?"

"Of course. I think of you and the moon as kindred spirits."

"How so?"

"You both have a very dependable light about you. You make others want to search for beauty in the darkness," I murmured, seeing deep, grey eyes transfixed upon me. I had seen that look years prior, and I knew what it meant. "And you both come and go as you must."

I withdrew from her balcony, stepping back into the warmth of her room instead. I could feel her shameless gaze still fixated on me, but I didn't tempt myself to look back.

"Do you find me so different, now I'm head of my house?"

"Quite the opposite. Honestly, I was happily surprised to see you hadn't changed."

"Then why won't you look upon me as you once did?"

I turned to see her directly in front of me. There was an air of experience about her, making her stand confidently. Her voice was bolder as well, perhaps from her years of instilling order and inspiring loyalty in her people. It was almost imperious.

I sighed while leaning against her dresser. "Because we are in different chapters of life now. We cannot play like we only have each other. I've had to depend on others while you were in Phora."

Her mouth morphed into small frown. "Do you dislike me because I stayed in Phora? Because I chose to run my house alone?"

"No, of course not," I contended, reaching out to her to reassure of my feelings. She took my hand into hers. "I could never fault you for finding where your soul belongs."

"I find you much different. You're more self-assured. There's a greater sense of serenity within you than I could have ever hoped to see."

"It seems as though we've both grown into ourselves."

"But without the other. I longed for you to step out of the shadows, but I can't help but regret not being the one to help you do so. Is that selfish to say?"

She was still gripping my hand, peering up at me. Her lips remained parted with the last word that had fallen from her tongue. Those grey eyes were darting from my gaze to my mouth, her body flush against mine. I swallowed. "You do yourself an injustice if you think you aren't part of me."

Suddenly her lips were pressed to mine. Her hands weaved into my hair while she released sultry moans into the night. Immediately, my body wanted to react. I was waiting for the thrill I had known; the intoxicating feel of melting into her. But my arms remained braced against her dresser. Her lips felt familiar, like being welcomed into a long-forgotten home. If anything, the feeling made me more nostalgic than aroused. I hadn't known the last time I saw her would be the last time I would kiss her, hold her. Her touch had been the only one I had known for so long. There had been a time where she'd embodied all my hope, but Eve—

Do not make me regret it.

My heart stalled in my chest.

I had promised her. I wanted to earn her, and that thought left me still as a corpse against Zae. I couldn't begin to indulge in Zae's advances because it wasn't her touch I craved.

Zae froze just as I had and peered up at me wide-eyed. "It is not me you're thinking of. I can sense it."

"Zae..."

She released me as if I had burned her and took two steps back, flushed and breathing heavily. "Are you thinking of *her*? Your little advisor?"

"You will speak of her with greater respect."

A heavy silence hung in the air between us. And then Zae did something I didn't expect. She smiled.

"Oh, Safir!" she squealed. "I could feel it! Have you given your soul to someone? Did I not say you would—"

"You're making assumptions."

Zae's head shook. "No, no. I see you perfectly. I saw how you looked at her."

"Currently, she's merely my advisor. There is no other arrangement."

"And I see how she looks at you. She would give herself to you if she knew."

My mouth ran dry as I struggled for words, eventually finding them. "If you really thought this then why lure me here?"

She waved me off while fanning herself to cool her blush. "I did not lure you anywhere. You followed me, just as you used to. If you had such feelings for this girl, why did you kiss me? I sense your confliction."

"I— you advanced onto me!"

She giggled. "I will say, I haven't let myself be that selfish for a long time. You're one of the few people I trust myself with. Now why didn't you my resist advances?"

"I …" I leaned back against the dresser with a huff, suddenly feeling as foolish as I had as a child. "I missed you, Zae." I truly had. I hadn't realized how hungry I was for another friend before Eve came along and brought beauty and laughter with a grace and a humility that would have even been beyond Zae. "You were my only friend the last you were here, and I wasn't aware that was the last time I would see you."

"Saf …"

"I apologize for indulging in your advances. I think I was looking for a proper conclusion to the relationship we had rather than having it concluded via letter."

"If I could have done it differently I would have."

"I know."

She reached her hand up to caress my cheek. I didn't flinch. "You lost a prospective wife, but not a friend, my dear Safir. I am remorseful I didn't allow you to bid farewell to the former." She placed her other hand on the other side of my cheek. "If you cannot have me as a wife, would you still have me as a friend?"

I felt a weight lift from my shoulders I hadn't been aware I was carrying. A sigh escaped me as I wrapped my arm around Zae, pulling her into a chaste embrace. She buried her face in my shoulder as I replied, "Thank you for not being afraid all those years ago."

"I would have been a good wife, you know. I would have tried."

"I know." I rested my chin on top of her head. "I wasn't lying when I said you are very much a part of me."

"But I am just *a* part of you now, not the *greatest* part of you, not anymore. That is a good thing." She clung to me, and it dawned on me that it was not just I who needed a proper conclusion. "I may never know love for a man, but being with you is the closest I've come to reaching it."

She withdrew, though a stray tear escaped her eye. Zae chuckled while flicking the dangling charm in my ear. "Well then, I bid you goodnight, Your Royal Highness. I look forward to our friendship blossoming throughout the rest of my stay."

"As do I." If it hadn't been for her, I wouldn't have been the kind of man who could've been a friend to Eve. As I left her room and ventured to mine, I couldn't help but feel lighter than I had in years. It was as if part of my heart had been liberated and was more open to whatever force was willing to fill it.

As I collapsed onto my own bed in a heap of exhaustion, I wondered what would fill the newfound void within my soul. I recalled the feeling of Eve in my grasp. It felt like a divine privilege to have her that close to me. I couldn't help but wonder if we were on the precipice of a great happiness together. I replayed our dance over and in my thoughts until I faded into a slumber, a smile left on my lips.

Eve

Sleep never came for me. Not for one second.

I lay amongst piles of heavy fabric with my eyes burning from staring up at my canopy. Next to me, Maisy slept with my hand clasped in hers. If it hadn't been for her, I would have sobbed myself sick. She never asked what happened. She didn't interrogate me for details. She only remained there. My thumping sense of stupidity coursed through me every time I recollected the sounds Safir and Zae had made. And I physically felt Arius' words:

Deceit is innate for House Astana, the driving force for why they have the crown.

In my memory, he said it with a slithering tongue and venom dripping in his voice. It would have given him great joy to know I was even considering his words. But Safir hadn't promised me anything other than healing, meals, and shelter. He hadn't professed any sort of affection to me, not aloud anyway. But I swore that night I'd felt something through his touch a powerful emotion growing from within him, and it had been for me. I had sworn it must have been for me. He couldn't have just fabricated such a beautiful feeling, could he? Would he really be capable of creating emotions just to manipulate me into staying? He wasn't his brother, and I didn't want to believe he was the creature Arius painted him as. Safir had always been afraid of being seen as a monster. Was he capable? Yes. But would he ever? No. Still, the hurt remained. The hurt of being made to feel like an idiot by someone who was supposed to feel safe.

I sat up in bed, which stirred Maisy. "You should eat something," was all she said, and she pulled me out of bed. I threw on my usual gym clothes, refusing to confine myself to a corset ever again. It was still early enough in the morning that the sun's rays scarcely cast light through the windows of the palace. I was glad to see the sun. I'd thought morning was never going to arrive.

Maisy dragged my sleep-deprived body down to the kitchen which was awake and lively. Milfred took one look at me over her pile of pounded dough before she patted a seat next to her.

"Here, love." She placed a plate of pastry in front of me. "Your heart looks empty, but your belly won't be when I'm done with you."

I sniffed, letting my head fall onto her rounded shoulder amongst her frizzy hair before I lifted the sweet pastry to my mouth. I could hardly taste it. I ate, nonetheless. A small girl slept on top of sacks of flour in a corner— the girl who had been given to Ashire by Arius. She was so still that for a second, I thought she was a corpse.

"Don't fret about the wee babe. She's been sleeping since she finished eating. You won't disturb her." Milfred's great arm wrapped around my shoulder and held me there. "You're going to be fine. Maybe not today or tomorrow, but each day is an opportunity for something better."

It was kind. More kindness than I deserved in a world that wasn't mine. My attachment to Safir had made it feel like I had a place in that realm, but there was a real world just a few hundred feet away that needed me more. I was only playing a part.

"Tell the prince I'm ill and wish to be left alone today," I told Maisy while walking out into the garden.

"Are you coming back?"

Maisy hadn't asked me that in months. I glanced back before I took the final step through my portal. "I'll try."

With one step, I was back in the world I knew and understood. I marched forward, trying to put as much distance as I could between me and my idiocy.

The air was heavy, thick with humidity. It was grey and overcast with a few scattered raindrops. I walked through dull streets and alleys, not a speck of beauty to be found, but somehow that made it feel more real, more transparent. At least the ugliness was honest. The city wasn't trying to hide its grotesque corners and underbelly. I never would have thought I would have preferred it to Walor.

I walked until I found myself in Nicky's room. His eyes flickered to me. His eyebrows furrowed with confusion.

"Eve? What's happened?"

My composure fell apart as I crawled into his bed and lay next to him, buried my face into the crook of his neck and sobbed. It came in waves, each more powerful than the last.

"I'm here," he rasped against me. "I'm sorry … I'm so sorry … that you're hurting." Even my paralyzed brother took it upon himself to comfort me from his hospital bed.

"This isn't what I thought it would be, Nicky. I really did think I was happy, that I could be happy. But now—" a sob caught in my throat, "I don't think I know how."

He smiled sadly. "I know how that feels … but Eve, you wouldn't … be like this if you hadn't … felt happy for one moment … That's worth hanging onto."

I lay there, lurching at the idea I had thought I had found someone I could be content with besides my brother. It was only what I deserved for daring to think I belonged anywhere other than next to Nicky.

Safir

"Still feeling ill? Are you certain?" I asked Selasi.

"That's what Maisy told me, Lord."

"I'm not certain what to do. I can't engage in tonight's activities if she isn't present." Most of the day had been spent recuperating from the night before, as many guests had suffered the consequences of too much wine. As the afternoon was fading, the palace was beginning to stir. Dinner was going to be served with a musical ensemble of players from the city. I sighed and rubbed my eyes, trying to think of a solution. "Why can't Lani heal her from her ailment?"

Selasi cleared his throat. "Perhaps it isn't an ailment Lani can easily mend."

"That's absurd. The engagements last night must have been rather overwhelming if she's this ill."

"Yes, Lord," he said plainly.

I peered up at him, allowing my skepticism to pulsate through the air. Selasi's eyes darted to the ground. "Selasi? Is there information that you are withholding from me?"

He paused before replying, "Eve appeared quite distressed after dancing with Lord Arius. She retired to her room soon after."

I stiffened. "With Arius? Vada only knows what he said to her. Why did I not see this?"

Selasi's eyes still could not rise to meet mine. "I believe you had just exited the dance floor with Lady Zae."

"I see," I muttered, a wave of remorse washing over me as I thought of leaving Eve alone in a room full of aristocratic drunks, worst of all Arius Rarke. "I was temporarily occupied."

"Of course," Selasi remarked with a notable edge of judgement. "I'm aware Lady Zae can be persuasive."

"Nothing questionable occurred last night. It was merely two friends establishing an understanding."

"I do not doubt it, Lord."

"Perhaps I should go and speak with her."

"Perhaps you should."

"She's here!" Maisy announced while bursting through my door. "I mean, she's ready. Eve is downstairs with the guests, waiting. She's waiting."

"Was there any insinuation Eve wasn't present?" I asked while rising from my chair.

"Of course not!" she yipped, throwing glances to Selasi. "It'd be best for you to hurry, Lord. His Majesty is waiting for you as well before dinner begins."

I heeded her warning, though not before throwing skeptical glances their way. As I traveled down the stairwell to join the others for dinner, I recalled the dancing we'd shared, feeling Eve's closeness, seeing her beam for me in that dress. It made me ache to see her again.

As I emerged into the dining hall, the room filled with lit candelabras and a splendid feast, my chest tightened. She was standing next to Lady Tesara, who was rambling to her newfound friend. Eve did not appear intrigued. She stood with stiff posture and clouded eyes. When she looked to me there wasn't a hint of joy— if anything she looked pained. I couldn't help but notice she was wearing trousers with her leather vest, plain and discreet, in stark contrast to the gorgeous ensemble she had worn the night prior.

I looked at her questioningly, but Ashire emerged beside me, dark circles under his eyes and wine in hand. "Remind me to never again try to out-drink Zae's advisor. That bastard's liver must be begging for the sweet release of death."

Emtias arrived and stole the goblet from his hand. "Perhaps had you been busier dancing you wouldn't have to worry about the wine."

"I was reliving old times with my uncle, and my brother danced enough for the both of us. Thankfully, Eve was able to relinquish you enough for you to engage in your duties."

"Yes, thankfully," I agreed absentmindedly, watching as Eve excused herself from Lady Tesara and made her way to my side. She hardly even looked at me, though she was taking deep breaths to suppress my Blessing.

"Kind of you to finally join us, Eve," Ashire chastised from the other side of me. "I take it you've recovered from your ailment?"

"Yes, Lord," she replied.

We stared in shock at her quiet demeanor. "Dear Vada, she must have been near death," Emtias simpered, but Eve did not appear amused and neither did I. Surely she could feel me watching her, trying to discern any hint of what she was thinking.

"Eve?"

"Safir."

"I see we will not have the privilege of seeing you in your dress tonight."

She cleared her throat while holding her chin high. "It wasn't worth it."

Her words were poignant, and she said them with such ferocity it stung. Her hands were clenched as she grimaced next to me. Whatever she was feeling was obviously a raging storm. It was even more painful to think I was the cause of it.

I reached for her. "Eve …"

"My dear friends!" Ashire's voice rang out, making me drop my hand to my side. "Last night's festivities were such a success that we'll continue tonight in our merriment. May we dine and enjoy each other's company further before the actors arrive. Enjoy!"

People cheered while taking their seats, piling their plates high. Ashire departed, sitting at the head where he could be most easily admired. I was to take my place next to him, but I hesitated. Eve had already taken steps to her seat, but I reached out for her, desperate to clutch her hand.

When my fingers found hers, she did something she had never done with me before: she flinched. Her sapphire gaze whipped around to mine, filled with ire. She did not recoil from me, refusing to make a scene, but her hand was limp in mine. "What?" she growled.

I dropped her hand like a hot coal. "Apologies."

"Don't worry about it." Eve paced across the room, but instead of sitting across from my seat, she took a seat beside Lady Tesara, much to our guests' delight. Lady Tesara beamed, although Eve couldn't feign similar enthusiasm as Lord Arius claimed the seat next to her. She glanced back at me, taking deep breaths, as if to show me she was still suppressing my Blessing.

It was as if she knew exactly how to drive a knife into my chest. I was grateful she was there, because everyone would have been in fits if they could sense my confused turmoil as I sat next to Ashire.

Eve's seating choice hadn't escaped my brother either, as he glanced between the two of us.

"Remember to focus on the reason behind this dinner," he murmured to me. "You'll have time to repair whatever fracture this is, but you must continue to engage with the noble houses while they're here."

I nodded, though hardly mindful of his words. Lord Arius bent far too close to Eve's ear and whispered something that made her wince. Yet she looked up at him and nodded, seeming to agree with whatever vile thing he had said to her. I had never wished for Eve to bludgeon a man to death more than in that moment.

"Your Royal Highness," came a voice from across the table. Zae had taken the seat originally meant for Eve. Her hair flowed around her bare shoulders as she descended into her chair. "It seems Lady Tesara fancies your advisor as a companion. Wouldn't you say, Lord Batrum?"

Lord Batrum had only been one seat over but nodded in agreement while plucking a peach from the pile of fruit. "Quite so. Forging relations can be quite hard when being buried in books. The king and I share such a fault. I know my dear wife is quite thankful to have made such a fast friend."

"Of course," I said. "It is unsurprising. Lady Tesara is splendid company and Eve is…very agreeable."

"Agreeable?" the grotesque voice of Lord Arius piped. "Yes, I think I concur."

What had he said to her? How did he know her well enough to understand how agreeable she was? I fought the temptation to reach for the dagger concealed in my boot.

Ashire reached out to my arm. "Safir, control yourself."

"I was informed you had a proposition for our excess grain supplies in Xard, Your Royal Highness," Lord Batrum added, clearly oblivious to my growing outrage. "Would you care to elaborate?"

I knew the idea had been Eve's, but obviously she had been trying to be strategic for my sake. "Yes, of course, uncle."

Arius continued to whisper to Eve throughout the evening. She hardly appeared enthusiastic and busied herself speaking to Lady Tesara. It was an exhausting night discussing diplomacy with Lord Batrum and Zae. Occasionally, Emtias and Ashire attempted to lighten my load, both aware where my attention was drawn to. It helped that Ashire and Batrum were never in short supply of reminiscing about my brother's trips to Xard as a child. Any stranger would have mistaken Batrum's admiration for Ashire as fatherly affection.

The mood did not improve when dinner concluded, and the actors put on their musical for Ashire. It was a clever comedy that had most of the guests giggling, but I dared not muster a smile and neither did Eve. She maintained her cold disposition throughout the rest of the night, only excusing herself once everyone had retired, even Ashire and Emtias.

"Are you sure?" I asked her, hoping we could take a walk in the garden like she usually desired.

"I fulfilled my part, and no one sensed your Blessing," she stated plainly.

I almost recoiled. Yes, hindering my Blessing was her original purpose but surely she understood that was a mere fraction of why I wanted her near. "Eve," I said softly, standing from my chair to slowly approach her. "You've always spoken so transparently with me. It's something I've always appreciated. Can you not do that now?"

She stood there frozen while keeping her eyes to the ground. How I would have loved to see her sapphire gaze. It would have been a comfort. "I want to go to bed, Safir." The way she said my name, she did not say it with a smile. I hadn't realized how much I had come to depend on it.

Eve departed the dining room, brushing past my hand that was already reaching out for her. I would have preferred her argue or scream at me than to leave me in silence. I would scarcely have time to devote to repairing whatever fracture had occurred in our friendship until the guests had left the palace, but I felt certain it involved Lord Arius' grotesque presence.

Eve

Overhearing Safir and Zae had been a wake-up call. Nicky only desired so much time left on this Earth, and I needed to focus on him. What tasted most bitter was knowing I had indulged in Walyre more than I should have. The temptations and mysteries of that realm made it easier to forget what absolute shit my reality was, and that was why I had never told Safir about Nicky. I had wanted a world where reminders of my pain wasn't lurking around every corner. That felt unforgivable. I had lived in a fantasy, and it felt like the time to let it go.

Earlier today, standing in the forest steps away from the portal, I'd pondered what made me return. Maybe it was what Nicky had told me, that I had been happy at one point and promised I'd be present for Safir to succeed in his debut, but that was all I planned to owe him.

I'd promised myself this was my last week in Walyre.

Seconds after I stepped into Walyre, Maisy emerged flailing in disbelief, joy, and panic. I couldn't help but feel too embarrassed to put that dress back on, to look the part but ultimately be made the fool. If Safir wanted company he could seek out Zae.

She seemed comfortable sitting close to him anyhow while I had Arius infecting my ear.

"Were you not deceived, my dear?" he asked.

His tone made me cringe. He was clearly too satisfied with himself at the sight of me avoiding Safir, but I nodded, nonetheless. I'd thought I had become Safir's close friend and maybe someone even important. I had wanted to be important to him. But whenever I recalled the sounds those two had made, and the way Zae had said his name, I couldn't help but wince. It made me feel as if I were a mere distraction from his Blessing.

"The week will be long. I suggest you brace yourself," Arius warned closely in my ear.

I refused to lean on him for advice. Even if I felt used by Safir, I had no doubt Arius' agenda was sinister. Safir caught my eye every now and then, but I returned my attention to Lady Tesara, who happily regaled me with the stories of her children. She knew all their stories, even the date each child lost their first tooth. I had never believed a person could be born to be a parent, but she was. I would have even believed it was her Blessing.

But she wouldn't tell me her Blessing.

Batrum, Arius, Zae and Tesara had joined us strolling through the gardens to fill the time but to also flex on the grandness of Walor Palace. "It isn't lady-like." She blushed. "Though my husband found it beautiful."

My curiosity was piqued. "What is it?"

She lingered behind as the rest of the party walked through the gardens. I took deep breaths to try to steady Safir's Blessing from afar as Tesara whispered to me, "Another time, my dear. It will give us something to discuss when you visit Xard. And then you may tell me yours."

I hadn't told anyone what my presence did to Blessings, not thinking of it as a Blessing but a side effect from being in a separate reality. I didn't care to talk about it and respected Tesara's request, despite never intending to visit Xard.

We arrived on the veranda to have lunch. A lighter spread was prepared so we could look out at the fountains and gardens. The breeze was light and the heat from the sun was alleviated by a few clouds passing through the mountains. Everyone ate slowly, only I struggled to do so when I noted the small girl who had been gifted to Ashire, Oberia, was serving us.

She appeared less terrified than days prior, but she threw nervous glances to Lord Arius, who acknowledged her presence with a sly smile. "I see you're not utilizing my gift to its fullest potential."

Ashire frowned.

"Show your king another story," Arius commanded while reaching for his goblet.

"I prefer to distract myself with the company of those around me," Ashire informed him, "rather than images drawn up from a child, as magnificent as they are."

"Perhaps you do not appreciate my generosity?"

"Perhaps you do not respect your king's wishes," Emilias hissed.

As Oberia refilled my goblet, I fumbled my hands and the wine splattered onto the girl's dress. She yelped and uttered hundreds of apologies as I stood from my chair. "Well, no need to let the poor thing serve in wet clothes. Return to Milfred and change." I hoped to Vada she would take her sweet time. There was the slightest hint of a smile on her lips as she bowed before scurrying away. "No need to debate something that is no longer an issue," I sighed while sitting back in my chair. "Besides, I'm quite capable of pouring my own wine."

Ashire chuckled while Safir snickered across from me. I glanced to him; fighting being pleased. Half of me ached for that smile while the other half was irritated by it.

"As much as I cherish children," Tesara added, twirling a curl around her finger. "I yearn for the company of adults. I much prefer this arrangement."

"I have no doubt you're raising the next generation of great leaders for the kingdom," Zae piped up. "Someone must do it."

Lord Batrum smiled. "We believe so, but it is a shame they will not be able to intertwine with your descendants, Lady Zae. Think of how agreeable our grandchildren would be."

"I cannot say such a life hasn't tempted me once or twice, but it has yet to win me over."

Arius leaned onto the dining table. "That seems to be a slight directed towards you, Your Royal Highness."

Safir held his hands up in defense. "I never claimed to be the perfect man."

"The prince was *more* than tempting," Zae coyly confessed. "But a different path was chosen for me. There is still much time left for me to worry about such endeavors."

I wanted to vomit.

"Now enough of exposing my life. Your Majesty, are you not troubled with producing an heir?" Zae asked boldly while sitting back in her chair.

Emtias' expression appeared similar to mine in that moment. Neither of us moved. Ashire finished off his wine. "I forget how free your tongue is, my lady. We're quite similar: I've yet to be tempted."

Zae did what I dreaded most: she directed her attention to me. I could hear the smile in her voice. "And Eve? As His Royal Highness said, you're rather agreeable. Do you ever intend to marry?"

The entire table fell quiet, and my heart pounded in my ears. I knew Safir's ember gaze was boring a hole into my head from across the table. I hadn't truly let myself look into his eyes for days, knowing my resolve would crumble if I did, but luckily Zae's tactlessness was a worthy distraction. I looked at her with my chin held high. "You said it perfectly: a different path was chosen for me," I retorted with too much ire.

Regardless of whether she was from a noble house, that didn't give her the right to pry.

"Dear Vada, my lady," Emtias sighed. "Do you intend to gut every poor soul at this table?"

"I have yet to be gutted," Arius whined.

Emtias whipped his head around. "It would be an honor to rectify that." "Emtias," Ashire said cautiously.

"One's prospects for finding a wife dwindle when one has to spend the majority of adolescence in hiding." Arius threw a scowl to Ashire.

"Thanks to the mercy of your current king, as you are sitting before him, that excuse no longer suffices," Emtias hissed.

Arius grinned. "Then what is your excuse, Fae?"

"My commitment is to the crown above all else."

"We're all aware of how admirable your commitment is to the *crown*."

Tesara squirmed as she stood. "The child tends to stir after I eat. Would anyone care to join me for a promenade?"

"That honor would belong to me," Batrum sighed while standing from his chair. "Perhaps it would be best to retire before continuing to engage in such vigorous conversation."

The choir of aristocrats, too tired after eating their light lunch, all agreed to return to the palace, leaving behind half-eaten meals I didn't doubt would be thrown out. Usually, I didn't mind indulging in that life, even letting myself feel grateful. But knowing my time there was coming to an end, I was able to see with a bit more humbled clarity.

"Eve?" Safir's low voice spoke from behind me.

I wondered if he was trying to reach for me as he used to. I craved his touch, to be the one he never needed to be afraid of, the one he shared his Blessing with.

"Could we talk when we return to the palace? Alone?" he asked with his tone pleading.

Sucking in a deep breath through my nose, I turned around but kept my gaze to the floor. I knew he was mere inches from me, and in that moment, I could feel the heat emanating from his body. My eyes closed while I breathed in his scent of fresh pines and crisp mountain air. It used to be such a comfort.

"Please," he breathed. I could feel his breath against my forehead.

I knew if I opened my eyes in that moment my composure would have been demolished.

"Eve?" a new voice came from afar.

My eyes shot open, seeing Safir's burning ember gaze. I whipped around to see Lord Arius looking at me expectantly. "Join me for our walk back to the palace. I would appreciate a more delicate presence."

As usual, he hardly asked and more commanded. It took a monumental amount of energy to pull myself away from Safir's warmth, his scent, his gaze. I swore I could even feel his hand reaching for me.

Safir

I would have burned that veranda to the ground if it meant I held Eve in my presence for one moment longer. Every moment I reached her we were pulled away in opposite directions. I had to walk briskly and engage in conversation with Lord Batrum and Lady Zae as if it weren't gnawing at my soul. Lord Batrum was more concerned with taxes upon his new export of ale than was his heavily pregnant wife, who waddled her way back to the palace.

While Ashire and Emtias settled with Lord Batrum regarding taxes, Zae clung to me, glancing behind her where I knew Eve and Arius were trailing behind. Despite being obviously cross with me, Eve maintained hindering my Blessing, even at a distance. Her range had expanded over that one week, and it didn't go unnoticed by Zae.

"So that is why she became such a good pet for you? I could hardly discern your feelings until now. You've become quite good at concealing them as well," she mused.

"I ask that you keep your observations to yourself. She doesn't need to be exposed to those who would take advantage of her presence."

Zae snorted and looked at me dubiously. "Like your brother?"

I grimaced. "We both stood to benefit from this arrangement, at least in the beginning. However …" I looked over my shoulder to see Lord Arius dangerously close to my advisor, and a surge of irritation coursed through me. Zae released my arm with a hiss. "Apologies," I muttered. "I think perhaps the trials that have come with my debut have soured her disposition towards me."

"Hmm, that can be easily mended with time." Zae leaned into me. "I wonder if she's wounded by my closeness to you, Saf."

I sighed while turning to her coy smile. "If you're correct you're being awfully cruel to her, and I'll play no part in it."

"But it proves I am correct. See for yourself."

We both turned to see Selasi fetching Eve, who looked irate to say the least. Her jaw was tight, and chin held high. I couldn't make out their conversation, but it ended with Selasi escorting Eve back to the palace, which left my Blessing exposed. Eve's sapphire gaze flickered to me for a single moment, making my chest swell with anticipation but then she looked away.

"It seems you are wounded as well. Has she yet to give herself to you?" Zae asked, as ever with little tact.

"My dear friend, you must know our antics cannot continue this way. We must outgrow them."

"You said you liked that I hadn't much changed."

"Yes, but as you observed, I have." She stilled, her mouth forming a slight frown, and casted her hardened gaze to the ground. "We will always be friends and allies, Zae. And though I think you overestimate Eve's attachment to me; I don't wish you to cause her any discomfort."

"I do not wish to do anything of the sort. But Safir, promise me you will not give your soul to her, not until you know she will give hers in return. You deserve that much." Her face was a mix of reluctance and dismay. "In the meantime, I shall consort with His Majesty regarding his outposts heckling my traders."

"You can always discuss such matters with me as well, Zae." Again, I saw her reluctance, and it struck a chord of annoyance within me. "If you truly wanted to help me step out from the shadows, you would do so by helping me shoulder some of my brother's burden."

She smiled. "Yes, of course. I merely look to your brother's experience for guidance, something you will attain in time."

"Something I can only do if I'm trusted by my subjects. Do you not trust me?"

"With my life, Your Royal Highness." Zae bowed and excused herself, seeking out Ashire while I stood there looking back to where I had last seen Eve. How would I ever grow, become what I was meant to be, if I didn't have the trust of those around me?

Arius stared at me, unmistakably smug. The gnawing in my soul grew. I needed the trust of my subjects, the ability to perform my duties, and faith to be able to do so. But how to do it? I remained behind, wondering and worrying so much that my thoughts scattered, like a rockslide with no force to stop it.

In that moment, I longed for Eve.

Eve

Arius spoke about himself as much as Tesara spoke about her children, only he was a less endearing conversationalist. Every question he asked and every word out of his mouth had a purpose. It was like talking to Ashire but astronomically worse. Each question served him somehow, which was why I elected to be cautious despite being willing to give up that realm within days.

"You haven't been in service to the crown very long," he said. "How did they procure you?"

"I found them, in a way," I responded coolly.

We paused momentarily when Arius drew his attention away from me and pointed at the swordsmen posted in front of my transparent portal in the forest. "There are two guards stationed in such a remote part of the courtyard. Why is this?"

Think of something.

"A colony of wasps was found burrowing underground. The king stationed the guards to prevent guests from wandering too far into the wasps' territory."

"Why not just douse it?"

"He only wanted to disturb the ground once everyone left."

Arius didn't seem satisfied with my spontaneous lie. His brow furrowed as he took a step forward. "I wonder …"

I wrenched his arm and pulled him back along our walking path, gripping him with fleeting patience. "You ask a lot of questions without giving me a chance to inquire about you." Surely he would be more interested in talking about himself than investigating the courtyard.

He scoffed as his focus diverted. "There is little to tell that isn't already common knowledge."

"You mentioned you spent the majority of your adolescence in hiding?"

"That is hardly a secret."

"But you're obviously not in hiding now. You have your home, your rank, your luxuries. Why?"

"Because of the *king*," he practically spat. "Under the reign of King Muire and King Ronire my family hid in alleyways and hovels for fear of being persecuted. House Astana was as paranoid as they were ambitious after usurping the crown from my grandfather. However, when King Ronire died, King Ashire lifted the penalty from my family. We were able to emerge from the filthy streets and had our house restored."

I paused, dumbfounded. "That's very kind of the king."

"Do not think I am standing here out of the kindness of his heart. I am only alive for as long as I serve him. Do you know the king to make any decision without a calculated purpose?" He scowled so fiercely that it twisted his face.

Swallowing hard, I looked away. His distrust was apparent, and I hated how I understood fragments of his perspective. Just being there, on the palace grounds must have been a reminder of how little power his house really had in comparison to the power they once held. "I can't say I don't understand your frustration, but it doesn't benefit you to tell me this."

"Then you underestimate the intent they have for you."

I froze and met his scowl with as much vigor. "And what do you know of my purpose here?"

An unnerving smile grew from the corners of his mouth. "A little more each day but trust me when I say you will only remain here for as long as you serve the crown."

"I'm certain that is the way of the world. We serve a purpose until we don't."

"But a free man should decide his own purpose, not have it decided for him."

I couldn't disagree considering what I had endured for Nicky's sake. "No matter what world we live in, we are never free. You're wasting your energy confiding in me."

He growled into my ear, "Again, you underestimate yourself. Do you realize the power you could possess should you choose your own fate? I would be willing to help you. Making that simple decision ourselves would create a ripple felt throughout the kingdom."

"You're insane," I seethed while pushing away from him, but he gripped my arm and yanked me back. I looked around for Safir, but Zae had pulled him aside and was whispering to him. His gaze was so far from mine, so detached. The last place I ever wanted to find myself was alone with Arius.

"Insane? I could offer you autonomy, Eve."

"You just want to decide my future rather than have Ashire do it."

"At least I'd be transparent with you. Can you honestly say the king and prince have been honest?"

My heart jumped into my throat as Lady Zae leaned against Safir. Her waterfall of hair cascaded over his shoulders as he blushed. He reached for her, sharing his Blessing. And there I was, barely withstanding Arius's presence. Alone as ever.

Arius must have followed my gaze, as he groaned and leaned away from me. "Ah, I see. That was quite inevitable, I'm afraid. Those two will circle each other for the rest of their years. Don't get caught in their riptide."

I began distancing myself from him. From anyone. From everyone. I could feel my hands tighten into fists, as I wished more than anything that another intruder would appear for me to crack my knuckles into. But it was futile. I had taken two steps before Arius' was clasping my arm. He didn't grip as hard as Hunter, but he was twice as confident. I allowed him to halt me for a single second. "I swear to you, give me the word and you will be liberated."

"I'm not imprisoned."

"You said yourself no one in this world is free unless we make it so."

"Eve?"

Selasi approached us both, a hint of concern hidden behind his professional façade. Arius released me while Selasi bowed. "Pardon the intrusion. Lady Tesara requested your company in her rooms."

"If you'll excuse me, Lord Arius." I curtsied half-heartedly and paced back to the palace. With each stride I was able to breathe deeper.

Selasi fell in step with me. "Are you all right?"

"Fine."

"Whatever he said to you, please don't pay him any mind."

"I understand what it means to be a pawn," I grumbled, glancing over to see Safir leaning against the palace wall with Zae draped over him, caressing and touching and why, why, why did they constantly have to be touching each other? Were they not about to suffocate each other?

Safir's ember gaze met mine, and my heart convulsed in my chest.

I turned away, leaving him to defend himself against his own Blessing. With Zae at his side, my purpose appeared null and void.

Safir

Despite being debuted, I had yet to ensure trust that I'd be able to perform duties in the name of the king. Understandable, but not an issue I had originally foreseen. My worries had been consumed by not wanting to impede anyone with my tainted Blessing, a worry that had almost completely faded because of Eve.

And Eve. Mere days before she had beautifully fitted in my grasp, as if she had made that place her own. She'd breathed life and warmth into my name, but then some fracture had occurred, and it led me back to Lord Arius. I had been certain that once the noble guests had departed and left us in peace, I could recover Eve, but with each passing day that hope was dwindling. She was slipping from me. I knew we had become close, close enough to know each other's thoughts and sentiments from across the room. We were still connected by a similar pain, but the pain she was feeling during my debut, I couldn't comprehend. Even worse, I felt truly ill at the thought of being the cause of it.

"I was afraid of this, was I not?" Ashire piped up from his chair. "I didn't want you to become dependent on her. Now see how she twists your insides without even having to be in the room."

I scowled out the window. "Something had to have caused it. We've been getting on brilliantly until now."

"Is she no longer content with the original agreement?"

"An agreement you made her feel she had no choice in?"

"Regardless, has she expressed wanting to change the terms?"

I stalled because I knew he was going to relish in being right. "About one month ago, she did request she be compensated with coin rather than meals and healing, but—"

"Ah, well, that took longer than I had expected. It seems our hospitality isn't enough for her."

"But that was one month ago. Our friendship has only just soured this week."

"I've noticed," he sighed while turning to look at the fire. "I take it you're aware how keen Lord Arius is on her?"

"Acutely aware."

"Yet she doesn't seem to fancy his presence anymore than she does yours."

"He is poisoning her against me, I'm certain."

Ashire's fingers drummed against his goblet. "It takes more than one poison dart to bring down a bull."

"You are comparing my advisor to a bull?"

"In terms of character, yes. Stubborn and forthright." My frustration spiked, making Ashire stiffen in his chair and snap his stare to me. "Regardless, she's proven herself, and she has been good for you. I'll admit that. It would take more than just Arius, an obvious oaf, to turn someone who is as devoted as Eve against you."

"Perhaps we've overestimated her devotion," I hypothesized sullenly.

"I've never overestimated anything," he quipped. "I'm suggesting another is poisoning our most promising investment, namely your former betrothed."

My eyebrows rose high. "Zae?"

"Yes, Zae. Dear Vada, she is relentless in everything she does." He groaned into his hands. "Just speaking to her makes a man want to crawl into his own ballsack and die. And it's not escaped anyone's attention how much she is still drawn to you."

"I've put a stop to that today."

"You might be a few days too late if you want to win back your Eve."

"She's not my—"

"Do you know how jealousy is manifested? One must care for an emotion so viral to conquer its host. She is emotionally invested in you, otherwise she'd be indifferent to the extent to which Zae has molested you the past few days."

I plopped into my usual seat, defeated. "I understand, but you've yet to offer me a solution."

Ashire leaned back in his chair and stared at the ceiling. I could see grey hairs emerging above his ears. "Honestly, Safir, if it were me, I would cater to the girl for as long as I could for her to stay. Feed her. Heal her. Throw her coin. Erect a statue of her if it meant I could act in my role."

I shifted in my seat, my heart pounding at the memory of dancing with her, holding her, smiling with her. Just living openly alongside her had been a greater comfort than I'd thought I would ever know. None of those moments had anything to do with the fact she hindered my Blessing.

Ashire grinned ever so slightly. "But I'm aware you are not me, and for that I am grateful. You are not dependent on her strictly because she impedes your Blessing, and I very much want to be happy for you. Just endure the next two days, and when the rabble have all returned to their homes with new promises from their king, you will be able to focus on Eve. For now, you must be a prince before you are a man, do you understand? Duty always before pleasure, no matter the cost." His voice dipped for a split second.

That was the very reason I had wanted to help lighten his burden.

"I understand, I only hope if I'm able to do so, the people will begin to trust me."

"Once the guests have left, I will allow you to lead the next meeting with the local lords. You'll still be fresh off your debut, but it will be a start. It's to take place the day after everyone has departed. Do you believe yourself and your Eve up to the task?"

"I have the utmost faith," I affirmed with confidence despite feeling cracks in my resolve.

"As do I," Ashire whispered, but not intentionally loud enough for me to hear. Despite that day's trials, I was still able to manage a smile because of my brother.

Eve

No one is permitted to enter or exit this area. My apologies, ma'am.

I cursed fiercely while peering through the bushes, seeing the same rotund guards posted in front of my portal who had just refused to let me leave. I hadn't expected it to be blocked off to me, and I didn't feel like asking Ashire for permission to leave. No doubt he would have an entire monologue prepared about putting the crown before my other obligations. Well, fuck that.

"Obi? Are you ready?" I asked.

Petite Oberia practically disappeared within the bushes. "Are you sure I won't get into trouble?" she squeaked in the night air.

Nodding, I crouched lower. "If anyone finds you, tell them to talk to me, but that won't happen because you won't be caught. I promise. I just need a quick distraction. Once you see me disappear you can return to the palace."

"What if they ask why I was out of bed?"

"Tell them you needed to take a walk. Obi, I need you to trust me. Everything will be fine."

She nodded firmly. "I trust you, ma'am."

"And I trust you."

It hadn't taken much to lure Oberia from her bed. She had become far too accustomed to doing what she was told. It felt shitty taking advantage of that flaw. I swore I would take responsibility if she got into any trouble, but I needed to see Nicky. It had been too many days without checking on him, and I could hardly stand those arrogant aristocrats any longer.

Oberia took a deep breath beside me, and words escaped her mouth, but made no sounds. A gust of wind shook the leaves on the bush we were hiding in, and her shapes started to take form. They were human-looking, dark, and hiding from the moonlight. Obi mumbled furiously as two dark figures emerged into existence. Suddenly, a crack drew the guards attention as the two figures dashed in front of them and out of sight.

The guards held their weapons at the ready. "Quick! I saw them over this way!"

"Should we alert the other night watchmen?"

"Not yet, wait to make sure it isn't one of the king's guests. Now come on!"

They both abandoned their post. "Thank you, Obi," I huffed while making a mad sprint to my portal.

It was only fifty feet away, and I covered that distance in seconds. I didn't stop even when I passed through into the humid night air that would have been alien to Walyre. The mountains were replaced with a smog-filled sky and narrow trees. Still, I ran, needing to make the most of the night before it was over. Only two more days, and I swore I would never have to go back there.

The back of my small shanty house approached as I exited the forest. But there was a light on. I slowed my sprint to a confused shuffle. My caution spiked as I neared the back door. I couldn't see a figure inside, but I never left the lights on considering I was hardly ever home. My hand reached out for the knob, despite my legs wanting to put as much distance between me and the house as possible. Twisting the knob slowly, hearing its usual creak, I opened the door and stepped inside.

Everything seemed to be where I had left it, my boxing gloves, shoes, and workout clothes piled on the floor. Why was the kitchen light on? When I turned the corner, already reaching for the light switch on the wall, my entire being froze as I saw Hunter standing against the kitchen counter with his arms crossed.

Somehow, he looked perturbed. "I don't recall you being this messy when you stayed with Mary and me."

"What are you doing here?"

"Why aren't *you* here? I've been trying to find you, but no one knew where you were. Nick didn't even know."

My ire surfaced. "You saw Nicky?"

"Yeah, figured he'd know, but he wasted just enough breath to tell me to fuck off. You know I'm not as patient as I should be."

"You will never see him again. Nicky's existence is already a nightmare without you!"

Hunter took two long strides towards me. "And there you go again, being the most ungrateful client I have ever serviced. I thought we talked about this, Evie. I'm helping you for Nicky. I doubt you've forgotten that."

"Well, I'm here, so what is it you need to tell me?"

Hunter scanned me up and down, seeming to relish every second, and it made me want to rip away my very skin. "I've got another fight for you in five days. A big one. Got a lot riding on this, but you seem otherwise occupied. What the fuck are you even wearing?" He pulled at the string on my leather vest.

My breath caught in my throat as I clamped his hands in mine. I hadn't even thought to change. It was going to just be a quick trip to see Nicky and that was all. It had nothing to do with Hunter.

"What, you role-playing for guys now? If you ever wanted to go into a different field of service, I can certainly be of use to you."

"It's not for role-playing."

"Whatever it's for, it suits you. I mean *really* suits you." Despite his hands clamped in mine, he still yanked and pulled a few laces loose. I shouldn't have flinched, but I did. It only made him lick his wet lips as his eyes were clearly drawn to my breasts that Maisy had hoisted up in that vest.

Suddenly both hands were on me. One was groping my stomach, and the other was attached high on my ribs, his thumb probing the side of my breast. "**Stop**," I seethed. I wanted to cry and vomit and scream and fight and run and hide all at once.

"I've got a fight lined up for you. But I can't have you moving out of your weight class. You've obviously put on a few pounds, not that I'm complaining. It's fallen exactly where God intended."

My teeth audibly ground together. I had never hated my body more, never wanted to tear away every lump he could pinch, every bit of flesh that he had tainted. But then his hand rose to clamp onto my shoulder. His other hand dropped to his side. "When did you last eat?"

"An hour ago."

"Good. Sorry about this."

A massive blow landed in my unprepared gut. Air rushed out of my lungs and bile shot into my throat. Pain screamed from my core as my knees gave out and I plummeted to the floor.

I gasped wildly; no air could enter. I could barely remember how it felt to breathe as Hunter sat me upright and pulled my hair away from my face. Suddenly, bile and morsels of the food I had ingested at dinner erupted out of my throat and onto the kitchen floor. It hurt even worse as my abdomen contracted with each heave. My nose and eyes burned with snot and tears that ran down my face.

I sniffled and choked, while Hunter rubbed my back. "I really am sorry, Evie. The worst is over with."

Wave upon wave of violent heaves racked my body before no more vomit came up and I was left shaking and curling around myself. A cool cloth swiped across my mouth. I leaned back and let Hunter clean my face, doing away with any traces of snot, bile, or tears. I didn't want there to be any reminders left. He even fanned me while my stomach settled, and I was able to lean back against the cabinets. "*Why?*" I croaked.

"We just gotta keep the weight off for the next few days. I promise you, if you win this next one, I'll buy you whatever you want to eat. We just have to make sacrifices right now. Evie, that hurt me just as much as it hurt you." He reached out and clutched my slippery chin. "I would never hurt you if I weren't helping you. Remember that." There was no rage left in me to fight him. I simply closed my eyes. One arm went under my shoulders and the other went under my knees. "Don't worry. I'll take care of this mess while you rest."

He hoisted me into the air, making my stomach tempted to endure round two of projectile vomiting, but the feeling subsided when he settled me down onto my unmade bed. It felt foreign to me. Too lumpy. Too cold. Too empty. It wasn't as if I had the strength to argue.

We are never free.

Every single heartbeat in my stomach made me sweat. While Hunter was cleaning up the consequences of his cruelty, I undid my vest and pulled up my shirt to see a grotesque purple bruise forming right in the middle of my stomach. There was no going to see Nicky that night. There was no moving. It was going to take all my concentration to even return to Walyre. I hated it so much it almost outweighed the pain, but I missed Safir. He would have numbed the pain, stayed beside me throughout the night. Even if it wasn't sincere, it still would have been nice.

That was what I dreamt about that night.

At some point I had fallen asleep. I awoke to the sun blinding me through the window. It was quiet in my small house. I made the mistake of trying to sit upright, swooning with pain as my belly screeched at me to stop moving. I fell back onto my bed with a groan as nausea welled up in my throat. Still, I didn't hear anything else.

When I convinced myself to roll out of bed, hoisting myself up by some bookshelves, I saw that I was alone. The only indication Hunter had been there was the ugly bruise left on my stomach. It was a deep purple and black in the middle, radiating blue and red towards the sides.

"Son of a bitch," I groaned while trying to tuck in my shirt and retie my vest.

At least the kitchen floor was relatively clean when I passed it on my way out. It felt like I was hiking for miles, trying to step over each stray branch without aggravating my bruise. My breaths escaped me raggedly as I stumbled through the portal.

The guards jumped back and gasped at me. "Ma'am? How did you—"

"I won't tell if you won't," I grumbled and kept on my way towards the palace.

The sun hadn't reached over the mountain peaks yet, so at least it was still early. It certainly didn't appear as if anyone was looking for me. Yet, I could barely stand upright without wanting to faint. Every step, every breath, every thought aggravated my sore abdomen. I needed Lani to heal it, but would she be suspicious? I wasn't scheduled for a fight, technically wasn't even permitted to leave, and she had seen my injuries after a boxing match. My one, ugly, singular bruise made it too obvious I had been *attacked*. She'd ask questions. She'd tell the king. He'd tell the prince. And then Safir would have to feign concern for me for the sake of his debut. The very thought made me sicker than the injury itself.

As I clawed my way inside, barely able to tolerate the stairs to my room, I wished for Maisy to show up, and ever dependable, she did.

"Good morning, Eve! Oberia wished to join me this morning and— dear Vada, are you all right?"

I had been kneeling against my bedframe, not even able to crawl into bed. Beside Maisy was Obi, who stared at me wide-eyed and pale. "I'm fine, Maisy," I grunted.

"You most certainly are not! What's happened?"

As she reached to help me stand, I doubled over and clutched my stomach. Maisy's attention shifted. "Ah, I see. It's that ugly time, isn't it? Tsk, never had good timing." She sat me on the bed as it dawned on me what she assumed my ailment was. "Don't worry. I will draw you a bath and fetch some soothing grass from Lani—always does the trick for me when I'm feeling horrid with the burdens of womanhood." She stood with her hands on her hips and smiled at Oberia.

"Don't look so frightened, my dear. You will know these trials too one day."

Obi's eyes grew wider when Maisy tasked her with "watching over me" while she fetched me some painkillers. When Maisy was gone, I reached out my trembling hand to the poor girl. "Thank you for being so brave for me."

She nodded. "Everything was fine, like you promised. Except you." She looked down at my other hand clutching my stomach. "I hate to see you in pain."

"It's only temporary, like all pain."

Obi swallowed hard. "Ma'am, I don't think that's true."

Maisy returned with a small vial for me to drink. She protested I needed to eat something first, but I downed the bitter liquid. Then I had to stop her drawing me a bath, mostly because a hot bath would make the bruise worse, and I didn't want to reveal it to Maisy.

"Just give me a wash rag and some fresh clothes."

She did so promptly, seeming to understand I wasn't in the mood to be argued with. It took me twice as long to dress myself, though it would have been impossible had Lani's painkilling vial not worked. It didn't take away the pain, but it made me not care as much. By the time I had finished getting ready I knew I was going to be late for breakfast with the nobles.

"Do I still look as horrible as I feel?" I asked.

"A little bit," Obi piped, but Maisy hushed her.

"You look much better than when we found you. Remember to drink up and keep that rag secure in your trousers! I'll give you a new one whenever you need it."

I was going to have to explain later why I hadn't placed that rag in my pants.

Sighing, I practiced standing as straight as I could. I could only hope the nobles would be far too consumed with themselves to pay any attention to me. I knew Safir would be waiting for me, unable to enter without me being there, and so I'd have to put on my best performance for him first.

As I approached, fighting the urge to support myself along the wall, I saw him standing outside of the dining room with Selasi. Always us three, or so it used to be. Safir stiffened. His ember eyes blazed at me from beneath his white locks, and it made me temporarily forget my pain. I stood straight, knowing I was also under Selasi's watchful eye. He had become increasingly observant since the beginning of the debut.

"Good morning," I greeted, though it sounded strained.

Safir didn't immediately greet me. I could tell he was studying me intently as I stood alongside him and waited for the doors to be opened. He didn't offer his hand like he used to, and even though I wouldn't have taken it, it still somehow stung he had stopped offering it.

"Do you sleep well?" he asked while turning towards the doors, though I could still tell he was looking at me from the corner of his eye.

"I haven't slept well in days."

His face softened. Somehow, I wanted to scream at him and be held by him all at once.

"Eve …"

The doors flew open, and we both fell silent. We walked into the dining hall to be met by faces I had grown weary of seeing.

I would play my part until the very end.

Safir

She was on the cusp of saying something. Her sapphire stare was glistening, cheeks flushed, mouth hanging open, as if she expected me to say the words she was thinking. I would have gladly taken any words she had to give me, even words of animosity. At least I would have known what she was feeling.

She remained as still as a statue, hardly eating, and scarcely appeared interested in any of the conversation, much to Emtias' irritation. She hardly even catered to Lord Arius' attention. If we had been alone, I knew I could have reached her. I'd hold her, say whatever it was she couldn't say, and make right whatever was wrong within her. But sitting there, engaging in conversation regarding new policies, I had no hope of reaching her.

Duty before pleasure.

No wonder Ashire was turning grey.

The agenda for that day was a tour of the city. Ashire wanted to portray the city as the epitome of his success as king. The streets were cleaner, the mercantile district thriving, the main square was a work of art, and the temple of Vada was newly refurbished. The city represented the efforts of the crown, and it felt only right we would tour it together for the first time in decades. The last time I had ventured outside of the palace was Mother's funeral.

Lady Tesara had elected to retire. "The child stirs if I'm on my feet for too long. But I will not deprive my lord of such an outing," she urged Lord Batrum with a kiss and dismissed herself to her room. Our parties were divided unevenly into two carriages. Ashire, Emtias, and Lord Batrum entered one while Zae, Arius, Eve, and I entered another. Selasi led the party on horseback.

Inside our carriage, the air was so thick one could have cut it with a knife, but hardly anyone could sense my discontent due to Eve. Each bump made her wince, something I was determined to ask about later. I wanted to scowl at Arius, debating whether I could throw him out of the carriage, while Zae and Eve exchanged sideways glances. The two of them hadn't spoken to each other since the ball, and I was certain Eve had no interest in speaking with me. The carriage was full of sour sentiments. I could feel it aging me by the second.

At least once we left the palace walls we could pretend to be distracted by the cheering crowds. Zae graciously admired the growth of each district and marveled at the apparent happiness of the people. "It has been so long since I've seen these streets. The people brim with love for their crown, don't you think so, Eve?"

Unimpressed with the branch of neutrality Zae extended to her, Eve kept her gaze on the windows. "You said it perfectly. Who couldn't love the crown?" I had forgotten Eve had never seen the city only admired it from the palace. Seeing her drink in the scene with her mouth slightly agape reminded me of how beautifully she'd viewed my world when I first gave her the tour of the palace.

Arius sneered. "I think you're quite fortunate to have an advisor with such high standards. We're similar in that we're not easily impressed."

"I agree. One cannot surpass expectations if those around him don't hold him to a higher standard," I asserted.

We entered the mercantile district where trading took place. Markets were lined with polished goods and workings to be sold. It was thriving. We passed refineries, bakeries, shops with fabric draped across the windows. Cheering crowds followed to get a glimpse of the elusive nobles.

Just play the part, Ashire would say. The people would build up an image of you, and it was your job to maintain it. It was easier to do in a moving carriage.

We arrived at Vada's temple in the great square. I exited the carriage first followed by Arius and Zae. Eve exited last, groaning. My hand rose to steady her but fell back to my side. She hadn't wanted me to touch her, and I respected that desire, as much as it pained me. With adoring crowds shouting from behind the rows of guards, Eve turned about to take in the scene in full. Vada's temple towered over the people with tall spires and grand arches, lined with carvings of ancient incantations asking for luck. In the grand, open doors the high priests waited for us.

Yet, as we all stepped forward, Eve remained behind.

I stalled, seeing she was looking at a building across the square. She wasn't even tempted by the temple. She walked towards 'Mira's

Refuge,' the orphanage my mother had founded decades ago. Outside of its doors were dozens of pale faced children staring in wonder.

"Pray tell, what is your advisor doing?" Ashire asked while emerging beside me.

"I'm not entirely certain."

"I guarantee this was not in our itinerary," Emtias grumbled.

Selasi stepped forward. "I shall retrieve her, Lord."

Zae brushed past me in Eve's direction. "I think she has the right idea. What better display of the crown's investment in the future of the kingdom?"

I focused on maintaining a neutral feeling as I began following Eve.

"Ensure they don't dally. We will meet you at the temple," Ashire urged while Lord Batrum and Arius fell into step with my brother. Emtias had already arrived at the temple steps.

Turning to Selasi, I ordered, "Linger at a distance. Remain vigilant," before joining the two headstrong women before me.

The crowds roared as Eve, Zae, and I approached the orphanage. I was less enthusiastic. We were so close to concluding that week. While I was sure Eve's intentions were pure, she was walking out in the open with nobles. It was careless, but we had exposed her so little to the city. However, as we approached the small horde of children, it was enchanting to see the people looking to me, cheering for my house, daring to reach out. I made sure to keep my distance, but being out amongst the people was exhilarating.

As we approached, I motioned for the guards to clear a path, allowing us to approach the steps. The children practically scrambled, leaping, and fidgeting while a young woman attempted to corral them. They ranged from toddlers to children well on their way to becoming young workers. Their clothes hung loosely, and they had toothy smiles and weepy eyes. Zae tutted, patting their heads.

Eve knelt, meeting the children at eye level, as a familiar pair emerged before her. It was a young girl with a large pair of boots and a boy with a long cloak. They clung to her. She smiled, genuinely smiled for the first time in days, and it made my heart lighter.

"I remember you," she greeted while ruffling their hair. "You've grown a little."

And then the boy revealed underneath his cloak a lumpy babe on his hip. He bounced the babe and offered it to Eve. She hesitantly took the child into her arms. She winced.

"Have you been taking care of each other?" Eve asked.

They nodded.

"Good. I hope I get to see you again soon." She beamed while nuzzling the dirt-smudged baby as if the child were as precious as her own.

An odd sensation stirred in me to see her so affectionate, so tender, all while knowing the depth of her fortitude. I could have watched her coo into that baby's ear for the rest of the day, possibly because I enjoyed seeing her happy and perhaps…

An elbow struck my ribs as Zae gave me a smug look. "Entranced, Your Royal Highness? You have other admirers right in front of you."

She gestured to a few children who had been gaping up at me. While I couldn't touch them, I grinned at them as each attempted to bow before me, feeling ridiculous to be treated so formally by children. "Thank you for coming to see us today," I told them.

Eve had returned the baby to its siblings as she rose and looked over to the only adult. "Are you responsible for all of them?"

The young woman practically tripped over the toddlers while trying to step forward. Her dress had questionable stains, and she blushed while bowing before us. "Hello, m'lords and m'ladies. Me and two others care for this lot, but there are many more children inside who were unable to see you in person."

"How absurd," Zae chattered. "Three of you to take care of this many children? Do you find your provisions adequate?"

"We're thankful for whatever is provided by the crown. But more and more children find their way through our doors."

I watched the sea of young faces stare up at us, pondering if it was hope or hunger I saw in their eyes.

But just because it's painful to look doesn't mean they don't deserve to be seen.

I sighed. "Your dedication will be noted, and I will do my best to see your needs are met. There is no better way to honor the crown and my departed mother than to invest in our children."

She smiled. They all smiled. Despite their loss, even after we departed from the roaring crowds to make our way towards the temple, they all smiled. It was humbling.

"Safir?"

Eve gazed up at me. She hadn't said my name in days, and while she didn't say it with a smile, she still called to me in a way all her own.

"Did you mean that? You'll look after them?"

We hadn't halted our pace towards the temple, but I felt as if everyone else had vanished. "I will do my best."

"Promise me," she commanded.

My hand jerked at my side. "I promise."

She tore her gaze away from me, appearing … relieved? "They just seemed like all they wanted was for someone to reach for them."

My entire core ached as her voice broke, but she gave no further indications as to her sentiments as we approached the temple, our party reunited. Yet I could tell Eve's heart was somewhere different.

Duty before pleasure.

I would come to regret it.

Eve

Vada's temple was the epitome of extravagance, something I detested considering there were children living in squalor just a few hundred feet away. The priests boasted about tithes and the murals donated to the temple from noble families. The grandest of them all was a giant statue of Vada, shrouded in her cloak with one large coin in one hand. She was painted gold, standing over ten feet tall, surrounded by a small pond *within* the temple. Inside the pond were hundreds of gold coins, tossed in by well-wishers. It was enraging.

While the priests boasted, Zae took every opportunity to engage in conversation with me. It at least distracted me from the aching in my core. Lani's painkillers had taken full effect but holding that baby had reminded me how sore I really was.

"You know, for someone who says the path of children wasn't chosen for them, you seem awfully keen."

Zae had a habit of standing closer than necessary. It made the air saturated in her scent of cinnamon and cardamom. How she was able to smell so good in a realm that hadn't perfected indoor plumbing was beyond me. "Even you said it's good optics for the crown to show investment in its children."

"It is one thing to acknowledge the children and another to *give* yourself to them. Hardly anyone would do such a thing for the sake of being seen."

I swallowed hard, maintaining deep breaths to hinder Safir's Blessing, though it was hard to breathe with my sore stomach. He was pacing in front of me, appearing to keep Arius too busy to bother me. "It seems ironic, doesn't it? That this temple, for the goddess of luck, would sit directly across from an *orphanage*."

"Yes, the irony is quite bitter. I'm not the greatest devotee to Vada. I much prefer Tove. At least he has a sense of humor."

The priests' voices echoed off the marbled walls, so I kept my voice low. "I take it there are orphanages in Phora?"

"One or two."

"What becomes of the children who live there?"

"Admittedly," she mused with her eyes downcast, "it's a breeding ground for future smugglers, petty thieves, and prostitutes. They know little else than how to survive from one day to the next."

I looked up at Vada, gleaming in all her supposed glory. *Well, if she's too busy to bestow luck on those actually worthy of it, then I'll do it myself.*

I couldn't help but recall my conversation with Clay when I'd been at my most desperate, hating myself for having no useful skills for Nicky. Without options, I'd been at the mercy of those around me and I remained at that mercy now. "Why can't we train them in a skill so they can provide for themselves? The more options the better."

Zae hummed as we rounded corner after corner of the great temple. "You have good intentions but vague ideas. Details, my dear, people will want to hear details. Besides, most places of charity are more concerned with needing resources in the present rather than gambling on investing in the future."

It would be a gamble, so how to sweeten the deal? What would make it worth it to take one child into one's trade? What did people hate more than poverty? What complaints did Safir receive the most from local lords? "We'd need to incentivize involvement. The businesses would gain easy labor, and any business that participates or any family that is willing to house and host the child will receive … a slight reprieve on their taxes. The bane of every businessman's existence."

Zae scoffed as we rounded a corner and sat in one of the pews while Ashire and the others offered prayers to Vada. "How would you expect these businesses not to take advantage of these children?"

"They could commit for one seasons of work, but then both the business and the child can elect whether to renew the contract on a season-by-season basis."

Zae slowly grinned. "Interesting. In the short term you'd be making less money but given a few years you'd have a more formidable work force and theoretically less petty crime and smuggling."

"I think if we give them a means to apply themselves, set up a system in which they can succeed, you would see less of the consequences of poverty."

"There will be loopholes for some businesses to take advantage of."

I huffed. "This program wouldn't be released until all shortcomings are anticipated. I would need help and resources for that."

"Then that is what you'll get. I fully support this program. I am willing to provide any resources you need." She pretended to bow her head in prayer.

My heart sank. It was a good idea, and seeing hungry faces reminded me the people in that realm were very much real. Their burdens were real, just as real as what Nicky and I had faced. Burdens we had sworn we would stand against one day. But I still needed to walk away from it all.

"I think if anyone should present the idea it should be you," I told Zae. "People will listen to you. Your words have more weight than mine."

"It only matters what your words mean to who." She glanced to Safir. "And your words mean more to the prince than mine do."

"I doubt that."

Zae pouted at me. "Your lack of self-assurance is not very becoming, my dear. It insults your allure."

"Regardless, you should present it."

"Well, if we ever get to leave this blinding temple I will," she huffed in defeat.

It was comforting to know something was going to be left behind that helped someone. Yet Safir's concerned stare landed on me repeatedly. I could feel myself gradually losing my will to leave. Yet it took little to remind me of why I needed to leave in the first place.

I had a less than agreeable impression of the temple. The priests boasted of Vada's good fortune though there were children left to fend for themselves. I doubted they looked past their own fortune to consider anyone else's. I offered no praise or thanks upon our exit.

As we emerged from the temple, hordes of people had gathered, their hands grasping at the air. Emtias handed me a sack of coins. "A custom which began with the late queen. You will bestow good fortune on the people, per Vada's example."

I peered down at the heavy bag of coins, seeing the other nobles already handing out money to outstretched hands in the crowd. They made a path through the people, like parting a sea of desperation, the crowds lined by guards keeping them at bay. As promised, I played the part and dipped my hesitant hand into the bag. One by one I handed out the coins to eager hands. They offered thanks and smiles, like Feast Day but somehow less fulfilling.

"Come now," Zae encouraged as she emerged beside me. "At least try to look as happy as the people you're bestowing good fortune on."

My cheeks felt frozen in place. "This is so fake."

"This is a custom established by the fair queen. Would you prefer to give them nothing? Their happiness is real, regardless, and that is what matters."

"More can be done."

"More will be done, but not all at once. Be patient," she snipped.

As coin was handed out, the crowds grew louder and flocked closer to where I would have felt swallowed had the guards not kept them at bay. A few times I stifled a cringe when a busy body brushed my side, making me coil around my stomach to protect it.

A commotion erupted from the center of the square where the carriages and horses were stationed. The horses began squealing, rearing in the air, bucking the carriages off the hitch.

Everyone in the crowd startled. "Someone control those damn beasts!" Lord Arius commanded over the crowd.

"They're going to stampede!"

"They've been spooked!"

Voices cried out as the mares, stomped their hooves and whinnied. The guards abandoned their post holding back the crowds to steady the horses. As the guards fled, the horde of people swallowed us and suddenly, I no longer recognized the faces surrounding me. Bodies bumped and scraped up against me, making me clutch my stomach while whipping around in search of someone familiar.

"Safir? Zae?"

Something strong clamped onto the back of my collar and yanked me back with such force I almost toppled. My feet scuttled and my arms flailed wildly, trying to keep me upright, as I was pulled back through the sea of people. I couldn't turn to look at my assailant, only seeing masses of people putting more distance between me and the square.

Without warning I fell backwards into a stairwell of darkness. My arms reached up to grab at the air as I bit my tongue to stifle a scream. The adrenaline rush was monumental. I hardly felt the impact when I collided onto a clotted-dirt floor. I should have felt pain, especially from my bruised core, but instead I scrambled to my feet as quickly as I could with my hand poised on my dragger. Everything was dark except for a few rays of light emanating from floorboards above me. Was I underground? I saw a shabby wooden stairwell I must have fallen through, perhaps into a cellar, and lying beside me in a heap was Zae.

She groaned and looked up at me. "Eve?"

I released my dagger and hauled her from the ground, but she flopped against me. "I'm sorry. I didn't know what to do. Someone put a rag over my mouth, so I held my breath and grabbed onto you. I don't—"

A rush of air whizzed by my face as an arrow cut across my cheek and embedded in the wall behind me. Blood rushed to my limbs as I slowly turned.

"What the *fuck* are you?" a voice snarled through the darkness.

I stiffened, positioning myself between Zae and the voice. In the farthest corner, a man visibly shook while pointing a short bow at us. His teeth were chattering, and his knees were locked in a narrow stance, not at all a steady fighting position. "How can this be happening?" he grumbled.

A gasp sprang from Zae, and she trembled against me. "Why are *you* here? How? After everything, Frederara? You dare to add me to your list!"

He was wholly too distracted to respond to her. "How can this be happening? How? *How?*"

Zae grasped my shoulder. "Something is wrong. He is confused."

"Stop talking!" he barked, shakily pointing the short bow.

Another set of stairs led upwards next to the assailant, and we were surrounded by barrels of what smelled like soured ale. At least there was one other route for escape, but we were better off escaping the way we'd come in.

"What do you want with us?" I asked.

"Nothing with you! You aren't supposed to be here. It's *her* I was paid for."

He was still shaking. If he'd been hired, a supposed professional assassin, then something was off. Zae was right, he was too confused to carry this out.

I whispered to Zae, "Take my dagger and run. Find Safir." I reached out for a barrel, never taking my eyes off the neurotic assailant.

"Stop!" the man cried and just as I grabbed a barrel topper another arrow was fired straight for us. The barrel topper caught the arrow just inches from my face as Zae wrenched my dagger free and dashed back up the stairs out of the cellar. She lunged to push the cellar door open.

With her out of the way, I felt such a surge of unadulterated ire that I hardly cared about my own self-preservation.

"What do you think you're *doing*?" he cried while stumbling to string another arrow.

I crouched low with a growl. "Blowing off some steam."

Safir

It was a nightmare drawn from my subconscious. The guards had lost control of the crowds while trying to keep the horses under control and preserve the carriages. Selasi put himself between me and the roaring masses.

"Stay close to me, Lord!" he barked, clasping the hilt of his sword, as did I.

I had lost track of most of our small party. While I believed the crown had the heart of the people, royals rarely allowed themselves to be submerged in a horde of commoners for good reason. Uncertainty and panic bled through the air, and I permeated that feeling through my Blessing. It was impossible to focus on any sort of neutral feeling. There was only one rattled thought that leapt to the other.

When a hand pulled on my arm, I began to draw my sword from its sheath when I turned to find Lord Arius gripping me. "Your Royal Highness, allow me to transport us to the others. We've established order near the carriages."

I didn't have time to ponder my pride and accept Arius' help. I sheathed my sword while pulling Selasi beside me. Arius wrapped his arms around us and took a deep breathe. It felt like my feet no longer touched the ground, my body whooshing forward with a gust a wind before finding ourselves emerged out of the crowd within the span of a blink. I could breathe free air as we burst away from the crowd and behind a new line of guards keeping them at bay. Lord Batrum kept his distance from the crowds. Ashire and Emtias struggled to manage the horses' reins.

My brother and I locked eyes. "Safir!" he commanded, motioning me to his side.

I paced towards Ashire and placed my hand against the neck of one of the mares, taking steady breaths and focusing on a sense of calm. It was easier to focus on neutral sentiments when not struggling amongst the crowd. It took mere seconds for the mare to slow her breathing and cease her whinnying. In moments, she was leaning into my hand, and her calm demeanor influenced the horse tethered next to her.

Emtias murmured an incantation to the horses attached to the adjacent carriage. Their eyes glazed over, and hooves ceased stamping as a subtle yellow glow grew from Emtias. Amid the chaos, it was easily missed.

With the horses having resumed some frail calm, Ashire ordered the remaining soldiers to control the crowds.

"This could have ended very badly," he grumbled. "Did you see what originally caused the disturbance?"

My head shook. "I only experienced the aftermath. I saw nothing."

"I think I found the cause!" Lord Batrum emerged with an arrow in hand. "This was found between the carriages. Could have spooked the horses." He peered upwards. "The angle implies it was shot from high ground. We're not safe here, gentlemen."

My blood ran deathly cold. "We should return to the palace."

Ashire nodded. "A gross understatement. Escort Zae and Eve to the carriage."

I stilled. "Are they not with you?"

For the first time in years, Ashire's eyes widened with panic. "I was under the impression they were with you."

Dear Vada.

I shouted for Selasi with every bit of authority within me. He rushed to my side. "Find Lady Zae and Eve at once. Question every man if you must!"

Selasi's face filled with similar fear as he turned and began barking at the guards. "Four men with me. Everyone else, hold back the crowds."

"I want every building searched," Ashire demanded of his guard commander. "Lock down the square. No one enters or leaves! Emtias!" he called as the Fae emerged by his side. "Can you locate them?"

"It will take a few minutes, but I should be able to." Emtias removed a lock of hair from his inner pocket. When I recognized the color, I resisted the urge to question why Emtias kept a lock of Zae's hair on him. He rubbed the hair between his fingers. Smoke billowed as he chanted, burning the remains of her hair into ash. I had no such patience to wait on his report.

"I'm going to search," I told him while readying to breach the crowds.

Ashire yanked me back to his side. "You'll do no such thing. I can't lose track of all three of you."

"They are under our care, and they are alone in this city!"

"We've dispatched our guard and locked down the square. Emtias will find Zae and then Eve. You must calm yourself."

"Eve has never been in the city, Ashire! I will *not* abandon her in this mob."

He braced me with his hand against my chest. "I know you're in pain, but Lady Zae must take priority in the search. Would you even be able to do that?"

"Absolutely not."

"Zae is near," Emtias barked and began scanning the crowd. "She will come to us."

"Batrum!" Ashire howled as our uncle arrived next to him. "Do you possess anything from Eve or Zae? Could you send them a message?"

"Alas, not on my person. Offer me something of yours, and I'll venture into the crowd for them and message you when I've found something."

"Safir!" a voice screeched from the sea of people.

We all turned to see a disheveled Zae waving her arms, attempting to burst through the line of guards.

"Let her through!" Ashire shouted. The guards obeyed as Zae burst forth and practically collapsed onto the cobblestone road.

Arius held her aloft, muttering, "By the gods, how did you manage?"

I was too distracted by Zae's frantic state to care. There was something unsettling about seeing a woman known for her poise racked with panic. Zae reached up and grabbed me with her bruised hands. I begged her to speak. There was a tremor in her voice, and she looked at me with frenzy in her eyes. "I don't know how it happened! He grabbed me, and I grabbed Eve. We were pulled into a cellar, and he attacked us. Eve gave me this and told me to run. So, I ran."

Zae held Eve's dagger tightly in her grasp. I began to shake.

"You left her alone? Take us back there." I hoisted her upright and supported her buckling knees. "Retrace your steps."

"I didn't look back. I just ran! I don't—"

"Try! You left her alone, Zae!" Anger pulsed through me at the thought of Eve alone with an assailant, having endured one attack only to face another. I had promised she would always be safe with me. She deserved to feel safe with someone, and I longed to carry that burden.

A sudden force separated me from Zae. Ashire stood between us. "She's in shock, Safir! Have some sense. Your Blessing is only feeding into the frenzied crowd right now. Control yourself!"

I could see the crowd growing more agitated. They roared like thunder. Innocents were toppled to the ground and buried amongst the chaos. I reached for the handkerchief in Ashire's pocket and gave it to our uncle. "Take this and report back if you find Eve."

"Take Lord Arius with you. If you encounter any violence you'll jump back to the palace, is that understood?" Ashire barked at both men. They both nodded before disappearing into the roaring crowds behind the line of guards as Ashire resumed his focus on me. "You can calm the crowd if you focus. Try. It'll help Batrum and Arius navigate."

"I am not capable of calm right now," I growled, but then I felt a pair of cool hands on either side of my face.

Zae's poise returned as she gripped me. "Saf, only the good things. You *will* only feel the good things. You will do this now because *she* needs you to."

I stilled in her hold. She released me as I fought to disregard my anger and panic to focus on that warmth and calm I'd created when rotting in the dungeon. They were just as powerful a part of my arsenal if I focused. I inhaled deeply through my nose to focus on emitting my Blessing rapidly and widely over the crowd. I had to reach them so I could reach for her. With each deep breath I could feel my energy waning, hearing the crowd's whooping die down and the stampeding slow. Sweat beaded on my brow.

I had suffered for the good of the crown. I had suffered for the good of the crown. I had suffered for the good of the crown—

"Safir." My brother's voice broke through my veil of concentration. "You've done well." I opened my eyes to see the crowd had stilled, no longer bulging against the line of guards. Then Ashire stiffened while looking past the crowds with widened eyes. He reached up to his ear. "It's Batrum. They found her."

Eve

The assailant had done away with his shortbow as I circled him. We were in too close quarters, and it would have taken too long to string arrows. Instead, he drew a dagger from his hip and pointed it towards me. Luckily, Selasi had disarmed me dozens of times, and each time I'd taken careful notice.

I waited. He rushed me, his dagger in poor grip. I took a last-second sidestep, gripping his wrist while my right fist made purchase in his jaw. A distinct crack cut through the air as a groan escaped the man. He dropped the dagger, embedding itself into the dirt floor. I didn't have time to pick it up as he began throwing punches wildly. It was erratic, but there was true force behind them. I felt the wind with each punch I dodged. Furious breaths escaped me as I saw an opening and punched straight into his gut. His core caved around my knuckles, and I could hear regret in his grunt.

And yet he had the gall to run up the adjacent stairs. I lunged to pull him back down to me, but he slipped away, planting a swift kick to my nose that made blood spurt from my nostrils. He scrambled up the rest of the stairs, leaving me screeching and clawing my way up. I could hardly see through my tear-filled eyes as I reached the top.

Dozens of stunned faces looked at me with mouths agape. The crowded bar had come to a halt with half-drunk pints held in midair. My attacker dodged across the bar for the exit.

"Get back here!" I screeched with whatever was left of my adrenaline driving me forward. Not caring. Not stalling. Not thinking past what was happening in that moment.

I slammed my body into his as my arms wrapped around his cowardly form. We catapulted through a pane of glass as I heard shattering, gasps, and the sound of my own gritted teeth as we landed with a thump on cobblestone. My arms and legs were covered in tiny stings. The attacker scrambled out of my arms, kicking, and shoving to try to escape. I flipped onto my belly and pulled him back towards me by the ankle, dragging him through the sea of glass.

He struggled, but I found my way on top of him, and my vision turned red. My knuckles delved into flesh over and over until I couldn't register what I was punching, swing after swing with no perception of pain or fatigue. The thrill was terrifying. Why couldn't I stop? Why didn't I want to? I became a never-ending reservoir of ire, unrelenting and unrecognizable, numbed to the rest of the world.

My vision returned when I felt myself being lifted in the air. I was still swinging my fists, trying to make purchase with my attacker when my name broke through the roaring in my ears. "Eve, stop! You're safe now! You're safe!"

My fists dropped and shapes came back into frame. Selasi gripped my shoulders, searching my eyes for signs of lucidity. I tasted blood. My fists were caked with blood. Fuck, it was everywhere.

The attacker groaned amongst the shards of glass while guards restrained him. His face … it was pulverized. He was embedded into the cobblestone. I felt a surge of disgust in myself for being the reason for so much pain. I didn't mind defending myself … if I was in control of it.

Horrified faces gawked at my blood-soaked person, and I felt the sudden urge to hide under a rock. Even Lord Batrum and Arius gawked at me.

Selasi carefully brought me to my feet. "Don't look at them," he urged. "Lean into me." He propped my arm over his shoulders for support, making me cringe. With the adrenaline having run its course, I was suddenly aware of sharp pain in my cheeks and nose. I could feel blood dripping down the back of my throat, mixed with mucus and bile. Tiny stings coated my body, my arms and legs were embedded with small shards of glass, and worst of all my core felt like it was going to collapse in on itself. I could hardly stand, let alone breathe, making my world spin. Lani was going to have her work cut out for her.

But both Selasi and I froze when Safir broke through the crowd. Part of me dreaded seeing him, and the other part wondered why he hadn't been the one to find me. I could see the relief mixed with unease on his face. His ember eyes blazed, darting to each wound on me, and I could hardly withstand his gaze. Even from a distance I knew he was filled with a vortex of anger, because that was how I had felt. I could hardly stomach taking deep breaths to suppress his Blessing, so I only hoped me standing there was doing the trick.

He'd seen me hurt before, but he seemed more disturbed. "You're hurt," he said with his voice strained and extended his hand to my bloodied cheek—

I recoiled from him.

Shock crossed his stare as his hand froze midair. Never had I retreated from him, even in pain I would always accept his touch, but not then. I couldn't then.

"What's happened? Eve, please tell me."

"My lord," Selasi interjected, "allow me to take her to Lani immediately." He was using more energy to try to hold me upright. I would never forget my gratitude towards Selasi in that moment.

"Allow me to assist," Arius imposed while hoisting my other arm over his shoulders. I was in too much pain to resist. "I can get her to the palace quicker."

Safir merely nodded and dropped his hand to his side, watching as Arius closed his eyes and took a deep breath. Immediately, I withheld the air in my lungs, not knowing if I'd affect Arius' Blessing.

"Hold on," he muttered as a whooshing feeling rushed past me like walking through a wind tunnel, and suddenly my tired feet landed on the palace ground. "That was a little rougher than I would have liked," Arius commented, though he sounded hundreds of miles away. My knees buckled to the dirt. I coughed and heaved, blood pooling in my stomach. As Selasi and Arius drug me to Lani's infirmary, I memorized the look of shock and hurt on Safir's face. Those past few days I hadn't wanted to return Safir's touch because he had touched *her,* been with *her,* yet looking down at my blood-soaked hands, I felt too disgusting to be touched by him. I had been just as angry, just as full of malice as those I hated most, and it was ugly. It was disappointing. It was repulsive. And it didn't deserve to be touched.

Safir

It took a great deal of strength not to finish what Eve had started on that pathetic monster. I would have endorsed his death there in that street had we not been surrounded by people.

Ashire ordered him taken back to the palace for questioning. There were still smears of blood on the cobblestone road when we vacated the city. Lord Batrum joined Emtias and Ashire in one carriage, while I accompanied Zae in hers. She was the only one able to tolerate being in a carriage alone with me since Eve wasn't present. Her bruised arms trembled against me as she stared wide-eyed at the carriage floor. "She's mad. She must be absolutely mad to do such a thing. He said he was paid *for* me. He was trying to kill me. Why?"

"That is the only reason he is still alive, to understand why."

"There was something wrong with him. He was confused and panicked not at all like a paid professional. It was like watching someone forget how to walk. I have had threats sent to me, but never assassins, let alone incompetent ones. What could I have done to deserve such an attack?"

"None of this is your fault," I tried to reassure, though my tone lacked sincerity. All I could think about was Eve. Blood had smothered her face and she'd had a vacant look in her sapphire eyes. What had happened to drive her to such a point of ferociousness that she had *flinched* against me? It felt as if someone had driven their blade through my chest and twisted it.

Zae winced. "I share your concern. I do. I see now why you two are so compatible. Each person born is broken in a unique way. Yet you two seem to be broken into the exact same shape. You match."

I fought the urge to beg her to stop talking. It made it hurt even worse that Eve rejected my touch. Rejected me. How could we "match" in any capacity if I felt that rotten?

"It is because you feel this way," Zae interrupted my thoughts, "that I can tell you match. She will be fine. I know it. Vada seems to

272

smile on Eve, despite her aversion to deities." A smile threatened my lips, but the feeling was fleeting. When we arrived at the palace,

Zae's poise fully returned. "Go to her," she told me. "I will be fine."

And I did. I didn't wait for a command from my brother. I didn't wait for Eve to be returned to me healed. My entire being was vibrating with urgency, demanding to see. She could be brought to me covered in mud, smothered with bloodied regrets, and depraved sins, yet I would still choose her. I was willing to tell her that, as many times as it took to convince her, but I was sure that, in her own way, she already knew.

I dashed up the stairs to Lani's infirmary at a frantic pace. When I arrived onto the top floor, winded but uncaring, I threw the door open, but I was halted by Selasi stationed outside.

"My lord?" he asked, stepping in front of the infirmary door.

"Move, Selasi."

"Please trust me, Lord. She's not fit to be seen, and you're not fit to see her."

And then I heard it. Sobbing and choking most heart-wrenching. Selasi looked away, seeming to hide his own discomfort. My blood stood cold in my veins as I looked through the crack in the door, and there she was: hunched over a bucket. Her shirt had been removed, only leaving her small-clothes to cover her breasts that heaved as she lurched a mix of blood and bile. Lani's gentle hands held her hair away from her brutalized face. Hundreds of specks of glass protruded from Eve's flesh, and in the middle of her abdomen was a bruise. It was the ugliest mixture of purple and black, a stain on her once-perfect skin. In that moment of seeing her sobbing so violently the bucket was wobbling beneath her, I understood it wasn't my confession she needed. It wasn't my touch she needed.

Selasi shut the door. "I hadn't wanted you to see her in such a state. I'm sorry, Lord, for having lost track of her in the square. I personally—"

I found myself taking steps back from the door. First hesitant, then hurried. The once cold blood in my veins suddenly regained warmth. Selasi might have called after me, but my heart was pounding in my ears. I headed downwards until I found the creature who had caused such pain. My unquenchable anger was growing and what remained of my self-control was saturated by fury.

I felt no fear, no dread as I dared to enter the place that had once repelled me. I continued onward while descending into the dungeon. Ignoring the sickening feeling in my gut, I saw Ashire already at the bottom of the steps.

"What do you think you're doing?"

"What I was created to do," I growled while brushing past him. "Fulfilling a purpose."

He gripped my shoulder and spun me around. "You'll do no such thing. The captive isn't even conscious, Safir."

"He will wake for me."

"Stop!" he commanded.

I halted. I snapped my glare back to him. "You allowed me down here with the last assailant."

"You had more wits about you then. I forbid you to use your Blessing—"

"*Curse.*"

"I forbid you to use it to harm the assassin!" Suddenly he was in front of me, snarling, "I did not pull you from the edge of depravity just for you to plunge back in headfirst!"

"I'm sorry my recovery was such a burden placed upon you." I sidestepped him, but he remained two steps ahead.

"On my honor, you were not once a burden, Safir. Do not jeopardize the progress you have made by indulging in the thoughts the previous king planted."

"I'll give purpose to her pain."

"Stop, Safir!" he shouted again as I took another step forward and we came to stand eye to eye. "I order you to not take another step." His stare pierced me, but I raised my foot from the ground.

"REPEL."

My entire body was flung through the air, dragging my limbs as I came to a skidded stop along the dirt floor. I bit back curses as I grimaced up at Ashire, who stood tall and unmoving.

"Do not make me do it again."

He had been gentle with that attack. I knew the true extent of his Blessing. I almost scoffed while standing. "You're so quick to use your Blessing when you prohibit me from using mine?"

"I am trying to protect you."

"And I am trying to protect her!"

"No, you are not! If I believed that I would let you pass. But I can feel you're indulging in your own guilt and self-hatred. This is the work of the king past, and I refuse to sit idly by!"

"Move, Ashire," I snarled while drawing my sword. It felt heavier when pointing it at my brother.

He glanced to the blade and back to me. "If this is what you need, I will oblige." Ashire reached across his person and drew his own blade, his being slenderer with an exaggerated point.

I had never fought my brother but circling him made the memory of my mother churn into something shameful. Regardless, I could hardly see past my fury and rushed to clash my blade against his. He kept one arm behind his back and blocked my attack, dodging underneath and emerging on the other side of me. I whipped around just in time to catch the brunt of his attack, withstanding the blow with a grunt. Ashire grimaced while I pressed my weight into my blade, making him brace against his sword. Within the final second before I overcame him, he threw his full weight to the side, dragging my weapon along with it, and whirled around me so quickly I barely had time to blink. He rebuffed one attack after another, hardly trying to take the offensive.

"You know Mother would be weeping if she saw us."

"This isn't about Mother."

"Then please tell me what this is about!"

"The fact—" I rolled beneath his blade and leapt to my feet. "— that I was given a purpose for this confounded curse, and you're impeding me from using it!"

"Hardly." He dug in his heels and released an onslaught of attacks. "You're guilt-ridden! And you're using the purpose of the king past to justify it! It's pathetic to watch your potential wasted over one woman who wouldn't want you to do this! If she wanted to kill that man, she would have done so." He paced back to give himself breathing room, leaving me panting after blocking his strikes. "So, what do you think you're doing?"

"I'm meant to keep her safe!"

"But you're not thinking of her!" he shouted, his kingly voice echoing against the walls. "I can feel it. You're consumed with your own weaknesses. An assassin was sent to kill our ally, almost kills your Eve, caused a stampede, yet you can only think of your own shortcomings?"

My grip weakened. "I know. I—" I couldn't make sense of my anger at that point. It hadn't been to avenge Eve; it had only been to numb my own pain. It had been self-seeking, and I was willing to do it in her name. "Then what fucking good is this curse of mine, what purpose was all of my suffering, if isn't able to keep her safe?"

The "shing" of Ashire's sword being sheathed rang in my ears, as did his footsteps as they approached me. "The past king's purpose wasn't meant to protect. Do not spend your entire life looking for the purpose behind your pain. You're burdening yourself and Eve if you're expecting her to justify your Blessing." I felt his hand on my shoulder, still never afraid to make contact, and I didn't mind exposing him to the emotional turmoil that was plaguing me. "Safir, today did not happen because you weren't *more*. Today happened because someone else was so much *less*. Make no mistake, that man will pay for what he did to Eve and Zae. He will pay for undermining your debut, but not in this way."

A weighty sigh escaped me as I sheathed my own sword, allowing the guilt to wash over me. I met his gaze, seeing nothing but affection behind his usual cool disposition.

"Ashire, I am sorry."

"You're truly an imbecile." He smirked. "There is no need to apologize, not with me."

***

The grotesquely bruised assassin huffed through his swollen lips, his nostrils clogged with blood. He was as inspiring as a conversationalist as he was an assassin.

"I am Frederara Bask," he slurred.

Ashire shook his head. "Not possible. Bask wouldn't be as careless as you were."

The man's ego was more brutalized than his face as he hissed, "Today was an anomaly. Never, never has this happened to Frederara. My skills never dull, yet today … I always finish the job, quickly and quietly."

"Yes, if you are who you say you are your reputation would make you a formidable foe. Yet today, you gave no impression you were a threat. If it had been left to me, I would have allowed my brother's advisor to bloody you until your brains were ingrained between the cobblestones."

"Agh, that bitch!"

I stiffened and tried to take shallow breaths. Ashire had only allowed me to be present under the impression that I had regained control over my Blessing. Seeing that man, chained to the wall, and growing more swollen by the second felt like enough revenge for the moment. I would have hated to sully Eve's hard work.

"What is she? What does she do?"

Ashire took a step closer. "What are you implying?"

"She made me useless! All my years of work, all my experience left my limbs. My muscles couldn't remember how to shoot a damn arrow! My arrows always strike true, yet Frederara had to resort to retrieving the lady himself."

Ashire slowly nodded. "Interesting. Why did you target Lady Zae?"

"I was paid."

"Who is your employer?"

The assailant smiled, exhibiting missing teeth and bloodied gums. "Ah, now that's where Frederara knows best. If I tell you, they will kill me. If I don't tell you, you will kill me."

"What if we offered you amnesty in exchange for what you know?"

I snapped my stare to Ashire who appeared unmoved by his merciful offer. I had to trust in his decisions because they were often five steps ahead of mine.

Bask hummed and chuckled to himself. "There is nowhere Frederara would be safe. Your promise would be an empty one."

"If you can't trust a promise from a king, you can't trust a promise from anyone. Perhaps think this through. I'm willing to give you ample time," Ashire sneered while turning away from Bask.

***

"Clearly, Frederara's Blessing is to kill. He never had to practice to be any good at it, and while he was in Eve's presence, he became as deadly as a pigeon," Ashire hypothesized aloud in his study. "That must be the only explanation."

We had tried to conspire discreetly, avoiding involving the other guests for fear of raising panic. Batrum had gone to reassure and see over Tesara. Knowing Ashire, I was sure he was relieved at Batrum's absence. He hid his embarrassment well in front of his idol. We settled

277

in the heart of Ashire's study with Emtias and my brother. My curiosity was permitted to permeate through the air.

"I agree," Emtias said. "But who would want Lady Zae so assuredly dead they would hire Frederara Bask?"

"And why here?" I asked. "If the true purpose were to kill her why not do it on her journey home where there would be fewer witnesses and she would be more exposed? Why in the city full of guards and during my debut?"

"It is *because* it is your debut it was orchestrated for today," Ashire said. "The impact would have been to undermine House Astana. To have a noble woman killed during your debut would have cracked the foundation of our authority, sowing thoughts of distrust from Phora." He pinched the bridge of his nose with a groan. "And no doubt numerous commonfolk were injured during the stampede. Emtias, remind me to dispatch Lani as soon as she's finished with Eve."

Emtias nodded. "Perhaps it was meant to undermine the crown, but leaving House Oska without a head would have created a void of power for another house to absorb. And who would be so bold as to orchestrate such an attack?"

A knock came from the door. All three of us turned to see Lord Arius step through in all his smugness. I excused myself to look out the window, putting distance between us. I didn't need my Blessing to give away my disposition towards Arius. He greeted us warmly.

"I took it upon myself to check on Lady Zae."

"And?"

"She's doing remarkably well, Your Majesty," Arius responded to my brother. "She's unnervingly resilient. I must say, today's occurrences were unexpected. I hate seeing such vile creatures dare to show their faces."

Emtias narrowed his eyes. "I find it interesting that you say such things. Do you not have influence with the goblin hordes in the south?"

Arius waved him off. "It takes little skill to win over such simple creatures. Their needs are far less civilized than ours."

"It's almost dismissible, if they swore their allegiance to the crown rather than to you."

"Yes, but I am loyal to the crown, and so indirectly are the hordes. Did the kings past put such pressure upon House Calista for their allegiance to the griffins?"

Ashire sauntered forward. "The griffins are the oldest creatures in the land, older than the Fae. They're not as governable as goblins."

Arius nodded slowly. "Then upon my return I will renew my friendship with the hordes to tell of the renewed strength of the crown, with His Royal Highness now able to *finally* address his royal duties."

"How kind of you," I remarked.

"Yes, your advisor seems to think so."

I stiffened.

His rotten mouth curled into a grin. He knew he held me in his hand. "I hated seeing her so bludgeoned today, although it was quite entertaining to see her deliver the bludgeoning."

"I doubt the prince appreciates you making light out of his advisor's endangerment," Ashire snapped. I appreciated his commentary, for I could think of little else to say to Arius other than threats of disembowelment.

Arius held his hands up in defense. "I mean no offense. It was painful to see, especially with how close she and I have become over this week. We're quite alike."

"In what regard?" I asked, not taking my scowl off him.

"We both agree no one is truly free in this world. Are we not all bound by something or someone? Whether it be by title, code, or," he looked to me knowingly, "emotion."

My hands formed fists at my sides. "You've overstepped your familiarity with me, sir. Tread carefully in the presence of your king."

He bowed. "My sincerest apologies. It's merely come to my attention this is not the first time your advisor has had an unfortunate encounter with an attacker."

"The first occurrence was a grudge-wielding commoner," Emtias rebutted. "Not a hired assassin."

"True, but it makes one question whether her safety is a priority in the palace." Arius glanced to me. I bit hard on the inside of my cheek to keep myself from opening my mouth. "I feel it is respectful to inform the prince and king I have given her an offer to join my service."

I bit straight through my cheek and tasted blood.

"That's a rather overreaching offer," Ashire commented coolly. "You barely know her, and Emtias can attest she has much learning to do regarding her position as advisor."

"I think she proved herself more than capable today," Arius chuckled. "I am not trying to make light of today's unfortunate events. I believe she will flourish in the south."

"It will be her decision to make," I reminded him, unable to restrain the obvious disdain in my voice.

Arius drank it in. "I am fully ready to accept whatever decision she makes. Are you?"

I swallowed a surge of rage, exhibiting greater restraint than he deserved. I didn't try to hide my disgust, only wishing he would take a few steps closer to fully experience my Blessing, but he kept distant.

Ashire emerged and stood between us. "Regardless, Eve's security is being seen to. The assassin has agreed to our terms in exchange for divulging his employer," he bluffed.

Arius focused his scrutiny on my brother. "Is that so? How will you know he is not feeding you false information just to buy his life?"

"I don't, but he gives himself away. Every man does eventually." His Astana eyes blazed at Arius, seeming to call on the Last Flame. It made one compelled to hold his gaze.

We all remained as still as statues and as quiet as corpses. *This is how wars start*, I thought to myself. But we all jolted as the doors were thrown open and Selasi stumbled through. He knew better than not to announce himself, making me wonder what could have happened to make him behave so informally.

He bowed before Ashire. "Your Majesty, it is Bask. He's dead."

Eve

For the first time in my life, I hardly felt a flicker of anger. It was as if someone had doused the embers of my outrage with a bucket of water. I tried to recall memories that used to infuriate me: being separated from Nicky, being taken advantage of by Hunter, being made to give myself over and over. All I felt was a melancholic exhaustion, but not anger. I'd had moments of happiness throughout life, fleeting as they were, but each minute of life had felt like a different flavor of anger. That was all I had defined myself by, and so as I lay in a heap of exhaustion, I wondered why I didn't feel as angry at the assailant as I had before. I had felt small and hopeless while hurling into that bucket, as if things were never going to change. I had always had that anger as my constant companion, and it left me battered in body and soul.

"I'm so tired of this!" I had choked into that bucket, gripping the sides for dear life as I couldn't stand the pain from my sore abdomen every time I retched. I was tired of being angry. Tired of being in pain.

Lani had held my hair and pressed cool cloths to my head, healing me minute by minute. "Let it go. Good, my lily, just let it go." She knew the tears were arising from a deeper source of pain, a pain that couldn't easily be reached even by me.

I doubted it would be as easy as "letting it go" but at least I'd acknowledged I was tired of it all. Anger never got me anywhere. And that face, the one that had become nothing but a lump of swollen flesh … It was haunting to think I could have done that so quickly and with so little thought.

I think I don't like myself very much.

Maisy stoked my fire and Oberia curled up next to me. She whimpered until I put my arm around her, and she nestled her head onto my chest. Her soft hair tickled my chin and would have made me smile if I could manage such an expression. Maisy sat next to me and squeezed my hand, waiting for me to squeeze back.

"I'm fine, Maisy," I told her. The sullenness in my voice gave no indicator that I believed myself.

Maisy shook her head, making her red curls bounce. "No, I don't believe you are, but that's okay. Milfred says each day is an opportunity for something better."

Damp warmth ran through my shirt. Obi wept silently in my chest. She didn't sniffle, hardly breathed. I soothed her hair, like Lani had done for me. "Obi? It's fine now."

She shook her head. "No. Terrible things have happened. And I—" She didn't finish. I opted not to press her like I would have preferred.

The whole palace had been buzzing with the news of Bask's death. I couldn't pinpoint how exactly I wanted to react to it, so, I didn't say anything, merely kept my stare on the ceiling.

Selasi had been the one to inform us moments prior. He'd sulked in the doorway, unwilling to look me in the eyes. "Two guards will be posted here. Please don't leave without their escort, Maisy. At least for now." She'd nodded, as quiet as I had ever seen her around Selasi. When she had turned to look at me and Obi, all the color had drained from her already pale face.

"The assassin is dead," Maisy stated, and my stomach dropped. I must have looked as ashen as I felt because she reached to squeeze my hand. "It was not your doing, Eve. He was killed in his cell. We're to have guards posted to each room."

I shot up from the bed. "So, there's another assassin who killed the assassin?" How desperate was someone to keep him quiet? And even worse, that implied the person who'd hired him was in the palace.

Obi groaned and buried her head in a pillow, her sobs growing. Maisy released me and reached for the small girl, scooped her into her arms. "We'll be safe, Obi. Selasi would never let anything happen to us."

"It's not that," she sniveled. "I cannot say. I should not say!"

Maisy and I exchanged glances, opting not to press the girl further, but I felt dread crawl over my skin. We shared the silence for what felt like hours with the sound of clanging and marching outside of the door while guards were posted. Part of me was left to ponder if Bask was supposed to be an accomplished assassin, then why had he been so useless? Even more perplexing, Zae had recognized him. How useful was a recognizable assassin? Or had she had dealings with him before?

Each thought pulled me back into that world more and more despite the fact I planned to leave. That world would keep going without me, and I was needed more in my own reality.

A soft knock at the door made both Maisy and I stiffen and glance to the other. I motioned her to stay put as I slowly stood, unraveling Obi from my grasp before approaching the door. At least I was able to defend myself if necessary, but I didn't hear the guards outside protest. I peeked to see Zae standing there. She scanned me up and down, faintly smiling. "Thank goodness Lani is a quick worker."

"What're you doing here?" I asked, not in the mood for pleasantries. "Didn't they tell you what happened to Bask? We don't know where his killer could be."

She motioned to the entourage of guards behind her. "Typically, I don't mind groups of men flocking to me, but this feels ridiculous. Rest assured, I'm well-guarded. I needed to see you. To know you were well."

"Well enough, all things considered."

"I never was able to thank you for today. It was mad but brave what you did."

"No thanks necessary." I almost wished I hadn't done it.

Her brows furrowed and mouth made a firm line. "Don't be rude. Please accept my thanks."

"I will, but only if you answer a question for me."

Her features softened. "Of course."

I lowered my voice to avoid eaves-dropping guards. "Did you know Bask? When we were in the cellar, it sounded like—"

"I'm aware how it sounded," she snapped in a harsh whisper. "And I cannot fault your suspicions, but please keep this observation to yourself."

"You're not helping yourself sound less suspicious."

"I don't doubt it, but all I can promise are my good intentions and reassurance my ties with Bask are not as you think." She leaned towards me. "From one lady to another, what lengths have you gone to in order to endure the people, *the men,* in your life?"

My stomach twisted into knots. There was a resoluteness in Zae I had seen when I had to suffer Hunter, when I had to suffer anyone who made me to feel afraid. Demoralizing didn't describe it enough. It was as if we weren't meant to feel human unless someone else gave us permission.

I gulped while nodding, dreading what waited for me in my reality. Zae released a sigh as her shoulders slumped, as if in relief. "Then I ask you not to pass judgement. I feared we had as much in common. Regarding Bask, I do regret how he met his end in this world. He could have at least had the courtesy of staying alive long enough to unmask his employer."

"Are you not afraid? That someone wanted you dead?" I asked, dumbfounded.

Zae coolly brushed her hair over her bare shoulders. "There's not much use being afraid of something one cannot control. There's plenty else to ponder upon. Speaking of," she let out a small groan and smoothed the skirt of her dress. "I wanted to apologize. Perhaps I indulged in something, or someone, that was not mine to indulge in. And I'm terribly sorry for the discomfort it caused."

"You did nothing wrong," I said, far quicker than intended. Zae gaped at me, surprised. I had no claim over Safir, and they had a richer past than I understood. It still hurt to think of it, but that was my own burden, not Zae's.

She smiled softly. "You're welcome to visit anytime for any reason in Phora. And thank you again, truly, from one great lady to another."

The offer was appreciated even though I had absolutely no intention of acting on it. We departed there. Her scent of cinnamon and cardamom lingered behind her along with her restored air of confidence. My original impression of Zae had been one of self-absorption, but it certainly wasn't the whole picture. My anger had felt like poison, and if it hadn't been dissipating from my veins, I wouldn't have gotten to see the kinder side of Zae. That made me want to keep my suspicions about her to myself. She had earned that trust from me.

I didn't believe that made that day worth it yet stepping back into my room to see Maisy and Obi waiting for me, *that* made that day worth it. I slumped back into my bed, wondering if my poisoned anger had died alongside Frederara Bask.

Safir

Frederara Bask had been found with his throat slit open. From the neck down he was coated in ruby-red-blood. The two guards posted outside of his cell had administered Bask his meal and returned to their post. He was offered no cutlery to be used as a weapon, and yet mere moments later they glanced back to see his throat slit and his bulging eyes staring up at the ceiling. They had heard no cry nor seen anyone enter or exit. There wasn't any weapon present, nothing that could have produced such a clean swipe across the throat.

My first thought was Lord Arius. I wanted him to be guilty, but he also would have been capable of it, especially if he were the employer and didn't want his assassin to have a loose tongue. His Blessing allowed him to appear and reappear in any room within a one-mile range. Yet, based on the guards' report, at the time of death, Arius had been accounted for in Lady Zae's room and then in Ashire's study.

Lani had estimated Bask had died two hours prior to when we were first alerted, yet he had been given his meal thirty minutes prior to being found dead and, per the guards' testimony, had been very much alive. How could a man die two hours prior, yet be given his meal and observed to be alive thirty minutes before being discovered dead? But Ashire and Emtias were quick to surmise it couldn't have been Arius acting alone. All other guests were retained in their rooms with guards posted while Ashire drew conclusions so rapidly his thoughts outpaced his mouth.

"That damn Rarke," he growled while leaning against the fireplace mantel. "How could any sane man think it wise to undermine the crown while in the very same room as its king!"

"I have no qualms about accusing Arius," I offered, "but how could Bask have been witnessed alive but had been dead two hours prior?"

Emtias stood and laid a hand on my brother's shoulder. "The traitor brought the means to do so with him."

Ashire turned and stared at Emtias, as if they were having their own silent conversation, before my brother shot his hellfire scowl at Selasi. "Where is Oberia?"

"Currently with Eve, Lord," he answered hesitantly.

"Good. Arius can't jump to retrieve her. She is his only witness."

I stood from my seat, trying to calm my own fear and fury as to not infect Ashire. It was easy to see his composure was at its limit. "Are you going to share what you're implying?"

He ignored me. "Emtias, do you have the means to place a bane on him?"

The Fae's head shook as he inspected the hidden pockets in his robes. "Nothing for the kind of bane I know you desire."

"Ashire!" I barked. "Would you speak plainly?"

He whipped around to me with a look of frenzy I had never seen. "That bastard is capable of more than swindling your advisor, Safir. Besides hiring Bask to assassinate Zae and undermine my authority, he brought the very means to mask Bask's death so he wouldn't be discovered as the employer. No doubt he's trained the child to create detailed illusions, so she was able to make it seem as though Bask was alive while Arius jumped into the cell to kill him before retreating back to his rooms. We've seen how capable her illusions are."

All at once, I felt the weight of my idiocy. The absolute gall of that rotten creature, to bring such violence into our very home, thinking his actions wouldn't have consequences. My blood boiled and seared my skin.

Ashire grumbled at sensing my wrath, "Now we feel the same. I want guards posted with my Uncle Batrum and Lady Tesara," he ordered at Emtias. "If a single hair on their head is disturbed than I will erect the gallows myself for whoever dares to test my command. Now, fetch Eve. She'll be needed."

I stalled my anger. "For what purpose?"

Ashire secured his scabbard to his belt. "We'll need her to ensure Arius can't use his Blessing to escape. I refuse to allow this sin to go unconfronted."

"Does that blade already have intentions?" Emtias asked, narrowing his eyes at my brother. "Do you think you'll still be seen as one of the few diplomatic kings if you murder a fellow nobleman without trial or evidence?"

"As much as I'd sleep soundly knowing he was done away with, I have no intention of killing him. If we can subdue him, we can secure him until he waits for trial. Which is why we'll need Eve," he repeated, but I shook my head.

"She's in no state to be used as a pawn. She's done enough service to the crown for one day," I protested. "You will keep her apart from this. That very first night she was here, you promised you would not weaponize her!"

Ashire gritted his teeth while standing tall, kingly even. "Selasi, go and fetch my brother's advisor."

"Stop, Selasi!" I ordered. Selasi froze and looked between the two of us. "There's no need to pit my swordsman against me."

"Then you'll assume her place. I would never ask you to use your Blessing to bring harm, but you can dissuade Arius with it."

"By what means?"

"What would you think?" Ashire spat. "Give him a false sense of calm. If you refuse to use Eve to keep him from escaping the palace, we need an element of surprise. You will provide that cover to keep him from being suspicious of my true intentions."

My mouth fell open in shock. "Ashire, do you find me capable of calm right now?"

"Yes," he hissed, "you will, or I will retrieve your Eve and put her to use a second time today. Do you want that?"

I wanted to throw my fist through a window as I simmered in silence. Ashire had been both the most supportive brother and most infuriating piece of steaming goblin shit all in one day. This response was enough for him.

"Then you will do what you must, just as you did in the city square. Coat his senses in some innocuous emotion as we confront and subdue him. Whether you like it or not, Safir, this is sometimes what it means to play our roles. Emtias, what means do you have if you cannot cast a bane?"

"Perhaps I can induce a slumber, but it is not guaranteed without better understanding Arius' psyche." Emtias reached into his pocket and pulled out a small bag of sand, rummaging through the bag with a sigh. "I haven't replenished my stock since I last used it on the guards who passed into Eve's portal."

Ashire raked his hands through his hair. "You'll have to make do. I refuse to waste more time. He could have already jumped from the palace by now."

I had thought the same, though uncertain if I preferred for Arius to have escaped or be confronted. I didn't know if I trusted myself to remain composed enough to mask Ashire's true purpose. The fact he'd been bold enough to approach Eve while simultaneously endangering her sickened the farthest reaches of my soul, the parts that recalled how it felt to take a life. It had been years since I had sat with a man who had the intent to kill, and I needed to act accordingly. For the safety of the crown and for those it protected.

"Come in," Arius voice goaded.

I had precious seconds to disguise my disgust. The only way I was able to do so was to think of Eve. At least my concern for her was genuine. My breathing slowed upon my opening his door. The traitor lounged by the window on a sofa, his head in one hand and his drink in the other.

"How are you, Your Royal Highness?" he asked.

The guards posted outside closed the door behind me. Granted, their presence was useless considering Arius' Blessing. My thoughts clung to Eve, her clear voice that had beckoned more from me. I thought of her poor condition. Her rebuking my touch.

The air was fuller of my fear for her than my disdain for the creature that sat before me. He huffed while setting down his drink. "I apologize for coming across so forthright earlier. I, too, merely worry for Eve."

"I worry more than you know," I told him, maintaining my distance. "This isn't how my debut was to unfold."

"That's an understatement."

"It's made me see things clearly."

Arius paused. His head was turned towards the window, but his eyes tracked to me. "Oh? How so?"

I swallowed bile, thinking of Eve.

"I disparaged it earlier because I was only thinking of my own needs, but …" I inhaled deeply through my nose. "I knew you were right. Eve would be better off in the south with you."

Arius' jaw dropped. "That is not what I expected," he said. "Have you discussed this with her?"

288

"She's in no state to speak. Given the shock of there being an additional assassin in our midst, I felt it better to leave the subject for another day." I folded my sweaty hands behind my back and lowered my tone. "My brother isn't in agreement, but we seem to struggle finding common ground recently."

"Is that so?" Arius squinted at me, as if studying my intent. I *was* truly consumed with worrying for Eve. It took little effort to exude that emotion around me. "I'm almost impressed, Your Royal Highness. Forgive me, but you didn't initially give the impression you were proficient at sharing."

"If we were discussing trading a possession I would agree, but considering we're talking about a capable human being I'll remind you it would be her decision. As you pointed out earlier."

"Delightful." He clapped his hands with a chuckle. "I can ensure she'll receive the utmost opportunities in Shey."

"Unfortunately, I don't feel comfortable with anyone traveling alone until this killer is found. To do that, I'm willing to swallow my pride and ask for your assistance. Another point on which my brother doesn't agree."

He stood and strode towards me. I had to think of Eve, only of her as Arius stuck his hand out to me. "I marvel at your humility. You have my word as a Rarke to offer all I can to help."

Without hesitation I clasped his hand, his fingers digging into my knuckles while he stared directly into my eyes, unblinking. I wondered about Eve's injuries, her reasoning for distancing herself from me, her true pain she had yet to reveal to me, burying everything else until only she remained.

Arius smiled and released my hand. "I never thought the day would come where I was able to touch the cursed prince."

"In complete honesty, I wouldn't have believed so either."

He chuckled harshly, turning his back to me. "How am I expected to assist?"

"I'm requesting your presence in the great hall. The other noblemen are joining us so all may be involved in the delegation to find the killer." I retreated to the door. "I don't want to lose any precious time."

"But of course," he hummed, unmoving from the middle of the room. I stalled before reaching for the knob, using every ounce of my energy to emit a neutral warmth into the air. My breath shuddered through my nose.

Suddenly, I felt a rush of air, and he was standing directly behind me with his hands clamped onto my shoulders. I held my breath as he leaned forward towards my ear. "But I will ask a question: what makes a king, Safir?"

I. Was. Failing.

His voice was low. "It is not the jewelry that sits on top of one's head. It is relentless ambition to die for what's yours."

Ashire, forgive me.

Flames engulfed my memories while I whipped around to the traitor, wanting to burn the hand that dared touch me. Arius' smug face had a wide grin as the door behind me flew open. I unsheathed my sword as Ashire and Emtias dashed forward, making us a trio of animosity. Emtias commanded forth his handful of sand, which sprang from his palm towards his target.

Arius vanished with a look of satisfaction, allowing the sand to float in his place before retreating to Emtias' hand. Emtias cursed in Fae before seeing Arius reappear in front of the windows.

"Your Majesty!" Arius cried. "To what do I owe this honor?"

"Arius!" Ashire bellowed with more ferocity than I had ever heard. "If you believe yourself innocent, you will stand down to have a fair trial."

"You must have not heard what I told your brother." Arius looked to me. "And I was convinced to begin with, I promise you. How proud you must be to lie with your touch as opposed to killing with it."

"I will remedy that failure," I growled, poised with my sword.

"If you care so much for that girl, you would have never released her to me. I wouldn't have."

Ashire slowly approached him, holding his hand midair. The guards posted outside had vanished, more than likely dismissed with Selasi to guard the others. All the while Ashire was trying to prevent what he had feared most throughout his reign. "We can do what our fathers and grandfathers never could. We can be diplomatic. We can bridge this gap of misunderstanding."

Arius laughed. "There is no misunderstanding, Ashire. I am doing you a kindness. I am leaving no doubts in you now. You don't have to wonder how safe the crown is." He stood taller and broader, confidence building with each second. Meanwhile we were circling the room. "I want you to know exactly how tumultuous this path will be for you, because it has been thrice that horrific for me."

"I returned your status and lands. Do you think either of our fathers would have done so?"

"A true king knows the difference between what is best and what is right. You should have left me to die in exile."

I wanted him to crumble beneath the weight of my indignation. He deserved to have his skin seared, yet I couldn't control my Blessing enough to impede hurting Emtias or Ashire. Arius had the audacity to tear his glare from us and glance towards the gardens. "Last I was here…twenty-three years ago, I did not think this day would come. But I am Chike's retribution." He looked back up to my brother. "Best of luck, Asta—"

"REPEL!"

The glass windows exploded and scattered shards to all corners of the room while Arius's body was flung backwards with such force it sounded like a clap of thunder. A surge of wind rushed past as we ducked and covered our heads from the raining glass. Just as quickly as chaos had erupted, quiet enveloped the room. I staggered and tried to stand upright, surveying the damage, and scouring for Arius. My eyes darted to each corner of the room.

He was gone.

"By the gods!" Ashire cursed while slamming his fists into the ground, not caring how the glass embedded into his flesh. "I am more incompetent than all of the kings past."

"There's no time for that," I chided. "He could still be here."

"He said what he needed to," Ashire said, defeated. "More than likely he's on his way back to Shey."

"Not all of him." Emtias stooped down to the floor, swiping a vial from his pocket and guided a small puddle of blood into the vial. "Very good, Your Majesty. Your attack was powerful enough to reach him before he jumped."

My brother collapsed into a chair with his face in his hands, unable to relinquish a clever word. Part of me was eaten alive seeing him like that, my fierce brother bested by the likes of Arius. Perhaps I had sabotaged the entire endeavor by wanting to kill Arius from the start. If I hadn't allowed my anger to—

"Enough, Safir," Ashire groaned from his chair. "No part of today has been your fault. The fault was mine years ago."

I said nothing. Dread filled the gaps in my mind. Knowing someone wanted to depose us clawed away at the comfort and security we'd once felt in our home. The wound was now exposed, and Arius had meant for it to fester.

Emtias sat next to Ashire and began plucking pieces of glass from his hair. Ashire remained still, his stare fixed on the ground, but allowed the Fae's nimble fingers to pull away the larger shards and dust away the smaller ones. "Worry not. Arius committed many mistakes today, but the grandest now lies with me." Emtias held the vial up to the light. "One should never surrender their blood to a Fae."

Eve

What was the point of sleeping? Maybe it would have helped time go by faster, but I felt vulnerable even while awake. It was a long night that stretched into an even longer morning.

I hadn't cared to see anyone, but I wasn't given a choice when Ashire, Emtias, and Safir barged into my room. Ashire carried a chair and set it directly in front of Oberia. His hands were bloodied, and all three men were covered in tiny cuts. What the hell had happened? At least Safir looked to me, apologetic for the intrusion.

"Now, Oberia," Ashire spoke coldly. "Now is the time to talk."

It didn't take much prompting for the poor girl to spill her guts. Most was hard to understand through her sobs and snivels, wiping her nose on her sleeve while sandwiching apologies in between each sentence. Ashire said nothing more other urging her to continue with her story.

She had been bargained for from her mother when Arius had learned about Safir's debut. Obi had been given one task by Arius, if it was not completed, her life and her mother's would be forfeit. He exploited her Blessing until her illusions would fool even the most observant man. Only when one interacted with an illusion could they tell if it were fake. Her purpose was to provide convincing illusions in place of Arius when he needed to enact his plan to undermine the crown. When Bask was brought to the dungeon, she maintained her illusion of Bask resting in his cell until Arius was accounted for.

By the end of her explanation, her eyes were beet red with snot pouring from her nose. Her lips trembled with her arms wrapped tightly around her person, making me want to reassure her. I hardly cared what she had done. Every few minutes I'd exchange a glance with Safir, knowing I cared for someone who had done far worse. Obi was just a child. Safir had been just a child. Forgiveness couldn't be in short supply.

Thank Vada Ashire seemed to agree with that.

He rubbed his eyes, asking her, "Oberia? Do you want to return to your mother?"

Her head shook.

"Do you want to remain here?"

She nodded emphatically. Ashire stood from his chair. He extended his bloody hand, making her flinch, but he placed it on top of her head. "Then here you shall stay." He stroked her head before turning and evacuating the room at a rapid pace with Emtias following close behind. "I recommend everyone bathe and collect yourselves. We see off our guests in four hours."

The rest of us remained in stunned silence for a few moments before Maisy embraced Obi. The young girl wept again, "I should have said. He told me not to say, but I should have said!"

Maisy hushed her, muffling her cries of relief into her bodice. "Come now, all is well. All is well, isn't it, Selasi?" she asked of the befuddled swordsman standing in the corner. "I think we'd feel better with some toast and jam, perhaps?"

Selasi paused with a snicker while rubbing the back of his head. "I'm not certain old Milfred would want to see me, but if I'm willing to protect against assassins, you'd think I'd be able to brave the kitchens." He winked at Obi. "I'll be back with some toast and tea, although I might be missing an arm." Despite joking, he did groan when turning and heading towards the kitchen, making Obi's sobs lessen.

Safir remained in place, wearily staring out my window to the gardens, and I wanted to know so badly what he was thinking or feeling. The closer I was to him, the more I could see tiny specks of glass shining in the sunlight, caught in his strands of white hair. He was a beautiful mess, and it made my heart tear. Just because I was leaving didn't mean I didn't care for him. I had to care for Nicky more, but Safir didn't need to hear that in that moment.

I brushed a few flecks of glass from his hair, hearing tiny clinks against the stone floor. I was careful enough to only brush his soft, white strands.

He turned to me. "Are you all right?" he asked huskily.

I couldn't give him a reassuring answer in that moment. "For now," was all I could muster. "Are you all right?"

Safir glanced to the pieces of glass that had fallen out of his hair before turning to look back out my window. "I cannot wait for everyone to leave."

"Me too," I answered instantly.

His warm gaze softly landed on mine, and I knew why his stare made me feel so warm. I understood why I craved it, and for a few fleeting moments days prior I'd thought I understood how he felt. I had to remind myself that it wasn't enough.

"I'll leave you to get ready," he murmured, excusing himself from my room. The silence that he left behind deflated me as I slumped against the wall. Knowing I was going to leave was going to make that week even more painful.

I eventually returned to bed, to try to let sleep have some part of me.

Fuck, what a day.

As time waned to where we would see off whatever guests remained— or hadn't betrayed the crown— I began counting the things I would miss: Milfred's cooking, Selasi's jokes, Maisy's hairstyles, Lani's miraculous healing, the dew in the morning, the way the sun set behind the mountains, Ashire's library, Ashire himself (a little bit), Emtias' motivation, and Safir…

I forced myself from my bed one last time, pulling away from Maisy and Oberia's warmth as they began to stir. "I should get ready to see everyone off," I said aloud, making Maisy rouse with a yawn and a stretch.

"I'll draw you a bath." There was no room in her tone to argue with her, and so another item on my list was added. I'd miss the baths. I'd miss the smell. Maisy filled them with essence of crawlsey flowers, which were in abundance in the gardens.

As always, I preferred my privacy as I enjoyed the warmth while it lasted. I wanted the smell to linger with me for days after I left. I wanted to remember that it was all real, that I'd been part of life in Walyre. It made me think of when I'd tried to steal a book from Ashire's library when first trying to leave. I felt no such desire to do so a second time. If I took a token of that place I would always wonder, always be tempted to return.

When the water cooled, I stood and wrapped myself in my warm robe. Maisy did my hair, pulling strands into braids on one side of my head and instructed Oberia on how to perform similarly on the other side. Obi almost giggled but apologized profusely if she pulled my hair. I didn't mind. It was nice seeing Obi even begin to smile. They left me looking delicate as ever, with sets of braids on either side of my head pulled back while remaining tendrils curled against my neck as my hair dried.

I stood and thanked them both, hugging Maisy. She hesitated at first, but then returned my embrace tenfold. "You have that look. I'll be here should you return."

My eyes widened at her understanding, but I said nothing. We parted, and I exited my room to meet the others in the courtyard. My steps felt heavy, and I found myself staring out the rows of windows that highlighted the landscape of the valley. The crisp air I was going to miss greeted my nose when I finally stepped outside. I inhaled deeply and enjoyed the morning sun kissing my skin. All the little things I had become so accustomed to in that realm, were going to leave me reeling the next morning when I awoke in my grey world.

As I approached the nobles, lined with their carriages and entourages ready to depart, multiple pairs of eyes landed on me. Lord Batrum was conversing with Ashire, and Safir stood with Zae. It made my chest ache, but there was no anger there. It shouldn't be surprising he would cling to her when I wasn't present to suppress his Blessing. I ignored the blood rushing to my face as I approached Lady Tesara first. She cupped my face. "I'm so happy to see you so well now. What a rotten way to end such a lovely week. I promise when you visit Xard no such travesties will occur."

"A lofty promise, my dear. 'Disgraceful' is a more appropriate way to describe yesterday's offense to the crown." Lord Batrum kissed my hand as I curtsied. "It was a pleasure meeting you. And Your Majesty," he called to Ashire behind me, brushing past to bow to his king. "You handled this week's tribulations like the scholar I'd hope you'd be. I am all too proud to see the fruition of your dedicated studies."

Ashire was borderline beaming. "Those words carry a great deal of weight and appreciation, Uncle. Please message me as soon as your return to Xard safely."

"You have my word. Until next time, my king."

"Perhaps when the conservatory is finished, we shall celebrate with a ball of our own. Eve and I long to dance together." Tesara beamed with wide eyes. "Isn't that right?"

I nodded, appreciative of her optimism, but skeptical any such endeavor would take priority over finding Arius. "It would be our pleasure. I wish you safe travels and a safe arrival for your daughter."

"Daughter?" Lord Batrum inquired.

Lady Tesara beamed. "Just a feeling, darling. Yes, dear Eve, thank you very much for your companionship. I will write to you often— I promise. And this," she reached into her sleeve and withdrew a flower. Its stem drooped to the side, holding one white flower shaped like a bell. "I made, er, found this for you. Just a reminder that something beautiful could grow amid turmoil." I delicately took it into my hands. She placed a quick kiss on my cheek before struggling to enter the carriage before Lord Batrum offered his assistance.

"We will be in touch," he told me, speaking low while glancing to Ashire. "As always, we will do what we must to support the crown." They piled into the carriage, and I felt relieved that they didn't have the burden of the crown.

Ashire allowed his disposition to relax, perhaps because people were leaving, and he must have been exhausted. His once-bloody hands had been healed and folded behind his back. "I believe you received a warmer farewell than I did."

"I doubt that."

There was a pause as he almost fidgeted where he stood. "How're you feeling today?"

I cocked my head to the side. "I don't think you've ever asked about my well-being before."

"I can certainly refrain from doing so in the future if you'd like. It'd spare me quite a bit of energy," he sneered, but he was waiting for my actual answer.

"I'm fine. Thanks for asking." And I tried to mean it.

"Give it a few days, and we will have recovered from the events of this week. I'm sure we'll find rejuvenation in time."

There was nothing else to say, so I said nothing. Safir left Zae's side and approached us. He didn't look to me, not even a glance. He stepped forward to say goodbye to Lord Batrum and Lady Tesara, smiling warmly but his eyes didn't flare like they used to. I focused on my breaths to do my job well enough one last time before Zae approached me.

Ashire made himself scarce as she stood in front of me. Her hair was combed to perfection and fell down the length of her back as she wore her loose dress despite the cool, morning air. Zae reached into her satchel and pulled out a scroll and my dagger. "My advisors and I drafted something for you last night. Also, this belongs to you."

I took the dagger and attached it to my hip while peering at the paper scroll. "What is this?"

"The beginnings of the program we discussed. I promised you would have my support. We laid out a general set of policies based on your ideas. It is only a beginning, but it felt like the least I could do. You seem so desperate to help those around you."

I hugged the scroll close to me along with my flower. "This is very kind of you. Thank you."

"My pleasure," she glowed. "And Eve, regardless of how you feel about me, I hope you know you do have a friend in Phora."

We bade each other farewell, with my flower tucked in my pocket, dagger attached to my hip, and scroll in hand. Safir did the same with Batrum and Tesara, leaving our guests to their journeys back home. The air itself around us felt lighter with each second the carriages gained distance from the palace. A few days prior I would have felt relieved, ecstatic even that the debut was over, and I could finally have Safir to myself. Yet events had changed so rapidly that it felt impossible to revert to the way we were.

I turned on my heel and made my way back to the palace. There were still no traces of anger left in me, only certainty. And because there was no longer a miasma of fury clouding my perception, I knew he was following me. I didn't hear his footsteps nor see him approach, but I knew it. Slowly but surely, he would follow me, and then we would say goodbye.

Safir

I had endured playing my part through gritted teeth. My debut had been a menagerie of thrills and shocks and questions for which I hadn't been fully prepared. I doubted anyone had. However, the fact it was over meant the time to truly engage in my new role had come. Even more so with newfound treachery threatening the crown. But I needed Eve.

Another reason I was glad the debut was over was that there was now *time* to repair the fracture in my friendship with Eve. We would need to be united more than ever given the previous day's treason, but more than that, I longed for the comfort of her once-warm presence. It had felt so alien to feel her so estranged from me, even though our arrangement had only existed for a few months.

When everyone finally departed from the palace grounds into the cobblestone city below, it was time for Eve and me to finally talk. We were once so transparent with each other, and I longed for sincere conversation.

She made her way back into the palace. I made no attempts in concealing the fact I intended to pursue her. Falling into her footsteps but allowing her to remain ten paces ahead of me, that was until Ashire grabbed my arm.

"Choose your words carefully," was all he said before releasing me.

I allowed his advice to marinate in my mind as I resumed walking in Eve's direction. A fraction of me wanted to be alone with her while the opposing fraction felt sickened at the thought. She felt wronged in some capacity, likely by me, but I couldn't remedy that hurt if I didn't know what it was. The sooner a remedy was found the sooner we could get along as we were.

Eve took an arduous path back to her room, but I followed. My ears caught the sound of her door closing just seconds before I arrived. Surely she knew I was close behind her. Upon opening her door, I found her staring out her window with her arms crossed over her chest. Her jaw was set tight, and her gaze appeared steely. A paper scroll and my gifted dagger lay on her bed. My curiosity was piqued, but I made a note to address that later.

I took long strides until she was directly under my gaze. I had no desire to open the conversation with simple talk. "I know Zae must have already thanked you, but I don't believe *we* have, on behalf of the crown, for saving our ally. You're developing quite the track record of Ashire being indebted to you."

Not a single muscle in her face moved, only her lips when she muttered, "I don't recall parts of it. It's kind of a blur. I lost track of what I was doing. I never want to feel that way again."

Her words struck me. My hand ached to reach out for her, but I stalled. "I promise I understand what it feels to lose yourself to temper, Eve. The emotional whiplash can be sickening. From my experience, the company that is there to greet you afterwards makes the biggest difference." She said nothing, only casting her eyes down. I continued while taking a step forward. "I love your bravery." I heard her audibly swallow. "But I loathed seeing you in such danger, in such pain. I never want to see you like that again."

"Done."

She spoke so curtly it made me uneasy. We still hadn't gotten to the heart of the issue, but we were closing in.

"Can your debut even be considered successful, given everything that happened?" she asked.

"Not as successful as we had hoped, but it is done. I showed I can shoulder some of Ashire's burden. He'll need us to assist in thwarting Arius. And he's asked that I lead the next meeting with the local lord, that is if," It was then it felt right to reach for her. I was so slow, so cautious, as I raised my hand to her soft cheek. I'd swipe my thumb across her jaw and feel her lean into my touch, and then I'd know all would be well.

But instead, she recoiled. Her furious sapphire stare snapped to mine, tears brimming. "No! No."

"Why?"

"Just, no," Eve huffed while settling her hands on top of her head.

"*Why?*" I asked. "Tell me why, Eve. What changed in these last few days where you would receive me before but not now?"

"Because…" Her cheeks became crimson.

I growled in frustration, "Because why?"

"Because you touched *her*!" she shouted. "The night of the ball I heard you and Zae, and now I can't bear you being as close to me without feeling like a complete idiot all over again, Safir!" Tears finally cascaded down her cheeks as horror washed over me.

She had heard us? Dear Vada, that first night felt like ages ago I recalled the night of the ball, how incriminating it must have sounded. I knew there was not going to be any suitable explanation.

Eve had retreated to her dying fire, wiping her eyes. "And at the dance, I thought, I swore that you were trying to convey something to me, that you felt something when it was just us dancing, but when I was left to fend for myself against Arius—"

"Arius only has poison for words, Eve!"

"Arius is a smug fucker, but he wasn't wrong about everything! Think about how it must have felt to think you *wanted* me, yet I hear you with Zae moments later."

I did want her. I still wanted her.

"I know there are bigger things to worry about now, not knowing where Arius is or what he's planning, and maybe I have no right to be this pissed off, but—"

"Who says you have no right?" I questioned boldly. If her affections matched mine then she had every right.

Eve stared at me wide-eyed. "What?"

I closed the distance once again, and she didn't retreat. "What if you had every right to be this angry with me?"

She sniffled and shook her head. "If you're saying I have the right to be angry with you, that's going to hurt ten times worse."

We were mere inches away from each other. I could feel the heat and smell the sweet scent of crawlsey flowers emanating from her formidable person. Dear Vada, I wanted to show her exactly what Zae and I *hadn't* done. "Nothing happened that night, between Zae and I."

Her eyes narrowed. "Did you sleep with her?"

"No."

"Did you kiss her?"

I hesitated for two heartbeats too long. Eve was already shaking her head with contempt on her face. "Bastard." She covered mouth with her hand to stifle sobs.

My heart tightened in my chest, and I wanted to impale myself on a spike if it meant repenting for hurting her. "I have failed you; I know that. I should not have kissed her. I wish I hadn't, but it wasn't sensual like you think. I hadn't seen Zae in years, and the last I saw her she was still my betrothed! Our relationship never had a proper conclusion, and I suppose that was our way of concluding the only other type of friendship either of us had ever known! That doesn't make it right, but it was not sensual whatsoever."

"It sounded to the contrary," she hissed.

Damn Zae for having been such an overzealous lover.

"In her own way, she told me as much." Eve sniffled. "If that kiss was platonic, in your mind, then what you were conveying to me when we danced, that was?"

"Genuine, only with you could I be so."

Her mouth scarcely hinted at a smile, and I was almost hopeful. "That's very good to know, but that's not enough to keep me here."

The air suddenly evacuated my lungs as my jaw fell open. It was my turn to recoil from her. "You're leaving?"

She nodded somberly.

I was rapidly becoming desperate as my thoughts raced. "Eve, please, after everything we've been through, I've just attained the ability to conduct my duties. I need you there if I'm to conduct the meeting with the local lords, and with Arius—"

"What did we expect, Safir? That I would come running between my world and yours for the rest of my life? That I would hang on you like an ornament until you were able to control your Blessing?"

"That is not the sole reason I want you to stay."

"Oh really? Because that's exactly what you *just* made it sound like!"

I growled while raking my hands through my hair. "Yes, per our original agreement your purpose here was to hinder my Blessing, but surely you're not as daft to think that is the sole reason I want you here. Your place, your purpose here, has expanded beyond anything I could have predicted! There was no way to predict you were going to do this to me, and I've accepted it."

"Accepted what?" she asked, daring me to confess.

I tried to slow my temper while approaching her, and that time when I reached for her, I was able to capture her face in my hands. She was warm, trembling yet steady all at once. I leant my forehead against hers so she would *feel* my words when I said them. "I've accepted that you are the first face I search for in every room I enter, that your presence has become a greater sanctuary than anything Vada could give me, and that I have given you such a power over my temper it is frightening, but I accept it gladly." Through the palms of my hands to the tips of my fingers, I tried to convey the overwhelming sincerity and longing I had for her. Her eyes widened and her breath shuddered. My heart stirred in my chest. I felt if I could hold her, let her sense my affection for her, it would be enough to convince her to stay.

Yet she didn't lean into my touch as she once had. After a few lingering moments, Eve reached and placed her hands over mine, clutching them tightly. She pulled my hands away from her face and placed them back at my sides. "Thank you for showing me that. I would have always wondered," she muttered before she turned away from my stunned person.

"Dear Vada, you're still leaving?" I asked, utterly gutted.

"I still have a fight I need to prepare for, and there are obligations in my world I can't neglect any further, regardless of how I feel."

"I have laid my soul bare before you, my brother's crown is under threat, and you're in a rush to get brutalized for money? Do you not care?"

"I care," she whispered.

"Is this about receiving coin instead? Is this really about money?" She stiffened, and I felt disappointed, though it was perhaps what I deserved. "If that's what it'll take I'll throw you coin! I'll pluck the very jewels from my crown if that's what it takes for you to stay. Is that what you want?"

"No." She swallowed a sob that rose in her throat, and I felt rotten all over again. "Not like this. You don't know what you're asking of me."

"I beg of you to tell me then!"

"You promised you would never ask that!" she shouted, finding more strength in her voice. "Just as you promised I wouldn't regret wearing that ridiculous dress. There are reasons beyond you for why I'm leaving, and those reasons belong to me and me alone. I refuse to be judged about how I survive in my world when you haven't spent one day in it. Meanwhile, I've nearly split myself in half to be part of yours. I'm done! It's not fair. It's not enough anymore. I'm done."

A tear cascaded down her cheek as she rapidly exited her room. I stood there a few moments longer, still feeling the lingering warmth of her face in my hands, waiting for her to reappear in the doorway. Yet she didn't. There was already a void forming in my soul that only she could fill. In a way, it felt worse than how I'd felt before I knew her. I had come to understand the peace and happiness I *could* have had.

I slumped against a nearby wall and slid until I hit the floor. My hands made fists in my hair as my grief grew each second until I could feel it pulsating in the air around me. My chest burned with frantic breaths. I had thought I had experienced every pain imaginable to man, yet somehow, she had created a new one. Amid my agonizing over what would become of Eve in her world that had made her as pained as me, I wondered if she could feel my grief reaching out to her across the ever-growing distance between us.

Eve

My heart felt like it transformed into lead. What he'd showed me through his Blessing hadn't been a lie. I was important to him, more important than anyone else had ever been. And as bittersweet as that revelation was, it felt right to leave knowing that. I knew whenever the demands of my world would reap the last bits of my resilience, I would think of that moment where he held my face in his hands, and I would be able to survive at least one more day. I hadn't realized how much I craved beauty in my life until I encountered Walyre, beauty in nature, in food, in companionship, or in finding a quiet peace. But no beauty was worth it when Nicky suffered.

I repeated that in my head when I went to visit him before my fight. It had been three days since I had left Walyre. When I went to see him, his breathing was heavy, more labored than usual. He was staring out his window despite having his television running. Even when I sat at the edge of his bed, he still didn't look to me.

"What're you thinking?" I asked while brushing a few strands of hair from his eyes.

He crinkled his nose. "If I concentrate I can imagine…myself running through the rain…I can almost feel it … I think I still remember … what it feels like."

"Is that the first thing you would do if you could? Run through the rain?"

He barely shook his head, keeping his gaze out the window. "No … I would kill Hunter."

"Nicky—"

"I mean it. He came by."

"He told me." My hand went to my stomach with the phantom pain of my bruise. "I told him to never come back here again."

"That's not enough," he huffed. "He looked at me with complete apathy …. but the way he talked about you—"

"I don't want to know."

"No, you don't," he snarled. "If me dying means you'll be …
rid of him then just … pull that plug right now."

I shot up from his bed. "Shut the *fuck* up. I would give up
everything to keep you alive!"

"You already have!" he wheezed, and I could see his frustration
growing in his limp body. He couldn't express in his anger, only
leaving more room for it to grow. "And Hunter knows that … He'll
play you forever."

I ran my fingers through my hair, fighting tears yet again.
"What do you want me to do? I've already conceded to letting you
die. What else could you possibly want?"

"He'll be there as soon as I'm in the ground … to take
advantage of you … don't let him … Get away from here … go to
the place where I can't see you and … find someone who will keep
you safe and happy."

He exhausted himself arguing with me, and it made my heart of
lead begin to stir. "What if I can't?" I murmured.

"Then find your own happiness … Promise me."

I returned to his side, nuzzling under his arm, not unlike how
Oberia had nestled against me. "I promise to try," I told him, and
breathed in his life as long as I could.

Safir

The passage of time escaped me entirely. I remained where she had left me until Ashire entered. The sun was no longer gazing through the window, and the fire was no longer emitting any heat. Hours must have passed, but I couldn't move from where I was. When my brother took calculating steps towards me, I didn't even try to predict what he was going to say.

"She's left," he stated.

My irritation spiked.

He grimaced. "I can feel you from out in the corridors, Safir. Please try to compose yourself. We cannot let your months of endeavors be for naught. She would detest it. Regardless, because of her, we now know there is a traitor in our land, and I will need your support."

I didn't dignify him with a response.

Ashire rolled his eyes. "That woman did not get herself stabbed and nearly killed just for you to wallow in your own self-pity! You insult her by acting like this."

He was clever to play upon my respect for her. It was working. "You were right. You're always right," I bitterly confided in him while rising from the ground, my legs numb.

"How so?"

"I was too late to reconcile with her. She appeared so grudgingly severed from me." I glanced over to the bed, to see her dagger and the paper scroll still sitting there.

Ashire followed my gaze and strolled towards her bed. I almost asked him not to disturb it before I realized how ridiculous that request was. He plucked the paper scroll from her bed, taking seconds to digest the contents of the document.

"What is it?" I asked him.

"A parting gift, but nothing of immediate importance." Ashire tucked it into his waistband. He looked to me with seriousness. I almost forgot for a second I was in the presence of just my brother rather than the king. "I can sense the depths of your pain, but you have now debuted yourself and instilled confidence in our house. We cannot regress now. You two were able to aid the other and perhaps you are meant to be severed. For now."

"For now? What possible reason do you have to think she will return?"

He lightly shrugged, a gesture most unlike him. "I believe your paths have yet to diverge. Vada has tossed her coin in the air and has yet to reveal what side it has landed on. It'll be interesting to see."

"How can you be so casual about such a prediction?"

"You affirmed it yourself. I'm always right." He sighed while motioning me to his side, which I obliged. "Come. The work does not stop here."

Eve

My knees bounced, tapping my knock-off shoes against the tile floor. Anxiety surged with each heartbeat when in the past I scarcely felt nervous before a fight. My teeth chattered and sweat dripped from my forehead.

"What the fuck?" I huffed while wiping it away, unable to quell the growing nervousness that made my blood jump.

I had avoided thinking of Safir, focusing on Nicky, but in that moment where I couldn't scrape together one second of peace, I felt most tempted to sink into happier memories. My eyes fluttered closed. If I focused intently enough, I could recreate the feeling of his hands holding my face. They possessed yet liberated me. They emitted such a sense of pride in being the one to hold me that close, a flicker of guilt for causing me pain, and a wave of admiration that flooded my heart, an admiration for every part of my being. No part was unwanted or denied of this warmth. While that made my heart stir in my chest, what I sensed at the forefront was the sense of peace, a peace one finds in a long-forgotten home, the peace of knowing where one belonged.

When my eyes opened my knees were no longer bouncing, but tears brimmed my eyes. I sniffed and gave my cheeks a hard smack. Just as I did so, the locker room door swung open, and Hunter lumbered towards me.

"Show-time, Evie."

I stood and slipped my bite guard between my lips.

His hand squeezed my shoulder. "You better give it your all. Finish this and Nick will be living in luxury for a while. You know what to do." He practically hurled me out the door.

A swarm of stumbling bodies greeted my sight. The spectacle was nothing special, but a pit formed in my stomach. Through the crowd I could see my opponent already in her corner with her trainer rubbing her shoulders and shouting in her ear. As I shuffled past bodies, I saw Clay taking bets. He threw a wink in my direction as I weaved underneath the ropes and settled in my corner. The air was heavy with expectation. I could have choked on it.

My knees started bouncing again, which caught the attention of my opponent on the opposite side of the ring. She narrowed her eyes and licked her lips, showing off her thick mouthguard. Her shoulders were pointed and her knees knobby, but obvious muscle twitched beneath her skin. She was eager, and I couldn't help but feel reluctant. Fulfilling Hunter's demand was going to be harder than usual.

Moments later we met in the middle, tapping gloves as the referee reminded us of the rules. My opponent didn't appear to be listening. She maintained her glower on me and already assumed a fighting stance. She was going to try to strike first.

Fine by me.

When the bell rang, within the span of a blink, air blew past my face as I ducked low to avoid her swing at my jaw, dodged upwards and back to avoid her following uppercut. She was opening the fight with vigor, no room to breathe or think. I had to be light. I had to feel lighter than I did to win. My gloves guarded my face as I tried to assess her, but she didn't give me reprieve. The second I felt my back against the ropes I ducked, narrowly missing a quick jab as I paced back to the middle of the ring.

Cries filled the air, shouting for us to "get on with it." My fists felt heavier than usual as they resumed defending my face. In any other circumstance my blows would have made purchase by then, but I felt too guarded. Hesitation weighed me down, and I would pay for it.

She was going to tire herself out soon enough. I should have waited for that moment, but the bell rang, signaling the end of the first round. We returned to our corners, no one bloodied or bruised yet, much to the dismay of the lumbering crowd.

As I sat in my corner, a jock, more than likely one of Hunter's friends, removed my mouthguard and squirted water into my mouth. I swallowed it as Clay emerged beside me. "What're ya doing, peach? You don't even look hungry out there!"

I didn't offer a response, only gesturing for my mouthguard to be replaced, and then I headed back in. The bell rang, like clockwork she resumed her earlier attack, making me dodge down then upwards, and in that moment, I tried to land my mark.

I swung for her, only for her to sweep out of the way. I felt the lost momentum in my arm as she parried. Swears were muffled by my mouthguard. *She* was playing *me*, and the second I whipped around to her, she made purchase in my jaw. My brain bounced in my skull as my hearing buzzed. I kept my fists up to block her following blows. The second I saw an opening I drove my fist into her ribs, feeling the air rush out of her mouth in a grunt. I had expelled too much energy in that one punch, making my follow-up not as strong as it should have been while my opposite fist landed in her side.

She paced back to regain distance. The roar of the crowd resumed in my ears. Over the noise Hunter called out, "Bring this home, Evie!"

And I wanted to. I wanted it to be over with. I hardly cared that I was leaving myself exposed as I drove jabs and uppercuts into her. My blows were absorbed by her body, eating away at her resolve. A hard drive to her face almost knocked her mouthguard lose, and her gaze became glossy.

Almost done.

And then his face flashed across my vision. The pulverized flesh of Frederara Bask. He begged me to stop, but I drowned out his pleas with the impact of my knuckles. Droplets of blood landed on my face, marking me with his blood. Too much momentum carried one punch after another, each landing in softer tissue until bone prodded into my fist. I had transformed a man into a monstrosity. I was going to kill him. I'm no better than the ones I hated. My anger, my poison, was going to kill someone.

I froze. That hesitation was all it took for my opponent to regain her senses and drive one, lasting uppercut straight into my chin.

My eyes rolled into the back of my head. The roar of the crowd dissipated, replaced with a high-pitched ringing, and I collided against the mat. My teeth rattled as every bone in my head screeched. I urged my body to move, but my limbs couldn't comply. I had to get up, for Nicky, but I couldn't do it out of anger, not anymore. My anger was poison. My anger would kill somebody.

It took ten seconds too late before my vision returned, and I saw the disappointed faces surrounding me. The fight was over. That revelation surged enough life through me that my limbs finally moved, and I scrambled off the mat.

My knees barely kept me upright as I slid out from the ropes and stumbled onto the floor. Someone jerked me past the sweating bodies, and I didn't have the energy to stop them. When a breeze swept over my face, my consciousness roused long enough to see it was Clay who had drug me outside behind the gym. "You gotta get out of here, peach. Go where he can't find ya. I'll buy you some time." His hand emerged with a pocketknife and cut me free from my gloves.

His eyes were wide, and for the first time in my life, he looked terrified. My concussed state hardly registered it. "Go, Eve! Now!"

I had lost the fight. I had lost *Hunter's* fight, and he would want me to repay him.

I started running. My knees were buckling, and I veered into brick walls, but I was still moving forward, leaving that stinking gym behind me. My arms braced me against whatever obstacles I encountered during my desperate sprint.

I hardly even felt pain during my adrenaline rush, but there was a sense of the pain to come if I didn't get out of there in time. But to where? Where was my body trying to take me? There was a more fundamental part of my brain that knew where I had to go, where I was safe, where I could always be safe.

You're safe here. You're safe with me. You know that, don't you?

It had only been three days, yet I was crawling back as bloodied as ever. The portal would still be open. I didn't have to see Safir. I could just hide there long enough to keep Hunter off my trail, and that kept my legs frantically moving forward, across streets and through alleyways, dodging around cars that didn't stop. I was running for my life, or whatever was left of it.

I didn't dare stop in my house. My legs were carrying too much momentum for me to stop. Hunter could be waiting there as he had before. I carried on with my fleeting energy. Past my house, through the trees, over bushes, and on the path I had come to know and would grant me safety. My hand stretched out to reach for the invisible portal, as I willed myself to disappear from that plane of existence—

My entire body collided with a sharp force as it hurled me to the side. I was flung through the air and then came to a sickening halt as my body wrapped around a tree trunk. Air was forced from my lungs while my back shrieked in pain. I collided with the forest floor, getting a mouthful of dirt. Gasping for air, I opened one swollen eye to look up through the darkness. I began to shiver with panic.

Hunter stood over me.

His head shook as he reached down. "I figured you'd be out here. Too smart to go in your house, and Nick can't help you." He yanked me up by my hair to stand at eye level. "You've cost me too much. And how is that supposed to help Nick? Hm? What are you going to tell him? Or what would you like *me* to tell him?"

Move!

That was all that screamed in my brain, and I swung wildly at him, feeling his nose crack against my knuckles. Hunter cursed and reached for his bloodied face. I took one hasty step before he yanked me back with such ferocity I landed on my back on the forest floor. I scrambled to my feet, but not before a steel-toed boot landed in my chest. I collapsed clutched my broken body. A searing, burning sensation emanated from my center and spread throughout my entire body. I couldn't gasp without feeling like knives were ripping through each vessel. He was going to kill me. His anger, his poison was going to kill me!

Hunter straddled my decrepit form. A brutal series of punches drove into me. With each attack I felt less and less. There was immense pressure against my skull, and a warmth pulsated around me, but the overall pain was fading, even the burning in my chest. I would have begged him to stop if he paused long enough to let me breathe. I could see the unfiltered rage that drove him, that crazed look. Had I looked like that? With each passing second, I cared less and less about dying. A gnawing thought willed the rest of me to try to stay intact, to keep my bones from breaking or my blood from spilling. To just keep me alive.

Nicky.

Oh fuck! Nicky!

The thought of Nicky dying alone made my consciousness rouse to the surface long enough to feel Hunter grab onto my foot and drag my broken body through the dirt. I looked back at the invisible portal, dragging my fingernails through the dirt as I screamed out for him, for my one friend who I knew would have kept me safe.

Safir

I was poised alongside my mother's tomb, as I had been the day I met Eve. Ashire tried to distract me with his theories of Arius' whereabouts, but my thoughts were fleeting.

"Lord, it's late. You should return and rest." Selasi's spoke in the darkness, but I didn't respond.

Rest for what? For a pitiful pile of obligations? To plot and hypothesize with my brother? "There are very few things that demand my utmost energy."

"We could spar, if you'd like to demand your energy."

"I appreciate your offer, but I hardly feel like being embarrassed by a man's sword skills that aren't even his Blessing."

"So, you admit that my ability with a sword is not a Blessing?"

He continually tried to bring levity to my dense air of sullenness. It was appreciated. I untethered my scabbard from my side, not having any use for it, and handed it to Selasi. "If you wish to dismiss yourself you may do so."

He plucked my scabbard and shuffled his feet but did not retreat to the palace. "I don't mind waiting a while longer. I appreciate any excuse to avoid Maisy's cutting words."

I did snicker at that. "Do you think she will adjust to resuming her role downstairs?"

Selasi shrugged. "She's happy to be useful, happy to take care of Obi, but she'll miss…She'll miss the work as a lady-in-waiting. She preferred utilizing her more personable talents."

"I'm sure. She was a good lady-in-waiting."

There was a heavy pause that weighed down the mountain air as Selasi took one step in front of me to obscure my view of the portal. "Lord, may I confide in you?"

"If you wish."

He looked to the ground. "I long for my family each and every day, and that longing has never left me, as much as I desire it to."

I shifted back onto my heels to observe his steely disposition. It was rare that he bared his soul so openly.

"Little things torture my mind. A certain scent, particular songs, the way old Milfred beats me with a spoon. Each day, I choose to dwell on the time I did not receive with them or appreciate the time I had." His jaw clenched. "I will never pass judgement on which decision a grieving man makes, but there is a choice, nonetheless. I can only choose whichever I believe would make them most proud."

"Selasi—"

"Goodnight, my lord," he interrupted with a coolness to his tone. He curtly bowed and returned to the palace in silence. I remained there, burdened yet liberated at the realization Selasi passed to me. My pain was inevitable, but my suffering was a choice.

My dreaded choice.

Was it even remotely possible to let her be? To relinquish her company and her memory to the passing time? Had my attachment to her become so great that I wouldn't be capable of giving up the notion of her entirely, if my devotion left me no choice but to…

I paced towards her invisible portal. Three days had passed. I was meant to experience that newfound pain, because it meant for a few fleeting months I had known happiness. I didn't mind the ache she left gnawing in my chest. It was all I had left of her.

Yet.

What if I didn't concede to that fate? The local lords be damned. My purpose be damned. Eve's existence lifted my life, and it had nothing to do with her hindering my Blessing. The crown be damned! I longed for her to know that regardless if she remained in my realm or hers. She gripped me with such ferocity even across the span of our worlds that it left me reeling.

Absent mindedly, my hand reached out and my fingers curled around the night air, wondering if she was also reaching for me wherever she was.

Eve

Mere yards from my only hope of rescue, anger had his hands wrapped around my throat. Pressure was building in my already broken skull as gravity pulled me downward. I tried to claw him away but to no avail. My last bit of life wasn't enough to save me. His grip tightened making the last bit of resistance flee my arms as they fell to my sides.

Blood or tears or sweat cascaded over what was left of my face. Darkness encroached. I would rather see blackness than Hunter's face anyway. Anything other than him. Anyone…

Safir.

It was more peaceful than I imagined. A wave of relief washed over me. No pain whatsoever! It was like being wrapped in a blanket of warmth that I only ever felt with Safir, and I gave into that warmth willingly. I was lifted and carried far away from that place. Far enough that nothing else would ever find me, except maybe peace and an undying love just for me. Just for broken me.

Safir

Precious seconds can determine the rest of one's life.

It took seconds to attack the former king to free Lani. Seconds for Ashire to kill him. Seconds for me to invite Eve to the palace. Seconds to decide I would never kill with my Blessing for fear of resurrecting the purpose of the king past. Every action to quell the surging remorse in me stemmed from wanting to silence the ghost that beckoned me to do his bidding. To bury him, I relied upon that decision to abstain from harming with my Blessing.

It took exactly two seconds to undo that decision.

The moment I dared to step into her realm my greatest nightmare was transfigured into reality.

I hardly knew it was her if it weren't for the vacant stare in her sapphire eyes. The rest of her was smothered in red, and I could have scorched the land when I saw the devil that tormented her.

His hands, sealed tight around her throat, were painted with her blood, and squeezed the very life that didn't belong to him. He stood strides from me, unwavering in his sickened endeavor. I darted forward, colliding with the assailant to free Eve from his grasp. He tumbled to the forest floor and looked at me with unfounded ferocity.

I didn't care for his name, his explanation, or his life. Before he even garbled some expletive at me, I pinned him to the ground and let my hand engulf his face.

He trembled.

"You will suffer ten times more than she, and it will be by my hand!" I brought forth the most potent pain my body had ever experienced, surfacing the stored memories so their sensations flowed into him. He twisted and howled beneath me, but I held him steady as I willed the memory of heat and flame engulfing the skin. My intent wasn't just to sear his soul. If that were all I desired the king past would have forever smiled over my shoulder. But it wasn't for him. His memory had never felt so far away. All I knew in that moment was that I had the undeniably means to protect *her*.

My teeth gritted as I forced all my weight onto the hand that grasped his screaming jaw, driving him further into the dirt where he belonged. I summoned such an authentic and calculated heat from my bones that smoke and the smell of burning flesh arose. Soon, he stopped screaming. His eyes became dazed, no longer focused on me. I lifted my hand from his face, seeing scorch marks in the shape of my hand along his jaw.

I turned to Eve's body. She lay mangled on the forest floor, caked in such dirt and red that I fought the urge to vomit. The heat running through my veins turned painfully cold. I shakily gathered her in my arms. The parts of her that used to be rigid, and tone felt malleable and gave away easily beneath my fingers. I tried to impart my warmth and devotion that through my touch to encourage her to live. Her eyes stared emptily when I frantically pressed my ear to her chest. I felt a sense relief and terror at hearing her fluttering heart, still fighting to live.

I whispered into her marred ears, "Y-you're safe now. You're safe." I stood with quivering knees. I would have flayed myself open if I were too weak to carry her.

Dashing forward until I re-entered the world I knew, the world where I would have never allowed such a thing to happen to her, it felt as if I were racing against Vada's coin toss itself. What side would it land on?

I fought the urge to vomit as her blood smeared across my body. As I threw myself into the palace, Selasi was already at the entrance. His jaw fell open and gasped at the body in my arms. "Go and fetch Lani!" I commanded with every bit of force in me.

He nodded with his footsteps sputtering while sprinting towards Lani's tower.

My entire being shook as I lowered Eve to the floor, hating how easily she spilled out of my grasp. I should never have let her leave. I tried to emit hope to her form, continually giving her heart reason to beat. Within moments, Lani was at my side with a winded Selasi, both staring wide-eyed in terror. Lani did not ask or shout. She merely acted.

Lani threw herself over the body and began hyperventilating so loud that I couldn't hear my own ragged breaths over hers.

Sweat soaked her clothes as she breathed deeply to maximize her Blessing. I didn't speak, only watched with dread as Eve remained motionless on the floor. In the light I was plagued seeing her existential external wounds. Her delicate features were swollen, smeared with blood. Teeth were askew in her splintered jaw. Her sapphire eyes stained red with broken blood vessels, and her nose barely clung to her face. Every fingernail was ripped from the nailbed. Black and purple hues tarnished her once perfect skin.

I shuddered, wanting to kill that bastard all over again.

"Your Royal Highness, please!" Lani hissed over Eve's body. "I can't concentrate with you here like this!"

My hands ripped through my hair as I turned away and attempted to focus on a neutral warmth, but to no avail. All I could see was red. *Her* red.

"I need to move her to my infirmary. Lord?" Lani asked, and I drew Eve's body back into my grasp. Seconds in Lani presence and I could hear Eve breathing gurgling breaths. "Selasi, go and fetch Maisy for me," Lani ordered as we stood, but Lani's hands never left Eve.

Selasi sprinted while we scaled to Lani's tower. Lani's breaths were deep and long. My fingers gripped Eve with hope when feeling her ribs once again rigid against me. When we finally reached the infirmary, I laid her on one of the beds.

Eve began to writhe. "Get a bucket now!" Lani commanded while wiping the sweat from her brow. I panickily fetched the nearest basin. Quickly Lani turned Eve on her side just as a river of blood poured from her hanging mouth into the basin. Eve did not wince or groan. The blood passively flowed out of her, varying in shades of sickly red.

"So much internal hemorrhaging. At least it's out of you," Lani wheezed.

"Will she live?" I asked, desperate yet hesitant to inquire.

Lani looked up at me from beneath her quivering brows. "The hemorrhaging isn't what I'm worried about."

My heart stalled in my chest.

Maisy charged into the infirmary with Selasi close behind. She tumbled to Eve's side. "Maisy will help me clean and dress her. Lord, I beg of you to wait outside. It will help me focus better," Lani beseeched over Eve's body.

My feet stalled. If I were a better man I would have made myself scarce immediately. Instead, Selasi pulled me away from her, steadying me backwards until the door shut between me and the infirmary. The second she was out of my sight, my knees collided with the floor and my fists slammed into the ground. "I'm sorry, Selasi, that you have to experience me like this." I had all but given up on controlling my Blessing.

"My sentiments match yours to a degree, Lord," his voice darkened above me. He gripped the hilt of his sword so tightly that his arm was trembling. "I'm practically blood lusting right now."

"Dear Vada," I seethed while rising to my feet. "It only took three days in that realm to reduce her to this."

"What happened?"

My thoughts flashed to the ugly creature that had held her precious life in his hands. "I don't know. His reasons will forever be foreign to me."

"I was informed that your brother is waiting for you. He's in the library."

"Should there be any news, you're to come to me straight away." He nodded and stood like a statue by the door.

I approached the library while her gurgling breaths echoed in my ears. Throwing the doors open, I saw Ashire standing in the middle of the library, looking up at his portrait of choice.

"Ashire—"

"So, she's returned?"

"Barely." I settled into a chair and let my face fall into my hands. "Just barely. I still don't know what side the coin has landed on, Ashire."

"I have a feeling we won't know for a while." He sat next to me. "This can't be the result of a brawling match."

"I don't believe so. This was an intentional attack."

"For what purpose?"

"If there is one, it will never justify this," I snarled when picturing that hideous man clutching her. My blood surged with such swiftness that I fought the urge to put my fist through a bookcase.

Ashire shuddered next to me. "Safir—"

"Do *not* tell me to calm myself."

He said nothing and allowed me to ruminate in my fury, my worry, my regret, and my indignation for the one who brought her to such a state. I dwelled on the notion of having Lani heal him just for me to rid the world of him once again. It would have given my anger purpose.

Later the library doors opened. My relief and disappointment were palpable as Emtias entered with a tray of steaming tea. "A rudimentary comfort, but a comfort, nonetheless. Milfred has awoken the kitchen staff in preparation for requests."

"That is kind, though unnecessary," Ashire remarked.

I said nothing, unaware if Emtias and Ashire continued their conversation. I had shifted my focus elsewhere, recalling Eve's liveliness during the ball, the way she felt within my grasp, the way she smiled breathlessly against me. She'd been so very *alive*. To think that would be the last I would see her that spirited, the thought reignited my infuriated grief all over again.

Then the doors swung open so wildly I jolted and looked to see Lani leaning against Selasi, her half-lidded eyes darting towards me. I had only seen Lani minutes prior, but new grey hairs protruded from her curls and her wrinkles were deepened in her face. Drenched in sweat and gripping Selasi, she panted, "A ruptured diaphragm. Lungs collapsed. Airway fractured."

I stood from my seat. "Is she alive?"

"Just." Her knees shook violently beneath her. "It's been years since I've seen such cruelty. Your Royal Highness? The one who did this to her—"

"I did away with him."

Ashire stiffened in my peripheral vision. Lani sighed darkly, "Good." She began turning away, still clinging to Selasi but I pursued her.

"Can I see Eve?"

Her head shook. "The internal bleeding ceased, and she is barely able to breathe on her own, but the damage done to her brain is going to take more time and energy than I currently have. She needs the least amount of stimulus possible for now."

"Please, Lani—"

"I will not leave her side, Lord. I'm willing to give all that I am." Reverence rang in her voice.

I knew she was— she always did. They left us there in the library, Selasi practically carrying Lani back to the infirmary. I couldn't ignore Ashire's scrutinizing stare.

"Did you sully your sword?" he inquired.

I shook my head while looking down at my hand, remembering my scorching palm on that man's face, the calculated heat I summoned so easily. "It wasn't on my person."

Ashire's hand struck my face with such ferocity that I spat blood from the corner of my mouth.

He glared at me with our family's eyes brutally burning. I almost froze thinking I was seeing the dead king before me. Hell was in his stare.

"I wouldn't give a damn if you ran the bastard through with your blade! But you will never again kill with your Blessing, indulging in the purpose of the king past!"

"It had nothing to do with him." I ran my tongue over my bloodied lip. "It was all to save her, Ashire. Would you have preferred I wasted precious time to defend her in a manner that you approved?" I turned my gaze back to my hand. "I even left scorch marks."

"Must I be there every time to keep your feet on the ground? For you to kill with it—"

"Was your 'repel' not intended to kill Arius?" I spat.

My brother stilled with his eyes flaring. "That is entirely different."

"Why is defending with my Blessing so much more damning in your eyes than when you use yours?" I fumed, watching Emtias and Ashire shudder in response to me.

"Because every time you use your Blessing as *he* willed it, you give him life!"

"But it was not as *he* willed it! It is my Blessing! I determine its purpose. Not you nor the king past! I chose to protect her with it." My fist slammed against my chest, still painted in Eve's blood. "And if I'm to be damned for it so be it. At least I'm damning myself rather than someone else deciding that for me." I slowed my breath, more shallow while refocusing wholeheartedly on Eve. The two before me notably relaxed. Ashire exhibited an almost look of relief. "With Bask you said I didn't have my wits about me. I was more consumed with justifying my sins than protecting her, but this was apart from that. I could only think of her. I know now what I want from this Blessing, and I won't be told otherwise."

Ashire raised a hand to stop me. His lips twitched, like he had forgotten how to smile. "I can tell. I can feel it. I never intended for you to feel you didn't have the autonomy to make such a decision. Very well. Let your Blessing be your own. It always should have been."

Ashire reached for his cup of tea, and we did not speak again for hours. I wondered if the sun would ever dare to show its face again. Time froze throughout the palace for the first time since the plague had swept through Walyre, and it brought forth an all too familiar and unwelcome tension. We all sat in silence as the night waned.

That was until the air became pierced with Eve's screams.

Eve

It wasn't what I'd thought it would be. There wasn't as much warmth as there had been, less of a sense of peace, more pounding sensation that racked my supposed corpse. Every fiber of my being burned, trying to rouse me from my earned slumber. Why was there no peace for me? Had I not earned it? Why was there pain, *pain*, **pain**!

Safir

I'd thought the silence was horrifying until ear-piercing shrieks cut through me swifter than any blade. It struck my core so savagely I immediately leapt to my feet and dashed to the infirmary. Selasi didn't stop me, in fact, he opened the door for me as we both rushed to see a scene of grotesque pain.

Eve's brittle body was bent backward on the bed as screeches escaped her gaping jaw with her hands clutching her head so fiercely I thought she was pulverizing her brains. Her screams sent shocks through me as I wrenched for her, seeing Lani and Maisy scrambling over the top of her.

"Maisy and Selasi, hold her down! Lord, try to calm her as well as you can," Lani commanded.

"What's happening?" I roared over the horrid shrieking of the woman beneath me.

Lani's hands shook. "H-her brain is swelling. Exuding pressure on the skull. She'll be dead in minutes if I can't control it," she wheezed while kneeling at Eve's head.

It took every bit of strength within me to stall my panic as I clutched Eve. Selasi held down her legs while Maisy pried her left hand away from her bursting skull. I did the same with the right hand, coaxing as much tenderness as I could into my touch. Perhaps I would be able to reach Eve in her unconsciousness, let her know she was not suffering alone.

Despite my best efforts, Eve's screams continued to fill the palace and would be stored in my memory as the most wretched sounds I'd ever know. Lani's hyperventilated so jarringly that her teeth chattered.

"Please, Lani!" I begged her, my voice giving away to grief. "Save her please!"

It wasn't fair to ask, but in that moment, all I wanted was for her to be whole. I would have been willing to strike down my own limbs, impale myself on any spike, whip myself as many times as needed if it meant she would be whole. And I knew Lani was giving every bit of herself.

Ashire appeared from behind Lani and placed his hands over hers, securing her grip on Eve. "Lean on me," he told her, commanding as her king.

Her eyes shot open. "Yes, Lord. I will *not* lose another."

The depth of Lani's strength must have been almost infinite. Her breaths became so ragged as she traded Eve's screams for her own. Blood dripped from the corners of Lani's weathered eyes and spilled down her cheeks.

Eve was still fighting against our hold on her. What if Lani killed herself to save Eve, only for her to be lost anyhow? How would we bear it? How was my soul to ever recover? I could hardly hear myself speaking to Eve. "Please stay," I begged while gripping her arm. Despair warped around me, and I couldn't stop it. I could only cling to her. "Please, Eve. My—"

My darling. My Eve. My—

"Beloved, don't leave me."

Both sets of screams gradually quieted as both women fell into unconsciousness. Lani fell back against Ashire who caught her, while Eve collapsed back onto the bed. Had Lani been able to heal her or was Eve so wounded that pain no longer reached her? Pressing my face close, I could still feel her faint breaths on my cheek and hear her heart. I dared to hope.

Ashire sat back with Lani in his arms and barked orders. "Maisy and Selasi, you will tend to Lani. Emtias," I stole a fleeting glance to see Emtias ashen in the doorway, "you will deathward her now."

Ashire carried Lani to another bed for Selasi and Maisy to aid. Emtias stood over Eve and mumbled to himself until the air around us began to vibrate. A glow grew from him and transferred itself to Eve, giving her a warming light around her otherwise tortured body. Emtias concluded with a sigh and the warm glow faded.

"Has it taken hold?" I asked, reaching for her wrist to feel her still beating pulse.

He nodded solemnly. "I'm sorry. It's been quite some time since I've had to cast a deathward. I performed it to the best of my ability."

"Did it take hold, Emtias?" I asked with dying patience.

"It has but understand that this is not healing her. It is merely holding her body in a moment of stasis, never allowing her to worsen, but she must heal either by Lani's or by her own volition. I'm merely freezing Vada's coin toss for the time being."

I leant my forehead against Eve's bloodied knuckles. "Thank you," I muttered. That was all she needed, a chance to invite life back into her. She just needed time, and at the very least we could provide that for her.

"Emtias, with me," Ashire remarked in the back of the infirmary. "Between the two of us, surely we can gather enough information from Lani's collection to be useful."

The only sound was that of opening and closing books as well as combing through pages. No more sounds. Only painful waiting and anticipation.

Waiting for her to decide to live.

Time passed excruciatingly slow. Each ragged breath that escaped her reminded me of her temporary stay from death. I longed to see her sapphire eyes staring up at me. I couldn't be privy to the battle that surely raged within her.

Her internal hemorrhaging had ceased. Her breathing had evened. Her brain must have stopped swelling as she stopped screaming. Her remaining injuries healed much slower. The swelling and bruising that clouded her once-delicate features lessened, patches of skin regaining their pink hue. I remained at her side every second that week to witness her attempt to thwart Vada's coin toss. Perhaps it was to her advantage to be averse to deities.

After ravaging Lani's entire collection, Ashire and Emtias were able to aid Eve and Lani. Ice adorned Eve's skull and we administered serums distilled from crawlsey flowers to decrease inflammation. Such methods were so sluggish, so time consuming in comparison to Lani's Blessing.

Lani remained comatose for two days before finally rousing from her bed. Her once dark hair became snowy white, and her skin gave away her many years of existence with a multitude more creases and wrinkles. Maisy had tended to her, bringing her hearty broths from the kitchen, and smothering her with blankets. I knew, and hated, that Lani's Blessing had been stretched to a breaking point as mine had. I wasn't certain what that entailed for her, but she spoke nothing of it. She would tend to Eve or correct Ashire and Emtias's technique when distilling serums before falling back into a deep sleep.

"Go and rest," Ashire ordered me one night. I had lost track of how many days had passed. "When she wakes, she shouldn't have to question which of you is the one closest to death."

"I'm fine."

He grabbed my shoulder and grumbled, "You're lying."

I didn't have the strength to withdraw from him, though I did momentarily hate him for reading my sentiments without my permission. "You didn't have to do that."

"If you don't rest you'll be of no use to her."

"If I were rested I'd still be of no use to her. I just sit and wait and watch and hope possibly for nothing."

Ashire knelt next to me. "I refuse to have a brother as absurd as to mistake his unwavering, albeit reckless, loyalty for 'nothing.'"

"That was *almost* kind."

"Please. Go and rest. She will not be alone."

A hint of desperation in his tone drew my attention away from Eve. While Ashire didn't appear quite as ragged as I felt, I could see fatigue smothering his stare. Days spent pillaging Lani's books couldn't have been that mentally taxing for Ashire. There was something else. He too worried. He worried for Lani, for Eve, but I could see his familiar concern for me.

But then Eve stirred in her sleep. Occasionally, she'd shudder and whimper a name that I didn't know. Yet, when I'd reach for her and convey a sense of warmth, she'd sigh and relax back on the bed. I'd fool myself into thinking she'd even lean into my touch as she used to, but I was fully aware my exhaustion was trying to thwart my rationality.

I settled against her bed, willing to rot in that position if necessary. "I will remain here."

Ashire ceased arguing and left me there with her, for as many days as it took before the result of Vada's coin toss would be known.

Eve

I found myself in a place whose name I couldn't quite recall. That frustration was beguiling as I stood in the middle of what I assumed was a park. But brick buildings with open windows surrounded me. Between the buildings were sidewalks with rows of purposefully planted flowers with trees and freshly cut grass. It was a real place. I had been there before.

Bodies flowed past me as I stood in the middle of the sidewalk, like water navigating around rocks in a stream. There was something missing. There was *someone* missing.

"Eve?"

People evaporated around me when I looked up to see Nicky standing there. He had a heavy backpack slung over his shoulder and a cocky yet perplexed smile.

"Hey, what're you doing just standing there? Come on, you might as well walk me to class if you're here."

How had I forgotten? Nicky was taking classes at the community college. He had been for almost one year, but there was something strange about his figure. There was a thought that tickled my brain, but I couldn't quite scratch it. I walked alongside him, though I couldn't help but stare at him.

"What?" he asked.

"You look … taller? So upright."

"That's a weird thing to say," he said while adjusting his backpack on his shoulder. "How was your shift? No pervs, I hope."

Shift? Oh, yeah, at the restaurant. I peered down to see myself in my uniform topped off with a faded nametag. It dawned on me how sore my feet were from hours of waitressing, but I didn't care while walking alongside Nicky. "It was fine. Got a lot of good tips. Don't you have an exam today?"

Nicky tousled his curly locks. For some reason, his hair seemed almost golden in the sun. "Yeah, but I'm not that worried. It's online anyway. Not too much longer until the semester is over."

Multicolored leaves cascaded towards the ground, and I shivered with the breeze. "You'll like it here. Though you should try to avoid Dr. Lyle's class. He makes you buy all his own books, but never even uses them in lectures."

"That's shitty," I remarked, wondering why I wasn't there joining him, but then it occurred to me that I had volunteered to work for an additional year while Nicky started classes. It made sense. He would offer me his notes and books, so we didn't have to buy them twice. Government assistance only went so far, as I worked full-time, and Nicky worked part time at the warehouse on the outskirts of town. It was barely enough to make it, but we both agreed it'd be worth it when we were both social workers.

It had been our goal ever since we had taken that first campus tour so many years prior, and we would achieve it. No matter how many grueling hours we endured, at least we shared them together.

"Did you hear the news? I saw it on television the other day." Nicky's voice broke through my thoughts. "About Hunter?"

I nodded, gradually recalling the revelation. "It's not surprising, he owed someone a lot of money. But what about Mary? And the baby?"

"All I know is what they said on the news. They didn't mention Mary. How do you feel about it?"

"I don't know. It's been a few years since we last saw him. I'm ambivalent, I guess."

"Ambivalent. That's a good way of putting it."

We were only a few steps away from the library entrance when Nicky turned to look at me. "I feel weird suddenly. Like we're both on the verge of a great chance, you know?"

I smiled. "Yeah, I know. I wouldn't have it any other way."

He stilled and everything became deafeningly quiet. "Really? This is all you want? Nothing more?"

I looked at him quizzically. "What do you mean?"

"You want to work your fingers to the bone to put us both through school, to become social workers, with Hunter cold in the ground. That's all you want?"

My words stalled as I tried to stutter a response. "Well, yeah, that's all we've ever wanted, Nicky. It's better than—"

"Getting your brain bashed in?" he asked so poignantly that I felt as if someone had landed one monstrous punch into my jaw.

I recoiled. That feeling. That feeling was so fresh. "Why did you say that? Why did you say it *like* that?"

"Because you know it. You know of the other life that could have been. I can even see it on you."

I glanced back down to see my uniform gone. Instead, I was clad in leather pants and a leather vest. A dagger gleamed on my hip, and the faint memory attached to it pinged in my heart. But then the pain came, growing from my face and my core. I almost doubled over in confused agony.

"What's happening?" I asked with fear shaking my voice. "What's happening to me?" Blood trickled over my eyes and chin. The rest of me began to tremble.

Nicky dropped his backpack and braced his hands on either side of my bruising cheeks. "Sh, sh, it's okay. You're okay. This is part of you, Eve. This is part of that life."

I looked at Nicky long and hard, at our matching blue eyes and the liveliness about him. He didn't seem troubled. I didn't understand his calm. I didn't understand his stature. I didn't understand…

"How are you standing?"

He smiled widely. "Why do you ask that?"

I wiped the blood from my eyes, smearing it across my hand. "It feels like I haven't seen you this tall in a really long time. Don't you want to lie down? You should lie down."

"I'm fine here. See?" He took my hand and placed it on his chest, inhaling a deep gulp of air. There was no struggle or wheezing. It was effortless for him, which felt so strange to me. "I can do this all the time here. Breathe. Walk. Talk."

"Why do you keep saying 'here?' Where else is there?"

"You know where."

The library faded. The trees became older-looking and the ground shot up to create giant peaks above us. The air became crisper, but it smelled so familiarly sweet. In the distance stood a white stone palace with great arching windows. I did but didn't know it. I felt myself being pulled to it.

Nicky looked in the direction of my stare. "So, this is where you've been going? No wonder I couldn't find you."

"Walyre," I breathed, though I didn't understand the word.

"I think you're torn between the two, and I can see why now."

"Can you stop this?" I asked, feeling desperate. "Stop it. I don't want to know. I don't want to see—"

"Just because it's painful to look doesn't mean it doesn't deserve to be seen."

I snapped my stare to him. Those words stabbed my heart, and I couldn't place the reason why. "Why did you say that?"

"It's too painful to look at me, isn't it? You'd rather be here than see me for how I really am. That's why you kept coming back here."

A crippling guilt welled in my throat. "No, no. I was here for you. I've done everything for you!"

His brow furrowed in confusion. "I don't blame you, Eve. You had to do something for yourself eventually, and I'm glad you did. You became something you hadn't been in a while." Nicky smiled as a wind blew, and he turned to face the breeze. "Happy."

"I'm happy with you here."

Nicky stepped towards me and took my hands into his. We both looked down to see my bruised and split knuckles. "You once said when I'm gone you wouldn't be too far behind. I want us to both stop being so hurt."

"Then let me stay."

He smiled again but appeared pained. "I would. I would, Eve, but I can't bring myself to be that selfish. I don't need you here, not yet. I'll need you out there, and so will he."

"He?"

"And when it's all said and done, you decide for yourself where you want to be happy, and please do it just for you."

His hands gripped mine so tightly my knuckles seeped blood, but I didn't mind. I had bled for Nicky for years. I pulled him against me and relished in the feeling of my brother returning my embrace. "I'll come back for you," I promised.

I felt him smile against my cheek. "I'll be here when you're ready."

Safir

In my delirium I had dreamt of her waking so many times, every time with gleaming sapphire eyes and a strong hand rousing me from my slumber. She'd breathe life into my name, and I would know all was well.

I had sat there with my fingers intertwined with hers for days. But when I felt her thumb brushing over my knuckles, I bolted upright in my chair.

I hardly risked taking a breath while watching her brittle body stir with life. Her fingers gripped mine, and I reciprocated while imparting my growing hope for her, praying it'd be enough to wake her. A hum rose in her throat. I watched with excruciating anticipation as her eyelashes fluttered open, revealing those sapphire eyes.

My chest tightened as she turned her head, settling her gaze on me, and smiled. "Safir." Her voice graced my name. I tightened my grip on her and reached with my other hand to cup her cheek. My heart raced when she leaned into my touch just as she used to. "So, you heard me?" she murmured, though I wasn't entirely aware of what she meant. Her voice was strained after the screams that had escaped her days prior. "Our last conversation … I'm so sorry."

My head was shaking before she had finished speaking. "No. I'm the one weighed with regret. If I had spoken with you earlier, if I hadn't been as atrocious as I am, you wouldn't have had to leave as you did. You wouldn't have—" The words caught in my throat as her broken image flashed across my thoughts. Eve stiffened next to me, gaping as she experienced my recollected horror. "I'm sorry. If I could have freed you from that I would have."

"But you did."

"I almost didn't, Eve!"

"Safir," she breathed while leaning her cheek into my hand. "How did you find me? And where—" Suddenly she froze next to me. "Where's Hunter? Did he do that to you?" she asked while looking to my healing lip.

"Eve," I began with all seriousness. "Who was that man?" I had wanted to know for days how she came so close to death within such a short time after departing my realm.

Her pallor somehow drained of even more color. When she released my hand, I almost regretted prying, but she braced her arms behind herself and pushed upwards. She winced while I tried to support her sitting upright. Lani and Maisy had removed her dirt and blood-smeared clothes and had wrapped her core in bandages to brace her fragile ribs.

Her head fell into her hand as she took shaky breaths through her nose. I swore I could almost hear her bones creaking. Despite the amount of energy Lani had poured into her, Eve was still recuperating. Death had been waiting for her. Certain death.

After a few moments surviving sitting upright, Eve picked up her gaze to me, her face mere inches from mine. "His name is Hunter. He's my foster father."

My blood froze within my already icy veins. "That *thing* was your father?"

"He's my foster father. He's a— wait, why did you say 'was?'" She stared at me, waiting, with her mouth hanging open.

I didn't know if I should have sounded more ashamed, but I couldn't hide my unabashed tone. "By my own hands, I ensured he would never harm you again."

"He's gone?"

I nodded.

She reached to brace her hands against her head. "He's really gone," Eve scarcely mumbled.

"Are you angry with me?"

She peered up and slowly shook her head. "No, no. I'm just … I'm afraid to feel relieved. And you— I'm so sorry."

I recoiled. "What could you possibly be sorry for?"

Her glassy eyes flickered from my hands and back to me. "You never wanted to use your Blessing to hurt anyone, Safir, and because of me—"

"Never *because* of you. Only *for* you, Eve, and I would do it again. I do not say this lightly. The past king did this to me for his own bidding, but I solely decide the purpose of this Blessing."

She said nothing, though she brushed her fingers over her throat. I recalled the deathly grasp that man had had around her delicate neck. I would have done anything to erase that memory. Her skin would never again know painful touch. I would make it my life's ambition to instill tender touches into her skin, to undo every bit of harshness that had befallen her. I must have conveyed that in my touch because she smiled while squeezing my fingers.

"Why would your father—"

"Foster father."

"Why did he do this?" I asked, willing to be bold.

"Because you and I only have the worst things in common." Her smile turned pained, but she didn't relinquish my grasp. "You never asked about my world, and I was always so thankful because it helped keep it that much further away, but that isn't fair, is it? You killed for me, so you should know."

There were years of accumulated sorrow in her tone. Regardless of the many horrid stories I had heard, my heart had never weighed heavier than when listening to Eve's. Touched by tragedy over and over. No wonder she had to hold her chin so high. And to know she had a brother left me taken aback as to why he was never mentioned. Nicky. I had heard her say that name in her sleep or whenever she was drunk. Eve painted him as a braver, smarter, cleverer person than she, and I hadn't thought such a person could exist. Why hadn't I met her brother? How had that grotesque 'Hunter' become involved?

Eve's story unfolded with terrible detail regarding the tragedy that befell her brother, and therefore became her burden, though she never painted the concept in such a light. Everything began to make sense, her asking for money, her brawling for coin, the involvement of her supposed foster father. Her temper made exponentially more sense. The way Hunter had used her for his own means, attempting to ensnare her virtue, made my hatred for him grow. Whenever she spoke of him, she brushed her fingers over her neck and swallowed hard. I could see the memory of him still fresh within her. It would take time to numb that memory. I knew that well.

When the horrific words ceased from her tongue, her sapphire stare became glossy, and her hands trembled in her lap. I grasped her hands to convey my adoration for her resilience. She smiled and leaned towards me, allowing her chestnut tresses to fall into her gaze.

"Can Lani not heal your brother?"

She shook her head. "I indirectly asked the first day you brought me up here. It's been too long, and it's too complex. He can only survive in my world, for however much longer he wants to survive." Her voice grew strained as she feverishly blinked away tears.

I detested never once understanding the depths of her angered pain. *Why?* I asked through my touch while reaching to swipe away a stray tear.

"Because," she whimpered, "it's selfish, but if no one else knew, I could forget too for a little while. You have to understand that for my *whole* life, we weren't wanted. *I've* never been wanted, and then suddenly I found myself here, and you—" She stalled and bit her bottom lip with a look that made me want to be brave. She flickered her gaze down to her lap. "I didn't want you to look at me as if I were incomplete."

She had to know better, surely. I didn't try to hide my reverence for her from my Blessing. A small smile dared to edge its way onto her lips, but that assurance wasn't enough.

I caught her proud chin between my thumb and forefinger, urging her gaze to meet mine. Incomplete? Perhaps. We were both broken, but into the same shape. We matched each other. She smiled wider as I leaned my forehead against hers, drinking in every bit of her life that she granted me.

So warm was her life. It felt like the warmth I'd spent days trying to recreate in that damn dungeon. I hadn't known I was already reaching out for her across our planes of existence.

"For what it's worth," she murmured so close that I could almost taste her words, "there towards the end, I could only think of you."

"Me?"

"You."

I couldn't help but capture her lips with mine, more needing than I had ever known. Her closeness was intoxicating as she leaned into me, sighing deeply while I held her face in my hands. Her tender lips were warm and somehow familiar when sealing themselves over mine, and I could have lived in that moment for eternity. Vada's coin toss be damned.

We parted as our trembling breaths washed over each other's face, but Eve's darkened, sapphire gaze remained transfixed on my mouth as she leaned forward and clung to me. She wrapped her arms around my neck, drawing me closer into her, in a sob as she reciprocated my kiss, her lips moving over mine in an enthralling motion that scattered all my thoughts. I tasted the slightest hint of salt, feeling tears cascade down her cheeks. There was a great deal of trust, grief, and admiration that neither of us needed a Blessing to convey to the other. Even greater was the liberation of finally finding where one's soul belonged, and I could taste her love on her lips and felt myself at home with my arms securely around her. The cruelty of passing time, the sins of man, even the end of days couldn't have pulled me away from that moment.

When her body slumped into mine and her head fell into my chest, I caught her against me. Small breaths escaped her as she fell unconscious with a smile on her lips. Thankful she couldn't see my sheepish grin; I settled her back on her bed. She had overexerted herself, but her contented expression led me to believe she deemed her expenditure worthy.

"Apologies, beloved," I told her while placing a kiss on her forehead. "One day we'll have time for moments such as this. I promise."

Eve

I hadn't thought it was possible to be such an overwhelming reservoir of emotions. Grief, shock, relief, and yet contentment violently churned every day. My confusion was only amplified by the nightmares of Hunter's grip, making me impulsively take a deep breath to prove to myself that I could still breathe. I'd reach for my neck to prove it to myself.

Hunter's ghost tried reach me when Safir was nearby. Yet there was little room for fear, doubt, or pain when I felt a caress so tender that my heart convulsed in my chest. It was so good and gentle and hopeful and everything my sullen soul had been craving my entire life. I threw myself into that bliss, melting into Safir, loving my newfound happiness. I had never allowed myself such a kindness.

Contentment rang in my ears every time I heard him echo the word "beloved" into my exhausted skin. The word sank into me and settled into my bones. I hadn't known I was capable of being so precious to someone.

The prolonged aching and creaking in every joint in my body slowly faded. I didn't know how many days passed before I felt alive enough to sit on the edge of my infirmary bed. Surely Nicky was worried sick. He never was able to see me in Walyre. The only distraction from that worry was when Oberia would come to my side, whimpering songs to bring pictures to life. They'd dance on the ceiling and act out stories, but Oberia's characters always looked sad as she nestled against me.

"I'm here," I'd remind her, and she'd nestle closer.

In her absence, books were often left behind. I'd hardly thought Emtias was one for displays of affection, but his care was present in the handwritten notes he tied to each book. Many of the books were poems and mantras meant for peaceful, mindful thinking. It was an entirely different flavor of thought— one I had hardly ever tasted.

"Ah, my fierce lily blooms," a warm voice rasped behind me one day when I felt well enough to sit on the edge of my bed.

I didn't turn and look, fearing my ribs would crumble into dust. Instead, the figure sat on the bed opposite me. Logic told me it was Lani, but her hair was white as snow, gleaming in the sunlight that streamed through the windows. The skin crinkled and sagged around her eyes and jaw as her now-frail hand reached out to hold mine. She gripped my hand with a look of pride on her wrinkled lips. And then it dawned on me …

"I'm so sorry," I whispered appalled. "I did this to you."

She smiled and patted my hand while sighing, "It's an honor to finally wear a face that reflects my true age. It was well worth every crease in this weathered skin."

"But your Blessing?"

"Has done its job. I've had so much of life. I'm glad I was able to impart some to you." She beamed with her brown eyes cloudy with apparent age. They'd never again be their clear and deep brown. "I can still heal, but its expanse has dwindled. I don't mind relying upon my studies to help the sick. In a way, I prefer it."

"I will never be able to thank you enough. Ever." I returned her grasp, trying to evoke my undying sincerity.

"You must live well with the life I have given you. That is all I ask."

I would have to. Safir's kindness had saved me and Ashire's mercy allowed me to remain, but Nicky was waiting for me. My world was still waiting for me, and I didn't know what it would be like without Hunter looming around every corner. I wondered if I would even recognize it.

"I won't ask," Maisy said one night when combing my hair. "When you plan to come back, or if."

I tried to stay still for her nimble fingers to do their work. "I'll come back, but I can't say when. When I do, it'll be because …" My barely mended windpipe ached.

Maisy didn't press it. "Selasi and I will look after His Royal Highness. I promise. Will you think of us?"

"It would be impossible not to."

Maisy wrapped her arms around me from behind, making her curls prickle my cheek. "And you won't be hurt?" she asked meekly, like a child afraid of the dark.

I fought off recoiling from her arms draped around my neck. "I won't. I'm sorry you had to see me like that, Maisy."

"I speak on behalf of a great many here when I say that we'll have you in any shape or form."

I believed her as I basked in the affection of my friend. I was going to miss it, but my energy was returning to me, and my joints groaned less with each passing day. There was a greater heartbreak awaiting me in my own world. I refused to make Nicky wait for me longer than he needed to. Bit by bit, my body hummed with the vitality Lani had given to me. Safir knew it.

"What will you do?" he asked, his words carried away by the wind. We sat on the edge of his mother's tomb. Safir was still as a statue while my knees bounced. Selasi stood a distance, appearing vigilant but stoic.

We were watching the sun disappear behind the mountains. "Wait," I admitted. "I'll wait. What about you?"

Safir brushed his white locks out of his ember gaze. "I'll help Ashire in any way I can to discover the whereabouts of our traitor."

"No leads?"

"None."

I pinched my nose. "The things that Arius said to me … he obviously wasn't grateful to the crown."

Safir scowled. "Arius' disdain towards my family has never been a secret, but his ability to be an actual threat was unknown. My days will be consumed in my study, reviewing documents for any obscure behavior. Unless …" he glanced to me hesitantly. "Will you be safe when you go back?"

The invisible portal beckoned and waited ahead of me. I could feel Nicky's wonder and worry, even if we were worlds apart. "I will be now. I should be."

If you go, I won't be far behind.

I cringed at the thought. New life ran through my veins given to me from Lani. What was I willing to do with that life?

Safir reached under his cloak and withdrew a leather pouch. He extended it to me. The pouch weighed heavily in my hand and jingled when I opened it. To my shock, dozens of gold coins and gems gleamed in my palm.

My jaw dropped, making Safir smirk. "Your proper earnings. If it means providing for your brother and abstaining from brawling, then accept it."

"Are you sure it's—"

"I would never insult you by giving you anything less than what you've earned, and besides Ashire dispensed the coin himself. I dare say it wasn't even painful for him to part with the money. He knows what a great service you've done for the crown."

"It wasn't just for the crown."

He nodded with a clenched jaw. "I know that. So does Ashire."

I inwardly cursed at the aching in my throat. "Thank you." I could only mouth the words, afraid of hearing my own voice break. The small fortune in my hands meant whatever was left of Nicky's life wouldn't be stuck in some soiled bed. That money meant truly getting to *live*. All the love I had for him couldn't have given him that.

"And this." Safir extended the dagger he had originally given me. "I was hoping you'd take that with you."

I jolted and pulled it back to me, noting a look of relief upon his face. "I'm sorry I left it. I thought it would make it easier to leave." I secured it tightly against my hip, allowing my palm to rest on the cool metal. My bouncing knees stilled as the time to leave approached, and all was silent as I stood.

Safir intertwined his fingers with mine and rubbed gentle circles into my knuckles. I squeezed hard and felt the wave of emotions flow through the tips of his fingers and consume my entire body. It was more than he had ever tried to convey, enough that I felt like I might burst, but for the first time his deep-seated grief wasn't the first sentiment I felt. There was already a sense of longing and an even greater anticipation that rushed over my being, so much worry, yet above all was such an enamored admiration. I wanted to cling to those feelings, and so I carefully pulled him along, both of us taking reluctant steps towards my invisible portal. Selasi slowly followed from behind.

With each step Safir's Blessing grew. I didn't dare turn away from it, wishing if anything I could convey just as much in return. When we neared it, Safir stopped and cupped my cheek. A deep warmth pulsated, as his grief surfaced, but it was different from the one that always lingered within him. It was a sorrow that reflected my own. I had to bite my bottom lip to keep it from trembling.

Safir inhaled before leaning his forehead towards me, brushing his nose against mine. "I can't ask. I won't ask when I will see you again."

Closing my eyes, I drank his words. For me to be able to stay in Walyre I would have to lose my only remaining family. Safir couldn't ask for me to return without also asking for Nicky to die. I couldn't even tell Safir I couldn't wait to return because it felt like saying I couldn't wait for Nicky to die. My two happiness' couldn't coexist.

"I can't keep Nicky waiting," I told Safir. My eyes reluctantly opened to see his stare, steely but understanding.

"And you shouldn't have to." Safir withdrew from me yet kept his warm hand against my cheek. His thumb so lightly caressed my skin that I scarcely felt it. "I'm tempted to pack away my crown now and come after you. Make you drag me along," he teased with a harsh chuckle. "You could show me your world. Your metal carriages. I could meet your brother if you wanted. Say the word, and I will follow you."

Both Selasi and I stilled. My head had already begun shaking in protest, but I still selfishly wanted him beside me.

"I don't wish to burden you with holding my hand while navigating your world, but this man, your brother, is so much of who you are. I know what I ask is selfish, but even just one day to see you safely into your realm and to meet your brother…I can't help but wish to understand that part of you."

"No, I can't pull you away from Ashire."

"Selasi can inform my brother of my whereabouts, and I'll be of no use to Ashire worrying for you."

"But…" I blinked, glancing to Selasi.

He smiled so warmly, almost reassuring me. "If you'll both excuse me, I have important news to deliver to His Majesty. I must also ensure Milred and Maisy are as abusive as ever towards me in your absence. It'll help past the time. I can only dread that Obi will grow to be just as cunning in their care. Until we next meet, Eve." He then bowed to *me* before returning to the palace.

Then it was just us two, waiting and wondering. I looked up to see Safir with a small glint of light in his eyes. Astana eyes. He guided me back into his arms, not ready to relinquish me even for a moment. I buried my head into his chest with a long sigh. He conveyed through my Blessing how he was willing to wait with me. It felt the least he could do, to help ferry me into my realm once I had departed that one in all its grief.

Unaware of how pressing time was, we remained there in a world of our own.

Slowly, I pulled him with me, and he followed. We stumbled silently into my world filled with grey and an anger that almost killed me. I didn't look to the place where I knew Safir had found me. The place where Hunter's body must have once laid. The only place that remained for me in my world was with Nicky. I couldn't take the time to acknowledge the significance of me standing atop of the ground that had been coated in my blood.

Safir's fingers squeezed around mine. Such strength imbued me to move forward, only thinking of moving forward.

It took over an hour for us to meander to Nicky's long-term care facility. I couldn't ignore Safir's rampant curiosity that coursed through him when observing my world. Everything appeared too "sharp" to him. Too angular. Too many reflective surfaces and not enough green. His senses were overwhelmed but I could tell he trusted my judgement and tried to focus on a soothing warmth for me. I felt half-dead by the time we got to Nicky's facility, as if Lani's life had drained out of me. But I regained a hint of vigor when we arrived outside of Nicky's door. "Wait here," I told Safir. He nodded, squeezing my hand before releasing me.

My fingers quivered while turning the door handle. How was I supposed to begin explaining to Nicky all that had happened? I staggered into his room alone. The second his eyes landed on me, his mouth dropped open, and he gasped so rapidly that he startled his ventilator. Nicky said nothing, his brows furrowed in concern as I slowly sat. Tears trickled over my cheeks once I settled the heavy coin purse on his bed, the weight of it sinking into the mattress. He gawked between the bag and me.

I sucked in a deep breath, trying to gather enough composure to say, "We don't have to worry now. You can die the way you want to."

And then we fell apart together.

Safir

Her roads were made of one continuous stone that must have taken ages to carve. Buildings and signs, metal posts jutting from the ground that emitted light, were all so angular as to cut oneself. Hardly any greenery graced my eyes. My ears drowned in the chaotic rumbling throughout her city. She was unphased by it all, moving automatically from one corner to the next with precision and apathy. People cried out on street corners and piled into their metal carriages, which released a horrid sound upon awakening. Bright illusions, like the ones that Oberia could create, were summoned on panes of glass, which exemplified the same report Ashire had been given about their absurd weaponry. It was an industrial hell.

I followed aimlessly alongside her, entering a great building with blank walls and people scurrying from one door to the next, holding vials and cups. Cries echoed from unknown rooms. The smell of decay hung in the air and explained Eve's lack of vitality. "It isn't the worst place to be," Eve murmured.

We navigated hallways until we stopped at one closed door. Eve squeezed her eyes shut, sucking in a sharp breath. "Wait here," she gently commanded. I released her, watching her enter and listening to her sob for the great tragedy that was on the other side of that door. I imagine she had to provide a lengthy explanation for her absence and even stranger reason for why I was present. Neutral warmth coursed through me, trying not to indulge in the crying and moans that also echoed down the hallways of that wretched place. It was far too reminiscent of my time in the dungeon…

I couldn't say how much time passed before Eve opened the door for me. She stood with her shoulders squared and her eyes glassy with tears. The extension of her hand beckoned me forward into the room. "He knows as much as he needs to," she whispered to me. She apprehensively led me inside, allowing me to behold what I could only guess was her brother.

Limbs curled around his trunk that appeared gaunt and twisted. A tube ran directly into the person's throat, seeming to take life rather than feeding it. The noises coming from the person were more terrifying than the ones emitted from the grotesque box of air. His breath sounded wet, gurgling with each strained inhale that instinctively made me want to clear my throat. I wouldn't have known that body belonged to Eve's brother if it weren't for the matching sapphire eyes. Despite death clearly tightening its grip, his stare remained just as fierce as hers.

"This is Safir. He's my … friend from my old job," Eve vaguely introduced me, and gestured to Nicky. "And this is Nicky, my brother."

I gave a curt nod. "A pleasure to finally meet you."

His head scarcely craned to the side. "Likewise?" he gargled. His direct stare followed me as I sat alongside Eve, trying desperately not to be distracted by the tubing, which had no place anywhere near, let alone inside, a human being. "So, you're the professor that … she took notes for?" he rasped.

It pained me to make him speak, yet it felt cruel to not converse as I would with any other man. I confused glanced to Eve. "Yes."

"Professor of what?" He scanned my clothes. "History?"

"Of sorts," I said, which made Eve chuckle. "I'm currently invested in politics."

"That's unfortunate." His cheeky grin made me see the hint of life in him that Eve admired so much. Maintaining a sense of humor had been beyond my scope while crawling towards death. "You don't look like you watch much … Golden Girls." He glanced towards Eve, making her roll her eyes.

I couldn't even pretend to know what he was implying. "The subject is lost on me," I admitted.

His eyes remained steadfast on his sister. "How could you have a crush … on this guy?"

Again, I was utterly lost in translation, but it earned a blush from Eve, who refrained from offering any explanation. I continued, "I'm told you've been confined to this state for some time."

The amusement faded from Nicky's face. That was when I observed he hadn't moved an inch of his body, not even to breathe, while I had been there.

I leaned forward in my chair. "I'd like to help," I offered while resting my hand on the rail of his bed.

His eyes narrowed. "How?"

Slowly, I enveloped his hand in mine. His fingers were bony, cold, lifeless in my palm. So, I started with that. I allowed him to feel how it felt to move my fingers, squeezing, and adjusting my grip before focusing on the feeling of my feet shuffling and moving within my boots. A startled gasp escaped Nicky as his eyes turned wide and his jaw dropped. I conveyed the feeling of taking in a deep breath that expanded my chest, allowing my back to stretch and arms to settle on the sides of his bed for him to experience what I could feel. I wondered how much he longed for it. His breath shuddered but he maintained a resolute stare at me, so I continued.

I took for granted the feeling of the grass beneath my feet tickling my soles. The feeling of the sun encapsulating my body. Submerging myself in a warm bath and holding my breath. A full belly on Feast Day, surrounded by pies and wine and smells of desserts. A tight embrace, warm and all-encompassing.

Nicky's gaze turned towards the ceiling with tears spilling from his eyes. We sat in silence while I imparted the experience of being caught in a rainstorm with drops pattering down my cheeks, a quintessential part of the human experience.

I paused when Eve reached for my hand. Her fingers weaved between mine with a look of sorrow that was masked with a smile as she watched him bask in all the sensations that world had unfairly deprived him of. She held her breath, allowing my Blessing to expand its range. I focused on the feeling of his sister's hand, warm and tight, just as I remembered from first meeting her. She would tremble yet hold steady all at once in my grasp. So secure. Strong. Unwavering. Just … Eve.

"Holy shit," he choked, breaking into a smile with tears pouring. "This is better … than morphine."

The afternoon gave way to twilight. I had never used my Blessing for such a prolonged period without reprieve. My joints were becoming stiff and my muscles fatiguing. I remained there for as long as I could, imparting something good with my Blessing. Something that brought value to a person rather than harming them. It couldn't have been further from the purpose of the king past.

We said little until Eve had fallen asleep in her chair. Her hair was tousled to one side, her limbs curled into a ball, an almost hopeful smile upon her lips. I savored it as Nicky cherished every sensation I could impart to him. Nicky glanced to his slumbering sister before focusing on me. "So …" he rasped. "You're the reason that I can't see her." My confusion was evident in my Blessing, prompting him to elaborate. "I could always find her … always … that is until she started her new job … She was much harder to find … I couldn't see her."

"Interesting," I murmured. "You've always been able to do this?"

He half-nodded. "Eve would run away whenever they separated us … I could find her and bring her back." My heart tore. Eve looked so peaceful in her sleep. She deserved every bit of that peace while awake. "How can you do this?" Nicky glanced down to my hand. "How is this possible?"

"Probably the same way you're always able to find your sister."

The breathing box sputtered with Nicky trying to cough, making him shudder. I directed as much warmth from my Blessing as I could. He relaxed with a wheezing sigh. "You're not from here," he stated. "There's no way."

I tried to paint a picture through my Blessing, allowing him to sense my realm through touch, the feeling of a place more wondrous, open, and hopeful than the world he knew, the sensation of crisp mountain air at dawn with the smell of spring and life emerging.

"Weird," he croaked. "You can let go … now."

I replaced his hand at his side, curious as to what had caused him to conclude experiencing my Blessing.

"Nothing personal … That was crazy … I never thought I'd get to feel any of that ever again … That being said, it's really weird sensing your feelings … for my sister."

Dear Vada, how awkward of me. "My apologies. That was unintentional."

His lips cracked into a smirk. "But I can tell … that you care," he said with a melancholic tone that grounded me in the circumstance of a man willing his own deathbed. "The place you showed me … will Eve be there?"

"I hope so."

He smiled. "She's a mess, you know … The best, but still a mess."

I chuckled. "I think I understand your meaning. I watched her bludgeon an assassin before. Twice."

His box of air sputtered with a harsh laugh that choked him. "I think you know that she won't always let you … love her but you have to promise that … you'll love her anyways." Nicky's expression became severe. "Promise me."

Even sustained by a godless machine, he still prioritized Eve. If I'd closed my eyes and listened only to his tone, I would have thought him ready to challenge me any moment. He was everything Eve had said he was. I understood that he had been the reason behind her relentless drive.

I stood and offered him a deep bow. "You have my word."

It was the easiest promise I had ever made.

Eve

I was confused at first when waking at Nicky's bedside to Safir's ember eyes, but my haze faded upon recalling the lengths Safir had gone to reach into my own world. He had given Nicky back the years of life he had missed in that bed while I'd barely scraped by to keep Nicky alive and miserable. Nicky had drifted into sleep as well, one more content than I had ever seen.

I'd known my world was going to be much duller than Safir was used to, but I wasn't as conscious of it until we arrived at a motel room. I didn't plan on spending my newfound fortune on anything fancy. It needed to last as long as possible for Nicky. The room was half the size of my room in Walyre, and I became acutely aware of the small space upon locking the door behind me. My eyes squeezed shut as I rested my forehead against the door. If it had been any other day, I would have been more self-conscious about the temporary living space, but I could only think of Nicky.

Hands settled on my shoulders, emitting a warmth and affection I knew well. I could sense his curiosity and admiration for my brother. "He's a good man," Safir breathed in my ear. My eyes fluttered open, and I slowly turned to see him standing inches away from me. My back remained flat against the door as I gazed up at him. Safir's ember eyes scanned mine from beneath his messy white locks. "A stronger man than most. Certainly stronger than me."

"And me." We both smirked and breathed each other's air. With Safir standing so close, I could feel myself fighting the tears. The image of him above me became blurry as I refused to let tears spill over. "I'm not ready," I whispered, like a secret that I wasn't supposed to have. "I'm not ready to let him go. Not the way he wants me to."

Safir leant his forehead against mine, expanding his Blessing. He wanted to take it all away from me, absorb every bit of my pain and make it his own. His comfort and affection made me feel like I could finally take a deep breath through the grief that wanted to suffocate me.

"Maybe," Safir murmured, "you have different ideas as to how you want the other to let go." He tucked a piece of hair behind my ear, and I leaned into him. His chest felt like a lean wall of force that contracted against me as his other arm wrapped around my waist to secure me there. "When you're far too bonded to think you could ever be without the other, you act as though you'll be eternally severed." My heart leapt into my throat with want, with drenching grief, as Safir's want grew bolder yet still cautious, waiting for me to initiate. "Understanding your brother better now, I can see you've carried him with you the entire time I've known you. And you'll carry him still."

I was so fucking tired of feeling alone.

My hands reached for his jaw, pulling him towards me with the force of all my grief and isolation. I felt a jolt like lightning course through Safir and into me when my lips found his. It wasn't like any of the kisses I'd known before. This wasn't tentative or tender. It was maddening. All I could do was *feel*.

Safir's mouth was burning, rapidly moving over mine, deeper and deeper until we could only taste each other. He worshipped my lips, and I could barely keep up in rhythm. I wanted to be closer, so there was no room for sorrow. I needed to be closer, and I could feel he needed the same. Suddenly, I was pinned between the door and Safir's body. He hoisted me up to his eyelevel with his knee wedged between my legs to keep me there. He groaned into my mouth when I weaved my hands into his hair, forming fists to keep him securely against me. Dear Vada, it was so good to feel so good. To not think about—

Don't think. Don't think. Don't think.

I squeezed myself around him, making another shock course through him and into me. I made a sound I didn't know I was capable of. An urgent desire pulsed through him, making a warmth build in us both. I rapidly undid his leather tunic so I could explore the toned planes of his chest. Not taking his mouth away from mine, he released me for a second to allow his tunic to slip from his shoulders. His white shirt was thin enough to feel the contours and indentations of strength underneath. His muscles twitched beneath my fingers, igniting an elation that just wouldn't let me stop. The knee between my legs ground against me and hoisted me up higher, making another sound echo from deep within my throat.

"By the gods, Eve," Safir huskily rasped. His hands slipped beneath my thin shirt, caressing my skin. He made a trail of burning kisses along my jaw, moving to my throat. But I felt constricted. My throat felt like it was caving in, but it was better than lingering grief. My fists remained buried in his hair to encourage him further. He ground himself against me. I jolted and cursed into his hair, burying my face into his white locks as he left me feeling light-headed.

"Hey, Evie."

Don't think. Don't think. Don't think.

Safir's hands had migrated to my sides, slowly rising, slow enough that he was asking permission as he paused his kisses at my throat. I sighed pleadingly in response, wanting to feel something good. Now. His hands resumed their path upwards until they were poised on either side of my ribs. The pads of his thumbs traced the creases beneath my breasts. My back arched against him, and I. Just. Needed. To. Feel. Good. His Blessing crashed over me with a thrilling, unadulterated need, a want for me. To marvel at me. To instill only bliss in me. To make me feel safe. To *love* me.

"Not that I'm complaining. It's fallen exactly where God intended."

Hunter's thumb smashed and probed the side of my breast. **"Stop,"** *I seethed.*

Everything did stop.

Safir had abruptly separated himself from me at arm's length with his hands on either side of my face. His ember eyes, drained of all lust, were scanning mine in a panic. I no longer felt his pulsating want. All that remained was horrified concern, and it made my stomach drop.

"Beloved? Speak to me, please."

I blinked over and over, seeing Safir before me. No one else. There *was* no one else.

I partially knew why my body had betrayed me. I pulled Safir's hands away from my face but held them tightly. My neck had begun to feel too warm, too constricted anyhow. I reached one hand to my throat to prove that I could still breathe. "You've done nothing wrong. I don't want you to think I don't want to be with you. I just—" I had just wanted to feel good, and Safir had just wanted to love me. My head shook in contempt for myself. "It isn't right, not right now. Not like this. I would just be trying to forget that Nicky wants to die. I want to be *present* with you," I confided while his fingers squeezed mine. "I want this moment to be as it deserves to be."

Safir nodded with a sheepish smile, and a hint of relief emanated from his Blessing. "You said I've done nothing wrong, but I will ask your forgiveness. I should never have taken advantage of your grief."

"You didn't. I can feel that you never would. I trust you." A warmth coursed through me, and it made the ghost in my head fade. "But will you stay here? With me tonight?"

Safir's ember eyes remained transfixed on me, the only person he had let himself come to love. "I am here in whatever way you need me to be. As your lover." He stepped closer. "As your friend." Another step closer. "I'd be the air in your lungs if it'd help you breathe easier." He cupped my cheek. I leaned into him with ease, feeling every bit of reassurance and affection revitalize my exhausted self.

That was the first night I didn't sleep alone.

Waking in a bed of warmth was a welcome change, making me snuggle closer to my source of heat. When an arm scooped under my waist and pulled me closer, my eyes shot open. Safir evoked a sense of peace through his Blessing that coated our bodies. I nestled into his chest, cherishing a few moments of tranquility before I knew the day would drain it.

And it did.

Nicky didn't wake that morning. Or afternoon. Or evening. He lay still, straining to take gurgling breaths. His lips trembled with the fever that had overpowered his body. I had seen him like that too many times before but then it felt… final. Death was coming. I felt sick and terrified that the night before had been the last time I would see his eyes. Countless times Safir tried to use his Blessing to numb Nicky's pain, if he could feel anything. Yet, despite Safir's efforts, there was no response from Nicky.

"Don't do this to me," I begged against his knuckles. "Not yet. Please, not yet."

By the time the sun had set, my limbs ached from being stuck in that chair all day. It made my guilt for trying to distract myself the night before even more intolerable. And then there was Safir, spending the day watching me agonize over my brother.

Safir fought me guiding him back to the portal, insisting on staying when I was adamant on the opposite. I couldn't have been more grateful for the kindness he had shown my brother, but that remaining time only belonged to us two. And it was fast approaching. When we made our way past the shack, I didn't even look in its direction, making a beeline through the portal.

It was a relief seeing Walyre again. It was all too easy to for me to forget my own misfortunes. Safir hesitated with his hand in mine. "Are you sure about this? I can remain with you. Ashire will not protest."

I looked away, almost embarrassed. "There was a time, years ago, when Nicky said he wanted to die. I told him that if he left I wouldn't be far behind."

"Eve—"

"And maybe that's why he managed for so long. Until now. Until I had you." I dared to look up at Safir, seeing his ember eyes wide with despair. I hated that look on him. "If his end is approaching, then it's going to be just the two of us. That time belongs to us alone."

I didn't doubt Safir would have his time watching me grieve, but in that moment I solely wanted it to belong to my brother. Safir slowly nodded, emitting a dread, and understanding in his touch that brought relief to me. "I'll wait," he told me.

I grimaced while backing into my own portal, keeping my eyes on him. Only him. Safir's gaze flared with the setting sun. His jaw clenched and fingers twitched at his sides as he stared at me, as if he were trying to drink in my image as much as possible until …

"You have to know," I blurted with quick courage. "You need to know how ruined I am because of this world, ruined in the very best possible ways." Safir's breath hitched as he listened intently. "Ruined for beauty, ruined for the cleverest company, ruined for love, Safir." One step was left between me and my own world. "You've all ruined me, and I am so grateful."

He vanished with the rest of Walyre and then there was just me, alone in a dull forest ten feet away from where Hunter had died. Intrusive dread tempted me to finally turn and look where it had happened. Finally alone, I envisioned my lifeless body, left in the dirt without a single care. If it hadn't been for Safir… I was the only remaining evidence of what Safir had sacrificed.

"Hey, Evie."

I found myself kneeling, sobbing while clutching my throat. I could still faintly feel Hunter's fingers squeezing the life out of me. I despised that Safir had been forced to use his Blessing for me, but I selfishly appreciated it so much that it left me doubling over into the dirt. And then my guilt-ridden grief found me, relieved that I didn't have to die. At least not because of someone as putrid as Hunter.

"I'm going to live a life free of you," I told the ghost in my head. "I'm going to find a life that's free of *you.*"

Safir

The day we officially parted I waited by her portal, as if it would help pass the time. I was certain, if I stood there long enough, weeds would wind around my feet and transfix me there. Yet I pulled myself back to the palace, to Ashire, to Selasi, to Lani, who had to continue about their lives as if nothing had transpired. Not one of them ever mentioned her, and most of the time I was grateful. It wasn't as if I needed someone to breathe a memory of her for me to recall her. I hadn't dared to ask her when she planned to return, knowing it was dependent on her losing her only family. To ask felt like I merely waited for more misery to befall her, and I couldn't bear for her to suffer further.

Returning to my realm lead me to discover that Ashire hadn't slept in days. He had looked a shadow of himself when I stepped into his study. Walls and floors were plastered with parchment and crumpled maps, his books tossed to the side.

I'd retrieved one book after another, stacking them on his desk. Ashire was reclined in his chair, staring blankly at the ceiling. His eyes snapped to me and tracked my movements until I sat across from him. My Blessing must have emitted the dread that had followed me back from Eve's world, which certainly didn't aid Ashire's disposition.

"Was your journey beneficial?"

The wretched sound of Nicky's breath rang in my ears. Both my brother and I shivered with my recollection. "In a way, but there was no changing the final outcome."

"And that is life." Ashire rubbed his eyes with a groan. "She will be returning to good company, as every being here has suffered from loss."

"It doesn't feel like a natural death, Ashire." I revealed the sensation of seeing Nicky's being fed life through mechanical means.

Ashire flinched in aversion. "A further indictment of her world. Emtias shall be returning soon, having restocked the necessary means to create his bane," he said, changing the subject.

"Have you decided on the effect you wish it to have?"

"We decided on a bane that will alert me if Arius is within a one-mile radius of my person. Emtias will cast the bane on a livery collar imbued with that traitor's blood that will create a signal should Arius jump near my location."

"Do you think this will provide you with the peace of mind to sleep?"

"I'm fine, Safir."

"I won't pretend you don't feel my doubt."

"Well, someone has to worry about the crown while you traverse realms in pursuit of your Eve."

I leaned forward in my chair, taken aback by his callousness. "I cannot hide my desire to serve the crown. If I were as harsh as you I would think my endeavors were necessary, considering you will depend on Eve to hinder Arius from being able to jump to the palace."

Ashire's head shook while he rubbed his eyes once again. "Yes, yes. My apologies. I am fatigued. It's drained any social talents I once possessed."

"A tragedy," I remarked while standing from my chair. "I'm going to employ Lani to administer you a tonic to sleep."

"Request that it mixes well with wine," he called as I exited his room.

It was late to visit the infirmary, but as expected, Lani was hunched over a grand book, using both hands to hold it upright to the candlelight. A small body snored in one of the cots. I peered in, gaining Lani's attention as she bowed her head. "Good evening, Your Royal Highness. I'm glad to see you back."

I trod into the infirmary, not wanting to wake the small person in the cot. It was Oberia. "Is she ill?" I asked in a low whisper.

"Worse. She's inquisitive," Lani joked with a smile, stretching the wrinkles along the corners of her mouth. "Milfred couldn't focus on her bakes in the kitchen now Obi has grown comfortable enough to be curious. She thought Obi would be better assisting me for the day. It was quite enjoyable to entertain such a malleable mind. I think I exhausted her." The book closed in her hands as Lani looked to me with cloudy eyes. "I sense there's a reason for you visiting me at this hour?"

I nodded. "Ashire."

"Ahh," she hummed while standing from the cot. Her knees and hips cracked but didn't wake Obi from her slumber. "I'm aware of what he needs, but I didn't want to intrude with my opinion."

"By all means, intrude."

She ushered me into her study, releasing a wall of aromatic smells. I didn't know how she could withstand being surrounded by such strong-smelling flora each day, but she hardly noticed while reaching into a cabinet for a tonic.

"He requests that it mixes well with wine."

"I've been here for many years. All my tonics mix well with wine." She extended the tonic to me, but her tremulous hand paused midair. "I too worry for our fierce lily," she said, sensing the depths of my Blessing. "I'm sure we'll all feel reassured when she's back where she belongs."

I couldn't fight my cringe. "In a way, that is what I'm afraid of."

There were not enough charters to read or letters to write to distract my thoughts sufficiently. There were torturous moments where I lapsed in my resilience and allowed myself to wallow in her image. I'd listen to my boots click against the throne room floor, a solitary sound when that room was once filled with music, thundering footsteps, and *her*. She had consumed the room with her presence. That night I'd believed our fragile happiness would be prolonged forever.

If I were truly feeling miserable, I'd request Oberia's presence.

She squeaked from behind me, "You asked for me, Lord?"

I cast my glance up towards the throne where Eve had once stood behind me. "Do you recall what she looked like that first night you were brought here?"

"Yes, I do."

"Can you show me?" I asked, longing yet begrudging all at once.

The girl's whispers seemed to spill onto the floor as wisps of color came into shape. Gradually the shapes evolved to show Eve standing there, clad in that dress that had left me stumbling, with her sapphire eyes piercing through me. My breath caught in my throat as my blood somehow ran ice cold, and the sensation burned my entire being.

I distanced myself from Oberia. "That is enough. I'm sorry to have asked that of you."

"Have I displeased you?" She was trembling.

"You've done nothing wrong. I'm sorry if my Blessing has brought you harm."

Her head shook, yet I still took ten paces away from her and tried to focus on a neutral warmth. "It is nothing I haven't already experienced before. I wonder about her as well."

"Do you?"

She nodded and kept her stare on the floor as she fiddled with her folded hands. "There was a time I aided her with my Blessing, and she thanked me for being brave. I never thought of myself as brave, but she made me want to try. She said once that all pain is temporary, but I disagreed. I still do."

I smirked darkly. "We share the same opinion, Oberia. Please return to your room. I won't require service further."

But on days where the longing was especially cruel, I'd summon Oberia to cast her image, just long enough to remind myself how much more painful it was to see Eve rather than imagine her. To even want her next to me meant wishing her remaining family would die, and I couldn't bear to wish her more pain for the sake of my selfishness. So, I stopped wishing for her there.

After two months I began waiting outside of her portal. I no longer expected her to appear, but I'd sit for hours each evening dreaming of finding her standing before me, and her realizing that I had been waiting, always waiting. I recalled her world, with curious alarm, the metal birds that divided her sky in a trail of white and the bombastic noises of her city. I didn't dare seek her out in her world, finding it more dangerous than her wandering aimlessly into mine.

Selasi remained alongside me, as stoic as ever. It was a welcome change from being suffocated in Ashire's paranoid study. Ashire couldn't breathe without hypothesizing Arius' location aloud, and it made me appreciate just how patient Emtias was to listen to each theory. I, on the other hand, fled the room after the fourth conspiracy.

Away I'd go to wait.

Time dragged insufferably. I clawed my way through the days with horrid sluggishness. Gnawing on the inside of my cheek, I tried to bitterly focus on Ashire's aggravation while he paced about his study with parchments scattered beneath his boots. He was right, if he had my Blessing, he wouldn't have been king for long. His frustration was endless. We were alike in that fashion, but I couldn't hide it.

"*Nothing?*" he seethed through clenched teeth. "No suspicious activities or mobilizations since the last letter was sent? No sightings from the outposts?"

"All of our correspondence with the outposts has been remarkably dull which usually would be a good thing."

"Not when we know there is an opponent in our midst."

"What of Emtias?" I asked, straining for hope. "Did he finish the bane before he visited his people?"

"No. He needs more time."

"Has he sent any word from the Fae?"

"Again, nothing!" He fell into his seat with sizzling irritation. "No sightings. No omens. They expressed their shared concern, but that's all they have to offer. We can't afford to lose them as our most powerful ally."

"One failed assassination attempt wouldn't topple the crown, let alone their alliances."

"It *could*. With time, distrust in our ability to maintain our power, our influence, is enough to topple any crown. Our alliance with the Fae was established under King Muire's influential Blessing, but it's maintained by the confidence the Fae have in House Astana." The stress carved worried lines into his face.

"Emtias would never allow the Fae to fall out of favor with our house. He's far too loyal to… our family."

Ashire offered a bemused smirk. "Regardless, my advisor's emotional investment in our house isn't enough to maintain our relations with the Fae."

I stirred in my seat. "Perhaps you should take some time, head south to visit Uncle Batrum, and feel the sun on your face."

"An idiotically considerate thought." He barely cracked his eyes open to peer at me. "I don't see how the sun would ease my nerves, and I'm quite certain I would burden our dear uncle and his newborn child."

It was a lapse in judgement on my part, to think he would even consider catering to his own well-being. Any suggestion had to be shrouded by some practical purpose. "I thought it would ease your mind if you were to observe the loyalty of your subjects yourself. There are no leads here in the city, so you might as well look elsewhere, or you're bound to drive yourself mad."

"Perhaps, but the local lords are calling for another meeting and that, I'm afraid, requires my attendance."

Despite my Blessing becoming more control, it still wasn't manageable enough for me to conduct business on behalf of the crown. It was a sickly feeling having to return to the shadows after my debut. Still, that wasn't the worst pain.

Ashire narrowed his gaze at me. "Safir, I don't want you to think that you're of no use to our family. I'm well aware of the burden you carry."

It wasn't that I cared for the family name or the crown, but for my brother I cared infinitely. Yet none of that needed to be spoken aloud. I wasn't diverting much energy into controlling my Blessing anyhow, tired of cursing myself for it. There were better ways to spend the solitary days.

My brother faintly smiled. "If anything, else, that understanding is a triumph."

The crisp breeze cut through the trees outside the window as the sky turned dark with dusk, signaling me to rise from my seat.

"Perhaps command the outposts to gather intel regarding any goblin activity. Could be linked to Arius," I offered while adjusting my cloak. "Do what you will, but that is where I would direct the majority of my efforts."

Ashire nodded as he watched me pace over to the door, initiating my ritual I conducted at the end of each day. "Three months to this day, has it not been?"

"Yes," I affirmed just as the door shut behind me.

Eve

The money served its purpose. Nicky's health scarcely rallied enough for him to be lucid enough to enjoy his final weeks. A power chair equipped with Nicky's ventilator allowed us to take walks in the courtyard. Seeing Nicky lift his face to the sun made every brush with death worth it. He grinned, but it wasn't without its bitter notes. "I tried to re-create this feeling … for years in my mind … I didn't think it'd feel this good." He beamed brighter than the sun.

He didn't ask. He never did. Ever since I'd walked into his room, with coin in hand and half-drained of life with Safir beside me, Nicky stopped asking questions. No prying into what had happened during my fight, or how it was connected to Hunter's death. We merely appreciated any moment we had together. We spent our time reading, playing games, watching TV, and taking walks. I secretly hoped Nicky's death wish would fade, but he promised not to give me hope where there was none. "It makes me enjoy it…all the more," he repeated one day. "And when the time comes … I'm ready… I'm content."

"How?" I asked, tired of me wanting him to live more than he did. I'd begged for him to try counseling or antidepressants or anything that would incline him to stay alive. Every option had been refuted with a smile. "How can you be ready when we've just started being together?"

He smiled and drank in the crisp air. "I know what the remainder of this life has … to offer me … I don't know what will happen after this … Maybe I'll be reborn as something else … maybe I'll find a heaven, or maybe … it's all oblivion … Whatever it is I know I won't be in … this chair."

"I am whatever the remainder of this life has to offer you." My voice trailed off in a whisper.

Nicky grimaced. "You're more than most can ever hope for … But a life watching me live in a chair isn't enough for you … I can tell … You fidget." It was moments like that where I had expected my tears to make an appearance, but they stalled. I thought they had run out. "I need you to accept it if you're ever … going to be happy again … Your own happiness … No one else's."

When I wasn't by his side, I was sleeping the bare minimum needed at the motel across the highway, stretching out the money as much as possible. I allowed the shack in the woods to rot. It was never mine anyway.

Meanwhile, news outlets flashed Hunter's face across headlines. It made me clutch my throat. The police had questions, but with my fortune from Safir, we lawyered up. The tables were turned to addressing Hunter's questionable practices, postulating foul play from his criminal associates. It had taken Mary over one week to call the police when Hunter was missing and another week for them to find him. Multiple rainstorms had already passed through and erased any physical evidence of me at that scene. Apparently he had died of cardiac arrest, but detectives were skeptical about the burnt handprint on his face.

I ensured he would never harm you again.

But to go to such an extent? For me? From Safir's Blessing? I didn't know if I had the right to question his methods. Ultimately, the detectives pursued Hunter's network of illegal gambling, counterfeiting, and fraud. No one in his family appeared particularly heart broken.

I mailed Mary and Lexi cash for them to start over fresh. Mary never gave her thanks. I never wanted it, but every now and then she'd send a postcard, having moved back west where she had family. Lexi was happy learning how to play the piano.

I maintained my focus on Nicky, trying to invigorate him with as much life as possible if he let me. After three months, his pneumonia returned. It felt like a knife twisting into my gut. He looked giddy when he refused the antibiotics. "The only control I have left … is this," he wheezed with a horrible grin.

If someone had laid out every drug known to man in front of me as Nicky willingly faded away, I would have snorted, injected, or drank anything to numb me.

"One more walk," he rasped from his hospital bed. His breathing was still labored, like a thick rhythm of death and pus, ringing in my ears. "Before they set me up … with the morphine drip."

His breaths crackled as we took one last walk through the courtyard. We sat at our usual bench just as a storm began rolling over the horizon. It was poetically shit. I knew it was only going to expedite his infection, but I couldn't refuse him anything. Not even his own death.

"So, what will you do … when this is done?" he wheezed. I decided to not answer, not trusting that I'd maintain my composure. "Classes? You can be a social worker…Or you could go back to that job you liked … the one that was far away … That sounded promising … You seemed to like that guy—"

"I'll—" I knew where I'd go, but couldn't say it, because it would make his death feel just on the horizon. "I don't know what I'll do."

"But you'll be happy?"

"I'll try."

"Okay, but I want you to know … that I'll be wanting you to be happy … I refuse for you to use me as an excuse," he said with a glint of smugness in his eyes.

"Not an excuse. I just don't know how or when it will be possible."

"It is … I saw it almost every time you came back from your job … Gone for days yet happier than I had ever seen … That had nothing to do with me … and I'm glad."

"Nicky—"

"Let him love you … Let him be happy with you … Let him protect you as much as you need … whoever he is. Not because you can't do it alone … but because you shouldn't have to anymore."

Fuck. This.

Nicky had clung to his life for me and seeing as I had hope to live outside of my grief for him, it made it easier for him to let go of me, and easier for me to let go of him. I would have never thought it possible until I had found Walyre.

Three months went by without a single reminder of Walyre. Nothing. All I had left was my flower that Tesara had given me. It never wilted. But the dreams that filled my head at night left wildly curious. Had they found Arius? Was everyone safe? Did they dream of me as I often as I did them? A war could be raging just a few miles from Nicky's room for all I knew. With Nicky doing his damnedest to die, my time to return to Walyre was approaching, an elating thought, yet horrifying since it was at the expense of my brother.

Nicky was growing tired of waiting to die. I was growing tired of him waiting to die. After only ever existing in my motel room or in Nicky's room, I took a walk. Nicky was being bathed, and I just needed to know. If that world, somehow more real than my own, still existed.

I knew the path all too well, although I hadn't walked it in months. Every now and then I would get flashes of sprinting through the streets, desperately seeking help. It felt like a rock sank in my stomach upon seeing the shack giving way under the neglect. My breath caught in my throat, making me reach to my neck to remind myself to breathe. It made no sense, but somehow, I was afraid Hunter was still in there. Waiting for me.

I trembled while putting the shack behind me and venturing back into the city. I hadn't gone there to be reminded of *him*. He wasn't supposed to be able to reach me. He wasn't supposed to be able to touch me. Finding my own happiness wasn't supposed to be that way. I was meant to find—

"Hey, Evie."

From that point on, I didn't bother going back to the motel room. I needed every second to belong to Nicky. How could dying be his happy ending? How could this be his grand exit? Nicky had lived and endured and loved me relentlessly, and all it would amount to was one last breath in a bed that had become his entire existence. In our world, our sorrow hadn't mattered. Our time trying to matter, still didn't matter. We were but blips on a spectrum of humanity that had ultimately left us as we were: twisted around each other in a hospital bed. Even to the nurses we were merely patients on their caseload. For everyone besides us, it was just a Tuesday. That world hadn't deserved our happiness.

Nicky opened his eyes for the last time. The pneumonia had become septic. His eyelids barely hung open, but his distant gaze settled on me. I'd been curled next to him, careful not to disturb any wires. His lips parted, only emanating a wet wheeze from deep in his throat. I reached for the sponge to wet his lips and tongue. "Are you in pain?"

The moisture helped him rouse ever so slightly. "Eve …" he gurgled. "Sometimes I think I've gone …" He paused before trying to lick his lips. "But then I wake up."

"It won't be much longer, Nicky. I promise." Maybe I'd never be ready. I choked while swallowing my sob back down into the pit of my core, tucking my chin into my chest. It felt like my ribs were going to break under the pressure of holding my breath. I wanted to unpack his pain into my empty body and make it mine. Yet no matter how much pain I caused myself, it was never going to unburden his.

"Every day," I panted through gritted teeth, "my first and last thoughts will belong to you."

"And mine you," he choked, his ventilator straining against his throat. One by one, tears spilled from his eyes. My arms wrapped around him tight enough to make him whole. "I'm not afraid … but I'll miss you … my only sister … my only friend."

He died that way. In my arms. Two days later.

Safir

I jerked awake, bolting upright with a sickening fear making my stomach drop. I wondered if it was time. I wondered if I could feel Eve's anguish across the planes of our existence. Dear Vada, I wished I had been there with her.

I knew what was to come. I was sure she was wasting little time, and so would I. After dressing in haste, I woke Selasi to accompany me to her portal, where it was only a matter of time before her arrival. I needed her to know I was waiting.

She was not meant to cross into her new life alone.

Eve

I stood alone with an urn for a brother.

Nicky had spent too much time confined to that bed, so I doubted he would want to be stuck in a box. A small hole had been dug in a park, next to a few almond blossom trees overlooking the world below. It was sunny enough to feel the warmth and breeze, far enough away from the city below to have some quiet.

I had always sworn Nicky's death was going to kill me, but it didn't. Sometimes I wished it had. My body was filled with grief, but my tears never came. It was as if they had dried up.

A haggard Clay staggered towards me with a cigarette in his mouth. "Couldn't he have chosen a more convenient location?" he huffed, leaning on his knees to catch his breath. "You look okay, peach."

I swallowed hard. "I'm sorry I never came by after my fight to let you know I was okay."

He struggled upright. "Forget about it. When Hunter's body showed up on the news, I figured he hadn't gotten the better of ya. Good to know you're still kicking."

I looked down at the urn in my hands. "Yeah, at least one of us is. I know Nicky would be glad you were here, and that you didn't die trying to walk up here."

"Yeah, well, I'm sure it's good for me or some shit. I'm trying to cut back to just one pack a day now anyway." He blew a plume of smoke out. "So just you and me here, huh? Probably oughta be that way." Clay coughed and clapped his hand on my shoulder. "I'll say this— Nick deserved more than what he got. He was a good kid, brave kid, who always did right by you, peach. If he had been my own son, I think I wouldn't have hated the idea of parenthood so much." Clay took a long drag and tapped his cigarette between his fingers. "I hope he knows the peace he wanted." He sniffled while releasing me. "I'll let you say your piece now," he rasped, but kept his back to me.

"I can't. There's nothing else for me to say. He knows."

"Well, then I'm glad I said that sentimental shit aloud." He turned back to me with obviously smudged tear tracks. "You ready to do this?"

I paused, knowing I'd never again be able to hold Nicky after this. Yet my knees descended to the ground. My hands shook as I settled the urn next to the hole, trembling worse at the idea of opening the lid. Seeing everything Nicky had ever been, thought, or felt reduced to an urn twisted my stomach. I almost decided to just leave it there before the painful sound of joints popping thudded at my side.

"I'll help," Clay muttered.

Clay opened the urn and was the first to tip it towards the hole. We both poured the ashes into the ground before smoothing the dirt over the top. Traces of earth remained caked under my fingernails, and I wished they'd remain there forever.

Then it was over. My brother was buried, and I remained. Years of grief hung on me so heavily I was surprised I was able to stand. Clay reached up and grasped my hand as I hauled him up from the dirt. We both stood back and looked at the freshly moved pile of earth. I think we were both surprised at how small it was.

Clay's dirty hand returned to my shoulder. "You did good, peach. You really did. He knows it."

I felt like my throat was going to swell shut. Still, no tears arrived. That world hadn't deserved my brother, and we weren't meant for that world. Our happiness wasn't meant for that time, that place.

"Do you know what you'll do? Where you'll go?"

At least Clay was asking the right questions, the answers to which I already knew but I had only allowed myself to focus on one day, one hour, at a time. To even look towards tomorrow opened a greater possibility than I had originally known.

To be happy, that was all Nicky had wanted.

I could finally let myself feel it. My own happiness pulled me so very far from that place, from my strongest grief. Away to a world that was my choice, to a love that belonged to me. It pulled me.

I took a step forward.

Safir

I strongly debated waiting there overnight. I stood there, deciding, with every fiber of my being, to live with her. Every action of mine would be an act of admiration for her, and maybe somehow that would help heal us both.

For the one who'd dared me to love, who'd taught me to grow through my sorrow, for the one my soul called home. I'd wait with empathy, to allow her to recover from grief. We could lean on each other. We could hold each other up.

It was frightening yet comforting to be so sure of someone. My very being ached to share that with her, and I welcomed my chance as-

She appeared before me out of thin air like she had that first day.

Standing perfectly still as I had imagined so many times.

I took a step back to brace myself with bated breath in my lungs. Eve stood there, gawping with similar shock. The time apart had been cruel to her. Dark circles were painted under her hollowed eyes. Dear Vada, those sapphire eyes had dulled so brutally it rocked me to my core.

If she were there, if she were truly there, did that mean—

I could see his death cling to her. She would always carry Nicky with her. And she had braced her shoulders to carry him still.

I took a step forward and stretched out my hand.

Then she did something spectacular.

She smiled for me.

Through ferocious tears, she smiled and ran to me, shattering any doubts that she wasn't meant to be with me.

I crossed the space between us, and Eve collided into my wide-open arms. I choked on my own longing for her, ensnaring her as tightly as I could manage as all my Blessing poured into her. She buried her face in my shoulder as she smiled and wept into me. My Eve fitted against me, real and warm, and perfectly broken. By the gods, she was meant to be there. My hands held her gaunt face while

I peppered kisses onto her hair, forehead, cheeks, and lips, over and over with all my longing pouring into her. Her breath hitched, and I silenced her growing sobs with my mouth gliding over hers in my never-ending commitment to show her how beloved she was. I couldn't deny how elated I was to see her there. Whole or broken, I'd have her in any form possible.

Hand in hand, readying to brave my world, I whispered the words I knew belonged to her.

Eve

The tears had finally come, not from grieving over Nicky as I had imagined, but from joy seeing Safir waiting for me. I knew my sorrow would find me later, when all had quieted, and I'd be left with my thoughts. But I let myself experience pure happiness while surrounded by a love I had never thought possible.

Safir took my hand, guiding me away from the portal, leaving my world behind one last time. He whispered the words my sullen soul had unknowingly craved to hear for my entire existence, words that buried themselves into my heart and bones, words whispered from my chosen happiness, and those words became me:

"Welcome home, beloved."

And we both walked forward.